Praise for *A Lovely Way to Burn*

'I was with Louise Welsh's gutsy gripping heroine Stevie Flint every terrifying step of the way' Kirsty Wark, author of *The Legacy of Elizabeth Pringle*

'I read it in two sittings, pausing only to sleep and dream about it. Gripping, perfectly paced and beautifully written' Erin Kelly, author of *The Poison Tree*

'A terrifying journey into the possible, this is dystopia for today. Feral, frightening and fascinating, *A Lovely Way to Burn* gripped and chilled me in equal measure' Val McDermid

'This intelligent thriller creates an alarmingly convincing picture of London on the brink of disintegration; it reminds us how fragile we are' Andrew Taylor, *The Spectator*

'I've felt for a while that we are in the mood for an intelligent slice of London-based dystopia, and I think Louise Welsh has cracked it with *A Lovely Way to Burn* . . . it kept me up all night nervously turning the pages' Cathy Rentzenbrink, *Bookseller*

'The London of the novel at once recalls sci-fi dystopia, Dante's *Inferno* and accounts of the 1665 great plague . . . Welsh's plot is ably handled . . . She has in Stevie . . . an engaging, stroppy heroine' *Sunday Times*

'A thrillingly dystopian mystery . . . It's a fine setup, and Stevie is a strong character, a forthright blend of sales sass and reporter brass. Welsh is particularly good at describing the institutional and social disorder that accompanies the outbreak of the sweats' *Guardian*

'This is a novel rich in the kind of iridescent word painting that has long been Welsh's speciality, and the vulnerable, often maladroit Stevie is a wonderful protagonist' *Independent*

'Welsh plays brilliantly on our worst fears, and the pace never lets up. Seriously scary' *The Times*

'Scary, shocking and touching by turns, this apocalyptic thriller will enthral. I haven't been so buried in a book in a while' *Irish Independent*

'Suspenseful and intelligent dystopian fiction. Welsh writes snappily and with filmic precision . . . Her setting, vivid and initially familiar, grows increasingly alien as the crisis worsens' *Sunday Business Post*

'Welsh develops a fantastically written mystery which keeps you hanging on to every word . . . A must read, which will leave you dreaming – or having nightmares – of apocalyptic London for weeks' *Irish Examiner*

'The writer [Louise Welsh] reminds me of most is Ian McEwan: both specialise in secrets, rather chilly sexuality, sudden reversals of fortune, and uneasy intimations of doom . . . *A Lovely Way to Burn* is superb popular fiction – a box-set waiting to happen' *Independent on Sunday*

'Louise Welsh writes elegantly and has visualised London in extremis with immense and detailed clarity' *Literary Review*

'The relentlessly taut suspense of *A Lovely Way to Burn* still lingers on my psyche. Such an apocalyptic crisis does not seem improbable and here's hoping freakishly foul weather and tube strikes are not an omen of things to come' *Stylist*

'A propulsive read, written in lean sentences and snappy cliffhanging chapters . . . Most impressive of all is the Scottish writer's evocation of a London that, with a Dickensian swagger, emerges as a pulsating untameable beast in its own right' *Metro*

'You know you're in for a seriously chilling read in this apocalyptic thriller when three very unlikely killers – an MP, a hedge fund manager and a vicar – go on a murderous rampage in the sweltering capital' *Marie Claire*

'A scary vision of London falling apart that's addictively readable' *Saga*

'A tense, claustrophobic medical whodunit with an apocalyptic tone that cranks the stakes ever higher' *Herald*

'The descriptions of London and society unravelling into chaos are utterly compelling and scarily realistic . . . Great if you like tense thrillers' *Heat*

'A taut thriller so involving that I missed my bus stop!' *Woman & Home*

'A brilliantly imaginative thriller with a compelling heroine and well-paced plot that keeps the tension high' *Hello*

Death is a Welcome Guest

Also by Louise Welsh

The Cutting Room
The Bullet Trick
Naming the Bones
Tamburlaine Must Die
The Girl on the Stairs
A Lovely Way to Burn

Death is a Welcome Guest

Louise Welsh

JOHN MURRAY

First published in Great Britain in 2015 by John Murray (Publishers)
An Hachette UK Company

1

© Louise Welsh 2015

The right of Louise Welsh to be identified as the Author of the Work has been asserted
by her in accordance with the Copyright, Designs and Patents Act 1988.

Extracts from 'The Horses' taken from *Selected Poems* by Edwin Muir
© Estate of Edwin Muir, reproduced by permission of Faber and Faber Ltd

A CIP catalogue record for this title is available from the British Library

Hardback ISBN 978-1-84854-654-7
Trade Paperback ISBN 978-1-84854-662-2
Ebook ISBN 978-1-84854-655-4

Typeset in Adobe Garamond by Hewer Text UK Ltd, Edinburgh

Printed and bound by Clays Ltd, St Ives plc

John Murray policy is to use papers that are natural, renewable and
recyclable products and made from wood grown in sustainable forests.
The logging and manufacturing processes are expected to conform to
the environmental regulations of the country of origin.

John Murray (Publishers)
Carmelite House
50 Victoria Embankment
London EC4Y 0DZ

For my nephew Zack Welsh

. . . darkness shades me,
On thy bosom let me rest,
More I would, but death invades me;
Death is now a welcome guest.

'Dido's Lament' from *Dido and Aeneas*,
libretto, Nahum Tate

On the second day
The radios failed; we turned the knobs; no answer.
On the third day a warship passed us, heading north,
Dead bodies piled on the deck. On the sixth day
A plane plunged over us into the sea. Thereafter
Nothing. The radios dumb . . .

'The Horses', Edwin Muir

Prologue

The *Oleander* left Southampton on 24 May under the command of Captain Richard Greene for a fourteen-day Mediterranean cruise. The liner had a crew of 1,150 and a passenger list of 2,300 souls. Many of the crew would be engaged in the essential business of sailing the ship, rather than catering to passengers' whims, but the cruise was advertised as luxurious and the *Oleander's* brochures made a feature of the ratio of one crew member to every two passengers.

The first casualties appeared on day three, not far from Monte Carlo. Travel is well known for broadening the mind and upsetting the tummy, but many of the *Oleander's* guests were elderly and so Captain Greene radioed ahead to let the harbourmaster know that there was a possibility of unplanned disembarkations.

The weather in the Mediterranean was bright and warm, the seas calm. Over the next two days more passengers and crew were confined to their cabins with vomiting, diarrhoea and worrying respiratory complaints. The sick people huddled in bed in their air-conditioned cabins, soaking their sheets with sweat and all the time shivering like it was winter in Alaska.

1

The first death was unexpected and was followed rapidly by another. Captain Greene radioed the news to the authorities and his boss at the shipping company. He was dismayed to receive the same command from both. The *Oleander* was to drop anchor immediately and await further instruction. He was equally dismayed to find that he was fighting the urge to throw up, and when the message came that the ship should *on no account, repeat, no account, approach port*, he was hunched over the ship's barrier vomiting into blue Mediterranean waters.

Perhaps it was the close confinement of the passengers and crew that allowed the virus to spread so swiftly. Or maybe it was the delay in getting extra medics to the ship, caused by onshore outbreaks of what was soon to be called the sweats. When a launch carrying medical personnel dressed in protective suits eventually arrived, there were fewer than fifty passengers still alive. Most of them were already showing signs of infection. Some determined souls had staged their own evacuation and lifeboats manned by the dead and dying drifted in the waters around the liner. Later some would wash up on pleasure beaches, but by then no one would care.

It was not the first outbreak of the sweats, but it was one of the earliest and it made headlines around the world. Magnus McFall imagined the *Oleander* often in the months ahead. The giant liner becalmed on sunny waters, looking from a distance like a picture postcard of luxury; the rescue launch hurtling towards it throwing plumes of white foam in its wake; the stench of decay awaiting the medics in the lower decks; the impossibility of salvation.

PART ONE

One

London was hotter than Mumbai that summer, hotter than Beirut, hotter than hell, or so people said. Magnus McFall believed them. The train's windows were open, but the air blasting through the carriage had a nasty, second-hand quality that reminded Magnus of sliding into a recently vacated bath, warm water scummed with soap. It did not help that the passengers were rammed together as if it were the last train out of Saigon. He breathed in through his mouth and tasted burning rubber. Some summers the tracks melted, stranding passengers between stations. It would screw him, but the possibility brought a smile to Magnus's face. He thought he might talk a wavering suicide bomber into sticking to his plan – *paradise is worth dying for, son, pull that string and shame the infidel* – if it meant the show would not go on, even though the show was the only thing that really mattered.

Magnus caught a girl glancing at him from across the aisle and grinned again. The girl frowned and looked away and Magnus wondered if he should practise smiling without showing his teeth. His agent, Richie Banks, had advised him not to get them fixed: 'They're as crooked as a pyramid sales scheme, but they're your best feature, chum. Make you look a bit less like your mother left you out in the rain.' Judging by the photographs lining his office walls, Richie had represented some odd-looking comics in his time. Magnus was not sure his agent knew the difference between a funny man and a funny-looking man.

Magnus glanced at his watch. Ninety minutes to go. He took a tissue from the pocket of his jeans and dabbed the sweat from his forehead, surprised by how calm he felt. It was the dead calm of the soldier about to go over the top, or an armed robber readying to storm a bank, but it was better than the gut-twisting that could cripple him before a show.

He looked down the carriage. Most of the passengers were also bound for O2. The crush of teenage girls in baseball caps stamped *Johnny Dongo Done Done Me Wrongo* was obvious. So was the group of middle-aged women, co-workers in some office, he guessed, large bosoms quivering with the motion of the train, bags clink-full of bottles that would be confiscated at the stadium entrance. There were couples too, the women better dressed than a night in the dark warranted in deference to the high ticket price; the men smart-casual in best jeans and trainers. They were out for a good time and that meant they would give him a chance. The Johnny Dongo look-alikes, Dongolites, were a different story. There were four of them smart-arsing by the door, dressed like 1930s history dons on their way to enlist for the wrong side, their floppy hair plastered with sweat and styling gel. They would be impatient for Magnus's set to end and for Johnny to take the stage. Magnus wondered how they could stand the combination of tight collar and

6

tie, the tweed suits heavy with perspiration. One of the Dongolites took out a Meerschaum pipe and stuck it between his teeth.

Magnus's own stage gear was zipped inside a garment bag slung over his shoulder, a white shirt and gangster-sharp, midnight-blue suit that looked like a safe choice until you caught a glimpse of scarlet lining. His guts were beginning to clench. He looked out of the window, trying to keep his eyes on the horizon, the way you were meant to on a rocky ferry crossing the Pentland Firth. London blurred by, a strip of blue sky above rows of apartments, precipitous graffiti and concreted back yards cast in shade. It was a world away from Orkney, but the tall buildings reminded him of Stromness, the shadows thrown by the houses along the seafront on to the jetties lined before them. The memory made Magnus think of school and all of a sudden he wished Mr Brown, his maths teacher, was going to be in the audience. 'You see, Mr Brown,' he would say, 'folk do find me funny. It turns out that I am a funny guy after all.' But Mr Brown was as dead as Magnus's father, both of them buried in the Kirkwall churchyard. The maths teacher felled by a heart attack he had cultivated as carefully as an investment banker might nurture his own pension, Magnus's father killed in a careless accident. Bad luck, everyone agreed, especially as Big Magnus never even took a Hogmanay dram.

He tried to picture his father swaying beside him, against the rhythm of the train, but imagined instead the old boy saying, 'You're the support act, son, not the headliner.' Though phrases like 'support act' and 'headliner' had never been a part of Big Magnus's vocabulary.

Was it a bad sign that the only people he wanted to invite to his gig were dead? Probably just a sign that he was kidding himself. Magnus would not have invited them had they been alive. His wee mammy would have jumped on a plane to London at the hint of a gig; the same went for his sister Rhona, her man Davie and a whole swathe of aunties, uncles and cousins eager for a spattering of stardust.

'No little lady you want to show off to?' Richie Banks had asked, looking up for a moment from the contracts splayed across his desk. 'Seeing a man on stage can do things to a girl, if you know what I mean.'

'No one at the moment,' Magnus had said, looking at the view of brick wall through the dim glass of Richie's office window and wondering how his agent could have stood to spend the best part of thirty years there. 'Come along if you want.'

'It don't have the same effect on me, son.' Rich had laughed. 'Anyway, sad to say, I'm already booked,' and he had mentioned another of his stable who was a regular on television panel shows. 'Gets the jitters before he goes on TV. Needs me to hold his hand.' Rich had pushed the contract for six nights' warm-up at the O2 across the desk to Magnus and pointed to where he should sign. 'This is a big gig for you, a good opportunity, don't fuck it up.'

'Why would I fuck it up?'

Rich slid the signed contract into an envelope. His grin was still in place, but he had raised his eyebrows, punting the question, which was no question at all, back to Magnus.

O2 was the next stop. The man in the seat beside Magnus was reading an *Evening Standard* he had folded into a pocket-sized square. Magnus glanced over the man's shoulder at the headline: 'Mystery Virus Wipes Out Cruise Ship'. A photograph of an impressive-looking liner illustrated the article about the latest outbreak of the sweats. He scanned the text. There had been cases of the virus in London, but nothing on that scale. The article listed instructions on how to act. People should observe hygiene precautions, phone NHS Direct if they felt unwell, avoid close contact with strangers. Magnus looked at the crammed carriage and grinned. London had not closed for the Blitz, the IRA, or al-Qaeda. It would take more than a few germs to shut down the city.

The train slowed. The man beside him coughed and then sneezed. He wiped his nose on a tissue and stuffed his newspaper into his jacket pocket. One of the Dongolites pulled out a spotty handkerchief and mopped his forehead. The boy was red-faced and shiny with perspiration; *gleaming like a . . . like a . . .* Magnus cast around for an image he could use on Dongolite hecklers, but nothing useful . . . *pig, conker, bell-end . . .* came to mind.

Magnus followed the flow of people on to the platform. There was work being done in the station. Some of the barriers that flanked the platform's edge had been taken down and temporarily replaced by traffic cones strung with fluorescent tape. They narrowed the walkway, pushing people even closer together.

Magnus saw the crowd before and behind him and realised that the rest of the train had been as full as his compartment. There were other trains, one every fifteen minutes, all crammed with people. Most of them were heading to the stadium. Magnus swallowed. It would be all right once he was on stage. For now he was just a part of the crowd, everyone moving at the same slow pace towards the exit, like one body composed of many cells.

The four Dongolites from his carriage paused up ahead. Magnus glanced in their direction as he drew level. The sweat-soaked youth was swaying gently on his heels, with the unfocused stare of someone about to be transported on a wash of acid. He was wearing black-rimmed spectacles, round and ridiculous, that made him look as if he had put his eyes to binoculars some *Beano*-reading wag had grimed with soot. The glass magnified the youth's eyeballs and Magnus saw them roll back in his head, pupils spooling upward until all that was left was white, greased and boiled-egg shiny. The Dongolite tottered backward. The heels of his spit-polished brogues knocked a traffic cone from the platform's edge. He swayed gently, took a step towards his friends, and then teetered backward again.

Magnus gave a shout of warning and moved towards the group. He heard the shrill blast of the guard's whistle, saw the Dongolite's knees crumple, his specs falling, smash against the concrete as he tipped off the platform, backward on to the tracks.

Christ! One of the Dongolites tore off his jacket, exposing maroon braces and matching sleeve suspenders. He froze. *Christ! Jesus Christ! Christ! Jesus!*

The other two Dongolites threw themselves on to the ground, ready to pull their friend up from the tracks below, but too slow, too slow. Magnus was with them now, face flat on the platform as if a bomb had gone off. He caught a quick glimpse of the boy's body, floppy hair corn-gold against the gravel, unseasonable tweeds rag-doll-rumpled and then the train was flashing past, the shouts of the crowd and the frantic scream of the guard's whistle not quite drowned out by its sound.

Richie Banks had once told him that 'Good comics have ice in their soul. I've known more than one cold cunt go up on stage and do their full routine, same day that their mother died. Unfeeling bastards, but a joy to represent. They don't let a crisis get in the way of a gig.'

It was like speaking to God, standing at the edge of the stage, facing the flare of lights that razed all view of the audience. Magnus did not mention the Dongolite's fall, the corn-gold hair shining bright in the dark, the rush of the train, or the shout of the youth frozen on the platform, *Christ! Christ! Oh Jesus Christ!* But the sound of the accident was in his head, the scent of blood and burning rubber still in his nostrils. When he took his bow and announced, 'Here's the man you've all been waiting for, Joooooooooooohnny Dongo!' the applause of the audience brought back the shouts of the people on the platform and Magnus could have sworn he heard the guard's whistle screaming on, so high his eardrums felt ready to explode.

11

Two

Johnny Dongo looked a mess. His hair had lost its comic bounce and hung in a lank cowlick over a forehead sheened with sweat. He spat into his handkerchief, raised a glass of milk cut with rum to his lips and said, 'What a fuckup.'

Magnus could not think of anything to say and so he kept quiet. He was on his fifth beer, one half of him still high on applause, the other still reeling from the shock of the accident.

'A fuckup,' Johnny repeated. 'A fucking fuckup.'

It had been a great gig, a show to be proud of, but nobody contradicted Johnny. Magnus took a swig from his bottle of Peroni and looked at his feet. There were six of them in Johnny Dongo's hotel room: Johnny's manager Kruze, a couple of Dongolites Magnus had not been introduced to and Johnny's girlfriend Kim, her face stern beneath her blonde beehive, but with a hint of a smirk that put Magnus in mind of Myra Hindley's mugshot. They were sitting on a trio of couches around a black coffee table that looked like it had been designed for snorting coke. The Dongolites were side by side, legs crossed in opposite directions as if to indicate that, despite appearances, they did not trust each other. Johnny was squeezed between his manager and his girlfriend in a too-tight arrangement that hinted at a power struggle. Magnus had the third couch to himself.

'A fucking fuckup,' Johnny muttered.

Kruze's eyes were red-rimmed and rheumy. He put an arm around Johnny's shoulder and gave him the kind of anaconda squeeze a wrestler might give a rival. His bald head gleamed. It looked solid, Magnus thought. Strong enough to batter down doors, but heads were fragile things, no match for speed and metal.

Kruze said, 'Kim's the only one who's going to suck your dick tonight, Johnny. It was a good audience and you did a fucking amazing show, same way as you're going to give another fucking amazing show tomorrow.' The TV was on, its volume muted. An aerial view of the abandoned cruise ship shone from the screen, followed by a shot of the Houses of Parliament. Kruze picked up the remote and killed the picture. 'If these bleeding emergency measures don't shut down the theatres, that is. A big fuss over very little, if you ask me.' It was not clear whether he meant the recall of Parliament that the sweats had prompted, or Johnny's tantrum. Kruze stirred the milky contents of Johnny's glass with a straw. Ice cubes rattled dully within. 'Drink your medicine. Time for beddy-byes soon.'

Johnny lifted the glass to his lips and drained it. A dribble rolled down his Roger Ramjet chin. He wiped it away with the back of his hand, then stretched for the carton of full fat on the table and poured some into his glass. He topped it up with a generous tot of Admiral Benbow, turning the white liquid a treacle-toffee shade of brown that tugged at Magnus's bowels.

Kruze sighed and got to his feet. 'Get him to bed some time before the call to prayers would you please, Kim love.'

Kim put a hand on Johnny's thigh.

'I'll make sure he gets back here in time for tomorrow's show, that's all you need to worry about.'

Kim's engagement finger sparkled with a ring that had caused some tabloid speculation, and her voice was smug with the assurance of possession. Magnus wondered if rumours about Johnny and the rotation of pretty boys who were always in his orbit were true. And if they were, whether Kim knew and thought them a price worth paying.

Johnny shifted into the space vacated by Kruze. He coughed and then sneezed three times, hard and painful, the sound of a small train crushing bone and flesh. 'Fuck.' He took his handkerchief from his top pocket and blew into it.

Kruze was halfway out of the room, but he turned at the sound of Johnny's sneezes and stood framed in the doorway, his pink shirt and pale blue suit Neapolitan-dapper, despite the late hour.

'Why don't I arrange cars for your guests and let you and Kim hit the sack, John?' Johnny Dongo flapped a hand, dismissing Kruze, but the manager persisted. 'If you come down with something, Magnus here will have to step into the breach, and you don't want that, do you?'

Magnus had once auditioned for Kruze, way back when he first arrived in London, his accent so thick he had to repeat everything he said. He had been working as a KP in an Italian restaurant, the only white boy in a kitchen devoted to 'authentic Tuscan cuisine'. Magnus had grown used to being ridiculed by boys with accents as thick as his own, but whose voices

14

lilted to different rhythms and whose journeys to London had been *sans* passport. Magnus had rolled with their jokes and contributed a few of his own. After all, he too was fresh off the boat and had had the privilege of an easy passage on the *Hamnavoe* rather than the long hikes, the stowaway goods trains, overcrowded night boats and container lorries his workmates had endured. But when Kruze had stopped Magnus in the middle of his routine about the *fear* that could hit you on your way home when it was after midnight and you were fu', and said, 'I can't understand a word you say, kid. Save up for some elocution lessons,' Magnus had bunched his fists. Later he was glad that there had been no set of golf clubs propped in the corner of Kruze's office, no handy paperknife, or pair of scissors on his desk, because the urge to score the smile from the manager's face had been strong. Perhaps Kruze had sensed the danger. He had leapt to his feet, like a man who knew life was short and had decided not to waste a second of it, opened the office door and ushered Magnus into the corridor with a 'Good luck.'

Magnus had put his foot in the door, leaned in close and said, 'Awa and fuck yoursel, ya big poof.'

But as Hamza, the best pizza maker this side of Islamabad, remarked later over a consoling beer, it didn't really matter what Magnus had said. Kruze wouldn't have understood a word of it.

Magnus and Kruze had run into each other a few times over the years since then. The manager had been polite and Magnus had wondered if he had forgotten the incident, but now the apologetic look Kruze threw Magnus told him that the older man remembered.

'Don't get me wrong, you did well tonight, Mags,' Kruze said, and something inside Magnus cringed.

Johnny flapped his hand at his manager again. 'Don't get your Y-fronts in a tangle. Your goose will be on stage crapping golden eggs tomorrow night.'

Kruze hesitated for a moment as if he were going to say something else, then shook his head and shut the door behind him. Johnny Dongo spat into his handkerchief again.

'Thank fuck for that.' He turned his bloodshot eyes on Magnus, his pupils microdots. 'I thought you were an island boy. Stop shaming your ancestors with that piss-poor stuff.'

Johnny splashed a goodly measure of Admiral Benbow into a glass and shoved it towards Magnus who took a sip. It was navy rum, dark and bitter, and it reminded him of late afternoons in the Snapper Bar, ship masts swaying at their moorings, giving a hint of what brand of wind would greet you when you went outside. Then, if you stayed longer than was wise, the ferry docking, blocking all view of land or sky, lit gold against the black of a winter's night.

Gold and black made Magnus think of the boy's hair shining on the gravel, the rush of the train. Bile rose in his throat. He drowned it with a swig of rum, finished the measure in his glass and helped himself to more.

'Take it easy, man,' said one of the Dongolites, but Johnny Dongo laughed. 'He'll be all right, he's Scottish. My old man was Scottish. He used to drink until his fists were full.'

Magnus could have gone home after his set, stood beneath a hot shower and attempted to wash the day from his skin, but he had stayed on to watch Johnny from the wings. Johnny had danced across the stage, skinny legs encased in

16

herringbone trousers of a lavender hue that would have made old Harris weavers fear for their souls. The audience were a storm of sound, out in the dark of the auditorium. So loud that Magnus wondered Johnny Dongo was not lifted from his feet and thrown on to his arse by the weight of laughter surging towards him. It rose from deep in the audience's bellies, firing out of wide-open mouths, each one with its share of teeth, and though he could not see them, Magnus could imagine the faces of the crowd, heads thrown back, tongues wet and shining, eyes squeezed into slits. The crowd had loved Johnny Dongo and he had steered them upward, ever upward, sending them rocket-fuelled out into the night. But now that Johnny was off stage, it was as if all his energy had turned to venom.

Kim coughed. 'Christ,' she said to Johnny. 'I think I'm getting your cold. I sound like fag-ash Lil.'

Johnny hoicked up a gob of phlegm and spat into his handkerchief. 'I don't have a fucking cold.'

Kim produced a small Ziploc bag from her purse and chopped out neat lines of coke, white stripes bright against the black coffee table, like an inverse barcode. Johnny took a note from his pocket, rolled it tight and handed it to her. 'Ladies first.' Kim rubbed his thigh as if she were testing it for quality and hoovered up three lines. She passed the note back to Johnny who followed suit.

'Whoa!' There was a glimpse of the man he had been on stage. 'That'll do the trick.' Johnny grinned and then sneezed. 'Fuck.' He sniffed and shook his head. 'I think I lost it.'

Johnny's pisshole-in-the-snow pupils had all but disappeared and Magnus thought the coke had met its mark

17

despite the sneeze, but the comedian fished the note from his pocket again and snorted another three lines.

'Sorry about that, lads.' He grinned at the Dongolites. 'Reduced rations. Share nicely now.'

Johnny's acolytes took their turn and then there were two lonely lines, thin and shuffled-looking, waiting for Magnus. There was plenty of the white stuff left in Kim's Ziploc and Magnus wondered if Johnny had orchestrated a shortage for his own amusement, but Dongo looked washed out despite his double dose of marching powder. The thought flitted across Magnus's mind that he should pass up his share in case Kruze's fears came true and he had to stand in for Johnny (*let's do the show right here!*) but the rum had tipped him beyond such precautions. He reached into his jeans pocket and pulled out a fiver. The blue note looked out of place in the upscale hotel room, but Magnus rolled it tight and snorted the good stuff up into his sinuses, tasting the chemical cut of it in the back of his throat. His nerves zingalinged in anticipation of the hit and, for the first time that evening, he smiled.

Time died in the hotel room and everything shrank and expanded into the moment that was now. Kim put on some music and got each of them up to dance, one at a time; all except for Johnny. The girl was broad-beamed and heavy on her feet, but she had a sense of rhythm and moved her hips in time to the music. Magnus wondered again if she was the comedian's beard and if Johnny would mind if he borrowed her for a while, just long enough for him to lie her down on the bed in the next room and fuck the sound of train wheels

18

from his head. He took Kim by the arm and drew her close, as if they were in some old movie and he was Frank Sinatra. Kim leaned in to him and put an arm around his back. She was shorter than Magnus and he found himself staring at her beehive. It looked hard and brittle and he felt a sudden urge to snap it from her head.

'I like your hair,' he said and ran an experimental hand across her rear.

Kim's face was shiny beneath its coating of make-up. She let Magnus's hand rove the globe of her bottom and then shoved him in the chest, dealing a blow that sent him reeling against the bathroom door.

'Rude boy,' she whispered, in a voice that might have been a come-on.

'Help yourself,' Johnny said. He was sitting between the Dongolites now, on the couch Magnus had vacated, all three of them laughing at something on Johnny's phone. Magnus saw that they were leaning against the stage suit he had carefully zipped inside its garment bag and hung on the back of the couch. 'That's sick,' said one of the Dongolites, pointing at the phone. Magnus still did not know their names.

Johnny had dispensed with his handkerchief. He spat on the floor. 'She's a bit of an armful, but islanders like their women big, don't they? It comes from being such little men. Go on, fill your boots.'

It was an odd image and Magnus laughed. He wanted to tell Johnny that his father, grandfather and no doubt his great-grandfather had indeed been short men, but they could hunt and fish and farm while he, the tallest known McFall in history at five foot nine (taller than Johnny, he seemed to

19

remember) could only jaw for a living. Then he saw Johnny's face and remembered a Lon Chaney line: *Nobody laughs at a clown at midnight.*

'No offence, John.' Magnus gave Kim a glance he hoped conveyed the right balance of respect, apology and sexual attraction. 'But I don't think it's in your gift.'

'I'm Santa-fucking-Claws, Mags. Believe me.' Johnny held his arms wide, and the Dongolites shrank into the couch. 'It's all in my gift. What do you think you're doing here? I gifted you this gig. Three nights in the biggest stadium in the country, that was my present to you.'

'And it's much appreciated, Johnny.'

Magnus had flung his jacket on a chair by the door when they had first entered the room (how many hours ago?). He picked it up and shoved his arms into its sleeves.

Johnny Dongo said, 'It doesn't fucking look like it. First you feel up my fiancée and then you refuse to fuck her. What's that all about?'

'You're a wanker, Johnny.' Kim went into the adjoining bedroom, slamming the door behind her.

'See what you've done,' Johnny said. 'You've upset her now.'

The curtains had been closed when they came into the room, but a thin sliver of grey dawn had reached through a chink in the heavy fabric and was stretching across the floor. Magnus took his phone from his pocket. The battery was dead.

'What time is it, John?'

Johnny leaned back into the couch, draping an arm around each of the Dongolites.

'Time you fucked off.'

The rumours were true then, Johnny Dongo liked boys.

'Don't worry, I'm gone.' Magnus held up a hand in good-bye and opened the hotel-room door, but instead of walking into the corridor he was confronted by the ensuite.

'I'm not jesting,' Johnny said, as the door swung shut.

Magnus emptied his bladder, zipped up and then splashed some water on his face, grimacing at his reflection in the mirror. He had what his mother called a 'baby face'. Some girls found the combination of shaggy black hair, wide eyes and gap teeth cute, but Magnus guessed they were not features that would age well. He drew his hands down his face, watching his eyes droop, feeling the scrub of bristle on his chin.

'You look like a discount rent boy,' he muttered.

The bathroom had a glass ceiling. He sat on the edge of the whirlpool bath and looked up at the view of lightening sky occasionally interrupted by a flash of high-flying gulls. Why did the birds gravitate to cities when there were wide-open seas out there? It was a question he might as well ask himself. Magnus wondered if the trains were running yet. Fuck only knew how much a cab home would cost. The thought of trains made the rum and beer in his belly threaten to slosh to the surface and he realised he would pay anything not to enter the station again.

The sound of banging startled him and he fell backward into the bath, knocking his cheek against the oversized tap jutting out from the wall. The porcelain was cold and hard, but the tub had been designed for couples to bathe comfort-ably together, toe to toe, or chest to spine if they were especially good friends, and it was wide enough for Magnus

21

to bend his knees and roll on to his side. He closed his eyes. The sound of banging grew louder and he opened them again. Getting out of the bath was not easy and Magnus fell twice, but eventually he managed it and unlocked the bathroom door. Johnny Dongo was on the other side, his face beaded with sweat, his shirt unfastened to reveal a view of bony, white sternum.

A wave of fellow feeling washed through Magnus. They were all human and alive in the dawn of a fresh day. Who cared what Johnny got up to with his Dongolites, as long as everyone loved each other?

'You're a good man, John.' He clasped Johnny's elbow. 'A good man. You want a bit of advice?'

'No, I want you to piss off,' Johnny said, pulling his arm free.

But Magnus had seen death that day and needed to share how important it was to live, while you still could.

'No one gives a fuck that you're a poof, especially not me.' He put a hand on Johnny's elbow and squeezed. 'You go for it, man, fuck all the boys you want while you're still young enough to get a lumber.'

Johnny Dongo pulled Magnus close. Magnus opened his arms, ready to receive Johnny's embrace. He had liberated him. Sex was sex and nothing more, whoever you had it with.

The comic whispered, 'If you call me a poof again, I'll kill you,' and smashed his forehead into the bridge of Magnus's nose. There was a moment of pain and blindness. Magnus's face was warm with blood and there was a fire klaxon sounding in his head. He grabbed a bath towel and held it to his nose.

'That is what is known as a Glasgow kiss.' Johnny turned to look at the Dongolites rumpled together on the couch. 'Did I tell you my dad was Scottish?'

'You did, John, yes,' one of them replied, his voice soft, as if he feared he might be next.

Johnny said, 'Trust nae cunt, son,' in an accent that would pass muster on Sauchiehall Street. He squatted next to Magnus who was crouched in the bathroom doorway, the bloody towel still clutched to his face, and ruffled his hair. 'Can you guess why I gifted the gig to you, Mags? Because you're an ideal warm-up man, no one has to worry about the crowd peaking too early. As my old dad would say, you're never going to set the heather on fire. I'm happy to have you on board, but don't take fucking liberties. Now piss off out of here.'

Three

Magnus turned into a lane by the side of the hotel and leaned against the wall, head tipped back in the hope that gravity would help stem the gush of blood from his nose.

The hint of light he had seen reaching through the curtains was merely a nicotine dawn. It was a while since anyone had punched Magnus, but the pain was part of his body's memory and it recognised and embraced it. Just as it had the time Murdo McKechnie 'accidentally' kicked a football into his face in P3. And on the night Rab Murchison decided Magnus was a 'bloody nancy boy' and smashed L O V E then H A T E into his 'poof nose'. And on the only occasion his father had punched him. That last one he had deserved.

He felt his face swelling and realised that there was a good chance it would be him, and not Johnny Dongo, who would need an understudy tomorrow.

'Fuck!'

Magnus spat a stream of blood and mucus on to the ground. He took off his jacket and shirt, held the shirt to his face and zipped the jacket over his naked chest. Blood was still running down into his throat from his ruined nose and he spat again.

He felt in his pocket for his wallet to check he had enough money for a cab, but it was empty. Magnus shoved his hands into the pockets of his jeans and drew out the crumpled fiver dusted with coke. He already knew what had happened. He had followed a routine formed by years of dodgy, shared dressing rooms and taken his valuables on stage with him. His money and debit card were in the pocket of his sharp blue suit, zipped in its garment bag, still slung across the couch in Johnny Dongo's hotel room.

Magnus slid down the alley wall and squatted on his haunches. He could probably face the humiliation of seeing Johnny again, but the night porter on duty at the reception desk possessed the bulk and Zen of Mike Tyson. The big man had been woken by the *ping* of the lift and raised his face from the reception desk as Magnus emerged into the lobby. Magnus had held his hands in the air and walked to the exit. But the porter had rubbed rabbit-pink eyes with grazed knuckles and shadowed him to the door, complaining about the bloodstains dripping on to the lobby carpet and detailing in a low voice, hoarse with a summer cold, the kind of things that happened to people who bled without consideration. Magnus could still feel the point, low on his spine, where the big man had shoved him into one of the rotating door's compartments and spun him from the hotel. There was no prospect of going back there.

He slid his mobile from his pocket and then remembered that its battery was dead.

'Fuck!'

He hurled the phone across the alley. It hit the brick wall on the other side and smashed open. The battery bounced from its casing, skittered across the ground and disappeared beneath one of the large container bins that serviced the hotel. This time Magnus did not bother to swear. He rose unsteadily to his feet, crossed the alley, lowered himself on to his hands and knees and looked beneath the container. It was dark, but he thought he could see the battery. He stretched a hand towards it, flinching at the touch of grit and detritus, but the battery was out of reach. Magnus stood and put his weight against the bin. Its wheels were pad-locked and it refused to move. It was a problem beyond his ability. He gave the container a kick that hurt his foot and then slithered to the ground, rested his back against the bin and closed his eyes.

Magnus woke slumped on his side. His mouth was dry, his face a dull thump of blood and bruise. He had no idea where he was except that it wasn't bed, it wasn't home. Something touched his feet. Magnus batted out a hand, and drew up his knees, sharp to his chin. He had been on stage bathed in the audience's laughter and then . . . *Oh God.* It all came back to him in a rush of shame and vomit. He wiped his mouth on the blood-crusted shirt still clutched in his hand, like a baby's security blanket.

He had no idea of how long he had slept. Magnus strug-gled upright and looked towards the mouth of the alley. It was brighter, the sun higher in the sky, but there was a lack of traffic noise that made him think it was still early. Something rattled at the dark end of the lane and he found himself drawing deeper into the shadows thrown by the hotel bins. His mother had warned him more than once of the fall that followed pride. And here he was, like an illustration of a cautionary tale for children, skulking in ordure just hours after his big bow.

Someone coughed. It was a harsh animal sound, loud in the early-morning stillness. Magnus looked towards the noise and saw a couple locked together in the gloom. His first confused thought was that they were dancing. The man had his arm around the girl, her head rested against his shoulder and they were swaying together. Then he saw the floppiness of the girl's limbs, the way the man was bearing all her weight, his legs scissored wide, spine pitched back for balance. The couple's shadows reeled against the alley wall and Magnus realised that they were drunk. No, the man's movements were quick and sure. The girl was beyond drunk, but her dancing partner still had his wits.

Magnus had made drunken love to drunken women in shadowy outside places. He spat on his ruined shirt and dabbed at his face, hoping to clean off the evidence of blood and dirt. There was a long walk ahead and whatever was happening at the other end of the lane had nothing to do with him. He was in no fit state to judge anyone. He thought, as he often did, of a woman he had met in a Belfast bar, late one night, after a gig. They had matched each other shot for shot of tequila and then fucked on the bonnet of a car parked in a deserted street, both of them reckless. Not so reckless he had not rubbered-up though. They had produced a condom at the same time, both of them laughing to see the other so prepared. 'Quick draw, McGraw,' she had whispered in exotic Ulster tones. And then she had kissed him.

Magnus got unsteadily to his feet. His legs had died at

27

some point during his sleep, and he felt as if he were fresh from a night's fishing, feet and knees skinkling at the firmness of solid ground. He looked back at the couple. The girl's head lolled to one side and he caught an impression of blonde hair shining. The cough that had woken him rasped again, harsh and fox-like. The man spat on the ground and then started to busy himself with his fly. He shoved a knee between hers, pinning the girl against the wall, sliding between her legs. There was no 'both' or 'together'. The man was alone with a human doll.

'Fuck.'

Magnus cursed his conscience and stretched a hand beneath the bin, searching again for the battery of his phone, but it was useless. The battery was dead and lost in ratty darkness. He looked towards the mouth of the alley, but the road beyond was silent. He was on his own. He stepped into the middle of the alley and walked towards the couple.

'Excuse me, mate.'

The man froze. He looked up and Magnus was reminded of the expression on the face of a cat interrupted in the act of dispatching a kill. He stepped closer and saw that the man's hand was not on the girl's arm, as he had supposed, but at the base of her throat. The girl's eyes were slits, open and unseeing.

'Like to watch, do you?' the man asked.

He was older than Magnus had thought, a craggy business-suited fifty, his white shirt unfastened at the neck.

'Only if both parties know what they're doing.'

'How fucking politically correct of you.' The man coughed again, his throat grating, metal on un-oiled metal, but the girl did not wake up. 'Don't worry,' the man said, 'she knows what she's doing, this is the way she likes it.' His voice was low and so assured that Magnus almost hesitated, but then the man said, 'You can have next go if you want. She won't mind.'

'You're a fucking rapist.' Magnus took another step towards him.

'Piss off, son. You don't know who you're dealing with.'

The man's arm must have been growing tired with the strain of holding the girl up, or perhaps he wanted to use her as a shield, because he let her fall against him, her face on his shoulder, his arms clasped around the small of her back. The girl's short skirt had ridden up and Magnus saw that her tights were shredded around her thighs, her underwear pushed to one side. She was wearing high-heeled yellow sandals and had painted her nails the same sunny colour.

Magnus said, 'Put her down and walk away.'

'So you can finish what I started?'

He had been wrong to think the man was sober, Magnus realised. He was drunk enough to have lost his inhibitions and lucid enough to carry through.

'So I don't kick your fucking head in.'

'Like someone did to you?' The man had shouldered the girl's weight again. He walked slowly towards Magnus, keeping as close to the far wall as possible. 'Don't worry. We're out of here.'

'Where are you taking her?'

'A nice warm bed.' The man's voice took on an apologetic tone. 'You were right to interrupt us. We'd been drinking. Things got out of hand. You know how it can be when you drink too much. Don't worry, she's safe with me.'

The man smiled. He was level with Magnus now, the girl still wrapped in his arms. It was easier to take the stranger at his word and let them go.

'Okay.' Magnus let out a deep breath and leaned against the wall of the alley, allowing the man a clear exit. Close to, the man's suit looked expensive, his shoes well polished beneath their scuffs. The girl's skirt and top might have been her best, but even Magnus's untutored eye could tell that they were chain store rather than designer. He said, 'Will you look after her?'

'Don't you worry.' The man grinned. Teeth shone white in his brick-red face. 'I'll see she gets what she needs.'

It was not easy to hit the man while the girl was still in his arms but Magnus managed it. He ducked to the right and slammed his fist into the stranger's cheek. The man crashed against the alley wall, still holding the girl close. Magnus grabbed her under her arms and they struggled together for a while, the girl between them like a rag doll. Magnus thought he could feel her waking. Perhaps her assailant felt it too because he let go suddenly, sending Magnus sprawling with the girl on top of him. It should have been enough, but Magnus pushed her to one side and stuck out a leg that sent the man sprawling. Then Magnus was on him, driving his fist into the man's face, one, two, three . . . he lost count of the punches in the rhythm of violence.

Magnus's hand had begun to hurt and he would have stopped soon of his own accord, but he was distracted by an unwelcome early-morning noise, harsh and mechanical, punctuated by regular, high-pitched beeping. He looked towards the source of the sound and saw a refuse van reversing into the alley flanked by bin men. Magnus heaved himself to his feet and gave the man a boot in the ribs. It was a good job well done. The girl had dragged herself to the side of the alley and was cowering against the wall, her hands over her face as if she could not bear to look at the world any longer.

'It's okay,' Magnus said. 'You're safe.' He sent his foot into the man's side again. The body moved with the impact of his kick, but the man did not make a sound and Magnus found that the silence pleased him. The bin men were running towards him, but they halted a foot or two away, as if scared to come any closer. They were big men, made bigger by their overalls and fluorescent jackets, but they looked hollow-eyed; deathly in the early dawn light.

'Call the police,' one of them said.

'Yes.' Magnus nodded. He was winded and his words came out in gasps. 'Call the police.'

He would have liked to have kicked the man again, but two of the bin men screwed up their courage and grabbed hold of him. One of them punched Magnus in the belly. 'Fucking rapist,' the bin man said. Then he punched Magnus again.

Four

Magnus sat on his bunk, staring at the small screen of the TV in the corner of his cell, watching a chef with a face as soft and smiling as the Pilsbury Doughman put a pastry lid on the fish pie he was making. On the bunk below, Pete moaned in his sleep. Magnus turned up the sound.

'Ask your fishmonger to dispose of the heads if you're squeamish,' the dough-faced chef said. 'But traditionally these form part of the decoration.' He started to insert dead-eyed fish heads into the pastry. 'This is why it's called Stargazey Pie.'

Magnus switched channel. A petite, blonde woman dressed in pastels was walking through an abandoned room. Whoever had lived there had not been house-proud. They had left in a hurry and remnants of their belongings were scattered around the space in dusty piles.

'Marcus paid £292,000 at auction for this derelict Victorian townhouse,' the woman said, stepping over a sleeping bag lying rumpled on the floor like the skin of some giant serpent. 'But with a bit of TLC the property has the potential to realise much more than that. Marcus, what are your plans?'

A sallow-faced man with large bags under his eyes stared nervously into the camera. He hesitated and then his words tumbled forth.

'I fix it up nice, nice fixtures and fittings, nice wallpaper, nice carpets, then I rent it out to young working people who want a nice place to stay.'

'That sounds nice,' said the blonde woman.

Magnus switched channel again. A good-looking girl with a wide smile and *café au lait* skin was displaying a set of exchangeable screwdriver heads.

'. . . you need never be scrabbling around to find the right size of screwdriver,' the woman said. 'Because the perfect tool for all varieties of screw is right here in this little box.'

She laughed in a way Magnus might have found appealing had he not been locked in a cell in Pentonville for the last two days.

He changed the channel again and saw an exterior shot of a hospital somewhere in India. The scene shifted to the hospital's interior, then to a full ward and then to a small child gleaming with sweat. A doctor with a cotton mask stretched across her mouth and nose placed a hand on the child's forehead. The doctor's hands were encased in thin plastic gloves. To avoid infection, Magnus supposed, but it seemed terrible to deny the sick child the consoling touch of flesh.

The child was critically ill, the voiceover said, and although it came from a poor family, poverty was not to blame. This was a virus that affected rich and poor.

Pete turned over in his sleep and started coughing. Magnus felt the force of his coughs reverberate through the bunk.

33

One of the warders had promised that Pete would be heading to the dispensary, but that felt like a long time ago. Pete had been ill but lucid then. He had not said why he was in Pentonville, but then neither had Magnus. They were in the wing reserved for vulnerable prisoners and sex offenders and the fashion was for discretion.

The television screen shifted to Beijing and the portrait of baby-faced Mao smiling out across Tiananmen Square. It flashed to the White House then to Big Ben and back to the newsroom. The World Health Organisation was co-ordinating responses to the virus, the newsreader said, his face stern. In the meantime it had recommended that theatres, sports stadiums and other places of public entertainment be closed. People should go to work as usual – the newsreader gave a reassuring smile – but the advice was to avoid unnecessary crowds. Someone coughed off camera. The newsreader's eyes shifted from the autocue to the studio beyond. He hesitated, as if unsure whether to comment on the interruption or not and then got on with the final item, a story about a family of chicks who had hatched next to a toy fire truck and decided it was their mother. Magnus watched a film clip of the chicks waddling in a line behind the red plastic truck and thought there was something obscene about it.

The television was getting on his nerves, but there was nothing else to look at except whitewashed walls and a barred window through which he could see a scrap of blue.

Sometimes in Orkney the land seemed like a thin strip between sea and sky. Few trees interrupted the view or the wind. He remembered how he and his cousin Hugh had played at superheroes when they were boys, leaping from

34

rocks and ridges, arms outstretched, their parkas around their shoulders like capes, in the hope that a gust would take hold and carry them across the fields.

Pete coughed again. The grating sound reminded Magnus of the man he had beaten in the alleyway. The police had told him that his 'victim' was a Member of Parliament, a man with connections in high and perhaps low places.

Magnus heard a click as the flap covering the Judas-hole on the other side of the door flicked up and someone looked through. He slid from his bunk. He was still bruised from the beating the refuse men had given him and the movement made his body sing with pain. He banged against the door and shouted, 'There's a sick man in here.'

A voice from the landing commanded, 'Step away from the door.'

Magnus did as he was told and was rewarded by the sound of a key turning in the lock.

The screw's mouth and nose were hidden by a cotton mask like the one the doctor on the news had worn as she tended the sick child. He was an older man, a heavy smoker from the look of his lined eyes and sallow skin. The screw coughed and Magnus hoped it was a reaction to a thirty-a-day habit.

'No association today.' He shoved two packets of sandwiches and two bottles of water into Magnus's hand and began to close the door.

'My cellmate needs a doctor.'

Magnus nodded towards Pete-the-Pervert curled beneath a blanket on the bottom bunk and saw what he had been avoiding. The man was slick with perspiration. He had thought Pete was deep in sleep, but his eyes were open and

35

Magnus realised that his cellmate was caught in a fever. The screw took a step back. Magnus asked, 'Is this what they're talking about on the news?'

'Do I look like a doctor?'

Across the landing someone battered against their door. The rhythm was taken up by the surrounding cells, a fast tattoo that reminded Magnus of the football terraces. The screw's hand moved to his keys. Panic tightened Magnus's chest, but instinct told him it was important to keep his voice reasonable.

'They say that whatever this is, it's infectious. He should be in isolation.'

'I'll see what I can do.' The screw's mask moved with his words. It was damp with saliva and Magnus saw the shape of his mouth, wet behind it. A clamour of shouting joined the banging. The racket boomed across the atrium, dissolving words into echoes, the music of fear.

Magnus said, 'I'm only on remand. All I did was to try and stop a girl from being raped. I'm innocent.'

'I know.' The screw glanced towards the noise and then back at Magnus. 'I can see it in your eyes. You've got a rapist's charm, but you won't get my knickers off without a fight.'

The cotton mask trembled and Magnus realised that the screw was laughing. He shouted, 'At least move me to another cell . . .' but the door was closing. Magnus heard the key turning in the lock and though he added his fists to the banging that echoed through the wing, the warder did not return.

Five

Magnus thought Pete might be dead. The wing had shaken to the sound of screaming, chanting and banging throughout the night, but the brightening dawn had stilled the noise, as if the prisoners were vampires forced to take cover from the sun. Pete had kept up a muttered conversation with himself for most of the night, but daylight had quietened him too and it was a long time since the bunk had rattled with his coughs, or swayed in response to his twists and turns. Magnus knew that he should rouse himself, get off his mattress and take a look at his cellmate, but the thought of the man curled beneath the blanket on the bed below, like a corpse shrunk in its coffin, gave him the horrors.

Magnus had kept the television on all night, trying to focus on something other than the noise around him, but Pete's ramblings and laboured breaths had insisted their way into his head. Pete had been talking softly to some girl, asking her to be nice to him, telling her she was *beautiful, a sweet thing, a real doll,* until Magnus had wanted to slide the pillow from beneath his cellmate's head and suffocate him with it. Men at sea shared smaller cabins, but this was a voyage he had been press-ganged into.

It had been Friday night when they locked Magnus in Pentonville. 'Emergency measures,' the warden who processed him said. 'You'll be in court Monday morning.' There had been no explanation of what had prompted the crisis or why he was being held in prison, rather than a police cell. Magnus had remembered the recall of Parliament Kruze had been dismissive of and selfishly hoped that theatres were under emergency measures too – at least until he got out.

The screws had allowed Magnus a phone call and he had rung his agent, Richie Banks. The phone had switched to Richie's voicemail and although Magnus had only left a short message, he was not permitted a second call.

Magnus's voice had grown higher, and more like a liar's, with every insistence that he had not touched the girl, except to free her from her attacker. Eventually tiredness won and he had surrendered to the indignities of prison admission. He answered questions about his medical history and mental health from a screw who looked like he had spent so long staring into the sun, it had all but burned the retinas from his head. Then Magnus had stripped naked, bent over to show there was nothing taped beneath his balls or secreted between his arse cheeks, and dressed in a prison tracksuit rough from rewashing. He had tried to comfort himself with the thought that the girl would clear him when she recovered, but the memory persisted of her huddled against the alley wall with her hands over her eyes, as the bin men set about him.

His thoughts were in danger of spiralling. Magnus looked at the patch of blue beyond the barred window. It was Monday morning. Someone would come to take him to court soon and, whatever the outcome, they couldn't leave him locked up with Pete. Magnus turned the television down and held his breath, hoping to hear approaching footsteps or the jangle of keys that would signal his release. His ears seemed to sing with the silence. There was nothing, not even one of Pete's rattling gasps. He turned the television volume up again.

Someone would come. First there would be the click of the hatch, the individual pack of cereal and portion of milk. Then a trip to court in a prison van and the chance to explain everything. If things went his way, he could be home in his flat by the end of the day. The thought brought warm tears to Magnus's eyes.

There was a name for the virus now: V596. Naming the disease seemed to make its existence more real, but the television had also shown images of people around the country acting normally. London was not bowed, a jaunty TV presenter had said, standing in Oxford Street among the usual chaos of tourists, shoppers and slow-moving traffic. As far as the city centre was concerned it was 'business as usual'. A couple of young Asian girls had bumped into the presenter in their haste to get to Topshop. The BBC had replayed the clip at intervals throughout the night and into the morning: the busy street, the reporter's laugh as the girls knocked him off balance, the girls' hands fluttering up to cover their mouths. Magnus had watched and re-watched it and thought he could see the reporter tensing in anticipation of the surprise collision.

'Pete? Pete?' Magnus's voice sounded puny in the still brickness of the cell. 'Are you all right, mate?'

He did not expect an answer and none came. Magnus tried to remember how the wing had sounded on previous days. He recalled slamming doors, the echo of footsteps, the shouts and laughter of men, but he had been caught up in his own misery and perhaps the prison always fell still in the early hours, at the intersection of early risers and the late to bed.

Magnus did an inventory of his body's hurts. The bin men's punches had buried the pain of Johnny Dongo's fist-in-the-face beneath their own ache. His head was groggy from lack of sleep, and his belly felt empty and sick, but he had none of the symptoms Pete had been tormented by, no cough or sweating, no vomiting or diarrhoea. He leaned over the edge of the bunk. Pete was a foul-smelling huddle on the bed below. Magnus remembered an ailing sheepdog his mother had nursed in her kitchen, the strangeness of seeing the dog in the house, his mother saying, 'It'll not be long now. He's turned his face to the wall.' Thinking about his mother made Magnus feel ashamed. She would never leave Pete to suffer alone, whatever his crime.

The Judas-flap scraped back. A second later Magnus heard a key turning in the lock and swung himself off his bunk. It was a different warder this time, a younger man with a broad, red face, cheeks like boiled ham and the beginnings of a beer belly.

'Fuck.' The screw's hand went to his nose. 'It stinks in here. Kildoran and McFall. Who's who?'

The warder looked like he had been up all night, but his skin was healthy beneath the tiredness, his voice free of the rawness that had made Pete's words sound as if they were being bled from him. The sight of the man, ugly and healthy in the doorway, made Magnus want to sob with relief.

'I'm McFall.' He held up a hand in a gesture that was part salute, part supplication.

The screw gave Magnus a sour look. 'Kildoran?' He squatted down and stared at Pete, keeping his distance from the bunk. There was no reply and the warder turned to look at Magnus. 'Turn him over.'

'What?'

'Roll him on to his back.'

Magnus took a step backward; his spine touched the wall. 'He might be infectious.'

'Just do it.'

Magnus saw a gun in the warder's hand. His stomach gave a queasy flip. No, he realised, it was chunky and decorated with yellow flashes. Not a gun, but a Taser.

He leaned in and touched Pete on the shoulder. 'Pete? Pete? Are you awake, mate?' *Are you alive?* he thought, but there was heat coming from the reeking body. Magnus looked up. 'I think he might still be with us.'

'I asked you to turn him over, not give me your medical opinion.'

Magnus took a tentative hold of the blanket Pete had cocooned himself in and rolled the man towards the edge of the bed. Pete groaned. He had been sick in the night and his face was soiled with vomit. Magnus tried not to gag.

'How long has he been like that?' The disgust Magnus felt was in the screw's voice.

'He might have been ill already when they put me in here on Friday. It got worse on Saturday and much worse last night.'

41

'And you didn't think to report it?'

'I reported it.' It was a struggle to keep his voice calm. 'I was told he'd be moved, but nothing happened. I've been locked in with him all weekend, watching the quarantine alerts on TV. For all I know I've got it too.'

The hand that held the Taser twitched. Magnus flinched again, but nothing happened.

The screw said, 'I wouldn't worry. You look like the kind of selfish bastard that always survives. Half an hour later and you'd probably have been chowing down on the poor sod. Come on.'

He stepped out of the cell into the landing. Magnus followed him.

'Am I going to court?'

The screw gave Pete a last glance and then locked the door on him.

'Courts are suspended.'

The screw touched Magnus's shoulder with the Taser, steering him to the left, along the landing, past rows of bolted doors. The air outside the cell was cleaner, but Magnus thought he could detect some taint beneath the usual prison odour of men, bleach and cheaply catered food. It was the kind of scent that might waft from a city three weeks into a refuse strike, bitter and sugar-cloying.

Magnus said, 'It's illegal to hold me in prison without a trial.'

'Bring it up at your hearing.'

Netting was stretched across the higher landings, like safety nets in a circus big top, to deter 'jumpers'. Discarded lunch wrappers and other detritus were cradled in it. Magnus wondered if it would be strong enough to hold a man. You would be taking a chance, unless you truly wanted to kill yourself. Either way, he guessed there would be a beating waiting when you got down.

Other men were being moved from their cells too. A warder accompanied each prisoner, as if the authorities had become nervous about being outnumbered.

'How many people are ill?'

The screw ignored the question. He took the one-size-fits-all key on his chain and inserted it into a cell door.

Magnus said, 'At least let me have a shower. I've not had a wash since I got here.'

'You're fucking lucky we're shifting you. If it was up to me nonces would be left to rot.' The screw's tone was amiable, as if he had grown used to hating and made his peace with it. 'The Home Office has told us to keep healthy prisoners together and that's what we're doing.'

He opened the door. A thin man was sitting on the top bunk staring down at his hands which were folded loosely in his lap. Magnus's first thought was that the man was praying, but then the prisoner turned his face towards him and Magnus saw the sullen twist of his mouth. His head had been shaved some time ago and his hair was growing back, dark and thick, like suede.

'I don't share.' The man's body looked spare, but Magnus got an impression of broad shoulders beneath the prison-issue tracksuit. 'Check with the governor. He'll tell you why.'

'I know why,' the screw said. 'But the governor's indisposed, so you'll just have to put up with it. Say hello to your new *cellmeat*, Mr McFall.'

Magnus hesitated on the threshold.

'Come on.' The screw gave him a grin and a shove in the small of his back. 'Mr Soames won't bite, will you, Jeb?'

Magnus would have liked to beg, but he stepped into the cell. The door slammed and he heard the jangle of keys, the sound of the barrels turning in the lock. The cell walls were the same rank yellow as the cell he had just left, the patch of blue beyond the window bars might have been the same scrap of sky he had been staring out at for the last three days. He slid into the bottom bunk. The mattress creaked above as the other man lay down, so close that Magnus could hear the rhythm of his breaths.

Six

It was seven in the evening. The time that Magnus should have been stepping up on stage to begin the warm-up to Johnny Dongo's show. He wondered if the show had been cancelled and pictured the empty auditorium, the rows of seats and abandoned aisles. Johnny would be furious, if Johnny was still alive.

Magnus was lying on his mattress listening to the racket of bangs and chanting coming from the other cells and looking up at the wooden base of the upper bunk. Names, obscene drawings and mysterious tags were scrawled across its surface. *Danny takes it up the arse . . . RICKY B IS DEAD . . . there's nowhere like home . . .* There had been points when the hammering fists and raised voices had been so loud that his bunk had tingled with their vibration, but now it was possible to distinguish individual voices among the clamour.

'They haven't fed us.'

It was the first time Jeb had spoken since the screw had put them together. Magnus wondered if his new cellmate found the drop in volume as unnerving as he did. He waited a beat before replying.

'No.' There was a television propped on a shelf in the

45

corner of the cell, a small flat-screen, not much bigger than the laptop he had at home. It had been blank-eyed and silent all afternoon. Magnus asked, 'What about turning the TV on, Big Man?'

The question hung there, ignored.

Jeb said, 'This your first time?'

Magnus had been held in police cells overnight once, on a drunk and disorderly charge, not long after he arrived in London, twenty-one and full of his own exoticness. The booking sergeant had been Scottish too, a big Aberdonian with more than a passing resemblance to the Reverend Ian Paisley. 'Cool your jets, wee man,' he had said as he poured Magnus into the police cell. 'You're in danger of getting your teuchter arse kicked.'

A disembodied pair of breasts stared down at Magnus from the base of the upper bunk, their nipples like eyes. He wished he had a pen to blot out their gaze.

'First time in Pentonville,' he said, hoping he sounded like a veteran. 'You?'

'I'm seasoned.' Jeb's voice had an accent to it, somewhere flat and northern Magnus could not place; one of those nowhere towns that used to have a mine or a factory. Jeb said, 'They shouldn't have put you in with me.'

Magnus kept his voice as expressionless as the other man's. 'Maybe not, but they did.'

Outside on the landings they had launched into a favourite in their repertoire: *Why are we waiting? Why are we fucking waiting* . . . Magnus closed his eyes. There were definitely fewer voices than before. He thought about what the penalty for being billeted with Jeb might be: a pair of hands around

46

the throat, a pillow to the face, a boot to the groin, or worse? He was growing tired of being afraid, but the fear persisted. Magnus took a few deep breaths, as if he were about to step on stage, and repeated his question. 'Any chance of putting the TV on, Big Man? There might be some news.'

'TV's fucked.'

'I have a knack with TVs.' It was a lie. 'I can have a go at it if you like.'

The body in the bed above shifted and then Jeb leaned down and stared at Magnus, his face large and too close; no smile, just the grim line of a mouth set in a blank face.

'I lost my privileges.' His eyes were brown with large irises and long lashes. Cow's eyes, Magnus's mother would call them. 'They took the digi-box away.'

Magnus wondered if the man was on medication and if so what would happen if it ran out. He was not much of a fighter. A fast jab of wit had always been his most effective weapon.

'Do you have a radio?'

The bunk creaked faintly as Jeb flopped back on to his mattress.

'I told you, no privileges. Who gives a fuck what's happening out there anyway?'

'How long have you been without privileges?'

'Haven't you learned not to ask questions?'

Jeb's voice was a slamming door, as final as the turn of a screw's key but Magnus had been alone with his thoughts for too long to keep quiet now that the silence between them had been broken.

'There's stuff happening on the outside you want to know about.'

Jeb snorted. 'You guys straight out of the van still believe outside matters. It doesn't. Not in here.'

'Maybe that used to be true, but the outside has found its way inside. What do you think that rammy's about?'

'The screws are on strike, or they've accidentally-on-purpose done some fucker in, or the government's cut prison food in exchange for more votes. Whatever it is doesn't matter, beyond the fact that they're not feeding us and that racket's beginning to mash my head.'

'It's more than that, it's—'

'I don't give a fuck. Not unless Jesus Christ himself's declared an amnesty and brought along a few beers to celebrate with the boys.'

Jeb's voice was bitter, but Magnus had detected a note of curiosity in it.

'There's no beer, but things are getting a bit biblical.'

He sat up with his back against the wall of the cell, and began to tell the other man about the virus. Jeb listened in silence. Outside, in the hallways beyond, the shouts and chanting grew and swelled and fell, and still no one came to feed them.

Seven

Magnus had watched scores of jailbreaks on TV. He knew the options. You could dig yourself out, through the wall or floor, depending on the structure of the cell. Or you might squeeze through the gap left by an easily removed ceiling tile and travel the mysterious space between roof and ceiling, unseen above your jailers' heads. Bars could be filed, windows forced, fences climbed, barbed wire negotiated, open fields traversed, the consoling shelter of a forest found.

Jeb said, 'We need one of the screws to open the door.'

'That'd be good.' The words came out more sarcastically than Magnus had intended. 'You believe me then?'

'Something's up.' Jeb's feet were dangling over the edge of the bed, his heels level with Magnus's eye line. The rubber soles of his trainers were imprinted, *Size 11*. 'Prison grub's crap, but cons live for their food. There should be a fuck of a racket out there.'

The almighty chorus that had shaken the halls had dwindled to occasional calls and shouting. The sounds were too distant for Magnus to make out the substance of their words, but their tone had shifted from anger to desperation. Once or twice he had heard sobbing and felt tears rising in his own

49

eyes. He would have liked to have battered against the door of the cell and added his voice to the protest, but the fear that it might annoy his cellmate had stopped him.

Jeb had kept silent, out of sight on the bunk above, while Magnus related what he knew of the virus. Magnus had wondered if the other man thought he was a fantasist and had paused to say, 'I know all this sounds mad, but believe me, it's true.'

Telling the story reminded him of other details: how pale and sweat-soaked the Dongolite had been before he toppled on to the railway track, Johnny Dongo's oncoming cold, the grating cough of the rapist in the alleyway, the hollow eyes and sallow faces of the bin men who had beaten him up.

Jeb's legs swung to and fro, to and fro; frustration and pent-up energy. 'We need to be ready for them.'

Magnus slid along his bunk, out of reach of the large feet. 'The screws?'

'Screws, cons, whoever comes through the door.'

'They've got Tasers.'

'So we get ready for Tasers.'

'And if no one comes?'

The legs stopped swinging. 'We draw straws for who eats who.'

Magnus made an almost-but-not-quite-decent living from his wit, but all he could manage was a weak, 'Very funny.'

'Laugh a minute, me.'

The north of England accent was more present. Magnus wondered if it signified anything. Jeb letting his guard down, or maybe trying to get Magnus to let his own guard down, so he could take charge and use him as a human Taser-shield.

50

His mind was spiralling towards panic. As long as Jeb had lain silent and calm on his bunk there had been the possibility that this was a prison crisis, unusual but not unprecedented. That the other man was taking it seriously, more than seriously, was spooked by it, made the virus real.

Magnus asked, 'How do you feel?'

Metal returned to the flat voice and Jeb's legs resumed their restless rocking. 'You sound like a woman.'

Magnus said, 'I don't mean emotionally. How do you feel physically?'

'Hungry.'

'But otherwise all right?'

'No. Otherwise fucked off, but I'm not sick if that's what you mean. How about you?'

'The same.'

'Good news for both of us then, if this virus is as bad as you say it is.'

There was a grudge of accusation in Jeb's delivery.

'Don't blame the messenger.'

Jeb slid from his bunk and leaned against the cell wall. Magnus saw the height of him, shorter than he remembered, five eleven or thereabouts, but broad-shouldered and barrel-chested. Jeb smiled for the first time. His voice was soft and reasonable.

'Best not to tell me *don't*. Not if we're going to try and get out of this together.'

The sky beyond the cell window crept to a blush-tinted grey that slid in turn to black and then back to a pink-grey dawn; another night, another day. Magnus had resolved

51

not to think of food, but his mind kept drifting to his mother's slow-cooked casseroles, more fragrant even than Hamza's Italian pastas, though Hamza's penne con salsiccia picante had been a masterpiece of bite and spice that barely left room for zabaglione. Places came uninvited into Magnus's mind too. The beach at Skara Brae covered in the large flat stones the ancestors had heated in their fires and used to warm water. They would have roasted fish too. Magnus could almost smell grilled sea trout. His cousin Hugh had always been landed with the job of gutting their catch, while Magnus and the other boys gathered drift-wood for the fire. Salmon was good, and herring coated in oatmeal or poached in milk, though he had hated it as a boy. Christ! He remembered his primary school classroom, the smell of wet coats drying on the radiators, Mrs Anderson's stern eye and quick smiles. Hadn't there been a Scottish prince thrown into a dungeon and so starved that he ate his own hands? Magnus held his hands up in front of his face. They were bony and unappetising, the knuckles red from clenching his fists.

'Listen.' Jeb's voice was a whisper.

Magnus kept his own voice low. 'What?'

Jeb slid from the bunk and went quietly to the door. Magnus followed him. There were footsteps on the landing. The sound was uneven and limping, but it was coming slowly closer. The terror he had been trying to keep at bay rushed at Magnus. He imagined some dreadful spindly-legged beast, distorted and unnatural, slouching towards them. Jeb gave his shoulder a shove. It was time to put their plan into action.

'Hello!' Magnus's voice was rusty from lack of use.

'Hello! Are you ill? I'm a doctor. I can help you if you let me out of here.'

The footsteps stopped. Magnus felt Jeb moving quietly in the cell behind him.

'Hello? My name is Magnus McFall. I'm a qualified doctor.' There was no response from the corridor, but the footsteps had not resumed. 'I studied medicine at the University of Edinburgh. I specialised in respiratory diseases before I got myself into this spot of bother.' There was a character Magnus used in his act, a bumptious Scotsman inspired by Mr Brown his maths teacher, whose certainty in the wrongness of the world had sent him into the St Ola Hotel every afternoon before the school bell had finished its final peal. 'Don't be scared. I saw a lot of this kind of thing in Africa during the SARS epidemic.'

Jeb whispered, 'Don't overdo it.'

But Magnus was sure he could feel the limping presence listening on the other side of the door.

'There are things I can do right now, as soon as you let me out, which will alleviate your discomfort.'

Somebody coughed. There was a sound of retching and then a faint voice said, 'Prove you're a doctor.'

Magnus had feared the challenge, but he put a smile into his voice. 'I can't very well do that from behind a closed door. Let me out and I'll prove it.'

There was a pause while the voice stopped to consider and then it said, 'Tell me something.'

'What kind of thing?'

'The kind of thing a doctor would know.'

'Fucking hell.' Jeb's voice was a low warning.

Magnus realised that if he failed, his cellmate would blame him. He thought of Pete's sickness, the pains that had racked him.

'I know your symptoms and what they signify. Your body is trying to expel the virus, hence your vomiting, diarrhoea and severe sweating. Unfortunately this kind of physical panic makes your body rather indiscriminate, and so it's also expelling a lot of useful and necessary stuff along with the bad. That's why, instead of feeling cleansed by the purges, you are shivery and disorientated. My first job will be to replace lost nutrients; thereby stabilising your condition; the next will be to—'

There was a sound of metal on metal as the person on the other side of the door tried to insert their key into the keyhole. It clattered to the floor and Jeb swore softly. 'Jesus Christ.'

Magnus held a hand up in the air, warning him to keep quiet.

'Just take it slowly,' he coaxed. 'Lack of co-ordination is a classic symptom, but you'll feel better soon.' At last the key was in the lock. 'You're doing well,' Magnus said. The key turned. Jeb tensed. The door pushed inward. Magnus stepped out of the way, just like they had rehearsed. 'Don't be scared,' he said and his voice wavered.

The screw's face might once have been a rich copper, now it was grey. He was clutching a Taser, but his eyes were unfocused, his hands trembling.

Magnus said, 'I don't think you need to—'

But Jeb sprang into his part of the routine. He raised the small, flat-screen TV in his hands and dashed it against the screw's face. The man slammed against the cell wall and crumpled to the ground. The Taser flew from his hand, rattled against the corner of the bunk and slid across the floor. Jeb pulled his foot into a kick.

Magnus grabbed hold of his arm. 'He's finished.'

Jeb's biceps were bunched hard, ready for action. He pulled himself free and for a moment Magnus thought he was going to follow through, but then Jeb shook his head, like a man trying to shake himself awake and said, 'Get his keys.'

Jeb's blow had stunned the screw and there was a gash on his forehead where the corner of the television had met its mark, but neither of these should have pinned him, gasping for air, on the floor. Magnus knelt down beside him.

'I'm sorry, pal. We were worried no one was going to come and let us out.'

The keys were on a chain attached to the screw's belt. Magnus stiffened, trying to keep his face as far from the other man's as possible, and pressed his hand into the softness of the screw's belly, trying to find whatever held them there. 'Sorry,' he said again. 'We didn't know what else to do.'

'You're not a doctor?' Disappointed hope quivered the screw's voice.

'No.' Magnus had found the clip securing the key chain. He unfastened it and shoved the keys into his tracksuit pocket. 'I'm a comedian.'

'A comedian?'

The screw was trying to get up. Magnus considered sliding his hands beneath the man's arms and dragging him on to the bunk, but the thought of coming into contact again with

55

the sweat-soaked body appalled him.

'Come on.' Jeb was already out on the landing.

Magnus pulled the blanket from the bed. He draped it over the man and shoved a pillow beneath his head.

'Sorry.'

'You said you were a doctor,' the screw whispered.

Magnus did not bother to tell him what he did for a living again. It wasn't funny any more. He closed the door gently behind him.

Eight

The landing was lit by emergency lights and hollow with silence. Magnus followed Jeb, the keys a weight in his pocket. The central hall looked as he remembered, a concrete and metal panopticon, designed to keep men on show. The walls were painted the same fatty-tissue yellow as hospital waiting rooms and school assembly halls. Perhaps it was the design that made Magnus feel their every step was being observed.

Jeb whispered, 'We can't be the only ones.'

Magnus kept his voice low. 'No, there's no way.'

'We need to get shot of here. Anyone asks, tell them we were moved here from D Wing and hope they don't twig the colour of our tracksuits. If cons find out we're VPs, you'll wish you'd caught the sweats.'

Magnus's confusion must have shown on his face because Jeb hissed, 'A vulnerable prisoner. A fucking nonce.'

'All I did was to try and stop a girl from getting raped—'

'I'm not interested. Same way you're not interested in why I'm here. They won't be interested in talking about it either, except with their fists.' Jeb paused and held out a hand. 'Give us the keys.' Magnus glanced at the Taser. It was chunky and made of plastic, but its shape was hard and menacing. No one would mistake it for a toy. 'Don't worry,' Jeb said. His voice had less of the north in it again. 'I'm not going to lock you up.'

'Hey!' The shout came from one of the cells further down the corridor, followed by frantic banging. 'Hey! Is somebody there?'

Magnus started towards the noise, but Jeb caught him by the shoulder.

'Leave it.'

'You must be joking.'

'No. He could be category A. They're the mad bastards murderers and rapists have nightmares about. You don't want those guys getting loose.'

'We can't leave him locked up.'

'We bloody can.'

BANG, BANG, BANG.

'Please, for Christ's sake.' The voice was raw and desperate. 'I'm shut in here with a dead man!'

BANG, BANG, BANG.

Other cells were taking up the noise. Magnus tried to work out how many prisoners he could hear. A dozen? Twenty? Maybe less. The solidarity of the first days' chanting was gone. The voices cut over and through each other, lost and ghostly, the sense of their words drowned in each other's appeals.

'They're not our problem.' Jeb held out his hand again. 'Keys.'

'They could starve to death.'

Jeb shrugged his shoulders. 'Shouldn't have got locked up in the first place then, should they?'

58

It was the shrug that did it, the casual dismissal so soon after their own escape.

Magnus turned his back on Jeb and ran down the landing to the cell that had started the noise, expecting to feel the sudden scorch of a Taser. He slid the key into the lock and turned to cast a quick glance at Jeb. The other man was gone. Magnus hesitated, but the prisoner must have heard him on the other side of the door. The voice within became soft and wheedling.

'C'mon, man, let me out. He died this morning. It's fucking horrible. I'm going crazy in here.'

Magnus glanced over the landing, wondering if Jeb could have made it down the stairs to the lower hall so quickly, but there was no sign of him.

'Come on, please, man. He died with his eyes open. They're staring at me.' The voice sounded tearful.

Magnus took a deep breath, turned the key in the lock, gave the door a shove and took a step backwards.

The man who emerged looked nothing to be frightened of. He had the beginnings of a sparse beard and his prison tracksuit was creased and grubby, but he was short and underweight, and the face beneath the beard looked young and tear-stained.

'You don't have anything to eat, do you?'

Magnus said, 'No, sorry.'

'Fuck, I'm starving.'

The stranger cast a look around the hall, as if he suspected there might be a buffet waiting somewhere. The noises coming from other cells were growing louder and more frantic. Desperation gave power to the banging; clenched fists and strong arms. Magnus hesitated, like a lion-keeper in a war zone, keen for his beasts to survive the bombing, but unsure of the consequences of opening their cages.

'I'd leave them to rot if I were you, mate.' The newly released man was walking companionably beside him. 'I mean, I know you let me out, cheers and all that, but this wing's full of nonces.' He realised what he had said and added, 'No offence meant.'

Magnus gave him the stare he reserved for hecklers. 'None taken.'

The man was dressed in the same incriminating blue sweats as he and Jeb. Magnus wanted to add something about not being a sex offender or a child molester, but then a cell door opened. There was a rush of movement and Magnus was knocked across the landing and into the guard-rail. Strong hands pinned him to the barrier.

'Keys!' Jeb's face was too close, his features tight with anger.

Magnus slid a hand into his pocket and brought out the keys. The noise in the cells was a discordant wave, a choppy sea at ebb tide, but it was not loud enough to drown out the slam of the newly released prisoner's feet against the stairs to the lower landings. Magnus handed the keys to Jeb. 'Please, don't lock me back up.'

Jeb shoved Magnus from him and jogged towards the stairs. Magnus followed, realising that he needed to stick close if he was to get through the series of locked doors that would take them out of the building and into the grounds beyond.

Nine

The main door of the wing led outside into a courtyard surrounded by high buildings. Jeb let it swing behind him and it was only luck that Magnus managed to catch it and slip out before the door slammed shut. 'Look, I'm sorry. You were right. I should have left the other cells well alone.'

It was hot outside, the sunshine glaring. Jeb moved, keeping close to the wall like a soldier in an urban combat zone. Magnus followed, sticking to the shadows. The buildings that formed the courtyard were punctuated by ranks of barred windows. Each window indicated a cell; a prisoner dead behind a locked door or abandoned alive; pairs of staring eyes following their progress. The sensation of being watched made him think of a recurring nightmare he had of being on stage, the audience getting to their feet and coming slow and zombie-like towards him as he struggled to remember his routine. There were fresh nightmares waiting for him in the thought of those barred windows. He wondered if he should try to get the keys from Jeb after all, go back, release as many as he could and damn the consequences, but he ran on, following his cellmate through the courtyard's shadows.

Jeb stopped at the corner of a wall, beneath a queerly

angled CCTV camera, surveying the last section of open ground they would have to cross before they reached the admissions building. If he wanted to, Jeb could leave him there, Magnus realised. On the outside-inside, surrounded by high walls and locked doors, exposed to the elements, the stares of the windows and the fading men inside.

'We can split up as soon as we get out of here,' Magnus whispered, 'but we stand a better chance of making it out if we stick together.'

Jeb glanced at him. 'You're a liability, mate.'

'We wouldn't have got out of the cell in the first place if it wasn't for me.'

'You think so?' Jeb's smile mocked him. 'It was me that smashed that screw in the face.'

'And it was me that persuaded him to unlock the door.'

'Then you turned into Jesus fucking Christ and started releasing random villains.' The smile was gone. 'Didn't you think there might be a reason I stick to my own fucking cell?' Every word was a bullet. 'Get yourself fucking killed if you like, but leave me out of it.'

'I apologised, okay?' There was no point in being polite, Magnus realised. Jeb was like a belligerent venue manager who needed convincing before he would agree to book a new act. Appeasement would get him nowhere. 'I told you, I won't get in the way and I might be some help.'

Jeb cast him a sceptical glance, but something in Magnus's words must have persuaded him because he whispered, 'Don't talk and don't try any Good Samaritan acts. First sign of trouble you're on your own. Understand?' Magnus nodded. Jeb cast a quick look around the courtyard. 'We need to get through the admissions hall' – he gestured up ahead with the hand that was holding the Taser – 'and then out through the front gate. I reckon these keys will let us into admissions, but I don't know about the gate. If you see anyone, keep your head down. Don't speak until spoken to and take your lead from me.'

Jeb did not bother to wait for Magnus to agree. He loped towards the door of the admissions block, keeping his body low. Magnus thought he heard voices shouting behind them, but all his strength was focused on keeping up with Jeb and he did not look back.

The key turned first time and they entered a small vestibule at the bottom of a steep metal staircase. Jeb clattered upward, the Taser clutched in his right hand. Magnus followed in silence, matching his pace to the other man's. The effects of his beatings were still upon him and his legs protested, but he forced them on, to an upper landing and another locked door.

'I feel like I'm in a fucking computer game.' Jeb shifted the Taser to his left hand and took the keys from his pocket. He slid them awkwardly into the lock. Magnus wanted to say that he would relieve him of one or the other, but knew the offer would be rejected. Jeb looked cautiously round the door. Something about the practised stealth of the move made Magnus wonder if the other man had been in the armed forces. 'Okay.' Jeb nodded to him. 'Keep up, and remember what I told you, take your lead from me.'

They entered a long corridor. Magnus supposed he must have passed through it on the night he was admitted, bloodied and bruised, still not quite sober, but he could remember little of that journey except a prison officer's hand steadying him when he stumbled. It had been a small kindness in a night lacking in compassion and Magnus found himself wondering if the man had caught the virus.

The thought made him think of his mother again. He had called her a week after her birthday, alerted by a caustic text from his sister Rhona, but had he spoken to her since? He didn't think so. She and Rhona would be fine, he reassured himself. London was an overcrowded airport terminal, jammed with travellers and the people who serviced them. The infection was bound to cut a swathe through the capital, but the Orkney Islands were at the butt end of the world and surrounded by sea. However hard the city was hit, the Orkneys would survive.

But what about tourists? an unwelcome voice in his head whispered. *What about the cruise ships and twice-daily ferries? The flights direct from Edinburgh, Aberdeen and Glasgow that connect with flights from London and beyond?*

'Where will you go when you get out?' he asked Jeb, to shut the voice up.

He expected the other man to tell him to mind his own business but Jeb said, 'Fucked if I know. Guess I'll cross that bridge when the time comes.' He bared his teeth; half snarl, half grin. 'If I haven't burned it already. You?'

'Up north, home.'

Jeb looked at him, his expression curious. 'Will they take you in?'

'Yes.'

'Lucky you.'

'Let's hope so.'

Jeb stopped and raised a hand in the air, silently telling Magnus to freeze. He cocked his head to one side. The pose reminded Magnus of the games of cowboys and Indians he and his cousins had played. Hugh had always been the tracker shaman, able to spot the enemy (for some reason the cowboys had always been the enemy) from miles away. Usually the memory would have raised a smile, but Magnus had heard the footsteps that had stopped Jeb in his tracks.

'In here.' Jeb pointed to a half-glass door marked *Education*. He unlocked the door and Magnus slipped in after him, closing it quietly. The room had been designed to allow tutors to be on their own with inmates, while also allowing screws to keep an eye on what was happening inside. Prisoners' paintings covered one wall. Perhaps the art teacher encouraged self-portraits, or maybe the inmates used each other as models. Bullet heads and staring eyes sent out blank challenges from the wall, fronts that must not be breached for fear of what might lie behind them. The prison featured too, its high walls and vertical bars looming aggressively towards the viewer. It was how the place made you feel, like it was alive and biding its time before it crushed you.

Jeb crouched beneath the pictures, his back against the wall, the Taser cradled in his hands. Magnus hunkered down beside him, under a large Dolly Mixture coloured painting of the Disney castle, complete with Mickey, Minnie and their weird chums. Some prisoner had painted it as a present for his small child, Magnus supposed. The thought depressed him and he wondered again what waited beyond the gates of the prison. Had the sickness taken hold on the outside, or had Pentonville been abandoned in some crude attempt at quarantine?

Jeb's breaths were keeping time with the approaching footsteps in the corridor beyond.

Magnus whispered, 'There might be safety in numbers.'

'Not for me.'

Fear had drained the blood from Jeb's face and tightened his features. He looked like a medieval church effigy carved by a mason with one eye on the old gods.

'What did you do?' The words slipped out before Magnus could stop them.

Jeb shook his head. 'Not what you're thinking.'

'You don't know what I'm thinking.'

'Don't I?'

He was right. A series of tabloid headlines were riffling through Magnus's mind, the kind of stuff that made you lay the newspaper face down. He started to get to his feet but Jeb sank a hand into his shoulder, keeping him there.

'They'll know you're a VP from the colour of your tracksuit. We're branded in here, remember? If they find us, our only chance is to attack first. Don't wait to see if they're going to play nice.' Jeb's voice was so low Magnus had to strain to hear it. 'They won't. If they smile, smile back, then hit them as hard as you can and run.'

The footsteps were close now. Jeb flattened himself against the wall and shut his eyes. Magnus focused on the window into the corridor. He saw the men's shadows approach followed swiftly by the men themselves, four prisoners, each dressed in green sweats, rather than the blue that he and Jeb were wearing. The men's complexions had the exhausted, stone-greyness of people denied the sun and they each had the loose-skin look of men who had recently lost weight, but none of them appeared to have the virus. A prisoner at the back of the line raised a hand in sly benediction and winked at them. Magnus recognised him as the man he had set free, now dressed in the colours of a different hall. The man nodded to let him know he wouldn't give them away and passed by.

They crouched beneath the paintings in the education room until the men's footsteps faded into silence. Magnus got to his feet first. Something in the intensity of Jeb's fear made him as keen to escape the other man as he had been to ally with him.

'Good luck.' Magnus was at the door before he realised that it was locked. Outside, in some distant corridor, the sound of screaming echoed. He turned and saw Jeb getting to his feet. The keys and weapon in his hands made him look more jailer than prisoner, despite his prison-issue clothes.

'Like you said, we can split up once we get out of here.' Jeb's voice was low and intense, as if he had found his courage and was making a conscious effort to hold on to it. 'But right now I reckon we stand more chance if we stick together.'

The screaming died abruptly.

Magnus asked, 'What did you do that makes you so frightened?'

Jeb stepped closer. 'Until you get these colours off you better be scared too.'

Magnus felt the heat of the other man's body and smelled the sweet funky smell of stale and fresh sweat mingling on his skin.

'All you need to know is that I never hurt anyone who didn't have it coming to them. I never touched up little kiddies and I never put my hands on a woman that didn't want me to put my hands on her.'

'Is that what the women would say?'

Jeb flinched. 'Women say a lot of things.' He unlocked the door and scanned the corridor left to right, like a sniper. 'I never met a woman who didn't say more than her prayers.' There was a catch in his voice, as if something in his throat's mechanism was broken.

Ten

The prison officers' locker room had already been ransacked, but whoever had been there had concentrated on money and valuables. The small space was littered with clothes, rifled wallets and gaping sports bags. Jeb undressed quickly and stowed his tracksuit out of sight on top of one of the lockers. Magnus stripped off his tracksuit. It was like trying to find an outfit in a jumble sale, sifting through a muddle of styles and sizes, looking for something that would fit and would not mark him out as a fraud.

'Hurry up. It's not a fashion show.' Jeb pulled on a Hope for Heroes T-shirt.

Magnus saw the Union Jack tattoo on Jeb's chest and wondered again if he had been in the forces. He found a bright blue mod T-shirt with a target on the chest and topped it with a brown hoodie. The hoodie was too warm for the weather, but he liked the idea of being able to hide his face.

'Here, these should fit you.' Jeb tossed a pair of jeans at him. They were long in the leg. Magnus folded the hems into turn-ups. Jeb was tying the laces on a pair of top-of-the-range Nikes. 'Try and find something you can run in.'

It was strange, wearing the clothes of someone you had

never met. Magnus rooted through the tangle of clothes and shoes until he found a pair of size eights. He wondered if the screws had left in such a rush there was no time to change out of their uniforms, or if they were still somewhere in Pentonville, coughing up their guts in the sickbay or dealing with a riot in the far reaches of the jail. He thrust his hands into the pockets of the jacket and found an Oyster card and a discount voucher for two classic margaritas and a bottle of wine at Pizza Express. He crumpled the voucher into a ball and let it drop to the ground.

Out in the prison corridors beyond someone bayed like a wolf.

'I'll be glad to get out of here,' Jeb muttered. He was rooting through the abandoned gear, pocketing car keys, checking ID cards. He found a Snickers bar, tore its wrapper free and shoved it into his mouth.

Magnus felt he might kill Jeb for a share of the chocolate but he asked, 'How will we do it?'

'Same way we came in, through the front door.'

The locker room was windowless and lined with steel cabinets. It was larger than the cell they had shared, but it gave Magnus the same trapped feeling and his skin itched with the urge to escape. A *Daily Express* lay folded beneath a wooden bench. Its headline screamed, *CONTAGION!* Magnus picked up the tabloid. It had been published two days ago. The first three pages were devoted to the virus. People were calling it the sweats and it was overloading hospitals in London, Paris, New York and Berlin. There was an editorial alleging that the poor state of the NHS had precipitated the crisis, but the criticisms were well-rehearsed and perfunctory, as if the journalist's heart had not really been in the story.

China and Russia had issued statements denying rumours of outbreaks in their major cities, but social media contradicted official accounts and the *Express* carried surreptitiously-taken photographs of a Shanghai hospital ward lined with beds full of failing patients.

A small galaxy of celebrities had been felled by the virus. Magnus searched for Johnny Dongo's name, but either the comedian was okay or he had been eclipsed by A-listers. There was something distasteful about the celebrity photographs, the rows of hot women in bikinis, all of them dead.

'Look at this.' Magnus passed the paper to Jeb.

'You can't trust tabloid rags.' Jeb tossed the paper on to the floor. 'They don't care about facts, or whose life they ruin, just as long as they can twist out a good story.'

Magnus lifted the paper from the floor and held it wide, showing Jeb the photograph of the hospital ward, flanked by sidebars of smiling female celebrities.

'People are dying.'

Jeb was riffling through jackets and trouser pockets. He glanced up. 'We already knew that.' He clicked a penknife open, checking its blade. 'How many of these actresses are holed up in some spa, ready to come back from the dead with a big *tada* when the time's right? And who says the people in that hospital have the chills? All that photo shows is exactly what I'd expect to see in a hospital, patients lying in bed.'

'They're calling it the sweats.'

Jeb clicked the penknife shut. 'Sweats, chills, I don't give a

71

fuck.' He slid the closed knife into his jeans pocket. 'Just concentrate on getting out of here. We can worry about killer flu after that.'

Magnus joined Jeb on the floor and rummaged in a sports bag. There was nothing useful in it, just a bottle of shower gel that claimed to double as shampoo and a towel, but touching another man's possessions felt intimate and wrong. Magnus shoved it out of the way and started on another bag. He wanted to find something to eat. He wanted a knife like the one Jeb had found, or, better still, a Taser. He said, 'What if the front door's locked?'

'I'm hoping someone will have already solved that problem for us, but if it's locked then we find a way of opening it.' Getting rid of his incriminating tracksuit had made Jeb more confident. 'Here.' He passed Magnus a prison officer's identity card.

The man in the ID photograph was older than Magnus. His hair was a similar dark brown, but it was cut short in a barber-shop no-style. His face was thin and intelligent-looking; perfect casting for a university professor, or a curator of rare manuscripts.

'I don't look anything like him,' Magnus said.

'Just flash it and only if you need to.' Jeb pulled on a beige jacket, shoved the Taser into one of its pockets and ran a comb he had found through his hair. 'Tidy yourself up.' He tossed the comb to Magnus.

Magnus glanced in a small mirror hung on the inside of one of the lockers. His hair was greasy, his chin covered in stubble too long to be designer, but too short to be called a beard. The bruises on his face were shifting to yellow, but the graze on his cheek had scabbed and it was obvious that his eye had recently been blacked.

'Ready?'

Jeb shoved an NYPD baseball cap on his head. His beard was slightly ragged, but the civilian clothes he had chosen fitted well and he might easily be mistaken for an off-duty prison officer.

'You look like a screw.'

'Good, that's what I was aiming for.' Jeb grinned. 'I'm not sure what you look like, but it'll have to do.'

The corridors up ahead echoed with the rumble of male voices. They passed a splash of blood blooming head-height on a wall, red and vital against the whitewash. Their eyes met, but neither of them said anything. Magnus wished he had the weight of a Taser in his pocket.

'Anyone who's got out will come this way,' Jeb whispered. 'So sooner or later we're going to meet someone. If anything kicks off, go in hard.' Magnus wanted to protest that he did not know how to 'go in hard', but he nodded. Jeb must have seen the fear on his face because he added, 'Fight dirty and don't hold back.'

Magnus's father had tried to teach him how to fight, shouting instructions while Magnus threw punches into a grain sack, *left, right, left, right, right, right, right,* but Magnus did not have the dexterity required of a good featherweight and he lacked the power to be a heavyweight.

'It's your mouth that gets you into trouble,' his dad had finally said. 'Let's hope it learns how to get you out of it too.'

They met their first prisoners in the next stretch of

73

corridor. There were two of them, both still dressed in green prison-issue tracksuits and trainers. Magnus detected a glimmer of sweat on the younger of the pair which spoke of the virus. That was who he would go for if it came to a fight, he decided, the under-fed youth whose hands were trembling. The decision prompted a familiar jolt of shame.

'All right, lads?' Jeb's voice was bold and confident.

The men froze and the boy Magnus had marked as his target muttered, 'Shit.'

'Don't worry, we're not screws.' Jeb took off his baseball cap and rubbed a hand through his suede head. 'Just treated ourselves to a couple of going-away outfits. Talking about going away, you're going the wrong way, aren't you?'

'Depends whether you want to get your head kicked in or not,' the elder of the duo said. He was a man somewhere beyond his mid-forties who looked like he knew what it was to take a kicking. The man's face was pitted with old scars that suggested a flight through a car windscreen or unexpected congress with a plate-glass window.

'Trouble up ahead?'

'You could say that.' The man's voice was heavy with resentment. 'A reception committee checking who's fit for the outside.'

'Too scared to go outside themselves, if you ask me.' The boy hugged his ribs, as if he were cold and trying to stop himself from shivering. 'They said I was sick. No one sick gets to leave.' His voice wavered, but he added bravely, 'I heard on the news that they're sending the army in anyway. That'll fix those cunts. The army have the best doctors too. They'll sort us out.'

'What about you?' Jeb asked the older man. 'You look well enough.'

'I didn't want to leave Jack here.' The boy was taller than him, but the scarred man reached up and put an arm around the youth's thin shoulders. 'Him and me's been mates a long time. He needs looking after, specially if he's ill.'

Jeb nodded as if he understood. His expression was neutral, but he stood stolid in the middle of the corridor, blocking the men's progress.

'Anything else we need to know?'

The man shrugged. 'They've got the prison records up on computer and they're checking what people are in for. They say they want to stop any nonces from getting out.'

Magnus snapped, 'Why don't they just mind their own fucking business?'

The older man gave him a shrewd look, but he said, 'The lad here's right. They're long-termers, big men inside, nothing on the outside. I guess they like being big men.'

Jeb said, 'We're both in for intent to supply, you know the sketch. Think they'll have any objection to that?'

'I don't suppose so.' The older man didn't sound convinced. 'Not unless your face doesn't fit.'

Jeb nodded again. 'Yes, there's always that.'

The young boy started to cough. The older man rubbed his back, but the boy's coughing increased, catching in whoops at the back of his throat. Magnus took a step backward, but Jeb held his ground. It seemed that all the air in the boy's body was being expelled, but then he bent forward and was sick against the wall. He crouched over his vomit, gasping for breath.

His companion put an arm around him. 'It's all right, Jack, you're going to be fine.'

'Piss off, you old poof. Can't you even keep your hands off me when I'm bloody dying?'

The man threw Jeb and Magnus an apologetic look. 'I'd like to find him somewhere comfy, where he could have a lie-down.' He gave them a sad half-smile, asking for permission to move on.

Jeb stepped to one side. 'Good luck.'

'Yeah, same to you.'

Jeb waited until the men were further down the corridor and then he asked, 'How many are in this reception committee?'

'A few.'

Magnus would have liked to have pinned the man down on exactly how many a few were, but the answer seemed to satisfy Jeb. He said, 'Are they armed?'

'Tasered up to the eyeballs, mate, wired too. That's why we're planning on bunking down and making the best of things. Prisoners make brutal jailers.'

Eleven

'The boy said the army were coming.' Magnus was crouched next to Jeb in a corner of an intersection in the long, white corridors that were a feature of the admissions block.

Jeb hissed, 'Ever been in army nick?'

'No, have you?'

A stretch of empty hallway loomed before and behind them. They had not seen anyone since encountering the two retreating prisoners, but a rumble of male voices reverberated through the building, echoing from all directions, like cries in an overcrowded swimming pool. There was something high-pitched and excited about the noise that raised the hairs on the back of Magnus's neck and he guessed it would not be long before they met more escapees.

Jeb said, 'I've heard plenty about them from guys that have. The army have their own rules. This isn't the cavalry coming over the hill to save us. We're the bad guys, remember?'

The wolf-man was howling again. It was hard to tell if he was in pain or celebrating his freedom to roam the corridors.

Magnus said, 'I've not even been properly charged. It was

different when I thought we were stuck here, but now help is coming . . .'

The baying noise increased in pitch.

Jeb said, 'I'll fucking throttle that guy if I get my hands on him.' He looked at Magnus. 'The army will help you into a set of handcuffs, kick you up the arse and into a cell that'll make your last place look like a fucking palace. If things are as you say they are, then we need to get out of here, pronto.'

Magnus thought of the headlines in the *Daily Express*. Jeb was right: tabloids were not to be trusted, but the contents of the paper chimed with the television he had watched and the sick prisoners, absent warders and abandoned prison all told their own story. He said, 'Scarface said there's a reception committee checking who's who. If they find our records on the computer they'll know we're VPs.'

'Keep your voice down.' Jeb glanced around as if he were afraid someone might have overheard.

The howling seemed louder, the yells and catcalls of the surrounding voices closer. Magnus would have liked to have found a cell, climbed into bed and hidden himself beneath the covers, until whatever was about to happen, happened, but the smell of Pete's illness was still sharp in his memory and he knew that once closed, cell doors were not so easily opened.

Jeb took a swift intake of breath and whispered, 'They're coming.'

The howling was upon them. A squad of men, most of them still in prison tracksuits, rounded the corner. The wolf-man gambolled beside them like a mascot. He was smaller than Magnus had imagined; a chubby, middle-aged man who it would be easy to imagine devoting Sunday afternoons to washing his car, were it not for the mad bluster of his dance, the crazy tilt of his head. The prisoners had broken up bunks and benches and armed themselves with chair and bed legs. A couple of them carried fire extinguishers. Magnus wondered why it had not occurred to him to arm himself in the same way. He leapt to his feet, ready to run in the opposite direction, but Jeb grabbed his arm.

'Stand your ground.' Jeb pulled his baseball cap low over his eyes, hiding his features in the shadow of its brim. 'This is our best chance.' He stepped into the middle of the corridor and raised a hand in greeting, like a man trying to stop a car on a country road. The group faltered to a halt. No one spoke and then Jeb said, 'Okay to join you lads?'

'We don't need any screws,' a voice from the back said.

There were about fifteen of them, Magnus reckoned. He wondered how they had got out and hoped that no one had seen him and Jeb crossing the courtyard, leaving other prisoners trapped in their cells.

'Do we look like screws?' Jeb's voice was hard and challenging.

The wolf-man waved a chair leg lightly in the air, the way a fool might wave his sceptre. 'You're dressed like off-duty screws, or filth . . .'

Jeb's head jerked at the mention of police. 'We look like screws cos we nicked these clothes from their locker room. We thought they might help us get away. We just want out, same as you do.'

One of the prisoners started to cough, a second man joined in and another spat on the ground.

'Anyone know these boys?' a tall man near the front asked.

There was no one in charge, Magnus realised, no one to make the decision to let them join the group. He said, 'I just got put in here on Friday, no trial, no lawyer. Emergency measures, the police told me.' He let some of the despair he was feeling leak into his voice. 'It's been a fucking nightmare. All I'm interested in is getting home. I've got family I need to get back to.'

The tall man nodded. He looked at Jeb. 'Do I know you?'

Jeb lifted his face and stared him straight in the eyes. 'Ever worked the rigs?'

'No.'

'Maybe we met somewhere.' Jeb shrugged. 'I work the rigs, three weeks on, three weeks off. It makes you stir-crazy. Occasionally it gets me into a bit of bother. Drunk and disorderly; expected a night in the cells, woke up in here.'

The tall man glanced at the men behind him. No one said anything and he gave Magnus and Jeb a curt nod.

'Plan is we go out mob-handed. Extra bodies should be a help.'

Magnus said, 'We met a couple of guys earlier. They told us there's a squad at the front door checking what people are in for and deciding who gets out.'

'We heard that.' The tall man snorted. 'There's always plenty want to make themselves fucking guvnor.'

'Fuck the guvnor!' the wolf-man shouted. A few of the men took up the cry. The wolf-man leapt into his dance again and the men stepped on, their voices rising once more. Magnus realised they were scared and the realisation tightened fear's grip on him. Jeb shoved himself into the huddle of bodies. He grasped Magnus by the shoulder, taking him with him.

Magnus pulled the hood of his stolen jacket up over his head. 'I'm not sure about this.'

Jeb's voice was low. 'Have you got a better suggestion?'

Once, on a Christmas visit to Edinburgh organised by the High School, his cousin Hugh had dragged Magnus on to the starflyer in Princes Street Gardens fairground. Joining the squad of escapees reminded Magnus of the sensation of suddenly being borne aloft by the ride. He felt the same swoop of danger in his stomach, the same loss of control.

Magnus had thrown up over the side of the starflyer. His vomit had been snatched away by the wind, travelling it seemed in one solid mass towards the south side of the gardens. Hugh had laughed so hard Magnus had thought his cousin might throw up too. 'I was just imagining some poor wee man walking his dog and getting hit in the face by your spew,' Hugh said later as the two of them walked along Rose Street in search of a pub that would not be too fussy about the age of its clientele.

Hugh had filled himself full of vodka and pills and walked into the sea, not long before Magnus had decided to hell with islands and left for London. Magnus had often wondered if Hugh had been scared when he did it, or if the drink and drugs had drowned his cousin's fears, even as the bitter sea slid over his head and into his lungs.

The wolf-man capered beside them like a fool at a Morris dance. He waved the chair leg he was carrying lightly in the air, like a sceptre. 'There'll be a squad of soldiers waiting to mow us down soon as we step out those gates.' The wolf-man's voice was high and excited. He pointed the chair leg as if it were a gun and made a rattling noise, aiming it at the prisoners behind him. Somebody knocked it from his hand and someone else kicked it away. The wolf-man scrabbled on the floor, among the feet of the men, searching for it. Magnus thought they had lost him, but it was as if the wolf-man sensed something different about him and Jeb. He soon returned to their side.

'Piss off,' Jeb said. 'Unless you want me to take that stick off you and shove it up your arse.'

'You would, wouldn't you?' the wolf-man said in a camp voice, grinning with delight. He thrust his face close and whispered, 'I know who you are.' Jeb made a lunge for him, but the wolf-man was faster. He ducked backward into the small group of men. 'Don't worry. I'm not a grass.'

'Prick.' Jeb's jaw bunched, but he let the wolf-man go.

The bodies of two screws lay slumped on the floor of the corridor, each of them marked with signs of the sweats.

Magnus whispered, 'What the fuck is this thing?'

Someone said, 'The army will have an antidote.'

Jeb touched the pocket that held the Taser, as if it were a talisman against infection. 'It was probably those army bastards that caused it in the first place.'

Magnus said, 'So maybe we should stick around and get vaccinated.'

Jeb laughed. 'Think they'd share it with scum like us? Who's to say they didn't drop a test-tube accidentally-on-purpose? It wouldn't be the first time inmates have been used as guinea pigs.'

The inmates' conviction that the authorities knew

everything reminded Magnus of the dying youth they had met earlier. *They'll sort us out*, he had said.

'The sweats isn't just killing prisoners.' Magnus jerked a thumb backward to where the screws' bodies lay slouched together in a corner.

The wolf-man was suddenly at their side. He did a twirl and then staggered with the dizziness of it. 'Collateral damage.' He giggled. 'Scratch a screw and you'll find a bastard, it's no great loss.' He waved his chair leg in the air. 'Me, you, these cunts, the whole stinking world. None of it would be a great loss.'

Twelve

Magnus had thought they would pause to work out a plan before they got to the reception desk, but the small band of inmates gained speed as they got closer to the front entrance. A man with keys ran on ahead to unlock each door and hold it open for the rest, who sailed through without faltering, as if they instinctively knew that to lose momentum would be to lose courage. The key-man waited until the last moment before opening the door leading to the entrance hall. He held it wide and they bombed through, keeping close, because the door was only wide enough for one man at a time.

It would have been better to keep quiet and hold on to the element of surprise, but the escapees were anxious and when the wolf-man raised his voice in a high ululating howl, others joined in. The sound was ghastly. Magnus thought that if he had been on the other side of the door he would have fled, but the self-elected cordon at the security desk were made of steelier stuff. They decked the first wave of trespassers with Tasers. The stun guns had been designed to fell with one quick blast, but the inmates pumped the triggers until the men snared by the wires stopped screaming and lay still on the ground. There were only a few Tasers to go round and no time to disengage the cables from their victims' bodies, but the cordon had planned ahead. They weighed in with batons and improvised weapons. Jeb had cannily positioned himself and Magnus in the second wave of the assault. He Tasered the largest of the men guarding the hallway and then took the penknife from his pocket and stabbed another in the neck. Blood gushed from the wound in a mesmerising arc. Magnus grabbed the man as he sank to the ground.

'Jeb, for Christ's sake . . .' He was about to tell his cellmate to get a grip. That he would end up killing someone if he wasn't careful, but then something hit him, hard and sickening, on the back of his head. He fell forward, landing on top of the other man's body. Jeb grabbed him by the scruff of his jumper and hauled him to his feet. They were in the middle of the tussle now, backed up against the admissions desk. 'Computer!' Jeb shouted in Magnus's face.

It took Magnus a second to grasp the command, then he realised what Jeb wanted him to do. He tumbled on to the counter, rolled behind the desk and grabbed the desktop computer. The cables snagged, *fuck, fuck, fuck, fuck, fuck*, but then Magnus managed to topple it to the ground, breaking its screen. He put a foot through the cracked plastic, making certain it was truly beyond use and no one could discover that they were VPs. His heel stuck in the computer's damaged frame. Magnus swore and pulled it free.

An overweight man was grappling with the electronics under the desk. He must have found the correct switch because he punched a hand into the air and shouted, 'Ya beauty!' and the front doors opened automatically. The gate to the outside world waited beyond it. An inmate dressed in jeans and a prison sweatshirt was running into the courtyard, a set of keys swinging in his hands. A prison guard raced after him, but the guard's movements were slow and weaving. He faltered to a halt and sank on to his knees in the middle of the courtyard, clutching his head.

There were only a few of them left tussling in the entrance hall. Magnus looked for Jeb and saw him in the centre of a small ruck. The men were squeezed together, limbs tangled, like Uppies and Doonies in close combat for the ba' and it was hard to tell who was fighting who.

'C'mon, lads. Have yous lot nae hames to go to?' Magnus shouted in the voice of Johnny Bell, landlord of the Snapper, who could empty a bar full of thirsty trawlermen, swift as the sea could sweep you from your feet. 'The bloody gate's open. Get yourselves through it.'

Some inmates took heed and ran for the door, a few continuing to exchange kicks and punches as they fled. A small knot of prisoners was too engaged in the fight to extricate themselves, afraid that if they turned their back their opponents would gain the advantage. Magnus had lost sight of Jeb, but it was every man for himself now. He scanned the foyer, plotting his route to the door. There was no way to avoid passing the cluster of fighters, but perhaps if he ran . . .

'He's a fucking nonce,' a voice screamed.

For a moment Magnus was unsure who had shouted, then he saw the weasel face of the hungry VP he had released from his cell during their escape. Magnus's cheeks flushed. He tore the computer keyboard from its shattered monitor, ready to use it as a weapon.

'I'm not . . .'

Denial started to his lips in a rush of breath and shame. Then he saw the cut across the small man's face, the bloody knife in Jeb's hand, and realised who the VP had accused. The fight faltered and eyes glanced in Jeb's direction, marking him. It was Magnus's cue to break for the door, but he shouted, 'He's lying to save his own arse. That guy's the nonce. I saw him earlier, straight out of the VP wing. He was wearing blue sweats.'

Two men had already grabbed Jeb. One of them pressed his hand to Jeb's throat, pushing his head back, turning his face crimson. The small inmate was on the edge of the tussle. He pointed at Magnus. 'He's one t—'

Eyes swivelled in Magnus's direction and he realised he was about to be lynched.

Jeb nutted one of the men holding him. He kicked the other one's knees, knocking him flat, and then kneed the weasel-faced VP in the groin before he could finish his accusation. The man crumpled and Jeb kicked him in the head, felling him. The weasel-man crawled towards the exit. Magnus saw the penknife shining in Jeb's hand and started towards him.

The fight was filtering away, more inmates making for the door. But the two prisoners who had fixed on Jeb seemed content to delay their escape. Blood was streaming from the nose of the man Jeb had nutted, but pain seemed to have given him strength. He sprang to his feet and caught hold of Jeb again. His companion shook the penknife from Jeb's grip.

'Just do him,' the other man said, his smile as wide as his gut. 'One less nonce, you'll be doing the world a favour.'

If Magnus ran now he might make it through the front gate and out into the streets beyond. The man raised the penknife in the air. Magnus fired the computer keyboard at the upraised hand. It dealt Jeb a glancing blow on the forehead that freed him from the smiler's grip and knocked the knife from the other man's grasp.

'Jesus Christ!' Jeb's attacker lunged towards Magnus who picked up a discarded fire extinguisher, freed its safety catch and pulled down on the trigger, blasting the men with foam. Jeb was back on his feet, grappling with the fat man, but the foam made the tiled floor treacherous and he slid backward, pulling his opponent on top of him.

'For fuck's sake,' Jeb shouted. 'This isn't fucking *Home Alone*. Hit him with it.'

Magnus swung the extinguisher; it was heavy and he almost lost his balance, but he managed to right himself and deal the other man a blow on the side of the head. His descent, sure as Wylie Coyote's after he had been hit with an Acme anvil, would have been comical were it not for the sickening crunch of metal against bone. Magnus retched, but his stomach was empty and all that came up was bile. The man groaned. The fingers of one of his hands fluttered. Magnus drove the fire extinguisher down again, like a crofter marking where he was about to begin digging turf. There was another stomach-turning crunch of bone and then the man lay still.

The fat inmate lost his grip on Jeb. 'Fuck.' He took a step backward, his eyes moving from Magnus to his friend lying still and bloodied on the ground, then back to Magnus again. 'Fuck,' he repeated. 'Fuck,' and made for the exit.

Magnus scanned the entrance hall, preparing for the next attack, but he and Jeb were the only people left standing.

'Shit.' Jeb leaned forward panting, his hands on his knees. 'I didn't think you had it in you.'

'I don't.' Magnus was gasping for breath. 'Do you think he's . . . ?'

Jeb looked up. 'Christ, that was a close one. I thought he had me there.'

Magnus held out his hands. They were trembling. 'I think I might have . . .'

Jeb said, 'You did what you had to do. You saved my skin and I saved yours.'

Magnus gave a crazy laugh. 'What does that make us? Blood brothers?'

Jeb folded his penknife and slid it into his pocket. 'It makes us even.'

There was a rumble of activity beyond the prison. Magnus looked towards the open gates and saw a flash of desert camouflage, a pale alert against the London brick.

Thirteen

'We could pretend to be screws and show them our ID.'

Magnus kept his voice to a whisper, even though the wall they were crouched against was too far from the gate for the soldiers guarding it to hear them. His heart was still pounding from the fight in the entrance hall, but the fear that had stalked him since his arrest had vanished. The drab courtyard gleamed with colours he had never noticed before and the air made his skin tingle. Magnus's eyes tracked a seagull flying high above. The sky was bluer than he remembered, the bird a soaring flash of white.

'If they don't believe us, it'll be game over.' Jeb was sorting through his pockets, examining the tangle of car keys he had lifted from the locker room. 'I'm not getting banged up again.'

'Going straight?'

Jeb glanced at Magnus. 'That kind of comment could get you into trouble inside.'

'Glad I managed to avoid trouble,' Magnus whispered. He had a hysterical urge to laugh.

'Save the jokes for later.' Jeb was all business. He nodded towards the gates where a small group of soldiers stood, cradling guns. 'It's up to you what you do. I'm going to drive through them.'

Magnus took a deep breath. His bravery had been all adrenalin and it was wearing off. He felt tired and hungry.

Jeb said, 'I'm not sure why these guys are hanging around instead of barging their way in, but my guess is that they're not sure what they're going to find inside and are waiting on reinforcements. We need to make our move now.'

It occurred to Magnus that he could hand himself in, throw himself on the mercy of the soldiers and take his chances. It was the phrase 'mercy of the soldiers' that decided him. The memory of news reports from Afghanistan and Iraq, film footage of men in orange jumpsuits being stretchered in chains into cages at Guantánamo Bay. He said, 'How will we do it?'

'Find a car, put the pedal to the metal and aim it at the gates. No finesse.'

'What if they shoot?'

'Duck.' Jeb shrugged. 'I don't know. Maybe we both end up with an extra bloody eye in the middle of our forehead. Are you up for it or not?'

This was how men landed in prison, Magnus realised, how he had got there himself, acting without imagining the consequences. He shook his head. 'Probably not.'

'Fuck you then.'

Jeb rose from their hiding place and ran the length of the wall, keeping his body low. Without thinking about what he was doing, Magnus followed. Jeb halted at a corner and peered round it. 'I thought you were crapping out.'

'I am,' Magnus whispered. 'But I can't hide behind this wall for ever. There might be another gate.'

'An unguarded exit?'

'You never know.'

Jeb let out a snort. 'The car park's over there. Don't make a show of yourself, if you're following me.'

The clothes Jeb had chosen were shades of grey that melted into the urban landscape. Magnus glanced down at the mod T-shirt he had stolen from the locker room. The red and white target on his chest seemed like a poor choice now and he pulled up the zip of his hoodie to cover it.

Jeb turned the corner and sprinted across open tarmac to where ranks of cars were parked. Magnus plunged after him, thigh muscles singing with the effort of crouching and running. 'They'll probably shoot me in the arse and blow my fucking bollocks off,' he muttered. But he made the shelter of the cars and hunkered down between a Mondeo and a Shogun. Jeb was flitting between the rows of vehicles, pointing one electronic key after another.

The Mondeo next to Magnus flashed its sidelights and gave an electronic chirrup.

'Fuck.' His voice was all breath.

Jeb jogged over, opened the driver's door and slid inside.

'Sure you don't want to come along for the ride?'

'I can think of pleasanter ways to commit suicide.'

'Don't jinx me.' For the first time since they had sheltered in the art room Jeb looked nervous. He adjusted the rear-view mirror and fitted the key in the ignition. 'You sit on your arse if you want. I'd rather take a chance than end up back inside.'

Magnus did not bother to contradict him. 'Look.' He pointed across the car park. 'That's our way out.'

The prison van was skewed across three spaces at the far end of the car park. It was long, with three small, high windows on either side, more like a large horsebox than a vehicle designed for ferrying men. Jeb complained that he didn't have keys for it, that Magnus was making him lose time and that the van was 'fucking impregnable', but Magnus suspected that he was secretly relieved not to be facing a cordon of armed soldiers through the Mondeo's wide windscreen.

Magnus pulled at the back door to the van, but it was locked tight. He skirted round to the front passenger side and Jeb took the driver's door. Magnus tried opening his side.

'Fuck, it's locked.'

Even as Magnus said the words he heard the door on the other side click open and the horror in Jeb's voice.

'Jesus Christ.'

It was impossible to know how long the prison guard had been slumped in the well of the driver's seat. But these were the hottest days of summer and it had been long enough to bloat the man's stomach and putrefy his flesh. Jeb held his bloodstained sleeve against his nose and mouth.

'No way, man, I am not getting in there.'

Magnus thought he saw something moving on the guard's swollen belly. He turned and retched, holding a hand over his mouth to muffle the sound. Bile stung the back of his throat. He breathed deeply, his hands on his knees bracing himself, and then straightened up, took off the brown hoodie and grabbed the dead man's arm, using the cloth as a barrier between his flesh and the corpse's.

The smell was worse than that of the Minke whale that

had been beached when he was fourteen. A group of volunteers had tried for hours to get it back into the water but the beast's radar was faulty, or perhaps it had been ill and wanted to die. Their efforts had failed. The next day he and Hugh had dared each other to climb up on its black mountain of a body. In the end they had done it together, the pair of them slipping and sliding until they reached its peak, standing triumphant until the gases in the whale had suddenly shifted, and they had tumbled off, laughing and swearing, sure that the creature had come back to life.

'Worse than a whale's fart,' he muttered. The dead guard flopped to the ground and Magnus saw the white stuff wriggling in the rotting flesh more clearly. 'Fuck, fuck, fuck.' Swearing helped. He dragged the man to one side, wiped the seat with the brown hoodie and dropped it on to the man's face. 'Rest in Peace.' The van's keys were resting in the ignition. Magnus turned to where his cellmate was crouched. 'Do you want to drive?'

Jeb's face was pale, but his voice had regained its edge. 'Think you'll go fast enough?'

Magnus nodded. 'If there's one thing island boys can do, it's drive fast.'

He would have preferred to have been dressed in a prison guard's uniform, but going back into the building to find one would take too much time and stripping the screw's decaying body was out of the question. Magnus steered the van from its parking space. The cab smelled foul, but he kept its windows closed, even though he doubted that its glass was bullet proof. He glanced at Jeb. 'Do you think the guy I hit with the fire extinguisher is dead?'

Jeb's knees were folded tight, as if he were bracing himself for impact. 'Concentrate on getting us through the gate.'

'I think maybe I killed him.'

'Why would that bother you?' Jeb took the penknife from his pocket and rolled it between his palms. Magnus remembered how the point of its blade had pierced an inmate's neck, the arc of blood fountaining from the wound. Jeb said, 'He was a piece of scum. He would have killed you, killed both of us, without blinking.'

'Doesn't it bother you?' It was a question Magnus would not have dared to broach before, but the closed-in silence of the cab and the waiting troops made it seem imperative.

Jeb pressed the point of the penknife against the palm of his hand, testing the sharpness of the blade or the elasticity of his skin.

'There's no point in thinking about it.'

They were crossing the forecourt now and the soldiers had seen the van. Their eyes were on the vehicle, their guns resting in their arms. Magnus drove slowly, hoping the van's insignia would make them think it was on official business. He felt the pure calm that always washed over him as he stepped on stage and into the spotlight, the fear that clenched his bowels before performances banished in the knowledge that, for good or for bad, it would all be over soon.

Jeb hissed, 'Speed up.'

One of the soldiers, a young man with fair skin and red hair, stepped forward. He held up his right palm. Magnus slowed the van and held up a hand in greeting. 'Smile, don't let them see you're nervous.'

'What the fuck are you doing?' Jeb spoke through clenched

teeth. His mouth was stretched into an expression that was more grimace than grin. 'Put your foot down.'

'Don't worry.'

Magnus nodded at the soldier, one foot on the accelerator, the other on the clutch, keeping the van slow until they were almost at the main gate. At the last minute he pressed a hand to the horn and floored the accelerator. The van was slower to gain speed than he had expected and for one horrible moment he thought that Jeb was right, he had left it too late. Then he saw the soldiers diving out of the van's path. He scraped the driver's door against the gatepost, knocking its wing mirror off. Then they were out of Pentonville and into the streets beyond. Magnus turned the van left and let out a roar. He kept his foot to the floor, going as fast as he dared along the city street. Jeb squinted into the passenger-side wing mirror, looking to see if they were being pursued.

'Anyone coming?' Magnus asked.

'Not so far.'

'Stupid fucking squaddies, lock the gate if you want to keep folk inside.'

Magnus slammed his hands against the steering wheel, drumming out a victory tattoo, light-headed with the buzz of escape and freedom.

'They were waiting on someone. That's the only reason they'd have kept the gate open.'

It was as if Jeb's words summoned the convoy. Two tanks flanked by soldiers turned out of a side street and drove towards them.

'Oh shit.' Magnus hit the brakes and slammed the steering wheel again, this time in frustration.

'Keep calm.' Jeb gripped Magnus's arm. His fingers dug into the flesh, forcing him to pay attention. 'They're heading to the prison, not away from it. They might not know about us yet.' He pointed to a side road. 'Turn first right.'

Magnus did as he was told. He was still going too fast and the van swerved on to the wrong side of the road as he rounded the corner, but the street was deserted.

'Okay,' Jeb said, looking at the road behind them in the wing mirror. 'Turn left at the end.'

Magnus obeyed him, taking the corner with more care this time.

He asked, 'Are they behind us?'

'No, I think we struck lucky. It looks like they weren't interested in us. The squaddies at the gate mustn't have radioed ahead.'

Magnus wondered if there were more bodies in the back of the van, prisoners who had never made it to their cells rolling from side to side, like slaves in the hold of a transport ship, each time he swung around a corner. That could have been his fate, locked in with men suffering from the sweats, watching them die one by one, and all the time being cooked alive inside the metal box.

'Keep going.' Jeb rolled his window down. Perhaps he was also wondering about the contents of the van, because he said, 'We'll ditch this fucking coffin asap.'

Magnus had grown used to the smell of decay inside the cab, but the fresh air blowing in through the passenger window was a relief. He opened the window on his side too and a breeze sprang in, ruffling his hair. They were alive.

Fourteen

It was only when he saw an old woman edging her way along the pavement with the aid of a Zimmer frame that Magnus realised what was wrong with the world beyond the van's windows. The streets were too quiet for a sunny London afternoon. He said, 'It's too quiet.'

'Not quiet enough.' Jeb had been monitoring the road behind them in the wing mirror. 'There's a truck behind us.'

'An army truck?'

'No, a VW camper van full of page-three girls.'

Magnus put his foot to the accelerator. The streets were too small for the cumbersome vehicle and it was an effort to keep it on the road.

'I thought you said you could drive.'

'Lewis Hamilton couldn't steer this thing any faster,' Magnus said.

You are in a controlled zone, an amplified voice announced. *Pull over and exit your vehicle.*

Jeb said, 'Keep going.'

Magnus glanced at the knife in Jeb's hand and wondered if it would go to his own throat should he slow the prison van.

You are in contravention of martial law. The amplified voice was calm. *Pull over and exit your vehicle or we will shoot.*

There was a tight turn up ahead, an alleyway that they were never going to make. Magnus dropped down the gears. 'I can stop and back up or we've got a choice between controlled crash and out-of-control crash.'

Jeb said, 'Don't fucking crash.'

'Trust me.'

The knife hand twitched. 'I don't trust you.'

We are prepared to fire.

Magnus increased their speed.

This is your final warning. Preparing to fire in five . . . four . . .

He heard Jeb fastening his safety belt and wondered that he had not fastened it before.

. . . three . . . two . . .

'Hold on!' Magnus skewed the van across the road, hitting the mouth of the alley sideways, blocking it with the cab of the van. The windscreen cracked and stayed miraculously in place, but both side windows shattered, spraying the interior with glitters of flying glass. There was a second dunt and the inertia-reel seatbelt tightened across Magnus's chest, as the truck pursuing them made contact with the rear of their van. The windscreen of the cab gave way and fell in on them in chunks.

Magnus opened his eyes and saw Jeb already out of his seatbelt, his face potted with stabs of blood, as if he had been attacked by sharp-beaked crows. He touched his own face and felt heat and broken glass.

'Come on.' Jeb was almost on top of him, reaching towards the handle of the driver's door.

'Lock your side,' Magnus said. 'It might slow them down.'

He felt as if his brain had been shaken around his skull like a dice in a cup, but managed to open his own door and jump out into the blocked side of the alley. He staggered as he hit the ground and righted himself against the side of the van. Jeb followed quickly behind him. Magnus looked for the soldiers, but the army truck was out of sight somewhere between the back of the van and the wall of the alley. He had no idea how badly it, or the men inside, were damaged.

'If this turns out to be a dead-end, then you've just given them a wall to shoot us against.' Jeb shoved Magnus on the shoulder, reminding him of the need to keep moving and they started to jog towards whatever lay at the end of the alley.

Magnus said, 'This is London, not New York. They won't shoot us.'

'I thought you came from Jockland, not another fucking planet.' Tears of blood were running down Jeb's face. His eyelashes glistered with shards of glass. He looked like a reluctant glam rocker, a bully boy drummer femmed up for the fans on his manager's advice. 'They announced on a loud fucking hailer that they were going to shoot us.' Jeb spat on the ground. 'Are you deaf as well as stupid?'

The alleyway was dark and lined with bins. It reminded Magnus of the lane behind Johnny Dongo's hotel, where he had beaten up the rapist MP. He should never have got drunk, should never have been there. 'Should never have been bloody born,' he muttered under his breath. He could hear footsteps but was unsure if it was the sound of soldiers following them or merely the echo of his and Jeb's feet against the cobbles. Jeb's movements were sluggish and twice he stumbled. Magnus realised that his own progress was slow and weaving and knew that if they had to face the soldiers they would lose. They turned another dark corner and saw a blaze of sunlight. The alley led out into a main street lined with shops.

'Thank fuck,' Jeb said. 'Come on.'

Almost all the shop windows that lined the road had been smashed. New clothes, some still on their hangers, lay scattered in heaps at the edge of the road, piled like storm-blasted seaweed at low tide. Trainers spilled from cardboard boxes inside a ransacked branch of Foot Locker and mobile phones were scattered like hand grenades outside EE Mobile. The bank sandwiched between the two plundered shops stood strangely intact, as if looters had decided they preferred solid merchandise to cash. Magnus picked up a smartphone. The plastic had been warmed by the sun. The phone's screen was cracked, its virgin battery uncharged. It would be no use for calling home. He dropped it with the rest.

'Do you know where we are?'

'Not a scooby.' Jeb's voice was a whisper although the road, like the others they had driven along, was empty of people.

A plastic carrier bag, caught by the breeze, wrapped itself around Magnus's leg. He peeled it free.

'Where is everybody? This is like something out of *Dr Who*.'

Somewhere there was burning. The breeze was tainted with the odour of melting plastic and charred wood. The scent caught at the back of Magnus's throat, nasty and acrylic, but there was an undertaste to it, a charred, summer barbecue smell that reminded him he was hungry. A Tesco Direct stood a few yards down the road. Someone had started to board up its windows, but they had given up halfway through and the plate glass on the exposed side had been replaced by fresh air and jagged shards.

'I need to eat something.'

'We need to get under cover.'

Jeb grabbed his elbow and kept moving, taking Magnus with him. Magnus shook himself free, but they crossed the road together, walking around cars that had been abandoned with no thought to parking fines or regulations. Magnus peered into a baby-blue Mini standing in the middle of the road, its doors wide open.

'Someone left this car in a hurry,' Magnus said. 'The key's still in the ignition.'

Jeb snapped, 'Don't start it.'

But Magnus had already leaned inside and turned the key. The engine growled into life. The sound was loud in the silent street and was almost immediately punctuated by the slap of boots pounding against pavement. There was movement in some of the abandoned shops as people who had hidden unmoving in the shadows fled. Jeb was already running for cover. The road was too jammed with cars for there to be any point in trying to drive anywhere and Magnus ran after him, leaving the car engine idling. He heard a crack of gunfire. He had been beater at enough grouse shoots to be sure that whoever was firing was not sending a warning shot over their heads.

'Fucking idiot,' Jeb panted and Magnus knew that it was not the gunman he was cursing.

A grille had been pulled half shut across the entrance to a

subway station, as if someone had started to lock up and then given up the task as too much trouble. A man in a business suit lay just outside. He was thin and might once have been rich, but death had made these things irrelevant. Jeb leapt over his body and Magnus followed, catching the toe of his trainer against the man's shoulder and landing flat on the tiled floor of the station. The fall saved him. Bullets rattled into the ticket hall, ricocheting against the walls and shattering the window of the information booth.

Jeb hurdled the ticket turnstile. Magnus crawled beneath the barrier nearest to him and followed the sound of Jeb's footsteps along the tiled corridors to the platform below. There were bodies in the hallways, men and women who had lain down and not managed to rouse themselves again, but the soldiers might still be behind him and Magnus did not stop to check if any of the sleepers were alive. He saw the black line edging the walls, and a sign directing him onwards and knew that they were heading towards the Northern line. *North*, the rhythm of his feet said against the tunnel floor: *north, north, north, north, north.*

Fifteen

There were other people on the platform, but Jeb was the only one standing.

'Can you believe it?'

Magnus did not need to ask what he was talking about. The reality of the sweats was stronger below ground than it had been in the looted streets. Up above there was still the chance that they had stumbled on the aftermath of one of London's riots; down here the evidence lay in the bodies slumped where they had fallen, waiting for trains they would never board. They were bodies, Magnus told himself, to be pitied and mourned. The thing to fear was flesh and blood, the soldiers who might yet appear and take him back to prison at gunpoint. But his skin crawled with the certainty that the lady who had pulled the folds of her orange sari over her face before she died was about to draw the gauzy material back, blink her dead eyes and come towards him. Or that the youth, whose yellow headphones were still coiled around his neck, might straighten his spine and get to his feet. Or that any of the people, so clear and sharp-edged, so there, but no longer present, would twitch awake, turn their heads and look at him with the jealousy the dead must surely feel for the living. It felt wicked to want the so recently deceased to remain dead, but they were gone and every horror movie and zombie flick Magnus had ever seen was crowding in on him.

'It's unbelievable,' Jeb said again, and Magnus saw that the dead stillness of the Underground was working on him too.

The electricity had failed and the platform was dimly lit by emergency lights. Along at the far end something moved, indistinct in the shadows. Magnus took a step backward; his foot touched the softness of another body and he almost toppled. He let out a gasp. The thing moved again, swift and undulating, and he realised that it was not one of the bodies restored to half-life, but the largest rat he had seen, sleek and busy, its whiskers twitching. The rat looked at him, and then it perked its nose in another direction, turning its ears, like radar towards some sound only it could hear. It scuttled down on to the tracks and ran into the waiting blackness of the tunnels beyond. A moment later Magnus heard the footsteps that had disturbed it. Jeb heard them too and held a finger to his lips. He nodded towards the tracks, where the rat had made its escape. Magnus shook his head. It was impossible. He had seen the Dongolite's face as the train consumed him. Prison was preferable to the rush of noise and steel that had sucked the boy under. Jeb shrugged, exaggerating the gesture to make up for not speaking. He jumped down on to the tracks and jogged towards the north tunnel, his feet crunching against the gravel.

Magnus heard his own breath, loud in his head. The soldiers' footsteps came closer. The dead woman lay still beneath the folds of her orange sari and the yellow wires of the youth's headphones remained coiled around his neck.

There were rats in the tunnels, rats and inky darkness that might be split without warning by the electric rush of a subway train.

The footsteps were very close now. The soldiers would be with him soon. Magnus wondered how they could be bothered to chase him in the face of so much death. Why they did not simply dump their uniforms and escape while they were still alive. But perhaps he already knew the answer. The only way to avoid going mad was to go on. Following orders was an enviable profession.

Magnus ran along the platform to a maintenance ladder and climbed down on to the tracks. The live rail glinted silver and tempting on his right. He marked the distance between it and him and ran northwards. A voice shouted behind him but Magnus ran on, into the dark.

Sixteen

Pitch-blackness folded around Magnus. The soldiers were still out there, somewhere in the dim-bright. Something scuttled through the dark and he imagined the same fat rat that he had seen on the Underground platform.

Between the ages of ten and seventeen Magnus and his cousin Hugh had spent many idle days shooting barn-rats with air rifles, competing for the highest score. Hugh had usually won, but they were well matched and Magnus was generally a close second. Magnus bent over in the dark and tucked the hems of his jeans into his socks, the way his father had instructed him to, to stop the rats from climbing up the inside of his trouser legs. He felt a sudden suspicious fear that they might somehow know how many of them he had murdered and decide to get their revenge.

Magnus stretched out a hand and walked into the blackness. Every atom of his body resisted, but he pressed on, humming the ghost of a song beneath his breath to give himself courage.

Scots, wha hae wi Wallace bled,
Scots, wham Bruce has aften led,

Welcome tae yer gory bed,
Or tae victorie.

Now's the day and now's the hour . . .

Something touched him and he sank on to his haunches gasping for breath.

'Shut the fuck up,' Jeb hissed.

Magnus would have liked to have punched him, but Jeb was a voice in the darkness and Magnus was finding it hard to breathe. He filled his lungs, trying to calm his hammering heart. 'You scared the shit out of me.'

He saw a flash of white in the dark and realised that Jeb was smiling.

'Don't worry. They won't come down here.'

'How can you be sure?'

'Would you?'

'No, but I wouldn't join the fucking army in the first place. They have lights on their gun sights. They're wearing stab vests and helmets and I'm willing to bet they've eaten recently. They can take us no bother, if they want to.'

'They don't have our motivation,' Jeb said. He was standing in a hollow in the tunnel wall, Magnus guessed. A recess where track workers had sheltered from passing trains, sucking in their bellies as carriages rushed past. 'Soldiers are pack animals. These guys looked like ordinary squaddies to me. They won't go far from the rest of their crew without orders. It makes them nervous.'

As if on cue, two pinpoints of light appeared in the blackness of the corridor. Jeb pulled Magnus into the recess beside him. It smelled of piss, mortar and loamy earth, a graveyard scent. It was a tight fit and Magnus felt Jeb's body against his, warm in the dampness. Jeb moved a hand to his pocket. Magnus knew he was taking out his penknife and resisted the urge to grab Jeb's wrist, for fear of feeling the sharp edge of the blade penetrate his side.

The lights came closer, no longer pinpoints but two fans of brilliance, illuminating the tunnel and revealing its red-brick walls, the high curve of its roof. The lights revealed rats too, larger than any that had graced his father's barn. Fat enough to make a good meal for a starving man, Magnus thought, disgusted by the eager way his belly responded to the image. He wondered if the army would feed them or if Jeb was right and they would be summarily executed; worse than dying would be to die hungry.

The lights were edging nearer and it would not be long before they exposed their hiding place. Magnus shrank against the wall. He felt Jeb's body tense, muscles bunching, readying for combat. There was a good chance that they would die here, wearing strangers' clothes and carrying other men's IDs. Magnus heard the sound of the soldiers' boots, crunching against the gravel, and felt sad that his mother would never know what had happened to him. He heard something else too, phlegm hacking in one of the soldiers' throats. Light ricocheted around the walls, bouncing across the roof of the tunnel in crazy circles and Magnus guessed that the soldier had bent over to be sick. He felt Jeb holding his breath, and realised that he was holding his own too.

'Mike, are you okay?' he heard a voice ask. The answer was low and unintelligible and the same voice said, 'Do you think you've got it?' The answer must have been a negative because the voice said, 'I think you're wrong, Mike. I think you've caught it. You're boiling up, man. You should have told me.' The voice sounded young and full of more regret than a young voice should be able to hold. It had a Liverpool accent, both soft and harsh, like a war ballad. 'You should have told me, Mike,' it repeated. Whatever Mike whispered next made the voice sadder. 'I'm sorry, Mike,' it said. 'Sorry, man.'

Jeb must have guessed what was going to happen next because a shudder ran through him. There was the sound of a gun being cocked and someone – Mike – shouted something that was all fear and panic, not a word at all, but unmistakable in its plea. There was a crack of gunfire, a flash in the dark, brighter than the lights on the gun sights that had led the men there. The soft Liverpudlian voice said, 'Sorry, mate.'

There was a moment of not quite silence, a sound of rustling and Magnus guessed the soldier was stripping his dead companion of useful kit, then the light resumed its stare down the tunnel. It puddled inches from where their feet stood, side by side in the recess.

They were dead men. Jeb's penknife was a child's toy, effective against a half-starved convict, but useless against an armed professional. Magnus wished that he could pray. Now was the time to commend themselves to their maker.

'Don't worry, lads.' The voice was stronger, as if the act of killing had fortified it. 'I've had enough. You go your way, and I'll go mine.' The soldier paused as if he were waiting for a reply, but speaking would give away their position, and Jeb and Magnus kept their silence. 'Okay.' The voice sounded at a loss. 'I guess there's nothing much to be said, except that I've got a gun for each hand now, so go the other way, if you want to keep on going.'

There was another pause, and then the footsteps resumed their contact with the gravel, fading into the distance. Magnus and Jeb stayed where they were, upright in the open recess, like mannequins in a display case, rooted to the spot until long after the sound of the soldier's retreat had vanished.

Seventeen

They travelled north through the dark, side by side, in silence. Magnus was glad of Jeb's presence. It was good to know that there was someone else alive, even if it was a man who knew how to kill quickly and who had been locked up for crimes unknown. Magnus would have liked to talk. Silence allowed too much space for his thoughts, which were all of home: his mother and sister, his cousins, even his brother-in-law. Davie was not a bad guy, just a wee bit too concerned with his own comfort for Magnus's liking. Rhona ran around after him as if it were the 1950s and Davie a limbless invalid. *They might all be dead*, a cruel voice whispered in his head, *dead and no one there to bury them*. He started to sing again, softly under his breath:

> *Scots, wha hae wi Wallace bled,*
> *Scots, wham Bruce has aften led,*
> *Welcome tae yer gory bed . . .*

'Shut up.' Jeb sounded weary. 'We don't know who's out here. And you've got a crap voice.'

Magnus had always finished his act with a song, like the

old comics on the circuit used to. Stanley Baxter, Frankie Howerd, Morecambe and Wise: those boys had known what they were doing and it was all there for the taking if you watched their acts. Not the jokes themselves, time had moved on and they had dated, but their patter, the way they moved, the way they were with the audience. They had honed their techniques over decades of performing live, before they got their big breaks. He would watch them late at night on YouTube, the screen of his computer glowing in a dimly lit hotel room, a miniature of Famous Grouse in a tooth-mug by the bed. He wondered if it was all gone, hotel rooms, the Internet, YouTube, Famous Grouse . . .

I fought at land, I fought at sea,
At hame I fought my Auntie, O;
But I met the Devil an' Dundee,
On the Braes o' Killiekrankie, O.

A hand slammed against his back and Magnus stumbled forward, only just managing to avoid falling flat against the track. 'What the fuck?'

'I told you to shut up.'

Magnus had not realised that he was singing. Jeb's voice brought him back to himself, back to ratty blackness and hunger.

'Who put you in charge?'

'You did.'

Magnus tightened his fists, but he was too tired for another fight. 'Soon as we get out of here we split.'

'Why wait?'

113

'Because this tunnel only has two directions and I'm not going back, not after walking all this way.'

'Reckon I could make you.'

Reckon you could, the soft voice in Magnus's head whispered.

'I won't sing if it annoys you that much . . .' Magnus stopped mid-sentence.

They had been stumbling like prisoners on an enforced march, along a curve in the tunnel, one or other of them occasionally touching the damp wall for guidance. Now they had reached the turn of the bend. A faint light shone ahead.

'Shit.' Jeb's voice was as soft as a bird's wing flapping into flight.

Fear cramped in Magnus's belly. 'What do you think it is?'

'Something.' The light was too far away for it to illuminate their features, but Magnus could hear the shrug in Jeb's voice. 'I don't know.'

'I don't like it.'

'Thank fuck for that. At least it means you won't feel a song coming on.'

Magus ignored the jibe. 'It could be anything.'

'Light at the end of the tunnel, that's meant to be a good thing, isn't it?'

Jeb's voice was resolute, but Magnus thought he could hear a shiver of apprehension in it. Magnus said, 'That soldier's probably clear by now. There's nothing to stop us going back.'

'If you don't mind being a poof.'

It was strange how the darkness Magnus had feared had become the thing to hold on to, the light something to be afraid of.

Jeb said, 'I had a girlfriend that was into hippy shit.' It was the first time he had mentioned anything about his life before prison and Magnus found himself paying attention. 'She used to say, put the bad stuff behind you and go forward. She was right about that. Always go forward, never back.'

'Ever gone too far?'

Jeb's laugh was deep and humourless. 'Far too far.'

He started to walk on, his feet crunching against the gravel and after a moment Magnus followed him. It was like a near-death experience, walking the long dark tunnel towards a pinprick of light.

'I keep expecting a voice to tell me to *turn back, it's not my time yet*,' Magnus whispered.

'Be nice to wake up and find out it was all a dream.' Something about the light in the darkness seemed to have made Jeb more confiding.

Magnus said, 'That'd be grand, right enough.'

He imagined himself in his old room on the farm, eleven or twelve years old. Woken by the sound of the kitchen door shutting as his father came in from early-morning milking, the rattle of metal on metal in the kitchen below, as his mother set the pans on the range, ready to make breakfast. His loathed school uniform hanging from the peg on the back of his bedroom door. Hugh still alive; knowing they would meet later at the turn in the bend where the school bus stopped. Nothing special, just an ordinary school day. Tears were running down his cheeks. Magnus let them take their course until the light threatened to touch his face and then he rubbed them away with the back of his hand.

It was a subway train, sitting tight against the walls of the

115

tunnel, its windows illuminated from within. Jeb slid along the side of the train.

'Check this out.'

Magnus followed. It was what he had wanted to avoid, being constricted between a subway train and a tunnel wall, another rock and a hard place.

'We can go through it.' Jeb pointed to a smashed window. He took off his jacket. 'Give us a leg-up.'

Magnus helped to boost Jeb up. Jeb slung his jacket over the jagged edge of the broken window and slid inside, head first. It was a tight fit and he kicked his legs as he wriggled through. He stuck his head out.

'You coming?'

'What's it like?'

'More of the same.'

Magnus muttered, 'More of the same.'

He took a deep breath and climbed on to the side of the carriage. Jeb reached out and dragged Magnus through. The jacket was still draped across the broken glass, but Magnus felt it scrape against his belly as he slid inside the compartment. They would have to be careful. Scrapes and cuts could turn septic and there was no longer the guarantee of a friendly doctor armed with antibiotics, ready to patch them up.

The brightness of the carriage hurt Magnus's eyes, but it was mercifully empty. Had he ever been in a completely empty London Underground carriage before? Maybe in the dim light of half-dawn after a heavy post-show session, but then his senses would be dulled by drink and tiredness, the taste of sulphate coating the back of his throat.

'You said it was more of the same.'

116

Jeb had put his jacket back on and was already starting down the carriage to the connecting doors and the next compartment. He glanced back at Magnus.

'What would you call it?'

'I thought you meant more bodies.'

Jeb opened the door and stepped through.

A thin man was slumped in the corner of the compartment, his face hidden by long dreadlocks that had fallen forward, obscuring his features.

Jeb said, 'Be careful what you wish for.'

The carriage smelled like long-ignored refuse from some downscale grill house. Meaty leavings that had been locked in a tin shed for days in the middle of a heatwave.

Magnus pulled the neck of his T-shirt up over his mouth and nose.

'It took some people suddenly,' Jeb said. A phone rested on the seat beside the dead man. He picked it up and tossed it to Magnus. 'ET phone home.'

'Don't you want it?'

The mobile was turned off. Magnus switched it on, wincing at the sound of its wake-up tune: loud and stupidly melodic. The battery was almost full, but as he had expected there was no signal. He glanced at the log. The last call had been two days ago, to *Mum*. It had gone unanswered. Magnus turned the mobile off again and stowed it in his jeans pocket.

Jeb was at the door to the next carriage. 'Guess you feel sorry for me. The end of the world and there's no one I'd like to call.'

Magnus caught the door as it was about to slam shut and followed Jeb through.

'Who said it was the end of the world?'

'Looks like it, from where I'm standing.' Jeb's voice was belligerent. As if he had just begun to comprehend the magnitude of what was happening and was working his way up to expressing it. The next carriage was empty too. A tatty copy of *Metro* lay crumpled on the floor. Jeb picked it up and shoved it at Magnus. 'Here you go. You like reading the news.'

The newspaper felt thin and insubstantial, a half edition. Its headline was to the point: *SWEATS KILLS BILLIONS*.

'We're not the only ones who've survived.' Magnus folded the *Metro* into a baton and slid it into the back pocket of his jeans. 'A bunch of lads left the prison with us, and there were plenty of soldiers about the jail. London's an overcrowded shithole.' He had loved the city, loved the anonymity it conferred, loved that he could walk for miles without anyone hailing him to ask his business and tell him theirs. 'It was bound to get hit hard. Things will be different in the countryside. I bet the sweats have hardly touched the islands. People are always behind the times up there.'

No they're not, the voice Magnus feared whispered in his head. *Once maybe, but not any more*. Orkney had Internet and drugs, a giant Tesco. There was no more relying on catalogues for clothing. Girls had the latest fashions delivered to their door and when they were dressed for a night out you would be hard pushed to tell them from Londoners.

Surely someone on the council would have got wise and set up a quarantine zone, he consoled himself. As soon as it became clear what was happening they were bound to have halted trains, flights and ferries, switched off the constant stream of tourists.

Money, the cruel voice whispered. *All those hotels, B&Bs and restaurants; the cafés, craft shops, excursions and galleries.*

The carriages were mostly empty, but occasionally they passed bodies lying where they had died. 'It's like going to sleep,' Magnus's mother had said to him of death. 'You close your eyes and don't wake up.'

His father had been caught in the combine, his flesh hacked, his bones and organs crushed. The doctor said death had been instantaneous, but Magnus had dreamed about the moment his father finished clearing the blockage in the combine's blades. There must have been a shit-sinking second when he knew, as the machine growled back to life, that he had neglected to take the keys from the ignition.

Windows and doors were shattered or forced open in some of the carriages, where survivors had smashed their way free. The driver must have died, Magnus guessed. They would find him slumped across the wheel, or huddled on the floor of the cab. He remembered the driver of the prison van, the squirming white of his belly.

'Why do you think we haven't caught it yet?' he asked Jeb as they slammed into yet another carriage, another stink of shit and rotting meat. 'Do you think we're immune?'

Jeb had pulled his T-shirt up over his mouth and nose and his words were muffled.

'Maybe, or maybe it's in the post.'

Jeb sounded as if living and dying were all the same to him, but Magnus had seen how hard he would fight to survive.

'Did you get ill?'

'Sicker than a dead dog.' Jeb looked at him. 'I caught it

119

early. They were about to take me to hospital when I got better. I tried to string it out, in the hope of meeting a nice nurse. I thought maybe some wild woman would fancy getting it on with a bad man, they say it happens sometimes. But the screws guessed I was faking. How about you?'

'The guy in the cell I was in got it. It took a long time for him to die. I had three days of close exposure.'

Jeb nodded, as if it made sense. 'Some people die slow, others die fast. The poor bastards on this train obviously didn't expect to catch it.'

Magnus made a mental inventory of his own aches and pains. So far there was nothing that tiredness and hunger could not account for. Perhaps the sweats would strike him down suddenly, the way it had hit the people on the train. He thought of the unanswered phone call on the dead man's mobile: *Mum*.

'Maybe they knew they had it and were trying to get to somewhere, someone.'

'Maybe.'

They made their way to the control cabin in silence. This time it was Jeb who moved the corpse, sliding the train driver out of the cab and into the corridor.

'Poor sod.' It was the first time he had expressed pity for any of the dead and Magnus glanced at him. Jeb caught his look. 'My old man worked on the railways. He wasn't a driver, you need connections to be a driver, but I know what he'd have thought about dying on the job; a fucking insult and not even any overtime to make it worth your while.' He was fiddling with the controls. 'Ever driven one of these things?'

'No.'

'Me neither, but how difficult can it be?'

The tunnel stretched ahead, dark and seemingly as endless as outer space, but they had walked a long way. Surely it wouldn't be far until the next station, the next assembly of bodies. Magnus could see his own reflection in the train's curved windscreen. He looked thinner, older, like the fishermen he had sometimes seen coming ashore in the early morning, battered by the elements, half-dead to the world.

'These trains need electricity to work.'

'I'm not completely fucking ignorant.' Jeb threw a few switches and pressed some buttons, experimenting with the dashboard. 'Just cos the station was out doesn't mean the points will be. If everything rode off one circuit the whole system would overload.'

As if to confirm what he was saying the engine shuddered alive. Magnus imagined the corpses slumped in their seats quivering in response. He saw them staggering down the carriages, heads bowed, hair hanging over their faces like the dreadlocked man in the first compartment, coming to see who had woken them.

Jeb let out a shout of triumph and the engine died. He slammed his hand against the dashboard, hard enough to hurt. 'Shit! Fucking thing!' He pressed a combination of levers and switches, but whatever charge the train had stored was gone.

They rested for a while in the shelter of the carriage, but Magnus sensed danger in sleep and though Jeb sank deep and snoring, he did not get beyond a half-doze. Then it was up and out, into the dark again, a long stumble through nothingness until they reached the next station and a weary climb up precipitous, stalled escalators. There was a moment of swearing and panic when they realised that the grilles to the Underground entrance were shut and bolted, but then Jeb found a key hanging from a hook in the ticket office and they were suddenly, miraculously, out into the brightness.

If the tunnel had been outer space, then this was a new planet of whose atmosphere they were uncertain. Magnus was getting better at un-focusing his eyes as he passed dead bodies, but it was hard to block out everything and so he knew that the corpse he was skirting had once been a woman in a summer dress. He glimpsed a tangle of long, russet hair and felt the pity of it all.

Jeb stepped through a smashed window of a Pret A Manger and grabbed a bottle of water. He threw its cap on the floor and chugged down its contents. Magnus followed suit. The water was warm, but the sensation of it going over his throat and down into his belly was delicious. He drank half of his bottle and then forced himself to stop, worried he would be sick.

The shop was a mess, but unless the contents of the till had been taken it was hard to see what whoever had broken in had been after. Tables and chairs had tumbled as if the seating area had been the scene of a fight, but there were no bodies, no spatters of blood. The glass counter was shattered and a display cabinet lay tipped on its side beside it. The wrapped food it had held was scattered across the floor.

He and Jeb squatted on their haunches and pawed through mouldering sandwiches, melted puddings and glistening sushi. They burst open packets of crisps and stale muffins that seemed impervious to decay. It was the kind of food Magnus hated, the sort of crap he resorted to eating on badly planned tours, where he arrived in towns too late for dinner and left too early for lunch. It was the best meal he had ever eaten.

When they were finished they packed a couple of paper bags they found behind the counter with more snacks and bottled water and crossed the road to a hotel. The doors were open and they walked silently through the carpeted lobby, their senses under assault from a surfeit of textures and colours after the grey of the prison and the black of the subway tunnel.

It was a five-star place, old-fashioned and gaudy with wealth. They passed the reception desk, unchallenged. Everything was neatly arranged, as if the staff and guests had simply left, taking their luggage with them. The carpet was decorated with floral medallions, the chairs figured with gold paisley patterns, the satin curtains embossed with thick, crisscrossing lines. Patterns vied with patterns, colours with colours; everything caught, reflected and refracted, over and over again in bronzed mirrors. Magnus said, 'You can check out any time you like, but you can never leave.'

'I can think of worse fates,' Jeb said and Magnus wondered how it would be to lie on a soft mattress and feel clean sheets against your skin.

The hotel corridors were a challenge to match the Underground tunnel. The lights were still on, the rows of closed doors a series of possibilities. Neither of them knew how to activate the hotel's electronic key cards and so they took turns at kicking and shouldering locks until they gave way. There were a couple of false attempts, rooms wrapped in darkness with bodies humped beneath their covers, but then they found two adjoining bedrooms. They made no plans for later, but their eyes met briefly for a moment before they each went into their room and closed the door behind them.

Eighteen

Magnus woke suddenly, aware that there was someone else in the room. Jeb was a shadow at the window. He had opened the curtains a few inches and was staring out at a view of the building's flat-roofed kitchens. He turned and looked at Magnus.

'I walked up to the sixteenth floor. You can see a good way across the city from up there.' His voice was calm, as if he were just back from buying a round at the bar and picking up a conversation they had already started. 'A lot of it's on fire.'

Magnus swung his feet out of the bed. He had intended to wash before going to sleep, but the lure of the hotel bed had proved too much for him and he had slipped between its sheets filthy and fully dressed, only pausing to take his trainers off.

'How close are the fires?' Magnus stretched. His head hurt. His back hurt. His shoulders, legs and arms hurt.

'Hard to say.' Jeb paused and Magnus got the impression that he was seeing the view from the top floor again and assessing the distance between them and the fires. 'Not so close you can't take some time to sort yourself out, but close enough for us to need to think about moving on.'

Magnus was unsure of how he felt about the 'us'. He got to his feet, rubbing his eyes. Jeb, he noticed, was freshly shaved, showered and changed. Magnus said, 'So there's still water.'

'Hot water.' Jeb nodded towards a chair where a neatly folded bundle of clothes waited. 'I got you these.'

It felt like a rival on the comedy circuit had just offered to swap the top slot for inferior billing. Some instinct within Magnus twitched, reminding him that kindness was a thing to be mistrusted, but he said, 'Thanks.'

He had been too weary, too fearful, to look at the television earlier. Now he lifted the remote and pointed it at the blank screen.

Flashing images appeared from a hospital ward somewhere in India. They were quickly replaced by similar scenes from somewhere in Europe and then Africa. The TV's volume was down and subtitles stabbed across the bottom of its screen.

```
V596 IS NO RESPECTER OF AGE OR SOCIAL
CLASS
```

The picture shifted to stock film of an anonymous scientist delicately inserting a pipette into a test tube.

```
SCIENTISTS ACROSS THE WORLD ARE TAKING
PART IN AN UNPRECEDENTED COLLABORATION
```

'It's showing the same stuff, over and over,' Jeb said in a low voice. 'I let it run on for an hour this morning. I reckon someone put it on repeat before they left the studio.' *Before they died*, the soft voice in Magnus's head whispered. He kept his eyes on the screen, where anxious men and women ushered their children towards hastily commandeered primary schools and community centres. It had been a sunny afternoon, but the children were dressed in coats and jackets, as if wrapping them up tight would help protect them from infection.

QUARANTINE CENTRES HAVE BEEN ESTABLISHED
IN TOWNS AND CITIES ACROSS EUROPE

The camera focused on unhappy-looking soldiers manning a barricade. Magnus thought some of them looked sick, but perhaps worry and lack of sleep had sapped the colour from their skin.

CURFEWS HAVE BEEN ESTABLISHED. NO-GO ZONES
PUT IN PLACE TO AVOID LOOTING AND DAMAGE
TO PROPERTY

Magnus said, 'We should check out the Internet.'

'It's down.' Jeb shrugged his shoulders. 'In the hotel anyway. I tried the computers behind the reception desk and a few laptops. Could be the server.'

'Could be.' Magnus nodded, though he knew that neither of them was convinced.

The scrolling banner at the bottom of the screen announced:

Military law established . . . Looters and
rumour-mongers   to   face   the   highest

126

```
penalties . . . Schools    cancelled . . .
Curfews in place during hours of darkness
. . . Dog owners urged to keep pets indoors
. . . Cabinet reconvened . . . Prime Minis-
ter set to make an announcement later
today . . .
```

And on the main screen the various images of hospital wards around the world were repeating.

```
V596 IS NO RESPECTER OF AGE OR SOCIAL
CLASS. SCIENTISTS ACROSS THE WORLD ARE
TAKING PART IN AN UNPRECEDENTED COLLABO-
RATION
```

Magnus switched channels, but they were either lost in static, guarded by test cards or running the same footage he had just watched.

'It's been like that all morning,' Jeb said.

Magnus wanted to make a joke about how he would have predicted endless repeats of *Frasier* or *Friends*, but he could not trust himself to speak. He lifted the pile of clothes Jeb had brought him and took them into the bathroom, not bothering to ask where they had come from.

Magnus showered with the bathroom door ajar. The water was tepid, but he could feel it restoring him to life. Prison had given him an awareness of walls and corners, he realised, a reluctance to be contained. Perhaps if he survived he would become one of those feral men who lived alone in the outdoors. There had been one of them on Wyre. Their mothers had told them to keep away from him, but one long holiday afternoon Magnus and Hugh had taken the ferry over and ridden their bikes up to the battered caravan where he lived. The man was outside, dressed only in baggy khaki shorts that looked like they had seen good service in the Great War. He looked wild, right enough, a Ben Gunn scarecrow with lunatic grey hair and a beard to match. He had been feeding something to his dogs, but paused to give the boys a gummy smile and then raised a hand and beckoned to them. Magnus had taken a step forward. Hugh grabbed his arm and without saying anything to each other, they had jumped on their bikes and pedalled off, as if the de'il himself was after them.

Hugh had been stupid to kill himself. It was a stupid waste, a stupid, senseless waste. Death would have come around eventually and in the meantime he could have lived.

The mobile phone Jeb had taken from the dead man in the subway carriage was sitting on the bedside table. Magnus wrapped a towel around his waist, sat on the edge of the bed and turned it on. He could hear his mother's telephone ringing, far away across land and water. For a moment Magnus pictured the old Trimphone that used to sit in the lobby, but it had gone years ago, banished by a cordless phone. His mother might have mislaid the handset. That was the trouble with these cordless numbers: you set them down somewhere and couldn't put your hands on them when they rang. His mother could be dashing between the kitchen and sitting room right now, looking for it.

The answering service came on. 'Hello, Mum?' He hated

the question mark in his voice. 'Hi, it's me. I hope you and Rhona are okay. There's been a bit of bother down here, but I'm fine. I'm coming home. I'll be with you in a couple of —' The phone beeped, cutting him off. He tried to remember his mother's mobile number and the number of Rhona's phones, but they had been programmed into his own device. He had summoned them by typing in their names and had never bothered to commit them to memory.

'Fuck.'

His mum was probably at Rhona's right now, the pair of them worrying about him and cursing him in equal measure. Magnus dialled the only other Orkney number he knew by heart, his Aunty Gwen's, Hugh's mother. Once again it rang out and he left a brief message. Cordless phones were useless, he consoled himself. If the electricity went down they went with it. His mother would have done better to have stuck with the old Trimphone.

He rang 118 118, thinking he should phone the Snapper Bar, or perhaps even the police or the hospital, but they did not answer either and he switched the mobile off, scared of wasting its battery. Things would be okay, he reassured himself. He would get home to find them all waiting for him.

Jeb was sitting at a low table in the lobby where guests had once enjoyed an aperitif while they waited for cabs to take them to that evening's destination. There was an unopened bottle of Highland Park and two whisky glasses on the table in front him. Jeb touched the neck of the malt gently with his fingertips as Magnus sat down.

'I never had a problem with drink, how about you?'

129

'I like a drink, if that's what you mean.'

'I meant if I open this bottle will you feel obliged to sup it all?'

There had been nights when he had killed a bottle and still been standing straight enough to make an assault on one of its comrades, but Magnus said, 'I can take a dram and put the cap back on the bottle.'

Jeb broke the seal and poured two measures into the waiting glasses.

'That's what we'll do then.' He passed one of the charged glasses to Magnus. The malt smelled of snugs and peat fires, of funeral breath and late nights. It smelled unbearably of home and Magnus was forced to look away. He cleared his throat.

'They made this not far from where I grew up.' He wondered at his use of the past tense.

Jeb raised his glass. 'To survival.'

Magnus echoed, 'Survival.'

They both drank. Jeb nodded, as if reaffirming the toast.

'When I first saw you, I don't know why, but I thought you were a soft lad.' He shrugged his shoulders. 'Maybe it's the accent.'

You decided before I opened my mouth, Magnus thought, I saw it in your eyes. He said nothing.

'We've been through a fair bit these last couple of days.' Jeb swirled the liquid in his glass, molten gold. This was another Jeb, no longer the sullen prison inmate or the crazed escapee armed with a ready chib. The military aspect that Magnus had noticed during their escape had returned. 'The odds were against us, but here we are.'

'These last days,' Magnus said. He took a sip of his dram. The whisky stung his lips but it brightened his perceptions. He could see the five-star hotel for what it was – a folly designed to make those who could afford it feel superior. That kind of swank was in the past; they had entered a new world where the only rank was survival.

Magnus had told Jeb that he could take a measure and put the cap back on the bottle, but he wanted to drink it dry and go into battle. Let whisky be his lieutenant and his linesman. He reached out, topped up his dram and gestured the bottle towards Jeb's glass. The other man shook his head.

'I'm not used to it.'

Magnus asked, 'How long were you inside?'

'I'd done three years, most of it in solitary.'

'So you're either a bad bastard, or an antisocial bastard.'

'A bit of both.'

The whisky was working on Magnus. He asked, 'What did you do?'

Jeb's voice was dangerously even. 'Like I said before, nothing you need to worry about. I ended up on the wrong side of the law, just like you. That's all you need to know.'

This was prison morality, Magnus supposed. Torture, robbery, extortion, violence of every stamp was tolerable, as long as the victims were male and over-age.

Jeb continued, 'What I was trying to say is, I can survive on my own—'

'Me too.' Magnus tipped back the last of his drink and reached for a refill, but the bottle was gone. His eyes met Jeb's.

'We need to stay straight,' Jeb said.

'That's your opinion.'

Jeb shook his head. 'It's like you're determined to make me change my mind. What I was going to say is, I can survive on my own, we both can, but we stand more chance together. At least until we make it out of London and work out what's going on in the rest of the country.'

'Going to organise a census, are you?' The over-patterned lounge seemed to sneer at them. Magnus wanted to take Jeb's penknife and shred the complacent cushions, tear the curtains, stain the carpets with red wine and worse.

'You should listen to your friend,' an American voice said. 'Two heads are better than one.'

Magnus turned and saw an old man leaning out of a winged armchair.

Jeb had sprung to his feet at the sound of his voice, but the man's age must have reassured him, because he sank back down into his seat, slowly. 'How long have you been there?' he asked.

'Long enough to know you were both in jail when this kicked off. You missed a time, boys.' He raised a drink to his mouth and Magnus realised that he was drunk. Not quite fleeing, but most definitely three sheets to the wind. 'Yes, boys,' the man repeated softly. 'You surely missed a time.'

Nineteen

The old man's name was Edgar Prentice, 'Eddie to my friends'. He was a professor in English Literature at Dartmouth College and lived in Norwich, New Hampshire. 'A nice town, but sleepy. You want an injection of culture then you get yourself to Boston or New York, Europe if you're lucky. I thought I was lucky.' Eddie had brought a loaded martini glass and a cocktail shaker over to their table. He raised his drink to his lips. 'Except the day before we were due to travel to London, my wife came down with a fever. I was all for cancelling, but Miriam wouldn't hear of it. She changed her ticket to a later flight, our daughter came to visit and I flew over on my own. Worst decision of my life.'

Magnus asked, 'How are they?'

The old man knocked back the last of his drink and refreshed his glass from the silver shaker. He was taller than any of the pensioners Magnus had grown up around, but his clothes hung loose on his bones and Magnus guessed that he too had recently lost weight. Eddie said, 'I anticipate a whole new set of taboos in this brave new world of ours. Asking about a man's family is going to be one of them.' He looked Magnus in the eye.

Magnus said, 'I was hoping immunity might run in families.'

Eddie tipped back his drink again. The electricity had died a few minutes ago and his hair gleamed nicotine yellow against the light of the candles Jeb had lit.

'Sorry to disappoint you.'

Jeb leaned forward in his chair. He had opened a bottle of San Pellegrino and the bubbles fizzed, straight and pure, in his glass. 'You stayed in London?'

'I didn't want to. It probably sounds lame, but as soon as that flight took off, I felt a sense of foreboding. I wanted to ask the stewardess to get the captain to turn the plane around and let me off. I didn't of course.' Eddie gave a sad smile. 'Just ordered a martini extra dry and found an in-flight movie I could tolerate. Soon as I got to London I phoned home. Jaime said that her mom was a lot better. I wished my girls goodnight and went to bed.

'The next day the TV news mentioned this new virus, V596, the sweats, but I didn't pay it any mind. I had tickets for *Richard III* at the Globe. I didn't know it, but it was one of their final performances. Richard overplayed his disability, but it was a good production.' Eddie shook his head. 'Sorry, old habits die hard. Like Jimmy Durante said, everyone's a critic.

'I wasn't worried when I phoned Miriam at home and on her cell the next day and got no response. I'd forgotten the premonition I had on the plane in my excitement of being back in London. As far as I was concerned, my wife was better. Miriam would be joining me in a day or two and in the meantime she was making the most of a visit from our

134

daughter. Sure, there was mention of the virus on TV, but where I was, in the centre of London, everything looked good. There was nothing to be concerned about. I didn't even bother to phone later, because of the time difference.'

Somewhere in the hotel a door slammed and footsteps rang out against a tiled floor. Jeb and Magnus turned to look across the dim lobby for the source of the sound, but there was no one there. Eddie said, 'We're not the only ones hiding out here. So far most people have kept to themselves, but I've seen them at a distance. You're the first folks I've talked to.'

Magnus glanced towards the dark part of the lobby, where elevators waited like upright coffins, ready to ferry guests up or down, to heaven or hell, but there was no one there. 'Why us?'

Eddie shrugged. 'Who knows? Maybe I'm just the right level of drunk. I always got sociable after a couple of martinis. It used to irritate Miriam. She thought I spent too much time talking to strangers and not enough talking to her.' He sighed. 'Nice as you fellows are, I'd give a lot to be talking to her instead of you right now.'

Jeb asked, 'When did you realise how bad things were?'

'That used to irritate Miriam too, the way I drift on to tangents. She'd say, "Get back on track, old man." She loved me enough to stay married to me for thirty-five years, but sometimes I drove her crazy.' Eddie gave a sad smile. His teeth were white and regular enough to be dentures. 'I'm not exactly sure when I realised things were serious. The hotel staff dwindled over the next couple of days. I was staying somewhere cheaper. Not here.' He affected an English accent. 'Even a professor's salary only stretches so far in jolly old

London.' Eddie sighed and resumed his own voice, dry and slightly slurred at the edges. 'I noticed there were less people around. The bar was closed, the maid service didn't freshen my room and there were no cooked breakfasts available, just stale croissants and little packs of cereal. I was irritated, but not worried. Brits have a fun-loving reputation. I thought maybe the hotel staff had had some party, gotten drunk and were sleeping it off. What concerned me was that I still couldn't get hold of Miriam or Jaime. I tried to get in touch with a colleague at the college, in the hope that she would drive round and check on them, but there was no response from her either. So eventually I called the cops. They told me they had no report of any problems, but said they would drop by the house and check on them. I don't know whether they did or not, they never phoned me back.' Eddie took a sip from his almost empty martini. 'The Internet was still operating. The sweats had gone viral, if you'll excuse the pun, but my own social media was more or less static. Usually I'm swamped by emails, even during vacation, but my inbox barely rattled.'

'Didn't you try to book a flight home?' Magnus asked.

'Sure I did. I packed my bags and headed for the airport determined to get myself on the first cancelled seat out of town, no dicking around. I started to cough in the taxi. The driver said he was sorry, but he wasn't taking any chances, and threw me out. I was beginning to feel bad, but I managed to hail another one and get myself to Heathrow. By the time I got to the check-in desk I must have looked bad too. They rounded me up and delivered me to a quarantine centre.' Eddie shook his head. 'They called it a quarantine centre, but it was a games hall with blankets on the floor. It was a place where they sent people to die in the hope that they wouldn't infect anyone else. I was there for four days. Like Charles Dickens said, "It was the best of times; it was the worst of times." I was too ill to worry about my family, but the sweats is no joke. There were some good Christian souls who tried to look after us, but I guess they mostly came down with it too. We were laid out in rows, as if we were already in a graveyard. There weren't enough people to clean us sick folks up, and we weren't capable of doing it ourselves, so we were left to lie in our own shit and vomit.' Eddie ran a hand across his forehead. 'I'm sorry. You boys both have people of your own to mourn. I guess it's a while since I talked with anyone.'

Magnus said, 'It's okay.' Eddie's words had conjured the gym hall in his primary school in Kirkwall. How it had looked the night high winds had disrupted their Boys' Brigade camping trip and the captain had arranged for them to bunk in sleeping bags in the hall instead. He tried not to imagine his mother and Rhona laid out on the hall's wooden floor, beside their neighbours.

Eddie said, 'I had weird dreams. Kept thinking I was slammed in the wagon of some overcrowded goods train headed for Auschwitz. Just shows how strongly those images are rooted in popular consciousness.' Magnus caught a glimpse of the professor the old man had so recently been, and then Eddie looked up and showed a face haggard by illness and grief. 'I thought God might come back to me. I was religious as a boy. Miriam used to joke that I'd relapse back to the Church on my deathbed, but He paid me the same no-mind He has for the last fifty-plus years.'

Jeb sipped his mineral water. His face was impassive. 'You didn't die.'

'No.' Eddie tipped the last of the martini from the shaker into his glass. His voice was weary. 'I didn't die.'

Magnus heard ice rattling inside the cocktail shaker and wondered that the man could take time to chill his drink when everything was falling apart.

Eddie said, 'I was in a crash on the interstate once, a long time ago. I had a blow-out in the fast lane. My car spun full circle, three hundred and sixty degrees, and crossed the barrier on to the other side of the carriageway. One moment I'm travelling north, the next I'm facing southbound traffic. I felt like I was moving fast as light, but I still had time to think about how much I loved Miriam. Jaime was just a little girl, she must have been around seven years old and I remember thinking what a shame it was that I would never see her grow up.' Eddie wiped away a tear. 'Well, at least I got to see her turn into a fine young woman.' He looked out towards the middle distance at the bar, still decorated with an elaborate flower arrangement as dead as the people in the darkened rooms above them. Magnus thought the old man was about to rise and refill the cocktail shaker, but he sat where he was, his eyes trained on the past. 'The sweats were in the newspapers and on television, but for a while everything seemed to function as normal. There were deaths in the news, sure, but there were always deaths in the news. I guess it had gotten to seem like death was no big news, just something the media were obliged to report.

'When I got out of the quarantine centre everything had changed. The city was under martial law. There were curfews at night, looting in the shopping districts, even the occa-sional dead body in the street.' He shook his head, as if he still could not believe the events he had witnessed. 'I don't know if it was a second wave of the disease or if the sweats just hit some people harder, but the deaths became sudden. I saw a young woman, a girl of about Jaime's age, drop down dead. One minute she was walking along, short skirt, cute red shoes, the next she was sprawled on the sidewalk. I went to help, but she was beyond help. A man shouted at me to leave her alone if I didn't want to catch it and so, God help me, I walked away and left her there, face down on the ground, her underwear on display, no dignity, no one to say a few words over her.'

'What else could you do?' Magnus thought about the bodies he had left lying on the Underground platform, the girl with long russet hair slumped on the pavement.

'I could have looked in her purse, checked to see if there was someone I could call. I know my girls are dead, perhaps her father is still waiting somewhere for her.'

Jeb held a hand over the bank of tea lights, watching the way the flames reflected against his skin. He looked up and met the old man's eyes. 'No one can bury them all. That's one of the reasons we're heading out of London. Other diseases will start to take hold. Cholera, typhoid . . .' He shrugged, acknowledging that he had come to the end of his under-standing of infections. 'Other things.'

Magnus thought about the fires Jeb had seen from the top of the hotel; soon it would be too late. 'We were shot at by soldiers. They told us we were in a controlled zone.'

Eddie nodded. 'The authorities couldn't keep up with the

number of deaths, but they sure were quick to stamp down on damage to property. Certain zones, shopping districts in the centre of towns, were meant to be no-go. I guess you've seen for yourself that it didn't work.'

Jeb said, 'It looked like people decided they wanted to die in front of a big flat screen, drinking a bottle of Chivas and wearing nice new trainers.'

Eddie nodded. 'I always thought of Brits as restrained, but the scenes I saw on television of your city centres reminded me of footage of the LA riots. I didn't want any part of it, so I maxed out my credit cards, booked myself in here and phoned home every quarter-hour in the hope that someone would pick up. Eventually Ben, my neighbour, answered.' Eddie's voice broke. 'He told me what had happened to my girls.' The old man covered his face with his hands and took a deep juddering sigh. When he removed them he was calm again. 'I never bothered to ask Ben what he was doing in my house. Anything there that he wanted, he was welcome to. I just wished him luck and hung up the phone. I've been here ever since, screwing up the courage to do what needs to be done.'

Jeb nodded. His face was blank, as if he were back in the prison cell he refused to share.

'We're heading north,' Magnus said. 'Far north in my case. I'm from Orkney.' It seemed crass to mention family after Eddie's tale, but he asked, 'I don't suppose you heard anything about how things are up there, in the islands?'

'No, son.' Eddie raised his glass to his lips. Magnus got the impression that this time it was an attempt to avoid meeting his eyes rather than an urge for alcohol that

140

prompted the move. 'I never heard anything about how things are up there.'

'Why don't you join us?' Magnus looked at Jeb, inviting his support, but Jeb stared unspeaking at the candles in front of him.

'I appreciate the invitation.' Eddie gave a polite smile and once more Magnus caught a glimpse of the person he had been before the crisis: a man with enough self-regard to stand by his convictions and enough empathy to do so graciously. 'But I don't have the energy left for that kind of trip. I thought I might hang around here, see if I can't find a way into the British Library and take a last look around for old times' sake. This disaster may have its compensations. I may never see another of Shakespeare's plays performed, but perhaps I can revisit his First Folio before I die.'

'There are fires in the city, diseases.' Magnus looked at Jeb again, but Jeb's face had regained its shuttered look.

'This isn't a time to be sentimental about strangers, not if you want to survive.' Eddie nodded towards Jeb. 'He knows that.' His eyes met Magnus's. 'You're a young man. You still have things you need to do, find a girl, start a family. I did all that. It was fun and I highly recommend it, but there's nothing left for me. I've lost my taste for life.'

His cousin Hugh had been a younger man than Magnus was now, but he had lost his taste for life too. Magnus wanted to say something about the misery of suicide, but the words were beyond his grasp. Somewhere another door slammed. All three of them turned towards the noise, but there was nothing in the lobby except a clash of colours and patterns it had once been thought worth a lot of money to sit among.

Eddie got up and walked slowly towards the bar as if his joints were hurting, though it might have been the shaker full of martini inside him that slowed his pace. 'There are more survivors than you might think.' It should have been a cause for celebration, but Eddie's expression was serious. 'Keep your eyes open, and be careful how you go. Like the bard said, "The world is grown so bad, that wrens make prey where eagles dare not perch."'

PART TWO

By then we had made our covenant with silence,
But in the first few days it was so still
We listened to our breathing and were afraid.

'The Horses', Edwin Muir

Twenty

The sound of Magnus and Jeb's motorbikes cut through the countryside, announcing their progress. Despite the heat they were both dressed in motorcycle leathers and crash helmets, both of them with scarves wrapped around their mouths and noses to guard against the dust and the stench of decay. The smell had grown worse as they left London behind. The summer had been a good one and crops had ripened earlier than usual. Now they lay rotting in the fields. Cattle also lay in the fields and some of them were rotting too.

The motorbikes had been Magnus's idea, the guns strapped to their backs Jeb's. They had planned to spend their nights sheltered in houses large enough to have spare bedrooms left unoccupied by the dead, but had encountered too many decaying corpses, too many families huddled together in death, too many blown-out brains and emptied pill bottles. Now they camped outside, taking turns to stay awake, like cowboys crossing the plains in some old movie.

Magnus reckoned that he could have reached the ferry terminal at Scrabster in two days, if he had bombed the journey. But they had met the aftermath of several accidents on their way out of London: a driver thrown through the windscreen of his car, a teenage boy impaled on the railings of a park he had somehow got locked inside, a little girl who had fallen from a high, neglected building; that last one had made Magnus cry. The tears had been a release, and he had hated himself for feeling better.

The accidents were a reminder that it was not only the sweats they needed to survive and they had agreed to stick to a steady thirty miles an hour, in the hope of avoiding a broken leg, or worse.

Magnus and Hugh had graduated to motorbikes in their teens. They had weathered the usual falls and near misses, raced each other past Maes Howe, the sky stretching wide and seamless above them. Neighbours had warned their parents of the speeds the boys went, but even his father's sudden death had not persuaded Magnus of his own mortality.

Hugh had let the waves roll over him, filled his pockets with stones, weighted his rucksack with boulders and then walked into the sea. His death had rendered life more fragile, but it had increased Magnus's recklessness. It was as if he had to live life twice as hard, to show Hugh, who was often with him, just out of sight on the periphery of his vision, what a fool he had been to give in.

The sweats had defeated Magnus's appetite for danger. He kept recalling the final frames of *Easy Rider*, Peter Fonda engulfed by flames, Dennis Hopper lying shot at the side of the road. Neither he nor Jeb had mentioned what provision they would make should the other fall ill, or become injured. There was no need.

It was late afternoon and the sun was at its highest point,

146

but the narrow road they were travelling was bordered on either side by tall verges which raised the surrounding fields three feet above them. It was like travelling through a shaded valley. Orkney was flat and almost treeless. You could see for miles. Here roads took dark twists and turns, the high verges and hedgerows deadened sound and it was impossible to know what might lie around the next corner, or who was hiding among the greenery.

They had started their journey on the M1 but, though the earth had seemed to be dying, it was as Eddie had said: other survivors haunted the landscape. Magnus caught occasional glimpses of them peering from curtained windows, hiding in verges, lurking in shadows in deserted towns. He wondered if it was death that had made them that way. Survivors had been abandoned by everyone they held dear and though their loved ones had had no say in it, their going made it harder to trust the living.

At first, Magnus had dismounted and taken off his helmet when he saw another survivor. But perhaps some of the prison menace still clung to him because so far people had melted away, except for an elderly man who came out of his cottage, levelled a shotgun at Magnus and told him to get going.

'We don't mean any harm,' Magnus had said.

The old man had kept his aim steady and repeated his instruction. 'Be on your way, boys.' But perhaps he believed Magnus because he added, 'And watch how you go. There are some bad buggers about.'

The old man had been dressed in work gear. His blue over-alls and battered wellies reminded Magnus of his father and

147

he had wanted to ask him what they should do. But Magnus had caught the light of madness in the old man's eyes, saw the tremble in his trigger finger and got back on his motorbike and rode away without another word.

He and Jeb had agreed to switch to the B-roads after an encounter with a souped-up Porsche. The car had driven alongside them, coming too close to their bikes and then drifting away, playing with them like a sheepdog harrying sheep. Magnus had known there was only one end to the game and had slowed his bike, bracing himself for the scud of concrete against flesh and leather. But Jeb had slid the gun from the inside of his jacket and fired at the car. They were still moving too fast for him to take proper aim and the shot had gone wild, but it had been enough to frighten the Porsche's driver and the car had zoomed off along the motorway.

They had come across the Porsche again a few hours later, parked at a service station. There were other cars skewed across the car park, all of them high-performance. A deep bass rock beat echoed from somewhere in the centre of the squat building. Magnus and Jeb had remained straddled on their motorbikes.

Jeb had flipped up his helmet's visor. 'They still have electricity.'

The services housed an M&S, a Burger King, and a Krispy Kreme Donuts concession. Magnus did not have to get close to know that it would smell foul inside. You would have to be unhinged to make your base there among the rats and putrefying food. He counted the cars. 'Twenty of them. Quite a gang.'

'Maybe.' Jeb leaned back, stretching his spine, his gloved hands still gripping the bike's handlebars. 'Or one *Top Gear* fan having the time of his life.'

He got off his motorcycle, unsheathed the Bowie knife he kept strapped to his calf and began slashing the cars' tyres. After a moment's hesitation Magnus dismounted, slid his own knife from his rucksack and did the same. They had been running low on fuel and had turned into the service station in the hope that they could switch on the petrol pumps or siphon petrol from abandoned cars, but had driven on without filling their tanks.

That was a day ago. The only people they had seen since were a couple of what Magnus had thought were youths, crouching in a ditch. Jeb had driven by without noticing them, but some movement had snagged Magnus's eye and he had seen two frightened faces, one brown, the other ruddy with sunburn, hiding in the shadows thrown by an over-grown hedge. It was only as he drove past that he realised they were girls in men's clothing. If he had been travelling solo Magnus would have slowed his bike to a halt, but he had looked at Jeb's broad, leather-clad back and decided it was better to travel on. The girls' fear brought back the alley-way behind Johnny Dongo's hotel, the man trying to force himself on the drunken woman.

Magnus's thoughts were dominated by the past, memories of home, his family, childhood, his cousin Hugh. The circumstances of his meeting with Jeb also preyed on him. Each night Magnus told himself he would ditch the ex-con and make his own way. Each morning they drove on together. Sometimes one of them was ahead, sometimes the other but, although their bikes ate up the miles at an even pace, they rarely travelled side by side.

There was safety in numbers, Magnus told himself. But he knew that he feared being alone in the changed landscape. It was too quiet, too full of the voices of the dead. As if on cue he heard his father say, 'A man is the company he keeps.' Magnus knew how his father would have reacted to his son teaming up with a prisoner who had been confined to a wing reserved for sex offenders. Thoughts of his father sparked more thoughts of home. Magnus had tried calling his mother several times, but though the phone rang on, no one answered. They would be okay, he reassured himself. His mother was the most resourceful woman he knew and Rhona came from the same stock. If anyone could survive it would be them. But survival had nothing to do with skills and good sense. It was a toss of the dice, a spin of the wheel of fortune.

Sunlight dappled through the hedgerows, strobing on the road ahead. Jeb had lengthened the distance between them. His body and the bike he was riding were figured with glimmering patterns formed from brightness and shadow. Magnus followed him, travelling through a discotheque of flashing light and dark. The birds seemed to have grown louder as the other sounds of the world had receded. A chaffinch was repeating the same phrase over and over, a piping refrain in a clamour of chirps, trills and flourishes. Magnus blinked his eyes. They had been driving for hours now. When the road widened he would pull ahead, slow the bike to a halt and call a coffee stop.

Another sound reached him, an alien hum that outstripped the noise of their motorbikes and the commotion of birds.

For one maddening, panicking moment Magnus thought a bee had somehow found its way inside his motorbike helmet, but then he realised the sound came from outside himself. It was an engine, high-pitched with speed, and it was growing louder.

Jeb's bike was up ahead, still in the centre of the road, travelling towards a blind bend. Magnus shouted at him to pull over, but his words were lost in the slipstream of noise and breeze. Magnus slowed his bike, steering it left, drawing closer to the verge to give whatever was coming towards them space to pass. He shouted again. Perhaps Jeb was caught in his own thoughts of the past and it was the lure of them, or other dreams, that stopped him registering the approaching engine. He heard it too late and pulled right as he cornered the left turn. A yellow Audi emerged around the bend and the bike skewed across the road, throwing Jeb beneath it. The wheels kept on spinning. They struck the tarmac and propelled the bike, with Jeb still pinned under it, across the road towards a ditch.

Magnus flung his own machine into a hedge and threw himself after it. The Audi skidded across the road, narrowly missing Jeb's still moving bike, and pitched to a halt in a cloud of burning rubber, facing the direction it had come from. The door of the car opened and the driver got out. Magnus's first thought was that he was just a boy. Magnus shouted, 'Help me get the bike off him,' and started to run to where Jeb lay trapped half in, half out of the ditch.

His second thought was that the driver wasn't a boy, not really. He was short and slightly built, but he was dressed in a palette of summer pastels that suggested rounds of golf with business cronies, followed by vodka and tonics in the clubhouse bar. The man grinned and his face creased into lines that were at odds with youth. There was something familiar about the aged-young face. Magnus realised that it reminded him of an old-fashioned ventriloquist's dummy one of the comics on the circuit had used as a prop. It was a horrible object, prone to obscene observations its handler would never have got away with. Time seemed to falter. Magnus took a step backward and the driver reached into the car.

Jeb let out a shout that broke the spell and Magnus started towards him again. 'Help me get this bloody machine off him,' he shouted at the man. Jeb must have managed to reach the motorbike's ignition because the engine died and its wheels faltered to a halt. There was a smell of oil and petrol and Magnus thought how easy it would be for the whole thing to go up. 'Are you all right?'

He lowered himself into the ditch. Jeb was curled as far forward as the motorbike would let him, clutching at his right leg. His face was twisted in agony.

'Don't worry,' Magnus said, his heart hammering in his chest. 'We'll get it off you.'

Jeb said something fast and urgent, but his voice was hoarse and Magnus could not make out the words. He put his gloved hands on the scorching metal, trying to work out how best to lift the bike free, without doing more damage. 'Fucking . . .' Jeb's voice was a struggle of pain and phlegm. 'Fucking . . . fucking . . .'

'It's okay.' Magnus tried to soothe him. 'We'll find a chemist's, fire some painkillers into you.'

The best option might be to take the bike apart, he decided. Remove its panniers and handlebars, its saddle and wheels and then see where they could go from there.

'Fucking . . .' Sweat spangled Jeb's forehead. His words were growing in urgency. 'Fucking look behind you!'

Magnus turned. The yellow Audi's boot was open. The puppet-faced man had taken something from it and was coming towards them. At first Magnus thought he had reached the same conclusion about dismantling the bike and had found a tool to do the job, then he saw the glint of the blade and realised it was a machete, or did he mean a Samurai sword? There was a man in Stromness who had killed his best friend with a Samurai sword that had hung blamelessly above the couch in his sitting room for years. Magnus's mind was racing. He pulled off his motorcycle gloves and reached for the rifle strapped to his back, but it snagged on something and he could not pull it free. 'Fuck, fuck, fuck, fuck, fuck . . .' Now it was Magnus who was swearing. Jeb said nothing, but his breaths came fast and heavy, like a horse after a gallop along the sands. Magnus pulled at the rifle again. This time it came free, but the man had reached the edge of the ditch.

He said, 'You're the vandals that slashed my tyres,' and raised his sword high.

Magnus was fumbling with the gun. *Fuck!* He had shot almost as many rats as Hugh, but now his fingers were groping for the safety catch.

'Shoot him,' Jeb whispered. 'Fucking shoot him.'

And the man's head exploded.

The spray of blood, bone and brain was warm; *body temperature*, Magnus thought. He wiped a hand across his eyes, trying to clear the redness from his vision, and felt a wild, hysterical urge to laugh. He stared stupidly at the gun in his hands, knowing that he had not pulled the trigger, but unable to comprehend what had happened. He looked at Jeb. His face was red, as if someone had peeled the skin from his flesh. His eyes were trained towards the road above. Magnus followed his stare. A tall man in a clerical collar and army fatigues walked to where the driver lay slumped at the side of the road. He prodded the body gently with the toe of his boot, though there could be no doubt that the man was dead.

Twenty-One

'**D**o you mind?' The vicar, if he was a vicar, nodded at Magnus's rifle. He had a Yorkshire accent and his voice was soft and slightly apologetic, but the gun that had killed the driver was still in his hand. Magnus placed his rifle on the edge of the ditch and raised his hands in the air. 'Thank you. I'd like your friend's weapons too please. Don't worry.' He smiled as if he had not just blown the top of the driver's head into a blizzard of shards. 'It's just a precaution.'

Magnus's hands were shaking and it was difficult to slide the rifle from Jeb's back, but he managed it. He had intended to ignore the gun tucked inside the leather jacket, but to his amazement, Jeb offered it up. The man raised his eyebrows as if he were also surprised.

'That makes me wonder what else you have on you. Check his socks for skean-dhu, please.' Magnus avoided Jeb's eyes as he took the Bowie knife from its sheath and laid it beside the other weapons. 'Thanks.' The man put the revolver into one pocket and the knife into another. He laid the shotguns in easy reach on the bonnet of the Audi and turned his attention to Jeb. 'How badly hurt are you?'

'I don't know.' Jeb's voice was compressed by the weight of

155

metal lying on his chest. He had wiped some of the sweat and blood from his face and his skin was pale beneath the bloodstains. His mouth grimaced, but when he spoke he sounded detached, as if he were discussing someone else. 'I've smashed my leg.'

Magnus could smell cracked earth and greenery beneath the butcher-shop stench of blood and brain. The gunfire had scattered the birds, but the chaffinches were singing again. *Chip, chip, chip, chooee, chooee, cheeoo.* A robin landed on a bush and tilted its head to one side. Its black button eyes seemed to take in the scene: the dead body with its ruined head, Jeb pinned beneath his motorcycle, the army cleric rummaging in the boot of the custard-yellow Audi. Magnus bent over and was noisily sick in the ditch. The robin flew off, chirping a warning call.

'Our luck's in.' The stranger lifted a tow chain from the boot of the Audi. 'The car's driver was a belt and braces man.'

Jeb's eyes were glassy. His words came out in painful starts. 'I thought slashing that bastard's tyres would keep him off our backs, but I forgot he had all the time in the world to get himself a new car and track us down. I guess he got lucky.' The grin tightened. 'If he'd taken another road he would have missed us.'

'The road less travelled,' the priest said, beneath his breath. He fastened one end of the tow chain to the Audi and swung the other end down into the ditch towards Magnus who fastened it to the bike.

Pulling the motorcycle free of Jeb was easier than Magnus had expected. When it was safely up on the bank the man slithered into the ditch beside them. Jeb's motorcycle trousers had stood the test of the accident. They were badly scuffed, but un-torn. The man squatted in the ditch, took the Bowie knife from his pocket and carefully slit the leather from hem to knee. He examined the damaged leg with a gentle efficiency that made Jeb swear between gritted teeth and Magnus ask if he was a doctor.

'I suspect I'm the nearest thing to one you're going to get, but no. I just picked up a few things along the way.'

The economy of his movements reminded Magnus of Jeb and he wondered if the altered world would be ruled by men like them, practical men who would not let pain or emotions interfere with getting the job done.

Jeb's leg was purple with bruises that seemed to deny the separation of blood and skin. It looked swollen and ripe, like a fruit ready to split its casing.

'Without an X-ray it's impossible to know if it's broken,' the priest said. 'We'll have to do this the old-fashioned way. Can you stand?'

Jeb pushed himself up and tried to put his weight on the injured leg, but his face buckled with pain and he sank into the side of the ditch.

'Well, that's that,' the man said, as if something he had suspected all along had just been confirmed. His eyes met Magnus's. They were bright Anglo-Saxon blue. 'Why did that maniac want to kill you?'

'I don't know.'

'Come on.' For the first time the vicar's voice was more army than Church. 'I may have lost my immortal soul to save you. I deserve to know why.'

'It's like I said.' Jeb had bitten his lip and spots of blood jewelled his mouth. He licked them away. 'We slashed his tyres.'

'He tried to run us off the road a while back.' Magnus glanced at the gun. The man had holstered it, but he had proved his willingness to shoot to kill. 'There was no reason for it except boredom or badness. We managed to get away, but we ran across him later by accident when we stopped at a service station. He was somewhere inside, but we recognised the Porsche he was driving. It was parked next to a fleet of around twenty fast cars. We thought he would be less likely to bother us again if we put them out of action.'

'And so it starts,' the vicar muttered. 'So few of us left, but already we're fighting.'

There had been no need to shoot their attacker in the head; a shot in the leg or foot would have put the driver out of action without killing him. Magnus said nothing and when the vicar hooked an arm beneath Jeb's left shoulder and nodded for him to take the right, he obeyed without a word.

In the end they pulled him from the ditch backwards, arse on the ground, ruined leg dragging painfully against the earth. Jeb kept up a low and steady stream of invective as they eased him out. It was hard work and all three of them were sweating and powdered with dirt by the time they reached the roadside. Magnus looked to see what kind of vehicle had driven the vicar to their rescue, but there was only the yellow Audi, abandoned diagonally across the road like a prop in a cop show. The priest opened the car's back door. Jeb lowered himself gently on to the back seat and slid, still swearing, until he was propped against the other door, his injured leg stretched out in front of him, the other in the footwell, bracing his body against a fall.

'Thanks.' Magnus unzipped his motorcycle jacket and

peeled it off. It was a relief to feel the air on his skin. He realised that he should have thanked the man before and added, 'You saved our lives.'

The vicar nodded. 'Were they worth killing for?'

Magnus looked at Jeb and then back at the other man. 'I hope so.'

'What are you going to do with them?'

Here it was, Magnus thought, the pitch for God. 'I don't know.' He gave the grin that had never worked on his school teachers, but which he seemed destined to greet authority with. 'Live them.'

There was another groan from the back of the car and Jeb said, 'If I don't fucking die first.'

The cleric in the stranger seemed to recede again and he reverted to army mode.

'We've a place nearby.' He looked at Magnus. 'I'll drive. We can send a truck to collect your bikes later.'

Magnus wondered who the 'we' were. He said, 'I'd rather follow on my bike.'

'I know these roads. You won't be able to keep up on that thing.' The man turned away as if the conversation was over and began unfastening the tow chain from the handlebars of Jeb's damaged bike.

The shadows thrown by the trees had lengthened. The crash and its aftermath had swallowed time. Late afternoon was edging into early evening and in a few hours the dark would start to drift in. Magnus leaned inside the car. Jeb was hunched on the back seat, clutching his leg.

'I don't fancy this.' Magnus's voice was a whisper. 'We could be walking back into prison.'

159

Jeb looked at his leg. 'I'm not walking anywhere. I've smashed this good.' His breath juddered and he said, 'I've done my ribs in too. A sudden move and one of them might puncture my lung; then I'd be truly fucked. Sorry, mate.' It was the first time Jeb had apologised for anything, the first time he had called Magnus 'mate'. 'I don't like it, but I've got no choice. I've got to go with the Righteous Avenger. You do what you have to do.'

It was in Magnus's mind to say that he could drive north while Jeb convalesced in the back of the car, but a look at the strained expression on the parchment face told him it would be impossible. He had planned to ditch Jeb, but the prospect of continuing his journey on his own made him uneasy.

The vicar was at the car now, the tow chain still in his hands. 'Ready to go?'

Magnus straightened up. He pulled his motorcycle jacket on and dragged his bike from the hedge where he had abandoned it. 'Where are you heading? An army base?'

'My base is a hundred miles south-west of here.' The chain clinked as the man dropped it into the boot of the car. 'It was hit hard, everywhere was hit hard. I'm the only survivor. I came here looking for someone I knew.'

Magnus noted the past tense and did not ask if he had found them.

Jeb mumbled something. The man glanced into the car and said, 'Your friend's going into shock. The sooner we get some meds into him the better.' He glanced at the bike. 'Don't worry. I told you, I'll send someone for it.'

'I'm used to country roads. I'll follow you.'

160

'Not on that.' The vicar nodded at the back wheel of the motorbike.

Magnus followed his gaze and saw an evil rip grinning in the bike's back tyre. 'Shit.' He knelt down and touched the torn rubber, though he did not need a closer look to know that the damage was beyond patching. It could have happened when he skidded out of the Audi's path, but he had heard no explosion, felt no tell-tale loss of control. Jeb groaned in the back of the Audi and Magnus got to his feet.

'I'll be heading north tomorrow, in this car if I can't find a way to fix my bike.'

He set the motorbike at the side of the road and slid into the passenger seat of the Audi, wondering why the vicar was so desperate to ensure he accompanied them.

Twenty-Two

The yellow Audi ate up the country roads at what felt like racing-track speed. The vicar had been right. It would have been impossible for Magnus to have matched the pace on his motorbike, even if its tyres had been undamaged. Magnus sat silently, trying to hide the urge to press his foot against an imaginary brake pedal. He pulled down the sun visor and glanced at Jeb in the vanity mirror. His eyes were closed, his lips moving silently. Magnus wondered if he was praying.

'What's your name?' the vicar asked.

Magnus snapped the visor back into place.

'I'm Magnus McFall, he's Jeb Soames.'

'Short for Jebediah?'

'I don't know, I never asked.'

The vicar ignored the road markings, keeping to the centre of the track as if he were confident of meeting no one coming the other way, though the whole reason for their haste was that the Audi itself had come the other way. The route was as winding as the man had implied. The old Magnus would have relished the challenge of its twists and turns. He had loved the sensation of speed and rushing air, the roadside flashing by, blurring on the edge of his vision.

162

'I'm Jacob Powe.'

Civilisation ran deep, Magnus thought. Everything was broken, but the man still felt an obligation to exchange names, as if they had met at a dinner party or a neighbourhood barbecue. He said, 'You're a minister?'

'An Anglican priest.'

Magnus had never got the hang of English religions with their married priests and un-Catholic masses.

'An army man?'

'A captain, if the army still exists.'

It was strange, a priest with a gun in his hand, though it was not so hard to imagine Jesus armed and ready to fight the good fight. It was the Messiah's beard and long hair that did it. The New Testament's hippy look brought back images of IRA and Afghan terrorists, or freedom fighters, depending on your point of view. There were the makings of a good routine there (a God routine), he thought, and remembered again that there was no comedy circuit, no audience waiting to be shocked into laughter. He wondered if they had anything to drink at the place where they were going. He had a thirst that would drain Christ dry.

'What do we call you?' he asked. 'Captain or Father?'

'Jacob.' The car slowed and Jeb muttered something as they turned into a driveway guarded either side by massive stone gateposts, each one topped with a carved pineapple, regal in its spikiness. 'Welcome to Tanqueray House.'

The driveway was hemmed on either side by an avenue of trees. The road's surface was tamped earth that had been covered some time back with shale. It was pitted with potholes and Jacob took it slowly. It was clear that the place

163

had been neglected before the arrival of the sweats. An explosion of rhododendrons reached across the drive from overgrown verges, occasionally tapping against the car windows, like paparazzi in search of an incriminating photograph. The flowers were the same bright reds and purples of the saris that had sometimes drawn Magnus's eyes on London streets; they had died too, the straight-backed Asian women with beautiful hair. Magnus rolled down the window and the scent of rotting foliage, more perfumed than the smell of decomposing flesh, but tainted all the same, slid into the car. He rolled up the window again. People went on about the beauty of trees, but Magnus had never felt easy around them. The branches bobbed and tangled above the drive, like mothers separated from their children, straining to touch even their fingertips. The image made him think of his own mother, how much she would be worrying about him. He pushed the thought away. There was no point in dwelling on possibilities. His task was to get home. He would leave in the morning. If he made steady progress he could be at the ferry terminal in a few days. The ferry would be no use, but it was the shortest crossing point. There would be other boats moored there and he would find one to suit him.

He asked, 'How many of there are you?'

'Seven – six.' Jacob stumbled over the number. 'Father Wingate was here before the sweats arrived. The house was a seminary and he was one of the brothers. He's eighty-two, but in good health for his age, sharp as a blade.'

'Eighty-two,' Magnus repeated.

'We're lucky to have him. Father Wingate remembers the

164

way a lot of things used to be done, before technology took over. His generation will be crucial to our survival.'

'And the others?'

'They came later. Waifs and strays, like you and Jeb. Like me if it comes to it.'

Magnus was about to say that he wasn't a waif or a stray. He had somewhere to go, but the car swung around the final turn, the rhododendrons gave a last desperate clutch and the house appeared at the end of the drive. It was larger than he had expected, three storeys high and broad enough to suggest that once there had been other wings balancing the structure.

'No vow of poverty,' Magnus said.

Jacob shrugged. 'It was Father Wingate's ancestral home. He donated it to the Church when he took holy orders, much to the outrage of his extended family, I imagine. The Church would no doubt have sold it in due course.'

'In due course,' Magnus repeated. Death was everywhere, and yet they still referred to it with euphemisms.

The mansion's roof was turreted and decorated with urns, like a house in an Agatha Christie movie where someone was due to topple to their death. Two staircases curved liquidly from an elevated porch down to a gravel courtyard where a Luton and a Transit van were parked. Each floor was defined by rows of windows, standing uniformly in line, black and secret. The house had been designed to impress, but it reminded Magnus of Pentonville, their flight across the courtyard uncertain of who was watching them. He wondered if people lurked behind the panes, observing their arrival and wondering in turn who the newcomers might be.

As if on cue the door of the house opened and a young woman trotted down the left staircase towards them. The girl looked like she had been born to the big house. She was in her early twenties, blonde and slender, with a pert nose that looked too good to be natural. Magnus thought that she might have been one of the girls he had glimpsed earlier that day, crouching in a ditch, disguised as boys, but he could not be sure.

Jacob slowed the car to a halt and the girl opened the driver's door. Magnus had thought their arrival would be an occasion, but she barely spared him a glance. She took hold of Jacob's arm, as if she were about to pull him from the car and said, 'Henry's gone.'

Twenty-Three

Jacob poured himself a small measure of whisky from the not quite full bottle on the kitchen table. He raised the glass to his nose and inhaled the malt fumes. The house was without electricity and the room was lit by a cluster of candles that threw weird shadows against the walls. 'This isn't a prison.' He had said the same thing as they sat down to dinner. His expression was serious, as if it were medicine he was about to put to his lips and not a fine Lagavulin. 'Henry was at liberty to move on.'

'He said he was going to stay.' Belle's voice had a rich-girl whine to it. 'He promised me.'

Magnus swirled the liquid in his glass, smelled a faint whiff of peat, took a sip and felt the malt slide down, warm and golden. The politics of the place were nothing to do with him. Now that they had eaten, only the bottle held him at the table.

They had laid Jeb on a door and carried him up to the main entrance. He was delirious and Jacob had sent the girl, whose name was Belle, indoors to find something to strap him to the makeshift stretcher with. Magnus had expected to deposit Jeb somewhere on the ground floor, but the priest had led the way up a grand central staircase and they had manhandled the stretcher to a room on the first floor. Now Jeb was in bed, tucked tight in a medicated sleep, his leg firmly bound, his ribs cushioned on either side by pillows. Father Wingate was sitting with him.

The elderly priest was a slight, shrunken figure whose head seemed too large for his body, the way the heads of children or anorexics sometimes can. His hair was thin, but brushed over his forehead in a style that might once, when the hair had been thicker and darker, have been considered foppish. Father Wingate looked too slow to avoid a coffin for much longer, but he had been quick to offer his help. Magnus imagined him in the room along the passageway, murmuring prayers over the bed, trying to inveigle God into Jeb's soul.

'Maybe something happened to Henry.' Injury tinged Belle's voice, as if the sweats had been a mean trick played on her alone.

'Maybe,' Jacob agreed. He stared at his barely touched glass, his voice as calm as the liquid it held.

Magnus wondered if the cleric had helped himself to something from the medicine cabinet when he had been dosing Jeb. There was a lifetime of whisky and pills still out there for the taking. If he got to Orkney and found it deserted he could drink himself to death on the supply in Stromness alone and if that did not work he could drink himself from house to house until he reached Kirkwall and beyond. He would take a man's way out, unlike Hugh. His cousin had died a hysteric's death. Stones in his pocket like some lady poet. *I was much too far out all my life and not waving but drowning.* They had learned that stupid poem at school, but

Hugh had not been out of his depth. The inquest had reported that the water had barely reached his chest before he sank beneath it.

Magnus must have muttered something out loud because Jacob and Belle stopped talking.

'Are you okay?' Jacob sounded smoothly unbothered, but then he had shot a man in the head without suffering any obvious ill effects. There was no reason why Magnus's drunken ramblings should trouble him.

'Aye.' Magnus took another sip of malt. So many dead and still his cousin haunted him. 'I'm okay.'

Jacob had said there were six people staying at the house, but so far Magnus had only met Jacob, Father Wingate and Belle. Henry was accounted for by his absence, but that still left two more survivors. There were too few people left not to be curious about those who remained. He remembered the brown face of the woman he had glimpsed crouching in the ditch with the girl who might have been Belle.

'What if Henry went the same way as Mel?' the girl said.

'Melody made her own decision. We should respect that.'

'What happened to Melody?' Something in the tone of Jacob's voice had already told Magnus, but the words were out before he could bite them back.

Jacob levelled his gaze at Magnus. His eyes were creased and tired-looking, but there was an alertness in them that suggested the cleric was not as relaxed as he appeared. He said, 'Melody struggled with the fact that she was a survivor. She couldn't understand why she had been allowed to live when everyone dear to her had died.' Jacob tipped back his dram and downed it in one, swift gulp. 'I'm afraid she killed herself.'

'She hanged herself in the barn,' Belle said, as if it were important to get the facts right. 'Henry found her.'

Jacob turned his gaze on Belle. 'That may be one of the reasons Henry decided to leave us.' He lifted his glass to his mouth, but it was empty and he set it down without bothering to refill it. 'Henry found it hard even to look at the barn after he discovered poor Melody's body. He made all sorts of detours to avoid the place.'

'He promised me he would stay.' Belle sounded tired.

Magnus finished his dram. He rolled the empty glass between his palms and realised he was staring at the bottle the way a well-trained dog will stare at its bowl before being given permission to eat. He pulled himself to his feet.

'I'd best get myself to bed.'

'Take the bottle with you, if you'd like.' Jacob slid the whisky towards him, but the moon was on the wane that night and the moment had passed.

'Thanks, but I've a long drive tomorrow.'

'You know your friend won't be well enough to go with you?'

Magnus nodded. 'He was never going to go as far north as me anyway.'

'Why does everyone go?' Belle asked.

The whine was back in her voice, but this time Magnus felt sorry for her. She was not far off a child, and the world was less fun than it used to be.

'Other folk will come along.'

Belle gave him a small smile. 'At least your friend is staying.'

Magnus heard the brightening note in the girl's voice.

He wondered if he should tell them where he had met Jeb, but it occurred to him that Christian charity might not extend to caring for a sex offender and he decided to sleep on the decision.

'You've got a captive audience there, but I'd leave him alone if I were you. He's a grumpy old git.'

'Belle might cheer him up.' Jacob was leaning back in his chair, his half-shut eyes trained on the girl. He looked and sounded like a pimp. Magnus wondered again if the man was really a soldier-priest. It was a new world. Perhaps everyone could be whatever they declared themselves, for a while at least.

'Trust me.' Magnus got to his feet, the floor pitched and he realised he had drunk more than he meant to. 'Jeb's used to being on his own. He prefers it.'

He took a candle to guide his way and closed the kitchen door gently behind him, leaving the pair of them still sitting silently in the dim light of the kitchen.

Belle had already shown Magnus the room where he would sleep. It was on the second floor, small and musty-smelling, but it had a bed equipped with a mattress and bedclothes. After nights spent on a bedroll on the ground it looked like luxury. Belle had lingered by the door, and Magnus had considered reaching towards her, taking her hand in his and seeing where things led, but her wrists were as thin as a child's and the thought of her fragile body beneath his had made him feel squeamish.

Magnus paused on the first-floor landing, wondering if he should make his way to Jeb's room and warn him to ignore .

the girl, unless he wanted his cover blown. The prospect of meeting Father Wingate gave him the creeps. His mother was an active Kirk member, but Magnus had never completely trusted ministers and their ilk. He had been a pallbearer at his father's funeral for his mother's sake, but had spent the day of Hugh's cremation driving his motorbike full speed to the far side of the island. There had been a moment on the Churchill Barriers when he had felt the urge to turn his wheels towards the water and plunge the bike, with him still on it, down into the depths among the wrecks of the German fleet, but it was only a moment and it passed. His Aunty Gwen had forgiven him for not attending, but Magnus was never sure that she forgave him for being alive when her own boy was dead, and he had avoided their house from then on, though it had been a second home to him.

He had been staring at the stair carpet without seeing it; now its pattern came into focus, an abstract arrangement of reds, greens and dulled yellows that coalesced into a sharp goatee-chinned devil's face, repeated over and over. Magnus closed his eyes and opened them again, forcing himself to unsee the image. It was a trick of the mind, like the faces he had conjured in the woodchip that papered his bedroom walls as a child.

He leaned against the banister for support as he climbed the stairs to his room. How could Father Wingate and Jacob Powe hold on to their faith in the face of so much death? What kind of god was it they worshipped? He pushed open the door to the room. The candle cast a thin pool of light over the worn carpet, the rose-sprigged wallpaper, the rumpled counterpane. The bedcovers shifted and Magnus saw the woman who had hidden in the ditch beside Belle at the sound of their motorbikes. Her long hair was spread across her shoulders, her expression was grave.

He said stupidly, 'Are you Melody?'

'No,' the woman said. 'Melody's dead.'

She drew back the sheets making space for him and he saw the curve of her breasts, her dark nipples.

Magnus whispered, 'I don't know you,' and thought what a ridiculous thing it was to say.

She said, 'I need to be with someone tonight. My thoughts are too loud in my head.'

Magnus could feel himself hardening, all his thoughts beginning to flee. He touched the doorjamb with his fingertips.

'You're grieving.'

'We're all grieving. The least we can do is comfort each other.'

Magnus stepped into the room and set the candle on the bedside table. His body threw dark shadows against the bedroom walls as he started to pull off his clothes.

Twenty-Four

Her name was Raisha and she had been a pharmacist in a large branch of Boots. She had also been married with two small boys. Her husband had died first, followed by her younger son, then the elder. She had had a mother, two brothers and a sister, none of whom survived. Those of her husband's relatives she had been able to seek out were also victims of the sweats.

Raisha told him all this as dawn stretched golden into the small bedroom. The birds were chorusing the arrival of the new day. Their songs seemed to stretch further and higher, as if there were more space for them in the new, unpeopled world.

Raisha said, 'I waited for the sweats to take me too, and when it didn't I went to one of the quarantine centres where I was sure to catch it. I worked there until there was no one left to help and then I started to walk. I didn't have the courage to kill myself, but I was sure that if I kept on walking I would die eventually. Every meal I took, every drink of water was a betrayal of my family. I knew I should die, but I kept on going.'

'And now?' Magnus asked. He had not told her about his own family and his hopes that they might still be alive.

Raisha was curled in the crook of his arm. The tears that had slid down her face as she recounted her story had dried.

'I keep on going. Father Wingate says that God has saved me for a purpose.'

'Do you believe that?'

'No, because that would mean He had a purpose in killing so many people. But Father Wingate is a nice old man who believes we can make a better world and so I keep my thoughts to myself.'

They had made love twice in the night. Magnus had put his arms around her by the glow of the candle, but Raisha had leaned over and blown out the flame before she allowed him to kiss her. Magnus wondered if she had been thinking of her husband and imagining that he was him.

'I think about them all the time,' she said, as if she had read his mind. 'Thinking about them keeps them alive. But sometimes it hurts too much and I need to shut out the memories. Her hand slipped beneath the covers and her smooth fingers began caressing his body. Raisha put her face to his and kissed him. He kissed her back and when she drew him to her, Magnus tried not to mind that she closed her eyes.

It was afternoon by the time they got out of bed. Raisha slid from beneath the sheets and dressed quickly with her back to him. She gave Magnus a smile before she left the room, but did not say where she was going or if they would see each other again. Magnus lay there for a while staring at the ceiling. The plaster was old and crisscrossed with thread lines. He saw a man's face in the cracks, a disjointed dog, a shape that might have been the outline of Australia. He had never been there. Never would now. Were there still people left alive on the other side of the world? Perhaps there was a man like him, way down under, lying somewhere in bed, his limbs heavy from sex, wondering about the future.

Magnus heard the sound of activity in the kitchen and hesitated before he entered. The man at the stove was tall and young with thick blond hair and a profile that would guarantee him an audition for a Boris Karloff biopic. It was an ugly, dignified face not made for smiles. The man took a pot of coffee from the burner, poured two cups and handed one to Magnus without asking.

'Your friend's awake.' His voice was a surprise. It was soft with a faint accent Magnus could not place: Scandinavian or perhaps German.

'Thanks.' He took the cup and held out his free hand. 'I'm Magnus.' He wondered where the man had been while he and Jacob had struggled to carry Jeb into the house.

'I know. Father Wingate told me.' The man was dressed in muddy jeans and a soiled sweater and Magnus guessed he had been working outside. He looked at Magnus's hand as if he were uncertain of what he was meant to do and then shook it. 'I'm Will.'

'Been here long?' Magnus asked.

Will shrugged as if to say, what did it matter, and raised his cup to his mouth.

'He was asking for you.'

'Who?'

'Your friend. Father Wingate said to tell you that your friend wanted to see you.'

Will topped up his own cup with coffee from the pot. He turned off the stove and went out into the garden, closing the door softly behind him.

At first he thought that Jeb was sleeping, but then his eyes opened and Magnus saw the weighing stare he had grown to know.

'I thought you'd be on your way.' He was back to the man Magnus had met in prison, the solitary inmate, bitter and self-reliant.

The room they had put Jeb in faced on to a kitchen garden. Magnus could see Will in the garden below, digging one of the beds. He was putting his back into the task, shifting soil as if his life depended on it. It was harvest, not sowing time. Magnus wondered if the task was therapeutic, or if Will knew nothing about the order of the seasons. There was a chair by the edge of the bed. Magnus sat on it.

'I will be soon. Someone said you wanted to see me.'

'They were lying.'

'It was the priest.'

'They're the biggest liars of all.' Jeb straightened himself awkwardly in the bed, grimacing against the pain. 'The old one or the killer?'

There was a slurred edge to his speech and Magnus guessed Jeb was still medicated. 'The old one.'

'That figures. That old bastard's having the time of his life.'

The room smelled of dampness, sweat and detergent, as if it had only now been pressed back into use after a long period of neglect. Jeb pulled back the bed sheet. He was wearing a

177

T-shirt and boxer shorts and Magnus saw the damaged leg bandaged tight to a splint.

'How is it?'

'How do you think?' Jeb held on to his ribs and leaned down to touch the bandages. 'Fucking sore. Christ knows what that bastard did to it while I was comatose.'

Magnus forced a grin. 'Maybe you should check your arse for love bites.'

He had helped to hold Jeb down while Jacob had pressed the bones of the broken leg into place as best he could and strapped them to the makeshift splint. Jeb had ground his teeth, groaning and muttering like a corpse fighting against resurrection. The cleric-captain had been grim-faced and efficient and Magnus guessed that this was not the first time he had performed triage. He said, 'You don't remember any of it?'

Through the window Belle was walking across the garden to where Will was still digging. They looked strange together, the large ugly man and the slight blonde girl; like different species. Will kept his eyes trained on the ground until Belle touched his arm. Something about the way he moved his head told Magnus the man had heard her coming and was impatient at the interruption. Will listened to what she had to say and resumed his task. Belle lingered for a moment, as if expecting him to give a response, then walked away. When she was gone Will stopped digging and leaned on his spade, staring down at the earth. Something about the way he stood reminded Magnus of the way his mother had been after his father's death; her silences, the half-finished tasks.

Jeb said, 'I remember the crash, that fucker coming towards us with the machete and Jacob blowing his head off, then nothing much until I woke up with Old Father Time snoring on the chair beside me.' He touched his bandaged leg. 'Jacob reckons we should slap some plaster of Paris on it. He's on the hunt for some now, but in the meantime . . .' He shook his head. 'I'm fucked.'

There was a cross on the wall above the bed, a skinny Jesus pinned like a fly on a dissecting board. Magnus gave it a glance and said, 'I haven't told anyone where we met.'

Jeb touched his bandages again, as if to check that his leg was still painful. He grimaced and looked at Magnus, his expression wary.

'Why would you?'

'There are girls here. Young girls.'

Magnus shifted the chair back from the bed, though he knew Jeb was in no condition to reach him from where he lay.

'Christ.' Jeb closed his eyes. 'You seriously think I'm a danger to them?'

'All I know is where we met.'

'Where *we* met. You were there too, remember?'

There was a sound on the stair outside. Jeb's eyes met Magnus's and he stopped mid-sentence. The door opened and Belle put her head into the room. She had tied her hair into sleek gold plaits and looked like a pretty supermarket assistant dressed up to promote Edam cheese. She said, 'Jacob has asked us all to assemble in the ballroom.'

Jeb pulled up the bed sheet, covering his leg, the borrowed boxer shorts. 'Did he say if he'd found any plaster of Paris?'

Belle stepped into the room. 'No, just that he wanted us all to assemble.'

Jeb looked away. 'You'll have to count me out.'

Magnus felt his face glowing. He wondered if Belle had overheard any of their conversation. Her foot kicked the back of his chair, though whether it was deliberate or because the room was small, Magnus could not tell.

She said, 'How about you? You've got both of your legs.'

It was in his mind to say that he was leaving, but the man had saved his life and it might also be a chance to say goodbye to Raisha.

'Sure, I'll be there.'

The girl looked at Jeb. 'How long will you be stuck like that?'

'I don't know. If Jacob gets some plaster on it I might be hobbling around soon.'

'You're going to be bloody bored stuck in here.'

Magnus said, 'Don't worry about Long John Silver. He's used to being on his own.'

Belle ignored him. She pulled on one of her plaits and asked Jeb, 'Do you want me to bring you some books? There are some lying around.'

'Sure.' Jeb glanced at the sheet again. 'Thanks.'

'Fuck, I miss the Internet,' Belle said. 'Do you think there's any chance someone might get it going?'

'Maybe.' Magnus shrugged. 'Who knows?'

He had seen photographs of giant warehouses in California where servers were housed. Other survivors might be battling to reconnect them with the rest of the world, or the computers may have exploded; a flash of light in a sun-bright desert.

'I still have my mobile.' Belle slipped an iPhone from the pocket of her jeans. 'It lost its charge ages ago, but I don't want

180

to get rid of it. I've got photographs stored on it.' She touched the phone to her lips and put it back in her pocket. 'I dreamed that they were all alive and living inside my mobile, my family, friends from uni, people I'd known at school, my mum and dad's neighbours. They all waved to me from the screen, as if they were in a YouTube video. I know it was just a dream, but it felt real.' Her voice sounded wistful. 'I heard my mum calling my name. I couldn't throw it away after that.'

'I have dreams about people I haven't thought of in years,' Jeb said. 'I had one about the guy who used to run the newspaper shop round the corner when I was a kid. I never thought much about him one way or another. He was just an old geezer who was permanently knackered from getting up at 4 a.m. He probably died long before the sweats, but I dreamed about him folding copies of the *Daily Mail* into a sack, ready for morning delivery.'

Belle nodded as if she understood. 'Father Wingate says we'll get used to it, but no TV, no video games, no Facebook, no Twitter . . .'

Magnus said, 'No cat videos.'

'Sure, some of it was stupid.' The girl kicked the leg of his chair again. 'But it was civilisation and none of us knows how it worked.'

Jeb said, 'Someone will.'

'Who?' Her voice was full of scorn. 'You? Him? All the useful people are dead. My dad was an architect. He knew how to make multi-storey buildings that would keep standing in an earthquake. What did you do?'

Magnus felt his face growing warm again. 'I was a comedian.'

181

'A comedian.' She shook her head. 'And you?' She looked at Jeb.

'I worked with disadvantaged kids.'

The answer was unexpected and it stalled her.

'I was studying art history.' Belle gave a small laugh. 'We don't know how to keep the lights on, or fix someone's broken leg properly. We survived the sweats, but there's no guarantee we'll see this year out.'

Jeb's skin was grey with tiredness and pain, but he seemed to be growing in confidence. He met the girl's eyes. 'My leg will mend and we'll see this year out.'

'And the year after?'

'And the year after.'

The certainty in his voice seemed to comfort her. Belle gave a sad smile. 'But there's nothing to look forward to any more.'

She was the kind of girl who had been used to new clothes and foreign holidays, to nightclubs and long lunches gossiping about the night before with other girls who looked and talked like her. She had friended, followed, liked, tweeted and smiled for selfies and a part of her had been lost in vanished cyberspace.

Jeb said, 'What do they call you?'

'Belle.'

Magnus had expected Jeb to compliment her on the prettiness of her name, but he merely nodded, as if acknowledging the rightness of it and said, 'I'm Jeb. It looks like I'm going to be hanging around for a while.' His smile was small and wry but it was a smile. 'Will you bring me those books when you have time?'

182

'Sure.' Belle's answering smile lit up her face, as if she had found some small event to look forward to after all.

Magnus said, 'I'll be stopping by for a chat with Jacob and Father Wingate before I go.'

Jeb turned his prison stare on Magnus. 'Do what you have to.'

There was bite in his voice and the girl glanced from one to the other, unsure of what was going on. She kicked Magnus's chair again. 'See you in the ballroom.' She closed the door gently, taking any good feeling with her.

There was a Bible on the table next to the bed. Jeb picked it up and flung it across the room, but Magnus had seen the move coming and ducked. The Bible splatted against the wall and landed splayed open on the floor. Magnus picked up the book and glanced inside. A sentence was underlined: *But Noah found grace in the eyes of the LORD*. He closed it.

'You wouldn't be doing this if I wasn't stuck here.' Jeb pulled the bed sheet back as if he were about to get to his feet. His body was lean and girded by prison muscle.

The sight of it made Magnus wonder if Jeb was right and whether he would have had the courage to press him had he not been imprisoned by a broken leg. He said, 'What do you expect me to do? You weren't locked in there for nothing.'

'Neither were you.'

'I tried to stop a rape. Things got nasty and when the police turned up they thought I was part of it. The whole thing would have been cleared up if it wasn't for the sweats.'

Jeb touched his leg as if the pain of it reassured him. 'You expect me to believe that?'

'It's the truth.'

'Where's your proof?'

'I don't need any proof.'

Jeb leaned forward, as if he would like to reach out and put his hands around Magnus's neck. 'Neither do I.'

Sticking his nose into other people's nasty business was what had landed Magnus in jail in the first place. If he had walked away from the man tussling with the woman in the alley he might have caught a flight to Orkney when the sweats had started to take hold. He would be home now and would know, for good or for bad, how things were. Magnus sighed and said, 'So tell me why you were locked in solitary in the wing reserved for sex offenders?'

Jeb looked away and for a moment Magnus thought he was going to refuse to tell him, but then Jeb leaned back and propped himself against the headboard. His eyes met Magnus's.

'It isn't just sex offenders who are classified as vulnerable prisoners. I was kept in solitary for my own safety. I used to be a policeman.'

Twenty-Five

Magnus had never been to a mass before. He sat beside Belle on one of the chairs that had been arranged in a line before the altar in the ballroom, stealing glances at Raisha who had chosen a place at the opposite end of the row, and mulling over Jeb's revelation. Raisha stared resolutely ahead, her features hidden by the black curtain of her hair. When she and Belle rose to receive the host from Father Wingate, splendid and smiling in his robes, Magnus remained seated, feeling awkward and resenting the trick that had been played on him. There were many miles to travel and a sea to cross before he reached home, but the priest had managed to imprison him indoors in fair weather. It was a hoax to rival transubstantiation.

The ballroom was large, with picture windows and a parquet floor. It had been a prettified marketplace, where daughters and sons of the rich were paraded and paired off in time to a band. Now the chandeliers that had graced the ceiling were gone. The room's only decorations were a suffering Christ and the Stations of the Cross. From where he was sitting Magnus could see Jesus being nailed up.

Will acted as altar boy, still dressed in his gardening clothes, but ringing bells and swinging a censer of sweet-smelling smoke and incense with casual confidence that suggested he was not new to the task. His face was blank and it was impossible to know if the duty brought him comfort, or if he was merely going through the motions to please the old man. Perhaps they were all dolls in Wingate's playhouse, puppeting through a semblance of a life because their real lives were over.

Jacob stepped up to deliver the lesson dressed in the same combination of army fatigues and dog collar he had been wearing when they met. He set his Bible on the lectern and rested his fingers lightly on its black cover.

'I had the privilege of serving in Bosnia during their civil war. It was a painful conflict, as all wars are. During one particularly savage battle, my troop and I took shelter in a bombed-out factory. It had manufactured tin boxes. One of the many strange aspects of war is the way inconsequential objects often survive, while other, stronger, more important things are ruined. Metal boxes were scattered everywhere around the factory floor, but the people who worked there were either dead or had fled.

'The glass windows of the factory had been blown out and as we sat there, steeling ourselves for the next round of fighting, a tiny bird swooped in through a window. It flew across the large cathedral-like space of the factory floor and disappeared through a rupture in the opposite wall. I realised then that we are like that bird. We appear on earth for a little while; but of what went before this life or of what follows, we know nothing.'

Prayers were said for Henry, wherever he might be, but Melody went unmentioned. Magnus wondered if her suicide had put her beyond the reach of the Church, or if she was now ranked among the amorphous dead, too numerous to warrant individual pleading.

When the service was over, Jacob and Father Wingate stood at the door to the ballroom, shaking hands with each of the small congregation as they left. Raisha was the first to go. Magnus slipped in front of Will, keen to catch her, but Father Wingate took hold of his arm and stayed him in the doorway.

'I know you are eager to leave us, but we have a favour to ask.'

Magnus caught Jacob's eye and knew that the soldier was calling in his debt.

'Don't worry.' Jacob put a hand on Magnus's shoulder. 'We're not about to ask for anything you're not equipped to give.'

The priest's words reminded Magnus of a phrase his mother had repeated in times of trouble: 'God never burdens you with more than you can bear.' He wondered if even she could believe that now.

Father Wingate led the way out of the ballroom, across the entrance hall and down a flight of stairs into a basement corridor. Upstairs the house retained glimpses of the stately home it had once been, but there had never been an attempt at grandeur down here. Everything was dark and meanly proportioned. Magnus recalled his granny telling him that big houses contained hidden networks of servants' corridors and stairways, so the gentry would not have to see them going about their work. The servants had been the blood of the house, running along webs of hidden veins.

Father Wingate opened a door and ushered them into a small sitting room. 'This used to be the butler's pantry when I was a boy.' The old priest's youthful smile was at odds with his wrinkles. It added mischief to his face and Magnus was reminded of an old Shakespearean actor who had been the stalwart of Sunday dramas before becoming the unlikely star of Hollywood science-fiction blockbusters, wizened in Spandex. The memory prompted another stab of loss. All the multiplexes were empty, the hotdog and popcorn concessions silent and mouldering.

Jacob had seated himself in a winged armchair, but Father Wingate hovered uncertainly on the edge of the hearthrug, still talking.

'Butlers are often rather magnificent creatures in literature, Jeeves and so on, but I'm afraid ours tended to be on the weaselly side. That's not very Christian, is it?' He turned the beam of his smile on Magnus. 'Ironic that I ended up with this room as an office. The Lord's way of quelling my ego perhaps.'

The room was austere. A desk sat at an angle with its back to a small window to avoid whoever was working there getting distracted by the view of refuse bins. A dark-wood bookcase, dreary with devotional hardbacks, stretched across one wall. A painting of a deserted lakeside, done in tobacco hues, hung opposite it. The obligatory crucifix loomed above the fireplace, as if someone had decided to add scorching to the list of Christ's tortures.

Magnus said, 'I would have expected God to delegate room allocations.'

Father Wingate lowered himself into a high-backed chair

that looked like it belonged at a dining table. 'God is all-pow-erful.' The priest's boyish smile was chastened. 'But I accept your point. My ego is not yet entirely repressed.'

'Take a pew.' Jacob nodded at the armchair facing his.

Magnus glanced at the old priest hunched in the straight-backed chair, still dressed in his robes. The minister in Magnus's mother's Kirk had worn the same dark suit to the pulpit for over thirty years. He would be buried in it, if he was buried. Magnus could feel himself beginning to despise the old priest with his frilly frocks and pretensions. The sensation felt too much like giving a fuck. Magnus said, 'You should have this chair. It looks more comfortable.'

Father Wingate's smile flashed again. 'My ancient spine won't stand it. Sadly it's the same when it comes to bedtime. It's been hard boards for me for some years now. I was never one for mortifying the flesh, but it seems that the flesh has decided it is time to mortify me.'

There was a trace of bygone BBC in the priest's accent, like a not quite mended speech impediment that returned at times of stress. The mention of hard boards put Magnus in mind of a coffin and the back of his neck tingled. He took the chair.

'Thanks for all you've done for me. You saved our bacon.' He would make his goodbye to Jeb short. 'You've got the makings of a good community here.' Magnus real-ised that he was glad to be leaving. There was something about the place that felt wrong. 'If I didn't have my family to think of I'd seriously consider joining you, but I need to be on my way.'

'I'll get straight to the point.' Jacob leaned forward, his

189

hands clasped. 'The sweats have wiped out centuries of culture, learning and technology. Those of us who are left are still in shock, but we don't have time to dwell on our grief. We need to assure our survival.'

It was an echo of what Belle had said in the room upstairs and Magnus wondered if he was about to receive a speech Jacob gave all his converts.

Father Wingate said, 'The good Lord will—'

Jacob nodded impatiently. 'The good Lord has set us a challenge. We need to meet it.' He turned his stare on Magnus. 'We want to create a community here—'

Magnus cut through his words. 'It's like I said, I can't join you . . .'

Jacob shook his head. 'We don't want to interfere with your search for your family.' There was a world unsaid, the slim chance of Magnus making it to Orkney, the slimmer possibility of finding his family alive. 'But we have all been through . . .' Jacob paused as if seeking the right words. It was a showman's gesture, Magnus decided, one priests were probably taught in the seminary immediately before being instructed on how to angle the collection plate to the best advantage. '. . . an incredible trauma . . .'

Father Wingate nodded his ugly head. 'Not since the time of Noah . . .'

Magnus remembered the words underlined in the Bible by Jeb's bed. The old man had been reading about the destruction of Sodom and Gomorrah.

Jacob touched Father Wingate's wrist lightly and the old man stopped mid-sentence, smiling to show he understood. The soldier said, 'We both think you need some time for reflection, to strengthen you for the undoubted trials ahead.'

Magnus was about to say that he had no time for reflection, no need of rest. Jacob anticipated his objections and held up a hand. 'And we also need your help. We hope that more people will join us. If they do we will need the means to sustain them. This estate is surrounded by agricultural land. There's a harvest waiting in the fields and livestock about to calve. There aren't enough of us to do it properly and even if there were, we wouldn't know how to. Jeb said you were brought up on a farm.'

Magnus had mentioned the croft one night, sad with memories. He silently cursed Jeb.

'It was only a smallholding. We sold it after my father died. I left home soon after and my mother couldn't cope with it by herself.' The selling of the croft had shamed him. He had thought his mother capable of carrying on, had not fathomed the depth of her debt until it was all but lost to the bank. 'I haven't worked on a farm since.'

'But you know about farming.' Jacob's voice was earnest. 'It's in your blood. You were brought up with it.'

Magnus shook his head. 'There are supermarkets stuffed with food for the taking. You don't need these crops.'

'We have stores of tins and other non-perishables, but the supermarkets are also stuffed with disease. There's something else.' Jacob glanced at the old priest. 'I didn't share this before because I didn't see any point in worrying you. The last time Belle and I went to gather supplies we came across the body of a man hanging on a lamppost outside a supermarket. Someone had strung a sign around his neck. It said, *Looter*.'

Father Wingate crossed himself. 'They will come for our stores.'

The soldier's voice was firm. 'We will grow in numbers and be ready for them. But the only way we can survive long term is to become self-sustaining.'

The old priest leaned forward and took Magnus's hands in his. 'This is a chance for you to do something good; surely your family won't object to your taking a little longer to reach them once they know you helped us to survive.'

The old man's hands were dry and horribly alive. Magnus pulled away. He thought of Pete dying on the bunk beneath him in Pentonville and of the inmate he had hit with the fire extinguisher. He was fairly sure he had killed the man. He had done little to make his mother proud in the fifteen years since he left the island. She would want him to do this.

'I'm sorry I can't . . .' He recalled the motorbike's shredded tyre and said, 'I'll be taking the Audi.'

Jacob's eyes were fixed on Magnus, too bright a blue for his tired face. 'Help us bring the harvest in, show us how it's done and then we'll let you go on your way.'

'You make it sound like the boy's a prisoner.' Father Wingate turned an anxious smile on Magnus. 'You're not a prisoner, but we would like your help.'

Jacob repeated, 'We need your help.'

'I can't.' Magnus rubbed a hand across his face. The crops were beginning to rot in the south, but they ripened later in the north. He could help and still be in time for the Orkney harvest.

Jacob said, 'We've already lost two people. I haven't shared this with the others, but I suspect that Henry may have chosen

192

the same path as Melody.' Father Wingate crossed himself. Jacob gave him an impatient glance and continued, 'Belle is demoralised, Will depressed. Raisha keeps her own counsel, but it is obvious that she's suffering. Who knows how many people are hiding in the woods and villages around here, tormented by grief? The sweats could be followed by an epidemic of suicide. We need to come together if we are to have any chance. A harvest is necessary for our survival, but it will also draw people to us and give them hope.'

Hugh was on the edge of his vision, just out of sight, but Magnus knew that no matter how quickly he turned his head, his cousin would be gone. He sighed and rubbed a hand across his face, defeated.

'I'll help you harvest three fields. That will be more than enough for your needs. Then I have to go.'

Jacob gave him a grim smile. 'It's a deal.'

'God requires a harvest.' Father Wingate smiled beatifically. 'And we are all His children.'

The three of them shook hands. Magnus remembered his slashed tyre again and wondered if it mattered that the soldier had not repeated the old priest's assurance that he was not a prisoner.

Raisha was standing in the hallway. There were fields waiting to be surveyed, equipment to find, jobs to be assigned, a harvest to plan. Raisha held out her hand, Magnus took it in his and she led him upstairs to his bedroom.

Twenty-Six

It was late by the time Magnus visited Jeb. He was surprised to find him propped up at a small table in his sickroom, a few pages of paper splayed in front of him, his injured leg set stiffly on a low chair. A single candle glimmered waxily from a saucer. Jeb looked up. His face seemed old and hollow by its dim light. He turned the pages face down.

'Want to sign my cast?'

Jeb tapped his leg lightly with a pen and Magnus saw that it had been plastered.

'I guess it's important to keep the old traditions alive.' Magnus took the pen from him and tried to scrawl his name on the plaster cast, but it was not quite set and the nib sank into it, leaving a shallow dent. He perched on the end of the bed. 'Maybe later, when it's dried.'

Jeb rested a hand on top of his papers. 'You going to be around that long?'

The candle wavered in response to a faint breeze reaching in through the open window. Magnus stared into the blackness beyond. He could see nothing, except the reflection of the candlelight in the glass pane.

'It seems so, since you told them I might be useful.'

'What did I say you'd be useful at? Fucking their women?'

Magnus felt his face flush. 'Helping them get the harvest in.'

'Shit, I let slip about your croft, didn't I?' Magnus nodded and Jeb said, 'Sorry.' He grinned. 'You've got to hand it to the religious. Not even a day off for the end of the world.'

'I guess that's the point. They don't want it to be the end.'

'Strange, when they believe they're in for pie in the sky.' Jeb scored a finger across his plastered leg and looked at the white powder caught beneath his nail. 'Do you ever think what a stroke of luck it was for you and me? A shame millions died, but the sweats did us a good turn.'

'I had a warm-up gig at O2 lined up.' Magnus wished he had not been reminded of his big break. It belonged to another life.

Jeb glanced at the door and then said in a low voice, 'You had a smashed-up face and an imminent rape trial. Entertainers have a bad rep. You could have been looking at a long sentence.'

This must be how long-married couples felt, Magnus thought. They had been over it before and there was no point in discussing it further. He said, 'If you were a policeman, how come you ended up in prison?'

'It's old news.'

'All the same . . .' Magnus let the threat hang in the air.

Jeb stared at him. 'You would, wouldn't you?'

'They have a right to know.'

Jeb sighed. He lifted the pages from the table and turned them over so Magnus could see the scrawled handwriting, the crossed-out lines and scribbled deletions. 'I was trying to write it all down. I don't know why. Scared I'll forget who I am, or maybe just too much time on my hands. I wasn't doing very well.'

'Perhaps you need to say it out loud.'

'To someone with a sympathetic ear?' Some of the fight had left Jeb, but his voice still held a challenge. 'Aren't there enough priests in this house?'

Magnus grinned. 'Too many.'

'That's the truth.' Jeb reached beneath the table and brought out a bottle of whisky. He nodded to a shelf above the bed. 'There's another glass over there.'

Magnus got up from his seat. Things were easier between them now. Perhaps it was their shared experience and imminent parting, or maybe being newcomers to Tanqueray House had united them in a way that saving each other's lives had not. A small stack of paperback novels sat beside the glass. He said, 'Has Belle been looking after you?'

'You'd make a good detective.' Jeb poured himself a tot and passed the bottle to Magnus who did the same. 'Belle's a nice girl. She isn't used to being on her own and she's trying to be brave about it. Helping me helps her.'

There was truth in what Jeb was saying, but the convenience of it made Magnus uneasy. He picked up one of the paperbacks to look at its title and saw a revolver secreted behind the pile. He lifted it by the barrel.

'Did Belle bring you this too?'

Jeb took another sip of his drink, hiding his expression behind the glass. 'Like I said, she's a nice girl. I told her I needed something to protect myself with and she gave me that. It's okay for you, you're heading into the blue yonder. I've no chance of running away if anything kicks off.'

196

There was truth in what he said. Magnus slid the gun back into its hiding place and replaced the book on top of the pile.

'You still haven't told me what you were in for.'

Jeb took a sip of his drink. Magnus thought he was going to refuse again, but he met his eyes and asked, 'What if I say I'm in for murdering the woman I loved?'

'It depends on circumstances, I suppose.'

'And what if I tell you a bundle of lies?'

'I'll have to trust my own judgement on that.'

Jeb's stare was level. 'I thought I could leave all this in Pentonville, but it's on me like skin. If it's going to come out, maybe it's better I tell you than someone else.'

'I'll be gone soon. I'll keep it to myself.'

'If you don't, you know I'll find you.' Jeb looked up towards the far corner of the room. His hair had grown out of the suede head he had worn in prison and was twisting into loose curls that gave his face a softer appearance. 'I said that I was innocent. That's not strictly true. I'm not a sex offender and I didn't do what they put me away for, but I deserved to go down.' Jeb's defensiveness was still there, but it had flipped to an insistence on his guilt. 'My trial was all over the papers, it was three years ago, but a lot of people still remember' – he paused and corrected himself – 'remembered, my face. There were two photographs that they used, one of me in uniform, smiling like every mother's dream. It was taken by a photographer for a local paper on a school outreach visit, not long after I completed training. My hair's long in the other one.' He touched his curls. 'And I've got a scruffy beard, like a tramp that's not had any attention from the Salvation Army in quite a while. There's a stupid expression on my face, as if I'd just sucked up an exceptionally long joint, which is exactly what I'd done.' Jeb came to a stop, as if he could see the photographs in front of him.

Magnus said, 'You don't sound like ideal police material.'

'I was superb police material. Perfect for what they wanted at any rate.'

'Which was?'

'Being a lying bastard.' Jeb knocked back the last of the whisky in his glass and freshened it with more from the bottle. 'I was an undercover police officer. Serpico, that was me, all cock and beard.'

Magnus took the bottle and poured himself another measure. A memory stirred. A documentary about police officers who had formed relationships with some of the women they were meant to be keeping under surveillance. One of them had had a wife elsewhere, a legitimate family.

He said, 'Were you married?'

Jeb gave a tight smile that hid his teeth. 'No, but you're on the right lines. My job was to infiltrate a group of environmental activists. I had to immerse myself in the organisation, dress like them, talk like them, act like them. I thought I was James Bond, though Bond wouldn't be seen dead in the grungy crap I wore undercover.'

It fitted with Jeb's shape-shifting personality, his swing from prison inmate to keen-eyed strategist. Magnus tried to keep his voice light. 'No nightclubs and casinos then?'

'No, but there were beautiful women. The main difficulty of infiltrating a network is that you come from nowhere and have to get people to accept you straight away. The easiest way to do that is to become involved with someone already on the scene, usually a woman.' Jeb made a face. 'If I'm honest it was always a woman.'

'You did it more than once?' Magnus had pulled on different personalities for his routines, but he had shed them when he came off stage. He tried to imagine how it would be to target a woman because of who and what she knew; to live with her and make love to her as someone else. 'Didn't you feel like a whore?'

Jeb put a hand over the candle flame and a shadow hand appeared huge and black on the wall. He took it away and looked at Magnus.

'I was a police officer, an undercover police officer.'

'And you could switch it on and off?' Magnus disliked the echo of the Kirk in his own voice, the black-suited minister passing judgement from the pulpit. 'Have sex with some girl and then report back on what she was up to?'

Jeb shrugged. 'Like I said, I thought I was James Bond. These people were talking about bombing laboratories, assassinating scientists, setting free animals that had been infected with deadly strains of viruses.' There was warmth in his voice now. 'Fuck, for all we know it was someone like them who set off this whole bloody disaster.' He realised that he was close to shouting and looked at the door. The house was still, but he lowered his voice to a whisper. 'I was flattered to be chosen. Our handlers made us feel special. We were in the know. Of course we didn't know the half of it. They targeted us the same way they taught us to target the people we were surveilling.'

The shell of aggression Jeb had worn in jail was fractured.

For the first time since Magnus had known him he looked sorry for himself.

'We were encouraged to identify vulnerable people in the movement. Cherry fitted the profile. She was a single mum struggling to make ends meet. Her passion for animals had tipped into radicalism and she'd joined a group who thought people involved in animal testing were akin to the Nazis. She was also gorgeous: big eyes, lots of red hair, petite. She looked like a Disney princess, but there was a bit of steel in Cherry. I liked that from the start. She was also unstable. I spotted that at the start too, but I thought I could handle it.' Jeb took another sip of his drink. 'I was arrogant enough to think I could make it into an asset.'

Magnus said, 'When did she find out you were a policeman?'

Jeb gave a sad half-smile. 'When I told her. These operations don't just last for a couple of weeks, a few months, they stretch on for years.' He shook his head. 'I should never have chosen a woman with a child. Cherry had episodes. She may have been schizophrenic, but she was too mistrustful of doctors and hospitals – they were Nazis too – to get a diagnosis. Her daughter was called Happy. She was one when I met her, three when I decided I couldn't stand it any more. It was partly down to her that I came out. She was a little sweetheart. Happy by name, Happy by nature. Cherry and I were squatting in a tower block that was due for demolition. It was a dump and Cherry insisted on a flat on the fifteenth floor, even though the lifts weren't working, because fifteen was her lucky number and she could keep a lookout on who was coming from up there. She thought people were spying on her.' He gave a small smile. 'What did they used to say? Just because you're paranoid doesn't mean they're not out to get you? It was squalor, but Happy didn't mind. Who knows how she would have turned out, but she was the most even-natured child I ever met.'

Jeb had made no effort to check up on Cherry and Happy after the escape from Pentonville. Magnus looked into the blackness beyond the window and thought how strange it was that he could still feel saddened by the deaths of two people he had never met.

'You said it was partly Happy that made you come clean. What were the other reasons?'

Jeb took another sip of his drink. He rubbed his cast gently with his fingertips as if to soothe the itching flesh beneath it.

'No one ever gave a direct order, but I began to realise that our handlers wanted us to do more than surveillance. The group I was with were disorganised. They were full of big talk, but they lacked leadership. I'm not saying they weren't committed or that they would never have done any harm. I learned the truth of that to my cost. What I mean is that they hadn't done any real damage yet. There was a power gap and one likely lad in line to fill it, a guy called Andy Cruikshank. He was a nasty piece of work. Cherry genuinely cared about animals, Andy just wanted a cause. It wouldn't have mattered what it was, home rule, nuclear disarmament, anti-capitalism: Andy would have found a way to turn the fight violent. As far as I was concerned he was our man. Remove Andy and all you had was a bunch of hippies dicking around, but my instructions were to cultivate him, become his right-hand man, see how far he would go. That included making suggestions for possible moves if his imagination failed him.'

'They were turning you into an agent provocateur?'

Jeb nodded. 'Spot on. I tried to kid myself, but eventually I decided that the only way out was to tell Cherry the truth. I think I was genuinely in love with her by then. I certainly loved Happy. I wanted to keep them so badly that I convinced myself that everything would be okay if I could just find the courage to tell Cherry everything.' Unshed tears gleamed in Jeb's eyes. 'I had it all worked out. I'd get a dishonourable discharge and sell my flat. I'd bought at a good time and once I'd paid off what I owed on the mortgage there would have been enough left over for a good deposit on somewhere in Wales. I'd taken Cherry and Happy camping there once and they'd loved it. We could have had our own animals, nothing big, a few chickens, a dog, maybe a goat or two, Cherry would have been in her element. And maybe there would have been enough space for her to get properly well.' Jeb wiped a hand across his eyes and lifted his drink to his mouth. 'So I told her what I was and what I'd done and as soon as I had, I knew it was the worst mistake of my life. Worse even than getting involved with undercover, because at least that had introduced me to her and Happy.

'She started screaming before I was even finished. It was like a mask had been stripped from her face. All the sweetness and softness disappeared and all the pain came out. She looked ugly, like a witch from a children's book. It sounds pathetic, Cherry was a small woman, a fraction of my size, but I was frightened. Then she stopped yelling and told me what she thought of me and my kind in a whisper that seemed to drive itself into my brain. It was like she was delivering a curse.

'I know I shouted, because other people told me I did. I wanted to explain why I'd done it. I know I told her that I loved her. But she wouldn't listen. Then she started shouting again, more than shouting, screaming. I'd waited until Happy was in bed, but she woke up and came through to find out what was going on. She wasn't used to people arguing and she was frightened. I went to comfort her, but Cherry was screaming so loudly at me to leave that I was afraid that, allergic as our building was to authority, someone might call the police. That was the last thing I needed.

'I went into the bedroom and started to pack my things, though why I would want to take any of that crap is beyond me. I should have walked out as soon as she shouted at me to go, then someone might have seen me. I would have had an alibi.

'Somebody started banging on the door to the flat. Cherry was still shouting at me to leave and screaming that I would never see her or Happy again. I should have ignored whoever was at the door, but I think I wanted someone else to shout at. I opened it and there was Andy Cruikshank. He had a squat a few floors below us. Cherry must have phoned him on her mobile when I went into the bedroom. He should have been the last person I wanted to see, but I was delighted. I punched him in the face. Then I heard Happy screaming. She had been crying before, but this was a different kind of scream, a shout of real terror. It was me she was calling for.'

Jeb's voice shifted. His eyes gleamed sad and distant in the candlelight.

'I ran through to the sitting room. Cherry was standing on a chair on the balcony. I yelled for her to stop, but she didn't look round, just took a step up on to the safety barrier and pushed herself into the air with Happy in her arms. She wasn't my child, but I loved her. I saw her face looking over Cherry's shoulder an instant before she jumped. Happy knew what was about to happen and she was terrified. If I had been quicker I could have saved her. I knew Cherry was desperate and hurting, but I stopped to hit Andy Cruikshank. That was all the time it took to kill her.'

The tears were running down Jeb's face now. He lifted a hand and wiped them away.

Magnus kept his voice soft. 'It's tragic, but I don't see how Cherry's suicide would result in your going to jail. She killed herself and Happy, not you.'

'Cruikshank told the police that I had pushed them both over the balcony. Cherry had told him I was a police spy. He blamed me for her death and he wanted to see me damned. The few people in the building who would speak to the police said they'd heard a man shouting and Cherry screaming that he would never see his child again. Someone even claimed to have seen me do it. It didn't matter that he was a junkie who had seen a spaceship land on the local play park the week before, he was treated as a credible witness. As for my bosses, as far as they were concerned I was on my own. They maintained they had already decided I was going rogue and were about to pull me. They pretended to think I'd killed Cherry and Happy too. The best they would offer me was a guarantee of vulnerable prisoner status in return for not revealing details of our operation. If I spoke out they would throw me into the general population. I didn't care much about what happened to me by then, but being a policeman in prison who had spied on his girlfriend and then killed her and her child? I knew enough to know I wouldn't survive that.' He looked at the floor. 'I was a coward.'

Magnus said, 'What about Cherry's medical records? Didn't they show she might be suicidal?'

Jeb's eyes met his. 'I already told you. She wouldn't go to the doctor. Even I didn't realise how far gone she was. If I had I would never have told her the truth.' Jeb stared at the ceiling. 'Andy Cruikshank was a star witness. All that fire and hatred made him seem righteous. I was a proven liar and he was a man of principle. Other witnesses for the Crown were a ramshackle lot. Junkies, hippies, the usual losers who end up in these squats, but Andy was good. He wore a suit and tie to court and he repeated his version of what had happened over and bloody over, until even I almost believed it.'

Magnus said, 'But he was lying?'

'Yes, he was fucking lying.' The warmth was back in Jeb's voice. 'I've just told you God's honest truth and if you don't believe me you can go to hell.'

Magnus said, 'I believe you.' He heard his father's voice, *Never trust a liar, son, never trust a liar.* 'Of course I believe you,' he repeated.

Twenty-Seven

They set out in an open-topped truck, Jacob at the wheel, Magnus and Will squeezed into the cab beside him. Belle sat in the back, her face shaded from the sun by a wide-brimmed straw hat Father Wingate said the abbot would have wanted her to have. Raisha had not appeared and they had left without her.

'She goes off on her own,' Belle said as they walked across the yard of a farm Magnus knew was too industrial in scale for them to manage, but which might have some useful equipment smaller farms could not have afforded to invest in. 'She misses her children.'

Will and Jacob were a little ahead, both of them with rifles slung across their backs. Magnus had been musing on the weapons Jacob had confiscated at the scene of the crash and had not yet returned. He wished Belle would leave him alone, but he said, 'Of course she does.'

He and Raisha had not used any protection. The sweats had made HIV look like a joke, but there were other reasons why people did not use contraception.

Jacob glanced back at them. 'What do you think?' Even when he was asking a question the priest's voice held an edge of command.

'It's big enough to have its own combine. We should check these sheds.' Magnus pointed to a series of flat-roofed buildings that looked more suited to a factory than a farm.

Jacob nodded. The day was warm, but he was still wearing his combat jacket. 'Stay close. You don't know who might be around.'

Now was the moment to ask for his gun back. Magnus tried to frame the words. The sun seared his eyes, blinding him for a moment.

Belle said, 'She goes into empty houses looking for children.'

Magnus glanced at her. The girl had tucked her hair inside the hat, which lent her a Huck Finn prepubescent look. Her nose was freckled and she might have been a boy.

Magnus said, 'Raisha?'

Belle nodded. Her features were lost and revealed again, as the shadows thrown by the hat brim advanced and then receded.

'At first she thought she would find one alive. There must have been children who survived.' Belle looked up at him again, her eyes wide with the horror of it. 'But they might have been too little to manage on their own.'

Magnus had not been able to forget the body of the toddler that had somehow fallen to its death. It had looked unmarked, like a large doll abandoned on the pavement, except for the bloom of blood around its head.

'Yes,' he said. 'It must have happened.'

'Raisha was obsessed by the idea. She started off by looking for her sons' friends. She knew where they lived and so she drove to their houses.'

Raisha had not told him any of this, only of her thwarted search for her relatives and her husband's family.

'They were all either dead or had left town.' Belle's voice was matter-of-fact. 'And so she started to check likely-looking houses, places with a trampoline, or a swing in the garden. Raisha says it's easy to spot homes with children.'

Magnus said, 'It's been too long now. If a child was locked in somewhere, or was too young to look after itself, it would be dead.'

'She buries them.' Belle's eyes met his, the hat brim a halo around her face. 'She wraps them in a sheet, digs a hole in the garden, puts them in it and says a prayer over the grave. I've told her she should stop. Things have got beyond burying.'

Beyond burying, a voice in Magnus's head whispered.

'What does she say?'

'She says—'

A deep-throated growl interrupted Belle's answer. They turned and saw a Jack Russell crouching on the other side of the yard. Belle said, 'Hello, sweetheart,' in a soft baby voice and sank to her haunches, holding out a hand for the dog to sniff. The terrier bared its teeth in a white slavering snarl.

Magnus put a hand on her shoulder. 'I don't—'

Jacob shouted, 'Get away from it.'

'The poor thing's scared,' Belle said, in the same silly voice.

'It's rabid.' The priest took his gun from its holster just as the dog began to edge towards them.

'Leave it alone.' Belle made kissy noises towards the dog.

Magnus grabbed Belle by the arm and yanked her to her

feet. The girl resisted, but he pulled her to him. He looked the dog in the eye and said, 'Sit,' in the commanding voice he had saved for the farm dogs. He saw a look of comprehension in the dog's eyes. Its steps faltered and though it gave a low, exploratory growl, Magnus knew that it wanted to obey him. 'Sit!'

He felt Belle stiffen. 'Don't!' Her yell was lost beneath the crack of Jacob's bullet. The shot hit the dog in its flank and it fell whimpering to the ground.

The girl shuddered in Magnus's arms. 'You fuckers! You fucking fuckers!' She punched Magnus in the chest and he let her go. The abbot's hat tumbled from her head, releasing a coil of blonde hair, and she ran to where Jacob was already standing over the small white body. The dog's ribs were moving up and down; quick and sharp and not quite final.

'At least finish the poor beast off,' Magnus shouted and Jacob squatted and put a bullet into the dog's head.

A splash of blood spattered all three of them and Belle screamed again. She put a hand to her face and shouted at Jacob, 'Why do you have to kill every fucking thing?'

The priest's face was pale. 'I don't . . .'

But the girl had turned her back on him and was running across the yard. Magnus made to follow her, but Jacob caught his arm. 'Let Will go after her.' And Magnus saw that the tall man had already left the corner of the yard, where he had stood silent while the drama played itself out, and was jogging to catch up with her.

Magnus bunched his fists. His biceps were tight with the urge to punch the priest in the face. 'Why did you shoot it?'

Jacob touched the creature with his foot. It was the same

gesture he had made after he shot the Audi driver. 'It was about to attack.'

'It was entitled to. We were on its territory. The dog wasn't rabid, Belle was right, it was frightened.' Magnus felt an urge to bury the thing, the way Raisha buried the children she found.

Jacob looked at him. 'How do you think it's been living since its owners died?'

A horrible realisation dawned on Magnus but he said, 'There are plenty of rabbits in the fields, sheep even.'

The priest touched the dead dog's belly again with the toe of his boot. 'I had a family too: a wife, two girls and a boy. The children wanted a dog and so eventually we bought them one. Spot, the not very originally named Dalmatian. Annie and the children didn't make it. Spot did.' The priest looked at Magnus, his features tight and bone-white. 'I would be a Herod to dogs. I would kill a whole generation of them if I could.'

'I'm sorry.'

The words were nothing, but the priest acknowledged them with a small nod. He turned and walked towards the barns, his gun still in his hand, and after a moment Magnus followed him.

They were cowsheds, as large as a car plant and full of death. Magnus and Jacob smelled them from yards away. Magnus would have turned back, but the priest was resolute and so he followed him inside, pulling the neck of his T-shirt up over his mouth and nose in the vain hope that it would help protect him from the stench. To his relief they did not venture deep into the buzz of flies, just stood in the doorway

210

of each outhouse taking in the swollen bellies, the exploded innards and dead, infected eyes.

Jacob said, 'I only had six months to go. I was a career soldier, I'd expected to retire in uniform, but I'd seen too much of this kind of thing. Replace those cows with people and you'll get the idea.' He nodded towards the yard where he had shot the dog. 'I saw some petrol up there. We should burn these sheds.'

Magnus said, 'There must be millions of places like this. How can you still believe in God?'

Jacob stopped walking and turned to face him. 'The reason I had decided to leave the army was that I could feel my faith deserting me. Annie said that she could see it in my face. She said my eyes had changed, grown harder, like bits of broken glass.' He smiled. 'Annie wrote poetry. I don't know if it was any good or not, but it spoke to me.'

'And now?' Magnus asked.

'And now?' The priest raised his eyebrows.

'Has your faith deserted you?'

'The sweats renewed my faith. This disaster wasn't God's doing, it was man-made. God has given some of us the chance to live. He saved us and however sad we feel we owe it to Him to make a go of things.' Jacob smiled at Magnus. 'I know you don't agree with me. But you may come to in time.'

'Perhaps,' Magnus said, but he knew that the priest was wrong. If God existed then the devil did too and it seemed that he had the upper hand.

They watched the sheds burn from a distance, but they could still hear the crackle and spit of the flames and smell the

211

spoiled barbecue rot of burning cattle. The cows had been swollen with gas and once the fire took hold there were small explosions. Magnus began to worry that they had made a miscalculation and that the surrounding fields would go up too, but the cattle sheds had been set far back from them on tarmacadam paths.

The byres on his parents' croft had been close to grazing fields, the livestock turned out on to grass as soon as the weather allowed.

'They never saw the sun,' Magnus said. 'The cattle were kept inside until it was time for them to be sent to slaughter.'

'We grew too big.' Jacob spoke as if he were reaching the conclusion of a long sermon. 'But we have a chance to learn from our mistakes.'

'No.' Magnus's own certainty surprised him. 'Isn't that one of the things your Bible tells us? We're greedy, over-reaching idiots who are destined to destroy ourselves over and over again.'

Belle and Will were waiting by the truck, Belle cradling something in her arms. Will said, 'I was going to come and look for you, but Belle was feeling sick and I didn't want to leave her.'

'It's that smell.' Belle had wrapped a shawl around her, though the afternoon was still hot. Whatever she was hold-ing shifted beneath the fabric.

Jacob said, 'There were barns full of dead cattle. We thought burning them might help stop infection spreading.'

Will gave a snort. 'Then you should burn the world.'

212

Belle's shawl slipped, revealing two squirming bundles of fur. She threw Jacob a disgusted look. 'She was protecting her puppies.'

Magnus said, 'Jacob killed the dog for a reason . . .'

The priest put a hand on his arm. 'It's okay.' He looked at the girl. 'I hope you'll forgive me.'

Belle climbed on to the trailer without answering and Will jumped up after her. Magnus reached in to stroke one of the wriggling balls of fluff. The puppy bit him on the hand, not quite hard enough to draw blood. He pulled it away quickly. They were old enough to be weaned, he realised, old enough to eat flesh. He was about to get into the cab, but the priest touched his arm.

'We didn't check the outhouses on the other side.'

The smoke was making Magnus feel uneasy. It was okay for the priest to say that he wanted people to see his community working and join it, but so far all he had done was light a fire that could be seen from miles around.

'There will be other places with combine harvesters. I think we should get going.'

But the priest was already walking across the yard.

Belle said, 'Let's go without him.'

'Jacob has the van keys.' Will's ugly face was blank, his voice flat, but Magnus sensed the anger coiled inside him.

'So let's take another one,' Belle whispered. Her voice was edged with panic, as if she too were worried about the fire's crowd-drawing potential. 'This place is full of abandoned vehicles.'

It was as if Will had not heard her. He picked up his shotgun, jumped out of the trailer and followed Jacob across the

213

yard, his footsteps scrunching quick and resolute against the gravel. Magnus saw Will's free hand clench into a fist and ran after him.

'For fuck's sake!' Belle shouted.

Magnus heard the truck's tailgate slam and the girl's swift footsteps behind him. Jacob had reached the sheds. He slid a door open and went inside. Will stepped into a trot. Magnus was running full pelt now, but the other man's legs were longer and he had a head start. Jacob had seemed not to notice he was being pursued, but he was a soldier, with a soldier's training and Magnus imagined him waiting on the other side of the door, his gun ready.

'Wait,' Magnus shouted. He felt sick with anticipation. Will followed Jacob into the shed and slammed the door behind him. Magnus faltered to a halt.

'Aren't you going to do anything?' Belle was beside him.

'We're too late.' Magnus's words came between gasps of breath.

'You're a fucking coward.' Belle still had the puppies shawled in her arms. She hugged them to her and ran awkwardly towards the outhouses before Magnus could stop her. No shot sounded and after a moment he followed her.

The darkness of the barn was almost blinding after the bright sunshine. The two men appeared like black shadows, side by side, facing away from him in the dimness. Belle came towards Magnus, pale and ghostly. He asked, 'What's going on?' but she ignored him and went outside, whispering softly to the dogs cradled in her arms as if they were in need of comforting. Magnus drew closer and saw that Will and Jacob were standing over the body of a man. He had

214

been dead for some time, Magnus guessed, but it was not the sweats that had killed him. Blood from deep cuts on the man's wrists coated his legs and belly. A gash yawned on his neck and a black bib crusted across his chest. Before the sweats Magnus had only seen two dead bodies, but now this was nothing to stare at.

Will said, 'It's Henry, he was with us for a while.'

Jacob passed the other man the keys to the van without looking at him. 'You and Belle should go back to base.' He was staring at the body as if something about it fascinated him. 'Magnus and I will take care of Henry. We owe him that much.'

It was in Magnus's mind to say that he was not one of Jacob's soldiers to be ordered around. He had never known Henry and owed him no more than the cattle they had burned, but then the priest's eyes met his and he caught an expression in them that might have been fear or a warning.

'She liked Henry. She'll be upset.' Whatever Will had been on the verge of doing was forgotten. He took the keys and left the barn.

Jacob waited until the sound of Will's footsteps had faded and the truck's engine gunned into life, then he hunched down beside the body.

'What do you make of this?' He touched dead Henry's wrists with the tip of his gun barrel.

Magnus squatted next to him. 'Things got too much for him and he cut his wrists.'

'Look properly and tell me what you see.' The priest lifted one wrist, then the other with his gun.

'Two deep cuts on each wrist, one crossed over the other like an X. He meant to do it.'

'And this?' Jacob let Henry's slaughtered arm drop and traced the gun along a dark bruise, striped above the wound like a bracelet. 'There's a matching one on the other wrist.'

'I don't know.' Magnus leaned forward to get a closer look. Each death had its own particular scent. Henry's smelled of freshly spread fields and iron. 'Perhaps it's something that happens when you cut your wrists like that.'

'It's something that happens when someone sticks a pair of handcuffs on you.' The priest's voice was as dead as the corpse on the floor between them. 'I'll tell you something else. No one cuts their wrists in one clean slice. It takes a few goes before the natural instinct for self-preservation is completely overcome. Henry didn't commit suicide. He was murdered.'

'Why are you telling me this?' Magnus whispered.

'You and Jeb were the only ones who weren't here when it happened. That means you're the only ones I can vaguely trust.' Jacob got to his feet.

Magnus followed him. 'Raisha and Belle . . .'

'Are as suspect as anyone.' There was a sheet of plastic draped over some machinery in the corner of the barn. Jeb pulled it free and dragged it towards the body. 'It's comforting to think of women as a higher species, less inclined to violence than men, but they do occasionally kill.' He put the plastic over Henry's corpse, slipping its edges beneath the body, as if he were tucking him into bed. 'We've been through an unprecedented trauma. Life is cheaper than it was before. Who knows what effect it will have on those of us who remain?'

'What are you going to do?'

Jacob pushed the final edge of the plastic beneath Henry's head.

'What can I do? Maybe it was one of our group, maybe it was a stranger. I'll keep my eyes open and try and make sure it doesn't happen to anyone else.'

'It could have been Jeb or me, we're strangers.'

Jacob gave a weird grin. 'Was it?'

'No,' Magnus said. 'It wasn't.'

Jacob nodded. He looked Magnus in the eye. 'It wasn't me either.'

Twenty-Eight

The combine harvester they had found was bigger than the one his father had rented each year for the croft and Magnus guided it slowly through the ripe field of corn. Jacob sat in the cab beside him to 'learn how it was done', but Magnus was aware of the gun on the priest's hip and his own lack of weapon. They were each wearing ear mufflers they had found on the driver's seat, ready for a harvest that had come too soon for some now-dead farmer and his mate. It was too noisy to talk and neither of them had mentioned Henry's body. Magnus was glad of the noise. Murder or not, there was nothing he could do about it. He liked the faint, familiar rumble of the combine's engine, the smell of newly felled corn and the uneven jolt of the field beneath the machine. Sweat was beading his forehead and trickling down his back, but the task felt clean. There was something purifying in the labour and even with Jacob riding shotgun it gave him space to think. He would leave Tanqueray as soon as he had cut the three fields of corn they had agreed on.

Magnus had visited Jeb and told him about Henry. One of the puppies had been curled on the floor of the room, chewing at the bedside rug's fringes. Jeb had stretched out a hand, caught hold of the dog by the scruff of its neck and pulled it to its feet. He rubbed the dog's ears. 'Are you sure it wasn't Jacob who did it?'

It was a typical police response, Magnus decided, blame the nearest person, but he kept the thought to himself. 'Why would you think that?'

The dog made a lunge for Jeb's shirt sleeve and he batted it away. 'You saw the way he shot the guy who attacked us. He blew his head off with no warning. Jacob's a soldier. He knows how to handle a gun. Okay, the man had a machete, but Jacob could have taken him out with a hit to the leg, a hit to the body if he wasn't sure of his aim.' The puppy jumped at Jeb's sleeve again. He cuffed it gently on the back of its head and it trotted out of the room. 'Jacob went for the execution shot. Don't get me wrong, I'm grateful, but if you're looking for a killer I'd say Father-armed-and-dangerous is an obvious candidate.'

Magnus had wondered at the way Jacob had shot the Audi driver, but he had seen the grim set of the priest's mouth as he looked at Henry's wounds.

'He took us to the body. Why would he do that if he had killed him?'

Jeb leaned forward, still stern, but more confident than Magnus had seen him since the accident.

'What's the point in putting on a display if there's no one there to admire it? We were trained to look out for the neighbour who's a little too nosy about the crime scene; the person who's over-eager to offer an opinion to the news cameras; the man or woman who knows a little too much.' Jeb opened

219

the desk drawer and took out a pencil and a piece of paper. 'Describe what you saw in as much detail as you can remember.'

Magnus looked out at the trees beyond the window. Jeb's story about Cherry and Happy was harder to imagine by daylight. It seemed to belong to the night. He wondered about the truth of it; the woman jumping to her death with the child in her arms, the last terrified look at the world the girl had given before she was plunged into the sky beyond the balcony. Magnus's trust in Jeb was wavering again, but he found that he wanted to tell him about Henry's butchered body, the way the priest had touched the wounds gently with the nub of his gun. How he had tucked the dead man tight in plastic, as if preserving him for another day.

Jeb listened silently, jotting down the occasional note. He nodded when Magnus mentioned the lack of defence cuts and the red weals Jacob had said were caused by handcuffs. When Magnus finished Jeb said, 'I'd like to talk to the priest about this. Do you think you can get him to visit me?'

Magnus had promised to see what he could do.

The corn toppled beneath the combine's blades in rows that were less straight than his father would have approved of, but which gave Magnus a forgotten sense of pride. He would find a van somewhere, pick up his abandoned motorbike, replace its damaged tyre and press on for Scrabster. The van would speed his progress and the bike would ensure he was not stalled by some obstacle: a tangle of abandoned cars, a collapsed bridge or a barricade that a larger vehicle could not negotiate. When he got to Orkney, Magnus would be able to tell his mother and Rhona (please God let them be alive) that he had done something good.

Jacob was saying something to him. Magnus lifted his muffler, but the words were lost in the din of the engine. The priest pointed at the ignition. Magnus killed the engine and drew the combine to a halt.

Jacob said, 'Ready for a break?'

'I can keep going for another hour.' Every moment he worked was a moment closer to leaving.

'I'm ready for a break and I think you should have one too. These are dangerous machines. It doesn't do to drive them for too long.' Jacob slung the bag with their water and sandwiches in it around his body, opened the cab door and climbed down into the field.

Magnus said, 'I've been driving these beasts since I was sixteen. I don't need to be told when to have a break.'

His father had been working his neighbour Bobby Bird's field since sun-up on the evening he died. Bobby supplemented the yield from his croft by working in a bank in Stromness. He paid for the combine's rental and Magnus's father cut Bobby's crop, then used the machine to harvest his own fields.

'I told him not to batter it,' Bobby had said tearfully to Magnus at the funeral, 'but you ken your faither, God bless his soul, he wouldn't touch his ain fields till he had done mine and he was feart the rain was coming in.'

His father had been right. It had rained for three days after his death; torrential, biblical, sheets of rain. Bobby and the rest of their neighbours had worked in it, Magnus, Rhona

221

and his cousin Hugh with them, to bring in his father's crop. But it had not brought the man back.

Magnus got out of the cab, slammed the door and jumped down into the stubbled corn. The sky was blue and almost cloudless. There were no jet streams intersecting in the sky, white on blue like ragged saltires. Jacob tipped a water bottle to his mouth. He wiped his chin with the back of his hand and then reached into his bag and passed another bottle to Magnus who unscrewed its lid and took a drink. Jacob was wearing dark Ray-Bans that contrasted oddly with his dog collar. It was hard to see his eyes, but Magnus could feel the priest watching him.

Jacob said, 'Did you tell anyone about Henry?' Magnus considered lying, but he hesitated a moment too long and the priest asked, 'Who? Jeb?'

'He used to be a policeman. I thought he might be able to tell whether it was murder or not.'

Jacob nodded. 'The same thought crossed my mind.'

Magnus said, 'He told you he used to be in the police? You're privileged.'

'He didn't have to tell me.' The priest smiled, his eyes still hidden. 'Jeb Soames is distinctive. He's changed, grown a decade older in two or three years, but I got a feeling of déjà vu when I was setting his leg. The pain brought out those big bones in his forehead. It took me a while to place him, but then I remembered a newspaper photograph of him wearing the same expression as he was taken into court on the first day of his trial.' The priest paused as if something had just occurred to him. 'Do you know his history?'

The sun was warm on the back of his neck. Magnus took a hanky from his pocket and mopped his face with it.

'He told me some of it. He wanted to convince me he was innocent.'

'Did he succeed?'

Magnus thought for a moment. 'I don't know.'

'The judge and jury thought he was guilty.' The priest's voice was neutral, as if guilt and innocence were all the same to him. 'The newspapers did too. Jeb was bulkier in the photo, like a human battering ram. I remember wondering how a man his size could bring himself to lay violent hands on a child.' Jacob stared up the field at the rolled bales of harvested corn. 'The girl who died was the same age as my younger daughter. Maybe that's why the story stuck in my mind.'

Magnus said, 'And you don't mind having him here?'

'If I'd realised who he was when we first met, I might have walked away . . .' The priest shrugged. 'He's here now. Maybe God intended it that way.' He tilted his water bottle to his mouth and drank. 'Is he getting close to Belle?'

'I think he feels sorry for her.'

The priest took off his Ray-Bans, wiped his eyes and put them back on. There were dark shadows beneath his eyes.

'Love is the thing that will make the post-sweats world bearable, love and children; new life. But it's probably best if Jeb doesn't get too close to Belle. From what I remember of the press coverage she's rather too like the woman he killed for any good to come of it.' Magnus was about to say that Jeb might still be innocent, but the priest asked, 'What did he say about poor Henry?'

Magnus shrugged. 'Nothing much, just that he'd like to talk to you about it.'

223

'Did he tell you that he thought it was probably me who killed him?'

'No,' Magnus lied. There were whole fields surrounding them and no one to care if Jacob should decide to aim his gun and shoot. *He went north*, the priest would say, *home to his family*. 'Why would he think that?'

'I would in his position. You've already seen me kill and I was the one who found the body. I reckon that makes me a prime candidate.' Jacob grinned. 'Don't look so worried. I've no intention of burying you among the corn. At least not until we get our three fields done.' He reached into his bag and took out the bread and cheese he had been wrapping in wax paper when Magnus had joined him in the kitchen early that morning. 'Next year at harvest we'll be eating bread made with our own flour.'

'I won't be here.'

Jacob passed Magnus one of the doorstop sandwiches he had made.

'Perhaps you'll come back.'

Magnus bit into cheddar and home-made pickle. 'I don't think so.'

'I don't blame you, I suppose, but you'd be a valuable asset to a new community like ours.' The priest sat on the step of the combine. He took off his glasses, though the sun was still skull-cracking sharp and his eyes creased against its glare. 'I know what Jeb was convicted of, but I don't really know anything about you.'

Magnus looked across the fields. The flatness of the land gave the illusion that you could see for ever, but there were plenty of places for people to hide among the long corn and he wondered if anyone was watching them.

'I was a comic. I was doing okay and had the potential to do better. I might have been at a turning point in my career, or it might have been another false dawn. I'll never know.'

The priest's eyes were almost as blue as the sky. Like bits of broken glass, his wife had said. He asked, 'Why were you in prison?'

Magnus's sandwich caught in his throat. He coughed, tried to swallow and coughed again. When he had caught his breath he asked, 'How did you know?'

The priest sat with his legs stretched out in front of him. He bit into his doorstop as if he were at a Sunday-school picnic that had done away with daintiness.

'I didn't. I just made a guess.'

Magnus shook his head at his own stupidity. 'I was innocent. I hadn't gone to trial and when I did, I would have been released.'

The priest had finished his sandwich. He took an apple out of his bag and polished it against his shirt. 'Why don't you tell me what happened?'

'What's the point?'

Jacob glanced at his apple, rubbed it against his shirt some more and then bit into its flesh. 'I want to be able to trust you.'

It was difficult to know where to begin and so Magnus told him about the Dongolite falling beneath the train, the drunken evening in Johnny Dongo's hotel room, the fist Johnny had put in his face and the man pawing at the drugged girl in the alleyway. Once he had begun, Magnus found he needed to go on and so he told the priest about

225

Pete dying slowly in the bunk beneath him, the man he had hit – killed – with the fire extinguisher. He even found himself telling Jacob about his father, caught in the blades of the combine and his cousin Hugh, walking into the sea, until the water covered him and the rocks in his backpack dragged him under. Magnus stopped suddenly, feeling lighter, but knowing that shame would soon follow. The priest tossed his apple core into the field beyond.

'The absence of so many people makes the past seem stronger. We need to grieve, but we need to start making a future too.' He took his Ray-Bans from his pocket and fingered them, as if he needed to give his hands something to do. 'I thought about telling Father Wingate my suspicions, he's my spiritual adviser.' Jacob smiled. 'We're each other's spiritual advisers. But however wise he is, he's an old man who has been through a lot. He views the coming of the sweats as an opportunity to build a better society. I'm not sure what discovering there is still wickedness in the world might do to him.' The priest looked up at Magnus, his eyes narrowed against the sun. 'I had my suspicions about Melody's death before we found Henry. There was something about the position of the chair she supposedly stood on to hang herself. It was lying too far from her body. I marked the spot and after we buried her I experimented with it. I'm taller and stronger than Melody was, but no matter how many times I kicked that chair away, it always fell short of where it was lying when we found her. I asked Henry if he had moved it, but he swore blind he hadn't. At the time I convinced myself he had forgotten he'd done it. He was in a state of shock. But now that we've found Henry . . .'

Magnus said, 'What's keeping you here? Why don't you leave?'

The priest put on his sunglasses, hiding his eyes again behind their dark lenses.

'We have a perfect spot. Father Wingate's right, it has the potential to be one of the foundations of a new society.'

'There are other perfect spots.'

'Which will also present their own problems. I've never been one for running away. If someone is killing people then I'd rather find them.'

There was something final in the priest's voice. Magnus said, 'What will you do with them, if you find them?'

The priest took a last swig from his water bottle and screwed its cap back on. He looked across the fields, as if he too wondered if anyone was watching them.

'I was always a New Testament man, but we seem to find ourselves in Old Testament times.'

Twenty-Nine

Raisha came to him that night. The image of her tramping the countryside, seeking dead children to bury, had lodged itself in Magnus's mind. He had wondered how he would be if she were to seek him out – could he stand hands that had cradled rotting flesh caressing his flesh? He was asleep when Raisha clicked open the bedroom door. A gust of cool air entered with her and Magnus woke a moment before she pulled back his sheets and slid naked into bed beside him. He flinched and she whispered, 'Is it okay?'

Magnus had begun to think of Raisha as a ghost flitting across the landscape in search of other ghosts, but now that she was beside him he could feel the heat of her body, the soft smoothness of her skin.

'It's okay,' he answered, keeping his voice low, though there was no one there to hear or care what they did. He wanted to tell her that he would be leaving soon, but then her mouth was on his, warm and sweet, with no hint of the grave.

A shaft of sunlight stretched into his room at dawn and prised Magnus's eyes apart. Raisha was gone. The sensation of having been used and cast away struck him as a feminine one, and he tried to be amused by it, but the feeling haunted him for the rest of the day, a kernel of sadness wedged in his chest that the motion of the combine could not dislodge.

There were four of them on the harvest crew now. Will and Belle worked the cut field gathering bales of corn with the aid of a forklift and a truck; a no-health-and-safety-team-of-two. Magnus and Jacob took turns on the combine, Magnus instructing the priest who learned quickly.

In the old days, before mechanisation, harvest time had forced communities to unite in hard work. Technology had killed that necessity. Magnus's father had complained about mega-farms and their obsessions with yields, but he had loved the ease of the combine, the blades that could fell a crop quicker than the sweats had felled London. Magnus tried to conjure his father's voice, but it was lost in the din of the engine.

Magnus remembered black-and-white photographs of his great-grandfather tilling his field behind a horse-drawn plough. He had risen with the dawn and gone to bed when the sun set. The misery of the long-bright, short-dark, repetitions of the seasons washed over him. London had been alive. Now it and all the other great cities, Paris, New York, Beijing, Mumbai and Moscow, were nothing but names on old radio dials. The loss of it all hit him again. If Magnus had been alone he might have stopped the combine and wept, but the priest was there and so he set his jaw and pressed on through the falling corn.

The sun was fading into a rose-blush sunset when they eventually arrived back at the big house. Father Wingate had promised to cook 'something hearty' for their return. 'Something hearty' turned out to be a large pot of brown lentils and another of brown rice. Father Wingate said a hurried grace over the food before slopping generous servings into bowls.

'I added some mushrooms I found in the woods. They're good for the blood.'

Magnus accepted his portion with a nod, resolving not to touch the mushrooms. Belle looked at her bowl with distaste. The puppies had greeted her with wiggling rears and wagging tails and she had both of them curled on her lap. She slid the dogs to the floor, poured a glass of water from the jug on the table and lifted the bowl Father Wingate had given her. 'I'll take this up to Jeb.'

Jacob looked up, his spoon poised halfway to his mouth. 'Eat first. I'll take him something when I've finished. Jeb and I have things to talk about.'

The girl ignored him. She left the room, the puppies trotting after her, the clack of their claws loud against the flagstones. Jacob and Magnus exchanged glances, but it was Will who said, 'Do you think she should be on her own with him?'

Magnus wondered what Will knew. He said, 'Jeb's still laid up, if it's her honour you're worried about.'

Father Wingate had stirred his lentils into his rice and was picking his way through the mess with the determination of a man doing his duty. 'A broken leg wouldn't have stopped me when I was a young sinner.'

They laughed, but Magnus noticed that each of them cast occasional glances at the door as they ate.

The dishes were washed and Jacob had lit the paraffin lamps he insisted on leaving on the kitchen and sitting-room window sills each night as a welcome to passing strangers, though no one had been drawn in by them yet. Raisha was still out somewhere in the darkening evening and Belle had not returned from Jeb's room. Father Wingate was sorting through a biscuit tin of odds and ends he had found, looking for 'anything that might be of use'. He had set a candle at his elbow and every so often he would lift an object from the tin and hold it near to the flame, examining it closely, as if it were an ancient artefact and he an archaeologist looking for the secret of what purpose it might have served.

Magnus's back ached from two days on the combine. He wanted to be on his own, but felt too weary to rouse himself and go up to his room. He sat at the kitchen table with the three men, an ill-considered bottle of malt and four glasses between them. The puppies skated into the kitchen, their paws losing purchase against the stone floor, mouths grinning. Jacob aimed his boot at them and they yelped out into the hallway and beyond. Something moved above and all four men looked up at the ceiling.

Father Wingate said, 'It's only the dogs. They don't know it's wrong to be alive.'

Jacob had spread an old newspaper on the kitchen table and was cleaning his gun. An actress Magnus did not recognise was flaunting her cleavage next to the headline *Royal Family Hit by Sweats*. Magnus watched as the soldier-priest oiled the gun's mechanism and then methodically wiped the grease from it with a cloth. He wondered if the actress had had something to do with the royal family, or if the photo had simply been intended to add some colour. The

231

world before the sweats already seemed strange. He would struggle to explain it to someone who had not been there.

Jacob took a sip from his glass. 'It isn't wrong to be alive. God gave us the gift of life. We should cherish it.' His voice was dark and bitter, thickened by the whisky.

Another noise sounded upstairs and again all four of them looked towards it.

'I'm turning in.' Will pulled himself to his feet.

Jacob said, 'You should tell her how you feel.'

'I don't feel anything.' Will's voice was a monotone.

'You stare at her.' Jacob had finished wiping his gun clean. He inserted the magazine into its chamber. 'There's no shame in it. But if you want her, don't stand there with your tongue hanging out, tell her.'

'I had a girlfriend. She's dead.'

Will started to leave the room, but turned back before he reached the door. The Dutchman had drunk less than Magnus and Jacob, but there was a whisky gleam in his eye.

'Boys . . .' Father Wingate's voice was a tremor.

Will put both hands on the table and leaned in close to Jacob. 'You are the one who wants her. Why don't you tell her, instead of playing with your pistol?' He straightened up and said in a louder voice, 'That man up there is the same type as you. He might enjoy sharing. Isn't that what soldiers like? Sharing the women they rape?'

Jacob's tone was weary; a headmaster disappointed with a particularly stupid boy, but his eyes narrowed and his hand sat next to the loaded gun. 'You had a girlfriend? Good for you. I had a wife and children . . .'

Magnus got to his feet and took hold of Will's arm.

'C'mon, man, it's been a long day.' Part of him was tempted to let them fight each other, but he tightened his grip and began to pull him away. 'It's up to Belle who she goes with. There are no rapists here.'

Will let himself be towed from the table. They were almost in the hallway when Jacob said, 'That's right, go to bed. You wouldn't have lasted a day on our squad. Where were you when the sweats took hold? Blubbing over your dead girlfriend? My men didn't have that luxury. We were in the bloody thick of it.'

Will jerked free of Magnus's grasp and bolted back into the room. 'You bet you were in the thick of it. The military made that bloody virus. You're the reason everyone's dead. Fucking murderers.' He made a lunge for Jacob, but the priest shoved the table forward, knocking Will off balance. He slammed into a kitchen cabinet and a plate smashed against the flagstones. The bottle of whisky toppled and the contents of Father Wingate's tin of odds and ends clattered across the floor.

'Jacob!' The old man had almost toppled too. He braced himself against his chair, thin and spectral, but a survivor all the same. 'We mustn't fight among ourselves.'

Magnus made a grab for the whisky and set it upright, but a good quarter of the bottle had leaked across the table and on to the flagstones. It scented the room; the smell of Christmas Eve, the Snapper Bar, night fishing with his cousin Hugh.

He shoved the memories away and slipped into the soothing tone his father had used to comfort sheep in labour; soft and coaxing.

'Father Wingate's right. Let's leave this till the morning.

233

We've an early start tomorrow.' By Christ, Magnus resolved, he would forget the deal he had made to harvest three fields. He would be gone, away from this mayhem, before dawn. Will righted himself and Magnus saw a kitchen knife in his hand. 'For God's sake, man.' Magnus could hear the fear in his own voice. 'What the fuck do you think that's going to do? He's got a bloody gun. Do you think you can out-stab a bullet?'

The soldier-priest was on his feet too, the revolver less than a hand's breadth from him on the table. Magnus looked at Father Wingate, but the old man seemed mesmerised by the knife. Will clenched it in both hands, as if it were a much heavier weapon, an axe or a claymore meant for cutting a swathe through ranks of enemies. Magnus saw the way it trembled and took a step backward.

Will said, 'You keep telling us this is a new beginning, but maybe Harry and Melody are the ones who got it right.'

'You're wrong.' Jacob unlocked the magazine from the gun and slid it out of reach across the table. The soldier's jaw was still clenched, but Will's words had hit some mark. Jacob picked up a small metal screw from the table, a remnant of Father Wingate's box of odds and ends, and rolled it between his hands. 'Harry and Melody didn't—'

A crash boomed from the floor above them. There was a moment of stillness and then Will ran for the door, the knife still in his hand. Magnus followed. The hallway was in darkness, the staircase a vague shape lit by moonlight. They sprinted up it, the sound of their work boots muffled by carpet. Magnus heard Jacob's breath close behind him and wondered if he had retrieved his gun.

Upstairs was silent. Will went straight to Jeb's room and

turned the handle, but something was jammed behind the door and it only opened a crack. A faint glow of candlelight reached into the blackness of the landing, illuminating the door's outline, like some sci-fi portal.

'Fuck off.' Belle's voice sounded high and querulous from inside the room.

Magnus said, 'Are you okay?'

'Go away,' Belle shouted. It was hard to tell if she was angry or panicked.

Jacob shoved him out of the way. 'Stop fannying about.'

Magnus said, 'She doesn't want us in there.'

Jacob shouldered the door. It refused to move, but then Will added his weight, there was a sound of splintering wood and the two men tumbled into the room, staggering into the remnants of the wooden chair that had been used to wedge it shut.

'What the fuck are you doing?' Belle had the bed sheet pulled up over her chest.

Jeb was in bed beside her. He did not bother to cover himself and his bruised ribs showed dark against the pale sheets. The moonlight shone stronger in the small bedroom than it had downstairs. It stretched in through the open window, touching the edge of the bed, bringing the night closer. A candle glowed softly on the table where Jeb's bowl of lentils and rice had been abandoned.

Jeb grinned. 'Nice of you to check, lads, but we're all right. Whatever that noise was it came from the next room, so you're welcome to bugger off.'

Will turned his back and left the room. Magnus hovered in the doorway. He saw the flush on the back of Jacob's neck and wondered again if he had pocketed his gun.

Jacob looked at Belle. 'Do you know what happened to the last woman he slept with?' His words were whisky-slurred, *schlept with?*

The girl had been proud in her fury, like someone acting a part; now a look of confusion trembled across her face. Jeb put a protective arm around her, but she shrank from him. 'What happened?'

Jeb pointed a finger at Jacob. 'I heard about Henry. You're in no position to start throwing accusations about.'

Belle said, 'What happened to Henry?' but Jeb's attention had shifted to Magnus. 'You let me down, big-time.'

Magnus saw what he thought was the stock of the revolver Belle had given Jeb, jutting from beneath a pile of papers on the bedside table. He forced his eyes away from it. 'I didn't tell Jacob anything about you. He used to read more newspapers than I did, that's all. It took him a while, but eventually he remembered where he'd seen you.'

'Where had he seen you?' Belle was hemmed in between Jeb and the wall, caught between a sudden impulse to get away from him and the urge to hide her nakedness from the other men.

Jacob lifted her dress from the floor. He held it between the tips of his fingers, as if it might be contaminated, and tossed it to her. The dress fell short of its mark. It landed in the beam of moonlight and Belle was forced to stretch across the counterpane to reach it. Her fingers scrabbled to get hold of its hem without exposing herself, but then she managed to grasp it and pulled the dress on over her head. 'Is no one going to tell me what's going on?'

Magnus said, 'Jeb will tell you.' He turned to Jacob. 'I

think we should go downstairs and give these folks some privacy.'

'He killed her.' The soldier-priest stood his ground, solid as a pulpit, straight as the barrel of a gun. 'Her and her child, tossed them over the balcony of a high-rise like sacks of rubbish.'

'That's a lie.' Jeb put his good leg on the floor and steadied himself against the bedpost. 'He's the killer. He slit your friend Henry's throat.'

Belle looked from one to the other, her eyes wide.

Jacob shook his head. 'Your boyfriend's a certified liar. He was an undercover policeman who went too far undercover. He forgot who he was, or maybe he discovered who he was. He was sent to jail for a long time. He'd still be there if it wasn't for the sweats.'

Jeb was struggling to get to his feet. 'You're a murdering bastard.'

'You've forgotten yourself, son. If it wasn't for me you'd be lying in a ditch with your throat slit and your belly cut open.' The priest and the soldier in Jacob had fused. He might have been in church preaching a sermon on vengeance, or in a dugout about to lead his men over the top. He turned to Magnus. 'Tell Belle where you two met.'

'Jeb can tell her.'

Magnus put his hand on Jacob's arm and tried to steer him into the hallway, but the soldier-priest shrugged him off.

'They met in prison. Magnus was in for rape, Jeb for double murder.'

Belle's hand went to her mouth.

Magnus snapped, 'It was a mistake. I was trying to save her . . .'

237

Father Wingate limped into the room, his breath creaking in his chest. 'The devil has got into this house. I thought we could keep him at bay, but he is here among us.'

Jeb pulled himself upright. He was naked and the battering he had taken was written in black and purple across his body. Magnus glanced again at the papers splayed on the bedside table. He was sure that the gun was beneath them.

'Jeb . . .' Belle's voice was soft and wavering. She reached out and touched his arm. 'Were you in jail?'

Jeb's hand was resting on the bedside table. 'It's not like he says.'

'But you went to prison for murdering a woman and her child?'

Jeb turned to look at her. The pain on his face might have come from his bruised ribs and broken leg. 'I went to prison for it, but I didn't do it.'

Jacob said, 'He did it.'

Belle looked at the soldier. 'Did you kill Henry?'

'Don't be ridiculous.'

Belle gave a high-pitched laugh. 'This entire fucking world is ridiculous. Why shouldn't I be?' She gathered her dress around her and crawled from the bed. 'I need to go.'

Jeb said, 'Don't worry about it. It's not like I was going to ask you to marry me.'

Belle shot him a look that was half hurt, half hate. 'And it's not like I would have given you shit from the soles of my shoes, before the sweats.'

She pushed past the men and went barefoot into the darkness. Will had returned and was standing in the doorway. He watched Belle go, but made no effort to follow her. 'It was the dogs that made the noise,' he said. 'They knocked over a table in the next room.'

Father Wingate stretched out his arms as if to gather the four men to him. 'Let us all get down on our knees and ask what God wants of us.'

Jacob pointed at Jeb. 'I should have sent you packing as soon as I realised who you were . . .'

Magnus said, 'All he did was to go to bed with Belle . . .'

'He deceived that girl the way he deceived the woman he killed.' Jacob's words were full of spit and fury. 'He's a predator, and that makes him a risk to our community.'

Jeb said, 'You're just trying to draw attention away from yourself. You're a stone-cold killer.'

Magnus grasped Jacob's arm again and tried to lead him from the room, but the priest shrugged him off with such force that Magnus guessed a third attempt would result in a punch. Instinct told him to shut his mouth, but he said, 'You don't have a community.' His family were in his mind again and Magnus struggled to speak. 'There's no kinship here. You're just a bunch of people huddled together because you're scared of being alone.'

Will said, 'That is how communities begin. People must co-operate in order to survive.'

Magnus laughed. 'You just pulled a knife on your spiritual leader.'

'I wouldn't have touched him.' Will looked at his hands as if he could not believe they had ever grasped a knife. 'I never used to get so angry but now . . .'

Father Wingate pressed his way into the centre of the room. 'We must all listen to God. His will is paramount.'

239

Jeb had pulled on a sweatshirt and was sitting on the edge of the bed struggling to ease a pair of jogging trousers over his plastered leg.

Magnus said, 'Want to hitch a lift out of here?'

Jeb's mouth was set, the skin around his eyes tight, and Magnus saw what Jacob had meant when he had described him as looking like a battering ram. Jeb gave an unhappy smile. 'I thought you'd never ask.'

Jacob put a hand on Magnus's shoulder. 'You still owe us two and a half fields.'

'Tonight breaks any deal we had.' Magnus nodded to Jeb. 'Can you get yourself downstairs?'

'Reckon so.' Jeb knotted the string of his tracksuit trousers. 'On my arse if needs be.'

'I'll grab a van and pick you up at the front.'

'Sure thing.'

Jacob's grip tightened on Magnus's shoulder. 'One of us will drive him somewhere in the morning.'

Magnus tried to shrug off the soldier, but the hand was clamped tight on the cords of muscle in his neck, the fingers a painful threat against his vertebrae.

Father Wingate fluttered, 'This is a time for prayer . . .'

Jacob said, 'Go to bed, James. You're right, everything will be better in the morning.'

Father Wingate's voice was high and urgent. 'God did not save us to fight among ourselves.'

Jacob reached into his pocket and took out a bunch of keys. 'Nor did he save us to starve.'

'You're not locking me in here.' Jeb steadied himself against the bedstead.

240

Magnus saw Jeb reaching beneath the papers on the bedside table where the gun was hidden and shouted, 'Don't!'

Jeb faltered and some instinct made Jacob jab a hand towards him. Jeb toppled against the bed with a shout of pain.

'Jacob!' Father Wingate tried to push his way towards Jeb, but Will put an arm around his narrow shoulders and half carried him to the hallway.

'This is not the best place for you tonight, Father.'

Jeb was pulling himself towards the table and the hidden gun, but he was too slow for threats or action. Jacob had Magnus's arms pinned behind his back in an arm lock that made his muscles sing. The soldier applied a knee to his kidneys and huckled him out into the hallway, slamming the door behind them. Will turned the key in the lock.

Magnus shouted, 'Sit tight for one more night or this mad fucker will shoot you. I'll get you out in the morning.'

He hoped that Jeb had heard him and was not on the other side of the door, cocking the hammer of the ancient gun, ready to blow himself, or them, to eternity.

Father Wingate was trembling at the top of the staircase. 'Jacob, I want you to know that I do not condone anything you have done tonight.'

'I realise that, James.' Jacob was more priest than soldier again. 'But there are facts you're not privy to. That man is dangerous. I should never have allowed him to stay, but I let compassion colour my judgement.'

'You're drunk,' the old man said. 'Drunk and jealous that he made love to living flesh, when all we have are memories to console us. It would have been better if we had died with the rest.'

241

'Perhaps.' Jacob's voice was a rasp. 'But drunk or not we're alive and our obligation is to live on.' He opened a door in the wallpaper and pushed Magnus towards a hidden set of stairs inside.

Magnus stumbled against a step. 'It's okay,' he whispered. 'I'll go with you,' but Jacob must have known that he was lying because he kept Magnus's arms pinned behind his back until they reached a door at the top of the house. He pushed him on to a dusty landing and then along a dark corridor, hollow with echoes. Jacob unlocked a door and shoved Magnus into a room bathed in moonlight and darkness.

'This used to be the nursery.' The priest's fury was evaporating into the gloom. He sounded tired. 'Father Wingate probably slept here when he was an infant. The bars on the window were to protect children from the fate your friend elected for that poor little girl.'

Magnus rubbed his arms, trying to restore their circulation. He was still uncertain of Jeb's innocence and did not bother to protest it. 'You know your way around the house.'

'I make it my business to know my way around any building I sleep in. This place is riddled with hiding places. People didn't like to see their servants in the old days. They kept them below stairs or in between the walls.'

There was a bed equipped with a bare mattress in the room. Magnus sat on it and waited for Jacob to leave, but the priest walked to the barred window and looked out. 'I don't want Belle, I'm still married to Annie.' The priest's back was towards Magnus, his expression lost in the dark.

'Why were you so angry?'

'I don't know. It hurt me to see her in bed with him.

242

Perhaps Father Wingate is right. I'm jealous of anyone with a future.'

It felt like their roles had been reversed; Jacob had become the prisoner, Magnus the priest. He said, 'As long as we're alive we have a future.'

Jacob laughed in the darkness. 'So much death has made me realise that ultimately all of our futures are the same.'

'I thought you believed in heaven and hell?'

Jacob shrugged; a shadow in the moonlight. 'I believe in hell.'

Magnus nodded. 'Me too.'

They stood in silence for a moment and then Jacob said, 'We need you here. I'm not going to put you in leg irons, but I can't let you go until we have more able-bodied men. Without the harvest we'll be completely reliant on what we can scavenge.'

Magnus said, 'My family—'

'Your family are dead. I wish it wasn't so, but you don't need to see their corpses to know that I'm right. The living need to stick together.'

'Whether they want to or not?'

Jacob turned away from the window, his face a white presence in the moonlit room. 'The dead are lost to us. Our duty is survival.'

'My family are survivors and my duty is to them.'

'It's natural that you should think so, but you're wrong.'

The priest touched Magnus's shoulder as he left the room. He turned the key in the lock, leaving Magnus alone in the dark.

Thirty

Magnus was woken by a bang. It was not quite light yet and it took him a moment to realise where he was. Then he made out the shape of the unfamiliar room, the barred window. 'Fuck.' The noise was still reverberating in his ears, but the world was silent and he wondered if the sound had been the remnant of an unremembered dream.

Magnus pulled on his boots and got to his feet. He had slept in his clothes and his limbs were heavy. He tried the door. It was still locked. 'Shit.' He was thirsty but there was no sink in the room, no glass of water. Magnus went to the window and looked out from between its bars, into the grey dawn. He pressed his forehead against the cool metal. Soon the sun would creep over the horizon and Jacob would unlock his door. The priest had been drunk and angry. There was a chance that morning might restore his equilibrium. If not, Magnus would take the first opportunity to escape. He had managed to break out of Pentonville, he could break out of here too.

Somewhere in the not quite dawn a blackbird was singing. The nursery looked down on the kitchen garden. It was the same view that he had seen from Jeb's room and Magnus wondered if he was imprisoned below. Jeb's ruthlessness had enabled them to escape jail, but this time his injuries would make him a liability. Magnus recalled the way Jeb had stuck his knife into a prisoner's gut during the final ruckus in Pentonville. It had been self-defence, but the action had been close to elegant in its swiftness. His own descent into violence had been messy. Magnus felt again the sensation of the man's skull giving way as he had hit it with the fire extinguisher and shuddered. This time there would be no deaths.

Magnus desperately wanted to pee. He searched for something to relieve himself into. The room had been emptied at some point and only the bed and a few sticks of furniture remained. He tried the window. It was locked, but the fastenings were the old-fashioned type that unscrewed without the aid of a key. They were stiff, but he managed to undo them and push up the casement. The window was too high and so he dragged a chair over and stood on it.

Magnus was peeing into the dawn, the morning air on his face, the salt scent of his own urine a small victory of streaming steam, when he noticed the dark shape lying on the grass beneath the wall that edged the garden. At first he thought it was a shadow but something about its outline perplexed him. For a moment he thought the dark blot might be a black bin bag blown in from somewhere else, but then he realised that it was a body, lying motionless on the lawn. The thought of yet another death made Magnus feel weary, but it occurred to him that whoever it was might yet be alive. He tucked himself away quickly, stepped down from the chair and broke it against the bedstead. He lifted the sturdiest of its legs and battered it against the door.

'Let me out! There's someone out there!'

It took a while, but eventually Will shouted from the other side of the door, 'I don't have the keys.'

'Get them from Jacob.'

'He's not in his room.'

A thought stirred in Magnus. He said, 'Someone's lying beneath the trees on the back lawn. I don't know if they're alive or dead.'

He heard Will's boots thump downstairs and went to the window. He reached the garden quicker than Magnus had expected. He ran across the lawn, leaving a dark trail of footprints on the dewy grass. Will faltered, unsure of what direction he should head in. He looked up. Magnus pointed to where the body lay and Will sprinted towards it. He slowed. Magnus knew that whoever it was, they were dead. Will raised his face towards the nursery window and shook his head. Magnus could tell from the heaviness of Will's limbs as he walked towards the house that it was someone they knew.

'Please God, don't make it Raisha,' he muttered beneath his breath. He waited until Will was below and leaned against the bars of his window. 'Who was it?'

'Jacob.' Will's face was taut and white with anger. 'That murdering bastard you came with shot him.'

Thirty-One

It was a terrible thing to see an old man cry. Magnus had never liked Father Wingate, but he put a hand on the elderly priest's arm as they walked away from Jacob's grave and whispered, 'He told me last night that he was still married to Annie. Jacob's with his family now. That's what he wanted.' Magnus did not believe in the afterlife, but Father Wingate did and he needed to comfort himself, by comforting the priest.

The old man patted Magnus's hand. 'I'm crying for the end of the world. All things must end, us too, it is the order of things, but I cannot help but mourn their passing.'

They were still alive and the world was not yet completely dead, but there was no point in contradicting him.

Magnus and Will had buried Jacob in a nearby churchyard, close to a recent grave marked by a simple wooden cross inscribed *Melody*. Father Wingate had delivered the eulogy and then watched as they put the soldier into the ground. *Ashes to ashes, dust to dust.* Neither Belle nor Raisha had been there, it had been an all-male funeral, like they used to have on the islands when Magnus's grandfather was a boy.

Magnus was aching and caked in mud. It had been hard,

filthy work digging the grave, but he had been glad of it. The priest had saved his life and they had parted on uneasy terms.

He took Father Wingate by the elbow and helped him into the passenger seat of the truck they had used to drive Jacob's body to the churchyard. Will was still standing by the fresh grave, his head bowed in prayer or resolution. Magnus watched him in the rear-view mirror and wondered if he was going to be a problem.

Magnus said, 'I'm leaving this afternoon.' The remnants of the hymn they had sung when they had buried his father were in his mind, the words only half-remembered.

Abide with me; fast falls the eventide;
The darkness deepens . . .

Father Wingate said, 'I made some bread yesterday. You must take some to help sustain you.'

'Thank you.'

The old man was a poor cook, but the gesture touched Magnus. The truck's cab smelled of rubber and burning dust. Magnus rolled down the driver's side window. Will had latched the churchyard gate and was walking towards the car park. Father Wingate shifted slowly to the middle of the seat and Will slid in beside them.

'Your friend's a murderer.' It had been his mantra since he had found Jacob's body dead on the lawn, his head a gunshot mess.

'You're wrong.' Magnus wished he had paid more attention to Jacob's theories about Melody's and Henry's deaths. He had tried to explain them, but Will's mind was fixed. Jeb was a convicted killer who had quarrelled with Jacob the night before he was shot dead. They had found a gun in his room, a room that had a clear sightline to where the priest had been shot.

'You can leave.' Will turned to look at Magnus. 'But he stays.'

'What good will that do?'

Will sighed. His eyes shut and then opened; sea-washed pebbles, brown and slip-shiny. 'It will prevent him from murdering anyone else.'

Twice in the last few days Magnus had thought Will was about to try to kill Jacob. First by the barn where they had found Henry's body, then in the kitchen, just before they had crashed in on Belle and Jeb. Both times had been crude and spontaneous, born of drink or frustration, but shooting a man in the head was hardly subtle.

Magnus said, 'It could just as easily have been you. You hated Jacob and now it looks like you're trying to take his place.' It would not hurt that Jeb would be out of Belle's way too, he thought, but did not say.

'I didn't hate him . . .' Will faltered, his almost perfect English momentarily deserting him. 'I would never have hurt Jacob . . .'

Father Wingate drew his cassock around his thin shoulders, as if he could feel the chill of the recently filled grave in his bones. 'It wasn't Will. He's a good Christian.'

Magnus started the truck and reversed out of the graveyard.

'Father,' he said and the word sounded strange in his mouth. 'We have a saying on my island. Old age does not always bring wisdom.'

249

The old man nodded. 'That saying existed well beyond your island and there is truth in it, but it does not follow that all old men are foolish.'

Magnus rolled up his window and steered the truck down the church road, into the village. This was the bit of the route he liked least. There were no bodies in the main street, but there were reminders of how things used to be: a post office with pictures of a smiling postman delivering a package to an equally jolly white-haired grandma; a pub decorated with decaying hanging baskets and the proud boast that it had been established in 1622; a row of terraced cottages, each one with windows behind which anything might lurk. Will stared straight ahead, but Magnus could not help glancing at the overgrown gardens, the drawn curtains and uninviting front paths. *Step inside*, the cottages seemed to whisper. *Why don't you stop and take tea? There's always someone home.*

Father Wingate was still talking. 'Jacob told me about how you were thrown into jail for trying to help a young woman. You were out of your element. Jeb helped you escape and you travelled a long way together. No doubt you shared trials and hardships. You may even feel that you owe him your life, but you mustn't let these sentiments blind you.'

Magnus said, 'And you mustn't let prejudice blind you. Any one of us could have killed Jacob: me, you, Will, one of the girls.'

A cat, sharp-toothed and feral, darted across their path. Magnus instinctively touched the truck's brake pedal. What did it feed on? he wondered. Rats or corpses? And was it just a difference of scale?

'I know an old lady who swallowed a fly . . .' he sang softly beneath his breath. 'I don't know why, she swallowed a fly . . .'

Will said, 'We took a vote this morning. The community decided to stay together. We also decided that Jeb is guilty.'

It was on Magnus's lips to say that four people were not a community, but he sensed it would do no good. He asked, 'Without a trial?'

'The evidence speaks for itself.'

'He didn't do it,' Magnus repeated. 'I'm sorry Jacob died, but I'm leaving this afternoon and I'm taking Jeb with me.'

'You can go, but he stays.'

The quiet confidence in Will's voice unnerved Magnus. 'You're not Jacob. You don't have his authority or his back-up. We're leaving.'

Magnus glanced at Father Wingate, but the old man nodded. 'An eye for an eye, a tooth for a tooth. We have to return to the old ways.'

Magnus slowed the van. He would have halted it, but they were not quite out of the village and the hairs on the back of his neck were still bristling. 'You want to execute him?'

'We haven't agreed yet.' Will sounded regretful. 'Raisha and Belle want to keep him locked up indefinitely, but even when our community grows it will be some time before we have the manpower to support prisoners.'

Magnus laughed. It was macabre. So many dead and here they were, preparing to kill one more. 'How do you plan on doing it? A firing squad? The electric chair? Crucifixion?'

Father Wingate sucked in his breath, but it was Will who spoke. 'I told you, we haven't decided. Raisha used to be a chemist, maybe she can make something painless.'

251

They slipped past the *Thank You for Driving Carefully* sign and the national speed limit sign, into a country road bordered on either side by wavering hedgerows, so high they almost formed a tunnel.

Magnus said, 'And if you kill him and then find out you're wrong?'

Father Wingate seemed to have forgotten that the earth was still settling on Jacob's corpse. He touched Magnus's arm and smiled. 'Then God will forgive him and us. Every death is a sacrifice to His name.'

A bird flew low across his windscreen, chirping out a warning call. Magnus tapped the brakes, though he was in no danger of hitting it.

'Even innocent deaths? Aren't you forgetting your Ten Commandments?'

The old man's voice was sure. 'We enter this world corrupted. Only death can purify us. That is what God revealed when He visited the sweats on the world. The plague is an act of love.'

Magnus stole a quick look at Father Wingate. He saw his arthritic fingers and trembling hands and knew that he would not have had the strength to force Henry's wrists into handcuffs or Melody's neck into a noose.

Leave Jeb behind, a mutinous voice in his head whispered. *Get on your way and never think of him again.* But he knew that would invoke another haunting, company for his suicide-cousin, Hugh.

Magnus said, 'I'll take Jeb north with me. You never have to see him again.'

Will said, 'But he would still be alive and Jacob would still be dead.'

252

'It wasn't him.' Magnus wondered why he was so sure of Jeb's innocence. He had been with Will when he had burst into Jeb's room, full of accusations and fury. He had seen the look of bewilderment on Jeb's face turn to anger as he realised what he was being accused of. But the man had been an undercover policeman who had fooled the people closest to him for years. Perhaps rage had got the better of Jeb and he had fired into the dawn, fired at Jacob. Magnus could see it in his mind's eye: Jacob walking the length of the kitchen garden, Jeb standing at his open window, the gun raised and aimed, Jacob falling to the ground, a swift descent driven by gunpowder and gravity. It was a scene he had witnessed countless times on the big screen and too like a movie to mean anything.

They had reached the gates of Tanqueray House. Magnus steered the truck into the drive, braking again as the tyres bit into the unpredictable gravel surface. He gave Will a grim smile. 'Killing is a poor foundation for a community. You don't want any trouble and neither do we. Jeb's a tough enemy, even with a broken leg. Take him on and you take on me as well.'

Father Wingate whispered, 'Your loyalty is misplaced.'

Will said, 'You never asked what I did before the sweats.'

It was true. Magnus had not been interested enough in the man to enquire about his life. He regretted it now. Perhaps if he knew what made Will tick he could persuade him to let Jeb go.

'What did you do?'

'I was a maths teacher. Maths is not the most popular lesson among rough boys. A teacher must learn how to instil discipline, or let their classroom turn into a madhouse. One of the first things I learned was to separate troublemakers. That's why I held a gun to Jeb's head and put him in the dungeon before we left for Jacob's funeral.'

Magnus stopped the truck short of its usual parking place. 'You put him in the what?'

Father Wingate said, 'Tanqueray House really is quite ancient and my ancestors were rather dreadful. They used to put their enemies down there and throw away the key.' His voice grew anxious. 'I don't think we should do that.'

Will nodded. 'We are civilised people. We want justice, not revenge. Taking a life is a grave responsibility. It was one Jacob shouldered when he saved you both and it is one that I am willing to shoulder in turn.'

Magnus shook his head in disbelief. 'Raisha and Belle won't agree.'

Will's smile was modest, a director announcing a star casting. 'Belle helped me.'

'And Raisha?'

Will nodded. 'She agreed.'

'You're mad,' Magnus whispered. 'All of you.'

'My son . . .' Father Wingate squeezed his shoulder.

Will said, 'We're alive and we intend staying alive, even if that means defending ourselves. This man is nothing to you. Go and find your family.'

Magnus closed his eyes. 'When I find my family I want to be able to look them in the eye.'

Thirty-Two

Jeb was a long way down in the dank and the dark. He said, 'I thought you'd be in Jockland by now.'

'You and me both.' Magnus had envisaged a cell more rustic than the one they had shared in Pentonville, but of the same basic design. Instead he was lying flat on his belly in a damp basement, looking through a metal grille set into the ceiling of the cellar below. It was hard to make out Jeb's features in the gloom, but Magnus recognised the hang of his head, the slump of his shoulders. 'I thought I'd stick around and try and save you from the gallows.'

Jeb was sitting on the ground, his good leg bent beneath him, his broken one stretched out straight. He looked up, his face a spot of white in the darkness.

'Is that how they're planning on doing it?'

Magnus shook his head. 'I don't think they have a plan yet. How did they get you down there?'

Jeb grimaced. 'The element of surprise. Belle unlocked my door. I should have realised when I saw her. She was wearing a beret and combat trousers, like a member of the fucking Angry Brigade. I thought she'd come to let me out, but she drew a gun on me. I could have handled that, I actually laughed when

255

I saw it. I didn't reckon on that ugly twat being right behind her. He put Jacob's gun against my head, ordered me into a rusty wheelchair that probably last saw service in World War One and shoved me through the house in it.'

The palms of Magnus's hands were damp and gritty against the cold flagstones, his flesh chilled beneath his jeans and T-shirt. He shifted a little. 'Was Raisha with them?'

'No, she went her own sweet way as usual. The old priest was there, flapping on about how they weren't going to hurt me. But he led the way to the dungeon sure enough.'

'How did they get you down the stairs?'

'A gun is a great motivator.' Jeb rubbed the plaster encasing his broken leg. 'I don't suppose you have one to spare?'

'Will searched me before he let me in here.'

'What's the chance of you laying your hands on one?'

'Slim to non-existent. He's on my back like a shadow.'

Jeb's voice was insistent. 'So fuck him up. Stick a knife in his guts, trip him down the stairs, poison him or suffocate him in his sleep. He's not the man Jacob was. You could take him.'

Magnus was not sure that he would be up to the job, but it made no difference. 'Will made a point of telling me he's hidden the key to the dungeon. He's the only one who knows where it is.'

The grille was too small for a grown man to pass through. Magnus put his face close to its bars, but he could not make out the interior of the cell below.

'What's the door like?'

'Fucking impregnable.' Jeb lowered his head. 'You may as well get going. I'm finished.'

'Not necessarily . . .' Magnus could no longer see the other man in the dim light of the dungeon. It was like speaking to the dead. He said, 'They want justice. If I can prove someone else shot Jacob, they'll let you go.'

Jeb's voice came soft and flat, out of the blackness. 'Do you know how often we solved a murder when I was in the police?' He did not bother to wait for an answer. 'Generally when the killer confessed, or we found them standing by the body holding the murder weapon. This isn't *Murder She Wrote* and you're not Nancy Drew.'

'Jessica Fletcher.'

'Miss Marple, Perry Mason, fucking Columbo: you're not any of them. If you want to get me out of here, get a weapon and take Will out when he's got the key on him.'

There had been too much killing for Magnus to embrace another death. He said, 'There are only four people to choose from: Will, Belle, Raisha and Father Wingate.' In his mind Magnus rejected the notion that Raisha might be the murderer. 'If I can work out who wanted Jacob dead, I'll have found the killer.'

'Just like that.' Jeb's laugh sounded hollow from the shadows below. 'What if it's a motiveless crime?'

Newspapers used to carry headlines of senseless violence. A stranger knifed in the anonymity of rush hour, a dog walker raped in a quiet beauty spot, a child abducted on its way home from school.

Magnus said, 'Even anonymous crimes have a motive, usually power. Jacob and Will locked horns. Now Will's in charge. Maybe I should start with him.'

'No.' Jeb's voice was low as if he were worried someone

might be listening, and Magnus had to strain to hear him. 'Always begin an investigation with the victim. Give Will the slip and search Jacob's room. Look for anything that seems out of place and see where it takes you.'

'And if I find nothing?'

'Raisha's your next stop.'

Magnus shifted his body again, feeling the cellar flagstones rough and damp through his cotton T-shirt. 'She's not the killer.'

'Maybe she is, maybe she isn't, but you're sleeping with her. She likes you and that means she'll be more inclined to talk.'

Magnus wondered how Jeb had known about the two of them. He said, 'I'm not you. I don't sleep with women in order to spy on them.'

'I'm sure your heart is pure.' Jeb's laugh turned into a cough. The sound echoed dimly against the stone walls of his cell. 'But from down here your honour seems a small price for my life.'

Thirty-Three

Magnus had expected Jacob's room to be in military order, but the bed was unmade, its sheets a tangle that spoke of sleepless nights and bad dreams. There was a Bible on the bedside table next to a half-empty glass of whisky. Magnus opened it and a photograph fell to the floor. He picked it up and saw a smiling woman sitting next to two little girls in summer dresses. Magnus had imagined Jacob's wife Annie as a frail brunette in need of protection, but the woman in the photograph was a voluptuous blonde; sexy and capable.

Belle was standing in the doorway. 'Can I see?'

Magnus handed the picture to her.

Belle glanced at the photograph of Jacob's wife and gave a small snort of amusement. 'That's how Marilyn Monroe would have looked if she'd eaten all the pies.'

Magnus took the picture back. He felt a need to defend the dead woman. 'She looks nice.'

Belle shrugged. 'You mean she looks like she could fuck and cook. I guess that's all men will want now.'

The girl had been sarcastic and skittish since Jacob's death. Magnus resisted asking if she was thinking about leaving the group in case she mistook the question for an invitation. He opened the drawer of the bedside cabinet and pawed through its contents: a tube of Savlon, a box of matches, a dead battery. He slid his fingers above and below the drawer, checking its hidden surfaces the way he had seen spies in movies do, but nothing was taped there. He thought Belle would ask what he was looking for, but instead she said, 'How's Jeb?'

'Locked in a dungeon, but otherwise on top of the world.'

'Perhaps I should visit him.'

Magnus lifted Jacob's pillow. He turned to look at the girl. 'Would Will give you the key?'

Belle said, 'Will thinks he's the big man now Jacob's gone. And you know how keen big men are on keys.'

'Would you be willing to ask him for it?'

She paused, considering his question. 'Probably not.'

Magnus dropped the pillow back on the bed and pulled the covers down. There was a stain on the sheet, stiff and familiar. He felt a quick stab of shame and drew the bedclothes over it. 'Because Jeb insulted you?'

'Because he killed Jacob.'

'You don't know that.'

'How sure are you that he didn't?'

'Pretty sure.' Magnus lifted the mattress. The slats below were empty. He had built a bed like it once, a flat-pack from Ikea he had assembled and then christened with a girl he had gone out with in college. He let the mattress flop back down again and sat on it. 'Why didn't you come to the funeral?'

'I couldn't face it.' Belle ran a finger through the dust on a chest of drawers by the window, leaving a wavy line on its surface, a river or a swimming snake. 'Jacob focused on survival so much it's ironic he's dead.' She dragged a hand through her hair. A wisp came away. Belle looked at it and then let it fall to the floor. 'He wouldn't have let you leave, you know. He'd decided you were crucial to *the community*.' She stressed the words. 'I thought about leaving after Melody died.' She raised her eyebrows. 'But where would I go?'

It was Magnus's cue to invite her to join him. He asked, 'How did you end up here?'

'It's not much of a story.' Belle boosted herself up on to the chest of drawers. 'I was working in the King's Cross Starbucks when the sweats started. My dad had a thing about his children learning to fend for themselves.' She swung her legs, watching her feet scissor to and fro. Belle had lost more weight and her limbs looked long and insect-like. 'They were at our holiday home in Portugal when the sweats got them. I should have been there too, but I'd had another row with my dad about money; a big one.' Her eyes met Magnus's. 'He was pretty tight, my dad, but he usually came round in the end. I thought staying in London might make him miss me.' She drew a circle in the dust beside her and dotted her finger into its centre, a glaring eyeball. 'Imagine if I had gone with them. I'd be all alone now in a country where I don't speak the language.'

'Are you certain they didn't make it?'

Belle stared at the surface of the chest of drawers and painted more patterns in the dust. 'Dad telephoned to tell me that Mum was ill. I could tell he was worried, but he didn't sound frantic. I thought she would be okay. He phoned back a day later. She had died and my sister was in hospital.' Belle added another swirl to her dustscape. 'I thought grief

261

had made his voice hoarse, but later I realised it was the sickness. I phoned him back, phoned all of that day, into the night, through the next day and the next, but that was the last time I spoke to him.' Her voice was flat, as if none of it mattered. 'I wasn't sure what to do so I phoned my aunt in Shropshire. We decided I should go and stay with her, but just as I was about to get on the train she called to say that she was unwell. I think she would have liked me to come anyway, but much as I was fond of my aunt, I wasn't willing to die for her.

'The girls I was sharing a flat with both went home. I had nowhere to go, so I stayed on, watching television and emailing and texting friends. One by one they stopped replying.' She gave a small, sad smile. 'I used to have some good friends.' Her eyes were slightly glazed, her voice far away. 'I ran out of food, but the Internet and television were trending riots and curfews and I was scared to go outside. I think I was ill for a few days, it's all a bit hazy, but I do remember hearing a woman screaming in the street outside, as if she were being murdered, and hiding under my bedclothes praying for her to shut up. Then the Internet went off. So did the water and electricity. I saw a rat in the toilet. I wasn't sure if it was real or if I was hallucinating, but somehow after that the flat didn't seem safe any more. I knew that if I was going to survive I had to get out of London.'

Magnus remembered his own flight from the city. The smashed shops, abandoned cars and dead bodies lying forsaken in the streets. 'That couldn't have been easy.'

Belle's eyes met his. 'There were gangs rounding up women, did you know that?'

'No.'

'I saw one. Men armed with rifles guarding half a dozen women who were handcuffed to a chain. One of them was only a girl, a tiny little thing with big eyes. Another was ancient, a pensioner. It didn't seem to matter what age they were or what they looked like, as long as they were female. A couple of the women were bruised and staggering, as if they'd been beaten up. I hid in a shop and watched the men force them into a van. After that I got myself a knife and only ever travelled at night.' Belle had lowered her head as she spoke; now she raised her eyes to his. 'I get so scared. I've thought about leaving ever since Melody hanged herself. But what if I met men like that?'

'You trusted Jacob.'

'Not straight away. I met Melody first. She was on a foraging trip. I followed her back here. She told me later that she knew I was there, but didn't want to scare me away. That was what Melody was like, gentle. She persuaded me to stay the night and introduced me to Jacob. I thought the priest's collar was probably a con. But by that time I was in bad shape. Melody and Raisha were living here and they seemed okay. I needed to be with other people and so I took a chance.'

'Jacob thought Melody and Henry had been murdered.'

Belle shrugged. 'Jacob wanted to live more than any of us. I think his lust for life embarrassed him, but he couldn't help it. The idea that survivors would kill themselves offended him.' She gave Magnus an apologetic look, as if the strength of her own opinion had surprised her. 'That's what I think, for what it's worth.'

263

'Maybe you're right, but Jacob was definitely murdered.' Magnus kept his voice gentle. 'Do you know why he died?'

Belle gave a frightened giggle. 'He died because someone shot his head off.' She slid off the chest of drawers. 'I don't know why you're so keen on getting Jeb out. Even if he didn't shoot Jacob he killed that woman and her child. Either way he deserves to be locked up.'

'If he didn't kill Jacob then someone else did. Doesn't that bother you?'

'It bothers me.'

Magnus touched her arm. 'Do you know the reason Jacob died?'

Belle gave him a brilliant smile, an underweight chorus girl whose grin could shine all the way to the back row. 'I think he must have really pissed someone off.'

Thirty-Four

Magnus spent the next hour searching Jacob's room, but there was no diary, no letter beginning *In the event of my death* . . . The closest he came was a scrap of paper tucked into the pocket of a pair of trousers.

> *Motives*
> *Love*
> ~~*Money*~~
> *Power*

The priest had scored a line through money, leaving love and power, like words waiting to be tattooed on the knuckles of someone's hands. Jeb and Belle had made love, but there was none lost between them now. Will had taken charge of the group, but he was not a natural leader and Magnus thought he might secretly be grateful if someone came along to relieve him of that power.

'Love and power,' he whispered under his breath. One of the puppies wandered into the room and nudged his leg. Magnus scrunched its ears and the dog, satisfied that all was well, jumped on to the half-made bed. Magnus stared out of the window, beyond the garden where Jacob had died and into the darkening evening. Killing was the execution of power and love could also be mercy. There was power in love too, he supposed. Father Wingate's all-powerful God killed for the love of humanity, or so the old man insisted.

'Love and power.'

The dog on the bed shifted in its sleep. A flock of birds swooped over the vegetable beds, into the woods beyond. He would go down to the lower basement and speak to Jeb through the grille before it got too dark to see.

He was about to turn away from the window when a slight figure dressed in a dark tracksuit darted across the garden. Raisha had pulled the jacket's hood up, hiding her features, but Magnus did not need to see her face to know that it was her. He left Jacob's room, hurried down the stairs, through the kitchen and out into the dusk. The garden was empty. He jogged past the vegetable beds, past the spot where Jacob had died, in the direction Raisha had taken. There was no sign of her. Magnus skirted the wall until he saw a wrought-iron gate he had not noticed before. He pulled and pushed it, but the gate was locked.

'Raisha?' He hissed her name. There was no reply, only the sound of the breeze lifting the trees. The air was heavy with a presentiment of rain. 'Raisha?'

Something caught his eye. He looked back at the house and saw the paraffin lamps glow into life on the kitchen windowsills, casting oblongs of light on to the lawn. Inside Father Wingate, dressed in a baggy jumper, crossed the kitchen and disappeared from Magnus's sightline.

Magnus found a foothold on the rough stone wall, and

boosted himself upward with the help of the gate's wrought-iron curlicues. The first time he lost his grip and fell on to the damp grass. But the second time he made it on to the top of the wall. He sat there for a moment hoping to spot Raisha, but the belt of trees restricted his view, nodding and bobbing in the twilight. Magnus dropped down on to the other side. There was slim chance of finding anyone in the woods, but he might catch a glimpse of her in the open fields beyond.

Magnus jogged into the knotty pine scent of the wood and went from gloaming into night. There was a path of sorts, but the men who had husbanded the trees were all dead, no one had cleared it for a while and it was littered with twigs and fallen branches. Magnus slowed his pace, careful not to trip. His death might be waiting here, far from the sea, in a foreign landscape of tree trunks and waving branches, but there was no anticipating death, not unless you took the path his cousin Hugh had followed. 'The road less travelled,' Jacob had said, after he shot the driver of the yellow Audi.

Magnus had thought the evening silent, but things moved everywhere in the wood, rustling the undergrowth, creaking in the treetops above. There could be people here too: canny survivors who hid in the troll darkness instead of making a show of themselves, cutting harvests that weren't theirs, burning barns, lighting lamps in windows and inviting murder. Magnus had assumed someone from their community had done the killings, but what if it was an outsider, some silent watcher picking them off one by one like a bogeyman in one of the video nasties he and Hugh had been thrilled by as teenagers? Something big shifted up ahead and

Magnus froze, catching his breath, until whatever it was – a deer, badger, escaped jaguar, all claws and hunger – moved away. Magnus forced his breaths into an even rhythm and walked steadily into the not quite pitch-dark. Ghosties and ghoulies were stories for children. Orkney was short on trees, but the islands had their own legends, stories of seal folk, beautiful selkies who beguiled mortals into the sea.

'Do you think something drew him there?' his sister Rhona had asked, not long after Hugh drowned. The two of them were in the Snapper Bar, both three sheets to the wind, though it was not yet dinner time. 'Hugh was always sensitive, maybe something called to him.' Magnus had walked away, out through the bar and down to the harbour for fear that he might slap her face.

There had been other nonsense spoken. 'The sea demands her due,' an old soak had said, his Guinness almost down to its last dregs of foam; low tide. Magnus had seen photographs in Tankerness museum of barrels of beer taken down to the shoreline and axed open. Men with waxed moustaches, flat caps and collarless shirts grinning as if the tradition was simply that and not a precaution; a nod to the old gods that they were not forgotten. When Magnus was around seven years old, his father had told him that in his grandfather's time it had sometimes been a sheep they had foregone, rowing the poor beast out too far for it to swim back. Magnus had imagined the scene too well. The creature's legs scrabbling as it was dropped over the side, the men careful not to upset the boat, the sheep trying to swim to shore, its head a speck of white above the water until the waves dragged it under. Magnus's father must have enjoyed the effect of his story because he had gone on to say that in the days of the ancestors the sacrifice had been more vital; a girl or a boy taken out and drowned. The prospect had given Magnus nightmares for years after.

'The sea demands her due,' the old soak had said and Magnus had pulled back his fist.

'The sea was not due my cousin.'

The quality of the light up ahead was different, the branches of the trees at the edge of the wood shifting against the brighter dark of the night sky. Magnus tripped in his haste to put the trees behind him. He righted himself and emerged into the edge of a field of yellow rape, looking down on to a low valley. Now that he was out of the shelter of the trees he could see the outline of the moon, a dim silver glow disappearing behind the clouds. He smelled rain on the air again and cursed himself for not stopping to grab a jacket. The crop of rape was beginning to rot. It added a sharp edge to the gunpowder scent of approaching storm. Raisha was somewhere ahead of him. Magnus started to walk. The fields beyond his were dark, but there was a patch of light further down the valley that might be a house. He would make for it and then, if Raisha was not there, turn back. The night boomed and he cursed again. When he was a young boy he had pictured thunder as giants' feet pounding across the islands, flinging standing stones this way and that in a mighty game. It would be easy to return to the old suspicions now that the comfort of electricity was gone. Another rumble sounded. Magnus felt a drop of rain and picked up his pace. He dreaded the prospect of the house up ahead, the chance that he might interrupt Raisha in the act

269

of tending some dead bairn. A fork of lightning jagged across the sky and he saw clearly for an instant the overgrown fields divided by neglected hedges and the white-painted house halfway down the valley. Magnus hurried on. Twice, three times he staggered and once he fell his full length. Rain stabbed his face, single drops that swiftened into a torrent, soaking through his T-shirt and jeans. Another bolt of lightning reived the sky and he knew that to turn back and make for the shelter of the woods would be foolish. He thought of Jeb listening to the thunder in the dungeon deep beneath the house and knew that the chance of proving him innocent was next to zero.

'A fool's errand,' he whispered into the rush of wind and water, his face streaming with raindrops. 'A fool's bloody errand.'

The house was bigger than Magnus had thought from the glances the lightning flashes had granted him. It was more modern too. A barn expanded and converted into someone's grand design. There were houses like it on Orkney, some of them barely used holiday homes, walls of glass juxtaposed with stones cut by the ancients and plundered from their sacred sites by Christian farmers. His father had made fun of them, but Magnus would have been happy to live in one; daylight streaming through an expanse of double glazing, a view of the Atlantic Ocean stretched out before him. There would be stylish homes for the taking now. The thought was no comfort.

The building was in darkness, his drowned face a miserable reflection in its glass wall. Magnus put his face to the glass, shielding his eyes. He could make out a long dining table, edged by chairs. Something moved within, or perhaps it was just a reflection of the driving rain.

'Raisha?' He tried to slide one of the doors open, but it was locked tight. 'Fuck.' Another lightning flash illuminated the night and Magnus saw his reflection again: slick-haired and wild-eyed; a seal-man. He stumbled to the front door and tried its handle. The door was made of heavy oak and Magnus thought it was not going to shift, but then it swung open and he lurched into the hallway. The floor was tiled in marble more suited to a metropolitan hotel. His feet slipped, but Magnus righted himself against a table, almost upsetting the withered remnants of an extravagant orchid display. The house smelled musty, but there was none of the foulness Magnus had feared. He shut the door gently behind him, feeling a sense of trespass. Water pooled from his clothes on to the expensive floor tiles. He was shivering and his jeans were waterlogged, but he resisted the urge to strip them off.

'Raisha?' Somewhere deep in the house he heard a sound. It was dark in the hallway and Magnus wished he had had the foresight to bring a torch with him. 'It's Magnus.'

There was a series of doors on either side of him, but the sound had come from up ahead. He walked slowly down the corridor, past framed photographs of the people who had once lived there, until he reached the family room. The noise was louder, a clicking sound too random to be code. A breeze touched his face and he noticed a small window that had been left ajar. The cord of its venetian blind was moving with the wind, tapping against the glass.

'Shit.'

Magnus felt a lowering of the soul. He closed the window

and the house became still. A dishtowel hung on a hook beside the sink. He mopped his face and neck with it and gave his hair a brisk rub. The room had been kitchen, dining room, sitting room and playroom. It was big enough to shelter a small herd of cattle. Magnus tried to picture his family sharing such a space when he was a boy, but the image eluded him. They had been close, but they had needed dividing walls to keep them together. Perhaps the family enshrined in the photographs had coexisted here, each with their own laptop, phone or tablet, in a small galaxy of virtual worlds.

Two large couches faced each other across a coffee table. One of the couches had a view of a garden equipped with a swing and a climbing frame. The other faced the kitchen area. The space was meant to be full of light and people, not this tomb-like silence. He wondered how Raisha could go on these expeditions and be reminded of all that was lost. Magnus had no appetite for searching the other rooms. He would dry off, wait for the storm to die down and then make his way back to the big house and see what was to be done about Jeb. Magnus kicked off his boots and peeled himself free of his sodden jeans, T-shirt and underwear. He hung his clothes over a couple of dining chairs to dry, shivering. A woollen blanket was draped over the arm of one of the settees. His skin was wet and his bare feet left a trail of damp footsteps as he crossed the room towards it. Something moved in the shadows and a curse escaped him.

Raisha was hidden, curled in the nook of the couch that faced the garden. She cringed as if she feared he might hit

272

her. Magnus grabbed the blanket and wrapped it around his body like a plaid. 'Don't worry. I'm not going to hurt you.'

Raisha sat up and drew her knees up until they almost touched her chin. 'Did you follow me?'

Magnus pulled the blanket closer and sat on the couch that faced Raisha's. It felt dangerous, sitting with his back to the countryside, but he could tell the woman wanted him nowhere near her.

'It was an impulse. I saw you crossing the lawn.'

'I didn't know you'd come after me until I saw your face at the window.'

Magnus forced a smile. 'That must have given you a shock.'

Raisha nodded. 'You looked different. Then I saw it was you.'

'You didn't answer when I called your name.' He tried to keep the hurt out of his voice.

'I told you, I was scared.'

'Of me?' Magnus had been wedded to fear since Pentonville, but he had not expected Raisha to be afraid of him.

She shrugged. 'Of everyone. We all saw things in the city. I thought it would be safer in the countryside but there's killing here too.'

Magnus adjusted the blanket. The wool was rough and comforting against his bare skin. 'Will said you voted to have Jeb locked up.'

'I voted for law.' Raisha looked at her knees. 'Belle told me what he had done to that poor woman and her child, so I thought it must have been Jeb who shot Jacob, but later . . .' Her voice tailed away.

Magnus said, 'What did you think later?'

'Later I thought it could have been anyone. We picked on Jeb because we wanted to find Jacob's killer and make ourselves safe, but what if it wasn't him?'

Magnus leaned forward. He realised that their conversations had always been conducted in half-whispers. 'Jacob told me that he thought Melody and Henry might have been deliberately killed.' He outlined the priest's theory: the chair that had been kicked too far from the corpse, the wounds that were too sure to be self-inflicted.

Raisha buried her face in her knees; he thought that she was crying, but when she looked up her eyes were dry.

'I'd already decided to leave. Now I know I made the right choice.'

'You think Jacob was right?'

'I don't know.' Raisha looked beyond him, out through the rain-spattered wall of glass and into the garden where children used to play. 'Melody was sad, we all are, but I was surprised when she hanged herself; hurt too that she hadn't come to me. Still, I wasn't shocked the way that I would have been before the sweats. As for Henry . . .'

'What about Henry?'

'Henry was like us, a survivor. I knew he liked Melody, we all did. Her death upset him, but I never for a moment thought he would kill himself. He was too selfish for suicide.'

Magnus wondered if Raisha had slept with Henry and felt an unexpected stab of jealousy.

He said, 'Where will you go?'

'I don't know.' Raisha had taken off her boots. She wiggled her toes and looked at her feet, avoiding Magnus's eyes. 'I'll travel on my own for a while, but I'll probably join some other community eventually. There are others out there, you know. I've seen messages painted on walls and heard the sound of car engines in the distance. They can't all be mad.'

'You could come north with me.'

'To Scotland?' Raisha's eyes met his. She smiled. 'No.'

He wanted to ask why not but said, 'Too cold?'

'I need to be alone for a while. You should go soon though, before anything else happens.'

'I need to get Jeb out first.'

'Why?'

Her question surprised Magnus and he stumbled a little over his words. 'There's no proof that Jeb killed Jacob and I wouldn't have got this far without him. I owe him.'

Raisha leaned forward and took his hand in hers, no longer frightened. 'The sweats have put us on the edge of a new world. Maybe we don't need people like Jeb in it.'

Magnus pulled free of her grasp. 'We can't start killing people just because we don't like them.'

'I don't mean we should execute him . . .'

'What do you mean?' The scent of Pentonville was back in Magnus's nostrils. 'We should lock people up indefinitely without a trial?'

Raisha's smile was chastened. 'You're right but . . .' She left the sentence hanging in the air.

'But what?'

'It would be nice to be like Father Wingate and believe that there was some purpose to all this. The sweats took my family, but it left people like Jeb. He's a child-killer.'

'He denies it.'

'And you believe him? He went to jail.'

'Innocent people sometimes end up in jail.'

'Including you?'

'I didn't get a trial, perhaps that's why I'm so picky about it.'

'Jeb got a fair one and the jury found him guilty.'

Magnus tried to conjure the words Jeb had used to recount the story of Cherry jumping from the balcony with her daughter in her arms, but it was as if the experience had become his own. He saw a red-haired woman teetering on a balustrade, a hysterical child reaching towards him.

'Jeb's no saint, but I don't believe he killed his girlfriend and her daughter.'

'I'd almost rather he had.' Raisha gave an involuntary glance at the window. 'If you're right, then Jacob's killer could still be out there.'

Magnus followed her gaze. The wind was making the plants in the overgrown garden dance, tugging at the untidy hedgerows and the trees on the ridge of the valley. The garden swing rocked on its frame and he reminded himself that he did not believe in ghosts.

'You said Henry was fond of Melody and sad when she died. How were the others?'

Raisha hugged her knees. 'Pretty much as you'd expect. Will never says much, but after Melody's death he shut down. We all dug her grave together, even Father Wingate took a brief turn of the shovel. It was Jacob's idea, an attempt at keeping the community together. We talked about Melody as we dug, what she had meant to us. I don't think Will said a word.'

Magnus said, 'What about Father Wingate?'

'Old people are programmed to accept death; if they

weren't they'd go mad. Father Wingate got dressed in his full regalia and led the service. You could tell he was grieving, Melody had spent a lot of time with him, but the ceremony seemed to buoy him up. By the time we got back to the house he was almost his old self.'

Magnus nodded. 'He was like that at Jacob's funeral, sad but energised. As if something necessary had been accomplished and we could get on with things now.'

'It's not so unusual. My husband's grandmother went to lots of funerals in her later years. She was a nice old lady, but she usually came back with a spring in her step and stories about who had said what to whom.'

Raisha sank into silence, as if the memory of her husband and his relatives had ambushed her.

Magnus went to the sink and poured them both a glass of water. He wondered how long it would be before the water system gave out and they had to resort to rivers and wells. There was so much he did not know. He set the glasses on the table between them.

'You said Melody spent a lot of time with Father Wingate. What did they do together?'

Raisha sipped her water. 'Melody became increasingly disturbed in the weeks before she killed herself. I wanted her to try anti-psychotic medication. Will and I even hatched a plan to scout chemist's shops looking for drugs that might work, but she refused. Father Wingate was counselling her.'

'Is he a qualified counsellor?'

Raisha shrugged. 'The rest of us were too stunned by our own losses to be much use to anyone else. Jacob gave Father Wingate his blessing and so the rest of us left them to it.'

'How did Jacob react to her death?'

'You know Jacob, he is . . . he was a practical man. Henry discovered Melody's body, but it was Jacob who cut her down, tried to revive her and when he couldn't, organised the funeral. I suppose his army training kicked in, but once she was safely in the ground he took to his room for a couple of days. I don't think I fully understood the phrase "drowning your sorrows" until Jacob finally emerged. He stank like a distillery and looked like a dead man.'

The phrase recalled his cousin Hugh so strongly Magnus could almost feel him at his elbow.

'Jacob's beyond suspicion now.'

Raisha gave an upside-down smile. 'The innocent dead.'

Magnus looked out at the garden again. The swing rocked to and fro, to and fro, and a shiver ran through him that had nothing to do with the cold. He asked, 'What about Belle?'

Raisha's smile died. 'Belle was jealous of Melody. Belle's pretty, but Melody was beautiful. Imagine how that feels, so few people left and even then there's someone better than you.'

'Better?'

'More desirable.' Raisha leaned forward. 'Belle's fragile. She needs men to find her attractive. Have you noticed how often she mentions her dad? Girls like her need a father figure, especially after their daddy dies. Belle might not know it, but she slept with Jeb because she wanted to make Jacob jealous.'

A laugh escaped Magnus. 'Jacob was at least twice her age.'

'Don't sound so shocked, it happens. Anyway, it wasn't on the cards. Jacob preferred mature women.'

The stab of jealousy surprised him again, warm in his stomach; a twist of the bowels. 'Women like you?'

'Not like me. Jacob's sort wants a woman who will look after him. Mothers they can sleep with. I was a mother to my children, not to my husband.' Raisha's tone deadened again. 'Jacob thought you were misguided, looking for your family. I think you are too, but for different reasons. As long as you don't go home you can imagine they're alive. The rest of us know we've lost everyone. We're like people who have been so badly beaten we're no longer certain which parts of us are hurting.'

Dawn would be on them soon. The room was beginning to lighten, its colours starting to reveal themselves: warm yellows and umbers set against a backdrop of white that was not white but some cleverly calibrated pink or blue.

Magnus said, 'For good or for bad, I need to know.'

'Of course you do. But you also know I'm right. The real reason you're trying to find out who killed Jacob is to avoid going home. You want to keep your family alive, in your head if nowhere else.'

Magnus got up and went to the window. The storm had almost blown itself out. The rising sun was still hidden behind the treetops, but the sky was tinged with pink and the landscape had taken on a rosy tint at odds with the heaviness in his chest.

He said, 'You surely don't believe Belle murdered Melody and then went on to shoot Jacob because of some love triangle?'

Raisha joined him at the window. Magnus was still naked except for the blanket and her closeness bothered him. She said, 'Of course not. Even if it was a serious motive I don't think Belle has it in her to kill anyone in cold blood. She's not as soft as she looks, but it's hard to imagine her as a murderer.'

He turned to face her. 'Perhaps it wasn't any of them.'

Raisha touched his bare shoulder with her fingertips. She leaned in close, as if for a kiss, and whispered, 'Or perhaps it was your friend, the child-killer.'

Magnus lifted Raisha's hand from his shoulder. His clothes were hanging on the dining chairs where he had left them. He crossed the room and felt his jeans. They were still wet, but he pulled them on, wincing at the cold cardboard sensation of damp denim against his skin.

'How was Belle after Melody's suicide?' Magnus shucked on his muddy T-shirt.

Raisha had returned to the couch and sat watching him with an amused expression on her face. 'True to character. The real tragedy wasn't Melody's death but that it made Belle feel bad.'

He pulled out a chair and sat on it. 'You're hard on her.'

'Perhaps, but you weren't there. She was so hysterical there was no space for anyone else to grieve. In the end I gave her something to help her sleep.'

Magnus wondered if Raisha had been jealous of Belle the way she said the girl had been of Melody.

As if on cue she said, 'You didn't ask about me.'

'Okay, how about you?'

Raisha levelled her gaze and her eyes met his. 'A big part of me was sorry Melody killed herself, another part envied her for having the strength to do it.'

Her words about medicating Melody and sedating Belle had reminded Magnus that Raisha was a chemist. He said, 'Are you planning on killing yourself?'

'I told you, I can't. I'm cursed with life.'

She gave the smile that signalled that Magnus could come to her. But the sun was fully up and all around the large room there were signs of the family who used to live there. Ghosts were meant to occupy the dark, but it felt to him that they had become more alive with the day. Magnus pulled on his socks and boots, ready to leave the house to them.

Thirty-Five

They embraced on the doorstep of the deserted house. Raisha's hair was damp. Magnus breathed in its rosemary and lavender scent and wished that they had braved the phantoms and grasped a last chance to make love. He felt the slightness of Raisha's frame, her birdlike bones beneath their thin coating of flesh, and remembered the women Belle had seen chained together.

'Be careful, there are dangerous people about.'

'That's why I'm travelling quietly.' Raisha pulled free of his grasp and nodded to a bicycle, a lightweight multi-gear affair, propped against the wall of the house. A cycling helmet dangled from its handlebars. 'It's the reason I came back here.'

'Did you bury the children who lived in this house?'

'It was empty. Maybe they're alive somewhere, with their parents.' Raisha's eyes met his. 'You think I'm mad.'

'Not mad, but I don't understand why you do it.'

She leaned into him, her arms circled his waist and she spoke into his chest. 'I didn't set out to become an undertaker. I wanted to find children who were alive and make them safe, but all I found were corpses. I couldn't leave them to rot.'

Magnus stroked her hair. 'And now?'

'That's another reason I have to move on.' Raisha pulled away. She tucked her trousers into her socks, ready to mount the bike. 'If there are children left alive, then they need someone to look after them.'

'Did you sleep with me in the hope of becoming pregnant?' The thought would have infuriated him before the sweats.

Raisha looked up. 'I slept with you to shut out the pictures in my head. My second boy, Imran, was a difficult pregnancy and an even more difficult birth. We were both lucky to survive, but I can't have any more children. I came to terms with it; after all I had two beautiful, healthy boys.'

A swoop of disappointment pierced Magnus's chest. 'I'm sorry.'

Raisha nodded, acknowledging his sympathy. She reached up and gave him a kiss on the cheek.

'I've decided not to dwell on how things were, or how they are. I'm going to try and imagine how they might be. You should do the same. Forget Jacob, Jeb and the rest of them, they'll only bring you more grief.'

It was good advice, impossible for him to take.

Magnus said, 'No one could save the people who died from the sweats, but I might be able to save Jeb. I've got a feeling that if I don't try, his death will haunt me.'

Raisha's voice was almost playful. 'What's one more ghost?'

'One too many.'

Raisha had the cycling helmet in her hand. She swung it gently by its chinstrap, as if trying to make up her mind about something. 'I didn't tell you this before, because I didn't want to encourage you, but I saw Belle leave the barn not long before Henry discovered Melody's body.'

Magnus took a step towards her. 'What are you trying to say?'

'I don't know.' Raisha caught the helmet with her free hand and then set it swinging again. 'I was sitting on the doorstep of one of the outhouses when I saw Belle head for the barn. Melody had gone past earlier, crying. I wasn't in the mood for talking to anyone and so I sat as still as I could and hoped they wouldn't notice me. I shouldn't have worried.' She gave the helmet another shove. 'They were both too caught up in themselves to see me. I was about to find somewhere quieter to sit when Belle ran out of the barn into the courtyard. I saw her face as she passed. She looked stricken, as if her whole body were screaming, but she didn't make a sound.'

'You didn't go after her, or go into the barn to see what had upset her?'

There was a bench in the centre of the lawn. Raisha crossed the grass and sat on it. Magnus followed her. The seat was small and their thighs touched. Raisha looked straight ahead, as if there had been no embrace, no lovemaking between them. 'I couldn't be expected to care that Belle was upset. We were all upset. It was only later that I wondered . . .'

Magnus finished the sentence for her. 'If Melody was already dead?' Raisha nodded and he asked, 'What did the others say?'

Raisha had set the crown of the helmet on her knee and was fiddling with its straps. She spoke without looking at him. 'I didn't say anything about it to them. I wanted to give Belle a chance to explain.'

Someone had planted meadow flowers at the steep end of the garden, where the lawn dipped down towards a secluded lane. Cornflowers, poppies, wild orchids and yellow daisies lifted open faces to busy squadrons of attentive bees. Raisha watched them as she spoke. 'Belle told me that she'd been reading by the library window and noticed Melody go into the barn. Belle wanted to speak to her, but something about the way Melody was walking made her think she was crying and so, uncharacteristically for Belle, she decided to give her some privacy. She stayed by the window and waited for Melody to come out.'

The garden was still except for the harried drone of the bees.

Magnus said, 'But she didn't.'

'She didn't. Eventually Belle's patience was exhausted and she went to find her.' Raisha let the straps of the cycling helmet go and looked at Magnus. 'She said Melody had already hanged herself.' Raisha's eyes were wide. 'All the things we saw in the cities, some of the things we did to stay alive, it's a wonder we aren't all insane. Did I tell you I sometimes see my children?'

It was a warm morning, but the hairs on Magnus's arms rose on end. 'No, you didn't.'

'They're always together. I catch sight of them standing by the side of the road, or on the edge of a room, watching me. It doesn't work if I look for them. They like to surprise me.'

Magnus glanced back towards the house, as if he expected to see two small boys watching them from the doorway. 'Do you think they're real?'

'You mean do I think they're ghosts or figments of my imagination?'

'I don't know what I mean.'

'I like to think they're real and that one day I'll be able to hold them both again.' A tremor passed through Raisha. 'Belle has her own horrors. She said that there was something about the way that Melody's body was turning on the rope that was too horrible to bear. It was as if she were calling all the dead into the barn. Belle ran out of there, back to the big house and hid in her bedroom. When Henry went looking for some tool or other and found Melody, Belle heard the commotion and came to her senses. By the time she reached the barn Jacob had cut Melody down. When Belle saw how hard he was working to revive her, it occurred to her that Melody might still have been alive when she found her. That was when she went into hysterics. She kept repeating, *She was alive, she was alive.*'

Magnus said, 'And no one else went into the barn before Henry, except for Melody and Belle?'

'They couldn't have without my noticing.'

A high-pitched whine sounded in the distance. It took Magnus a second to grasp what it was and then he recognised the faint roar of motorbikes coming from somewhere towards the south. There were more than two of them, but beyond that he could not be sure. Magnus realised that he was holding his breath. He whispered, 'Did you hear that?'

Raisha nodded. 'I've heard them before, always at a distance, but from different directions, as if they're circling the district.' She had lowered her voice as well, as if the distant motorcyclists might be in danger of overhearing her. 'I think there are more of them this time.'

'More survivors.'

Raisha got to her feet. The view of open countryside was blocked by the high hedgerows that edged the lane, but she stood on her tiptoes, as if there might be a chance of catching sight of the motorcyclists. 'More survivors.'

Magnus said, 'Are they the real reason you're going? They might be a better prospect.'

Raisha turned her back on him and crossed the lawn to her bike. 'Being too eager to join up with people hasn't worked out well. I'll take more care next time, if there is a next time.'

The sound of the motorbikes had dislodged Melody's death from Magnus's mind, but the realisation that Raisha was about to leave focused him. He followed her across the grass.

'Belle could have knocked the chair away from the body in her panic to get out of the barn.'

Raisha had fixed a tent and two saddlebags to the back of the bike. She tugged at their fastenings, checking they were secure.

'If she did, then Jacob was mistaken and Melody's death was exactly as it seemed: a straightforward suicide.'

Magnus said, 'But it still wouldn't explain what happened to Henry or Jacob.'

Raisha bundled up her hair, put the cycling helmet on her head and buckled its strap beneath her chin. The helmet was sleek and modern. It tapered in a point down the nape of her neck, like the skull of an extra-terrestrial in a sci-fi movie. Her brown eyes met his and this time there was no flirt in them.

'As far as I'm concerned Henry committed suicide and

287

your friend Jeb killed Jacob. If you really want to find your family you should stop wasting time and be on your way.'

Magnus said, 'You know there was more to it. I can see it in your eyes.'

Raisha held his gaze. 'You can see nothing in my eyes. There is nothing left in them to see.'

Magnus stood at the gate and watched Raisha cycle away from him. She wobbled a little as she rounded the bend. He held his breath, half expecting her to take a tumble, but she turned the corner and disappeared out of sight. As soon as she had gone a sense of his aloneness hit him, as hard and as sudden as Johnny Dongo's fist. Magnus sank into a squat and took a series of deep breaths. He should not have let her go, but even though Raisha had told him there was another bike in the garage of the house he waited, breathing in and out, while the distance between them grew longer.

Thirty-Six

Six motorbikes were propped on the gravel outside Tanqueray House, waiting for their riders like horses tied outside a saloon in a cowboy movie. Magnus stood on the edge of the overgrown drive under the shelter of the trees, willing his brain to work. He had cycled back on the companion to the bicycle Raisha had commandeered. The sleepless night had exhausted Magnus, his damp jeans had chafed his skin and the lanes' twists and turns had been testing. Newcomers were not necessarily bad news, but Magnus felt uneasy and ill-equipped for strangers.

He could ride off, find a clean bed, sleep the day away and then head north under the cover of night. Magnus thought of Jeb locked in the dark foundations of the building. If their positions were reversed, would Jeb take risks to save him? Magnus doubted it, but the only way to vanquish the sweats was to return to a point where life was sacred. Freeing Jeb and discovering Jacob's murderer was part of that.

It was cold and dank-smelling beneath the trees. He hid his bike in the undergrowth and made his way past the barn where Melody had hanged herself, to the back of the house. Magnus pressed his spine against the kitchen wall,

289

remembering the escape from Pentonville and the way Jeb had kept his silhouette narrow. The wall's rough stone snagged against the back of his T-shirt as he edged towards the window.

The men in the kitchen looked as tired as he felt. There were five of them, hunched round the table, spooning soup into their mouths. Father Wingate was with them. The priest's face was animated. He was talking, moving his hands in the air to illustrate a point, but Magnus could not hear what he was saying. He moved closer to the window, trying to see if Belle or Will were in the room. Father Wingate's eyes met his through the glass. The old priest looked away and Magnus drew back, knowing that if everything had been okay Father Wingate would have beckoned him inside.

From where he was standing, his body flattened against the wall, Magnus had a clear view to where Jacob had been shot. Jacob or Jeb would have been better equipped to deal with the invaders, if that was what the men were, but the soldier-priest was dead and Jeb locked in the dungeon. Magnus edged his way to the side of the house and the door Father Wingate had half-jokingly referred to as the trades-men's entrance.

Voices rumbled deep and masculine from somewhere in the front rooms of the house, but the passageway was empty. Magnus jogged along it until he reached the door to the basement. He had eased it open when he heard a clatter of claws against the tiled floor and saw the puppies rushing to greet him, their tails wagging wildly. One of them gave a welcoming bark and a hand grabbed Magnus's arm. *Fuck!* The word escaped him; a whisper of breath and spit.

290

Belle put a finger to her lips. She nodded at the door and followed him into the damp darkness beyond, careful to leave the puppies in the hallway. They whined and Magnus feared the dogs would give them away, but then he heard them clattering off on some new adventure. Belle clicked on a torch and led the way to a twisting stone staircase. Magnus waited until they were another level down before he spoke.

'Who are they?'

'I don't know.' Belle's face shone pale in the gloom. 'But I'm staying clear of them.'

'Do you know what they want?'

'They say they're just after a bit of food and shelter, then they'll go on their way.'

'But?'

'You remember the gang I saw in London?'

'The women chained together? These are the same men?'

'No, but they remind me of them. I hid when I heard their bikes, but I've been watching them. They're like a pack of dogs, growling at each other, competing for position, out for what they can get.'

'They don't know you're here?'

'As long as Will doesn't tell them, I think I'm okay, so far. This house is full of hidden stairways and passages.'

Magnus remembered the concealed staircase Jacob had led him up, on the night he had died. It seemed a long time ago. He said, 'Will's not completely stupid. He won't tell them there are women here.'

A woman, he reminded himself. Raisha was gone.

Belle said, 'That's the bad part. I think he wants to impress them. The pack has a leader, I don't know his name. He's the shortest of the bunch, but the rest of them seem to defer to him. He's Will's latest bromance.'

'Will's gay?' The thought had never occurred to Magnus.

Belle's whisper was sharp with impatience. 'I mean he admires him. You must have noticed, since Jacob died it's like Will's been trying to be him. He wouldn't deliberately set out to harm me, but these guys are "real men", the way Jacob was a "real man".' Belle lifted up the hem of her T-shirt and showed him the gun stuffed into the waistband of her jeans. It was the same one she had given to Jeb, the same one that had supposedly killed Jacob. 'It's loaded.'

'It's also ancient. Be careful it doesn't blow your legs off.'

'Ha bloody ha.' Belle danced the torch up and down his body, seeing him properly for the first time since they had snuck into the darkness of the basement. 'What happened to you? You're a mess.'

Magnus told her an edited version of his night: the flight through the forest to the house where Raisha was hiding; Raisha cycling away, in search of children to help.

Belle said, 'I guess this is where I'm meant to say, plenty more fish in the sea.'

She giggled and Magnus joined in, both of them laughing more than the joke warranted.

A distant shout echoed up the stone staircase. Magnus turned towards it. 'It's Jeb.'

Belle said, 'I don't want to see him.'

But Magnus had taken the torch from her and was hurrying down the winding stairs to the lower depths.

Thirty-Seven

Magnus shone the beam of the torch through the grille in the floor, down into the cell below. Jeb was stretched out on the cold flagstones and for a moment Magnus thought he was dead, but then he groaned and sat up, shielding his eyes with his hands.

'Who's there?'

'It's me.' Magnus turned off the torch, but he had already seen the pale skin flaking from lack of sunlight on Jeb's face and hands. He had only been down there for a day and a night, but the man looked drawn and Magnus wondered if Will had bothered to feed him. 'How's the leg?'

Jeb sounded as if his throat were made of sandpaper. 'The rest of me's so fucked it's hard to know.'

Belle was standing out of sight by the staircase. Magnus heard her intake of breath at the sound of Jeb's voice and resisted an urge to turn and look at her. He pressed his face close to the bars. 'I've not made much progress.'

'I told you, you wouldn't, fucking Jock.' There was a sound of rustling as Jeb shifted in the darkness below. 'Have they decided how they're going to do it?'

'Do what?'

'Kill me.'

Magnus turned the torch on again, angling it across the grille so he could make out the substance of the room below, without blinding Jeb. 'I don't know.'

'Don't know much, do you? Did you bring me any grub?'

Magnus did not want to mention the men congregated in the kitchen. 'I've just got back.'

'Christ, prison's a distant memory for you, isn't it?' Jeb curled his body forward, hiding his face and stretching his spine. 'I've been thinking about how I want to go.'

'There's no point in—'

'Get Raisha to make something that'll knock me out. Something painless, she'll know how to do it. And keep that old priest away from me. I don't want the last thing I hear to be him blathering on about God's forgiveness.'

Belle was quietly sobbing in the turn of the staircase. Magnus wanted to tell her to shut up, but he said, 'Raisha isn't here any more.' Jeb looked up. It was hard to make out his expression, but something about the way he cocked his head made Magnus say, 'She knows as little as we do about Jacob's murder, less.'

'It's the guilty who run. I don't know why she did it, but I'm betting it was her.' The sour stoicism Jeb had cultivated in Pentonville was gone. In its place was fear. 'You let her escape.'

Magnus said, 'I think I can persuade Belle to change her mind. I'll ask her to talk to Will and Father Wingate with me.'

'You won't turn that bastard. The only way to change his mind is to put a bullet in his head.'

'A life for a life?'

'Live by the sword, die by the sword.'

Magnus said, 'That sounds like an argument for not killing him.'

A grating metal-on-metal sound came from somewhere beyond Magnus's line of vision. He switched off the torch, sending the space back into darkness. There was a creak of hinges and a scraping noise that Magnus guessed came from an untrue cell door dragging across flagstones. Magnus jerked away from the grille, just before a light arced into the dungeon. A voice he did not know said, 'That's him. I remember his face.'

Jeb's voice was hard and belligerent. 'Do I know you?'

'He definitely did it?' Magnus recognised Will's voice.

'No question.' The stranger sounded convinced. 'You'll be doing the world a favour.'

Magnus risked a quick look through the grille. Will and the stranger were standing in the cell doorway and he could only make out the shadows they cast on the floor. Jeb was struggling to get to his feet, but his damaged leg would not co-operate. He gave up and half sat, half lay; sprawled on the flagstones like a man who had suddenly plummeted to earth.

'Who the hell are you?'

'I'm no one.' The stranger had a pleasant voice, mild and lilting, with the reasoned delivery favoured by newsreaders. 'We're all no one now, except for you. You're a murderer.'

Will set something down on the flagstones. 'Water and sandwiches.'

Magnus heard the scraping sound of the door closing.

'The key witness at my trial was a fucking liar!' Jeb tore off his shoe and threw it at the door but the key was grating in the lock. He waited a moment, gathering himself, then looked up towards the ceiling. Magnus's eyes met his; a powerless god's-eye-view. Jeb said, 'Either find a way to get me out of here, or find a way to kill me. I don't want them to have the satisfaction.'

'I'll get you out,' Magnus promised. He stood up, his mind empty of escape plans. He had almost forgotten Belle, waiting in the staircase behind him.

She whispered, 'Was it the short guy with the longish hair? He's their leader.'

'I couldn't see him.'

'I bet it was him.'

The girl began to climb the stairs. Magnus caught her by the arm.

'Raisha told me that you were the first one to find Melody.'

Belle's features were lost in the dark, but her voice was clear of tears. 'She said she wouldn't tell anyone.'

'Being frightened is nothing to be ashamed of.'

'Is that all she told you, that I was frightened?'

'Weren't you?'

'I'm always frightened.' She shook him free and resumed her climb.

Magnus asked, 'What happened in the barn?'

Belle's footsteps halted. Magnus remembered the gun tucked in the belt of her jeans and recalled again that it was supposedly the same one that had been used to shoot Jacob. He heard her turn towards him and felt the warmth of her body as she leaned in close and whispered, 'I killed her.'

The basement was as far as the staircase descended. There was nowhere to go except upwards, and so he followed her, his mind numb, into the deserted hallway of the main house and then through another unmarked door in the wallpaper and up to the attic storeys. She led him into a room that had been converted into an artist's atelier. The north side of the ceiling and much of the wall was composed of panes of glass. But it was not the room's bright contrast with the murk of the basement or the unbroken view across the countryside that drew Magnus's breath.

Images of death danced over the walls, across a landscape that drifted between green countryside, seas that raged then shone glass-calm, and towering cities in skyscraper-wonder. There were cramped suburbs of identical houses and ancient monuments: the pyramids, the Coliseum, Stonehenge. Sometimes death took the form of the laughing skulls that had decorated bags, T-shirts, scarves, even children's clothes before the sweats. But it also came clothed in flesh, in the shape of beautiful women, bare-breasted mermaids and aged crones. A hooded figure equipped with an hour-glass and scythe crept a steady path through the scenery, touching people on the shoulder, proving that death is no respecter of age, piety, wealth or beauty.

At first Magnus thought all the images had been cut from books and magazines, but then he saw that some of the figures had been painted. The style was naïve, with little concession to perspective, but somehow that intensified their effect.

'Did you do these?'

'I used to make collages from photographs I cut out of my mother's fashion magazines when I was little. I got quite obsessive about it.' Belle smiled. 'Sometimes I'd see a picture I liked, a beautiful model, or an amazing building, and tear out the page before she'd read it. I knew I'd get into trouble, but I couldn't stop myself.' She shrugged her shoulders. 'I thought I'd grown out of it.'

Belle had seemed like a spoiled child-woman bemused at her sudden lack of advantages in the post-sweats world, but the images on the wall formed a map of sweltering pain. Magnus stepped closer. He recognised the origin of some of the photographs, others he guessed: here was a smile culled from a toothpaste commercial, here a child that had been used to advertise cereal, here a rose that had once blossomed from a garden centre catalogue. He ran his fingers lightly over the collage, feeling the roughness of the pictures' edges. It was all there: the pain of loss, the petty frivolousness of things he missed, the hopes – some of them so ludicrous it was strange to think of them now – that would never be realised.

'It's amazing.' It was obsessive too. How many hours had it taken to find and clip the images? How many more to piece them together in a way that made such skewed but perfect sense? Magnus turned and looked at Belle for the first time since they had left the cellar. 'Did you kill Henry and Jacob?'

Belle gave a small snort of amusement. 'I wondered if the collage looked a bit serial-killer's bedroom. I guess I know now.'

The girl sank on to the floor, among a mess of discarded books and magazines. She winced, pulled the gun from her waistband and set it on the floor at her right hand.

Magnus kept his eye on the gun. 'You didn't answer my question.'

Belle's voice was incredulous. 'Are you serious?'

'You said you killed Melody.'

'I had nothing to do with Jacob's or Henry's deaths but yes, I feel responsible for Melody's.'

Magnus's relief was tempered by a snap of irritation. The

confession had been a piece of melodrama. He sensed time draining away, like sand in one of the hourglasses that decorated the wall.

'You didn't actually kill her.'

'You don't know what you're talking about.'

Magnus sat on the floor beside her. He knew he should formulate a plan, but he was weary to his bones.

'Someone close to me drowned himself. It's a long time ago now. The guilt doesn't go away, but I didn't kill him. He did it to himself.'

'Did you see it happen?'

'No, he was on his own.' The sweats had not cured Magnus of his horror of how alone Hugh must have been.

'Melody was a mess. She was sweet and kind and beautiful, but the sweats had fucked her up.'

'Raisha thought you were jealous of her.'

Magnus had expected Belle to be angry, but instead she smiled. 'Maybe I was a little. Like I said, Melody was beautiful, but I wasn't jealous of her demons.' She picked one of the magazines from the floor. 'Raisha brought me some of these. She's a strange woman, maybe we're all strange now, but she cares. It's a shame you let her go.'

It was in Magnus's mind to say that Raisha had never been his to keep, but instead he said, 'They're going to kill Jeb soon. Is there anything in all this that might lead me to Jacob's killer?'

'I doubt it.' Belle took his hand in hers. 'Was your friend in pain?'

'He must have been, but I didn't notice.'

He had not seen much of Hugh in the weeks before he

killed himself. Magnus had been waiting tables at the Kirkwall Hotel and trying to get a French student who was working there for the summer into bed. He was not sure what Hugh had been up to. His cousin had phoned the week before he walked into the sea, but the tourist season had been drawing to an end and Isabelle had been due to return to Nantes.

Magnus would exchange the opportunity of reliving all his audiences' laughter and applause for a second chance at his cousin's phone call. He had told Hugh he was busy and that he would catch him later.

Belle said, 'Melody was in agony.'

'Was she sick?'

'Not physically, but in herself, yes. We were all depressed of course, still are, but Melody took it to another level. Raisha gave everyone happy pills. I swallowed mine down like a good girl. I think the others did too, but Melody refused to take any. She said she needed her emotions to be authentic. I told her the pills don't stop you feeling bad. She just needed to look at Jacob or Will to know that. All they do is take the edge off things and make it possible to think without falling apart.'

The long night was catching up with Magnus. In another life it might have been pleasant to sit on the floor of the art room holding Belle's hand and swapping failures, but he had to think about how to free Jeb. He said, 'You couldn't force her to take them.'

'I thought about putting them in her food. I wish I had now. Melody was in so much agony it hurt to be with her. We went swimming in the river together once. She always wore

300

jeans and men's shirts with long sleeves. I should have guessed the reason, but it was such a hot summer I thought she was covering up against the sun, or that maybe something had happened to her that made her wary of showing her body. When she took her shirt and trousers off, I saw the slashes on her arms and legs. Melody said cutting herself made her feel better.' Belle gestured at the collage. 'I make these pictures for the same reason. It hurts, but I'm in control of the pain.'

The light was stinging Magnus's eyes. He closed them. 'You couldn't have predicted what would happen.'

Belle's voice was small. 'She wasn't dead when I went into the barn.'

Magnus kept his eyes shut. He could feel sleep coming for him. 'Raisha told me about that too. I know Jacob tried to revive her, but that's the kind of man he was. Even when it was hopeless, he wouldn't let death win without a fight.'

'I didn't tell Raisha everything.' Belle took her hand back and something in her voice made Magnus open his eyes and look at her. 'Her feet were still twitching. The chair she had stood on to reach the beam was standing next to her. I could have climbed on to it and supported her weight until some-one came to help cut her down, but I didn't.'

Magnus already knew the answer, but he asked, 'What did you do?'

'I dragged the chair away and ran out of the barn.' Tears were running down Belle's face. 'She was in so much pain, letting her die seemed like the right thing to do.'

Hugh lifted his head from the water. He raised a hand and then sank into a sea that was too calm to drown a grown man. Magnus shifted along the wall, putting a space between them. 'You let Melody die because her pain made you feel bad.'

'That's not true.'

Magnus sat on his hands to stop himself from raising them to her. 'Melody dragged you down, so you turned your back on her.'

'No.'

There was a sink in the corner of the studio stacked with paint-crusted pots and brushes. Magnus went to it, stuck his head under the cold tap and then peeled off his soiled T-shirt and began to wash himself.

'Do you know why you can't get the image of Melody kicking on that rope out of your head? Because it's against human nature to watch someone harm themselves without trying to stop them. Compassion for other people is what makes us human. The only person you feel sorry for is yourself. What does that make you?'

Belle was hunched against the wall, hugging her knees. 'I was frightened of her.'

'Because she was mentally ill?' There was a soiled-looking towel on a nail by the sink. Magnus dried himself with it. It was like rubbing his skin with sandpaper. 'You're going to be fucking terrified from now on. I'm guessing ninety per cent of whoever is left are off their heads.'

Belle looked up. 'I loved Melody. It was her who brought me here. She saved me.'

A black hoodie was slung over a chair. Magnus pulled it on. It was musty-smelling and paint-spattered, but cleaner than his mud-stiff T-shirt. 'If you want to confess, go to Father Wingate. I've got things to do.'

Belle's words came out in a rush. 'I keep thinking that maybe it was Melody who killed Henry and Jacob and that I'll be next.'

Magnus's hand was on the door of the studio. He turned and looked at her. 'Is this just another bit of drama?'

Belle raised her eyes to his. 'Melody was pretty crazy before she killed herself. She'd started to say that God intended the sweats to be the end of the world. Father Wingate spent hours with her, but Melody was convinced that the people who had survived had interfered in some divine plan. She was adamant that everyone was meant to be dead, including us.' The gun was still on the floor by Belle's hand. She pushed it away. 'Melody was sweet and good, but I'd started to think she might poison our food or stick a knife in us all while we slept.'

'Did no one suggest locking her up?'

'I think Jacob would have liked to, but Father Wingate was against it. He was sure he could save her through talk and prayer and Jacob agreed to let him try.'

'Why didn't you just leave?'

'I was scared. I didn't want to be on my own.' She looked at Magnus. 'I have dreams where Melody comes back for the rest of us. I saw her body, she looked dead, but what if Jacob managed to revive her after all? You used to read stories of people digging their way out of their grave and coming back for revenge.'

'Not in newspapers you didn't, not broadsheets anyway.' Magnus crossed the room and crouched next to her. 'These stories are fiction. This is just guilt and suspicion.'

Belle's eyes were wide. She grasped his hands in hers and

he saw that retelling the story had pushed her close to panic. 'What if she's a ghost?'

Magnus pulled Belle to her feet and hugged her. 'Ghosts don't exist.' He held her at arm's length. 'If they did, this place would be hooching with them.'

Belle whispered, 'I need to get away from here. Can we leave together? I don't want to travel on my own. Neither do you. That's why you teamed up with Jeb.'

Magnus let go of her. 'I can't leave yet.'

Belle caught his arm. 'You can't help Jeb. Even if you manage to prove someone else killed Jacob and Henry, they're going to execute him. He was found guilty of murdering that woman and her little girl, that's enough for them.'

'But he didn't kill them.'

'Don't you get it? When the community voted to execute Jeb it was because we wanted justice. If you'd proved that he hadn't killed Jacob, we would have backed down—'

Magnus interrupted her. 'That's not the way the law works. People are innocent until proven guilty.'

Belle held up a hand. 'There is no law. Will and these new men will make a big deal of having right on their side, but what they really want is to prove that they're in control. Melody cut herself and I make my collages; men like that turn their pain outwards. They want an excuse to show how strong they are by making a spectacle of executing someone. The best thing we can do is go, before they do the same to us.'

Magnus said, 'If we leave now it will be like walking away and leaving Melody to die alone in the barn all over again.'

Belle shook her head. 'No it won't. I loved Melody; I don't give a shit about Jeb.'

Thirty-Eight

Nobody ever slept in action films, but Magnus was an obsolete stand-up who had only ever shot rabbits and barn-rats. The thought of being unconscious with the strangers in the house frightened him, but he was dazed with tiredness. He left Belle in her studio with the gun, crept into his room and changed his clothes. There was no lock on his door and so he pushed the bed against it and slept, fully dressed.

His dreams were filled with noise: the hiss of the sea as it receded, dragging sand and shale in its wake, the boom of the waves as they hit the shore. He dreamed that he was chained to the seabed, trying to keep his head above an incoming tide. The sea was quick and choppy. He lifted his face to the sky, but the waves pressed on and his chains held tight, grabbing him back against the swell. A dark slab of salt water rolled over his head, filling his mouth and nose and Magnus surfaced, gasping for air.

He woke to the sound of voices and hammering. *Christ.* Magnus had hoped that sleep would revive him, but a shaft of sunlight had fallen across his face and he had the sensation that someone had felted the inside of his head. He lay there, hot and uncomfortable in his clothes, trying to formulate a plan, his thoughts a fuzzy choice between fight and flight.

Magnus dragged himself upright. He peeked out from behind the curtains, but the view from his bedroom fell short of the lawn and so he shuffled to a room with a better outlook. Four men were building a rough structure out of planks of pine. Their features were hidden by beards and it was hard to make out their ages, but the men were awkward with their tools and materials. Magnus guessed they were more used to communal offices and Center Parcs holidays than joinery. One of them had the slack skin and cautious gait of someone who had suddenly lost a substantial paunch. Another favoured one leg. All of them wore the blank look he had learned was caused by grief. He might only have shot rabbits and barn-rats, but watching the men on the lawn, Magnus was willing to bet the only contact they had had with guns was paintball. It was a big assumption and he had not yet set eyes on the short, well-spoken man Belle had called their leader.

The men might not be the outlaws he had feared but they had found planks of wood and were busy with their task. Magnus tried to make out what they were building. The group had none of the easy anticipation of each other's needs he had been used to on the croft and the Italian restaurant where he had been kitchen porter. They subtly challenged each other, holding on to tools longer than needed, blocking each other's paths. He could not hear what they were saying, but Magnus had been on the stand-up circuit long enough to recognise the stiletto stab and twist of criticism disguised as advice. It was the memory of the stale-beer-stinking comedy clubs where he had spent so many nights that made Magnus realise what they were making: a rough platform equipped with stairs. The sight of it was bewildering. Magnus wondered what kind of show the men were planning and then it dawned on him – *shit, shit, shit* – it was a stage for an execution. He hurried back to his room, changed his mud-spattered clothes and went in search of Father Wingate.

The old man was not in the chapel or his bedroom but Magnus heard voices in the study that had once been the butler's refuge. He pressed his ear to the door. Father Wingate sounded composed, but his voice was grave. 'I will offer to walk the route from his cell with him. He may not accept spiritual comfort, but regardless of his wishes I will say a prayer, committing his life to the Lord.'

An Irish voice said, 'I would have thought he'd be headed for a warmer place.' The stranger laughed, pleased with his joke.

Father Wingate said, 'The devil is among us, that much is true.'

Magnus would have liked to have heard more but it was too risky, standing in the open hallway. He tried the door next to the office and discovered a large cupboard that might once have served as a pantry. He slipped inside and left the door slightly ajar. A sliver of light cut into the cupboard's dark recess. Magnus wondered how they intended to execute Jeb and why they had gone to the trouble of making a stage. Who was the theatre for?

Cut and run, the treacherous voice whispered. *Cut and run.*

He was tempted to sit on the floor, but was wary of being ambushed by sleep and stood, leaning against the corner of

307

the cupboard, his eyes trained on the small slice of hallway. Magnus was not sure how long he had been hiding there when he came to with a start. He had been in a half-doze, leaning with his face scrunched against the cupboard's wall, listening to the faint rise and fall of voices; the distant hammering from the lawn.

The door of the office opened and Father Wingate said, 'The house has been in continuous occupation since ancient times. It started as a simple settlement which grew into a castle. My ancestors built a manor house on the castle's foundations some time around the 1600s. Of course it's been much altered since then, but for centuries all the farms and homesteads in the district paid fealty to it.'

'And it belonged to your family for all that time?'

'Until I bequeathed it to the Church.'

'So you speak with God as one Lord to another.'

'No one is equal to God.' Father Wingate's voice was frosty.

'You'll have to forgive my sense of humour, Father.' The man was unapologetic. 'It's not PC, but it's helped me survive.'

Magnus caught a quick impression of dark hair and blue shirt as the stranger walked past the cupboard.

Father Wingate called, 'Malachy?'

'Yes?' The man sounded impatient. He stepped back into Magnus's line of vision. He was not as short as Magnus had anticipated, just an inch or two beneath his own height, he guessed, but stockier, barrel-chested and broad-shouldered in a way that made him look bullish and out of proportion. His blue dress shirt was more suited to a business suit than the pressed jeans he was wearing, but he had left the shirt untucked, to hide a weapon or in concession to a permanent post-apocalyptic dress-down Friday.

Father Wingate said, 'You'll remember to tell your men about distributing the punch? It's always been the duty of the big house to offer some hospitality to the district. My mother used to arrange for urns of tea and fruit scones when she hosted the garden fête. Even after I handed the house over to the Church we held the occasional open day; tea for the grown-ups, orange juice for the children, that kind of thing.'

'They're not my men, but I'll tell them.'

Father Wingate said, 'I think alcohol will be the right thing on this occasion. Strong drink can be a great comfort.'

Malachy laughed. 'I'll say amen to that.'

Magnus waited until the sound of the newcomer's boots had faded and then stole from the cupboard into Father Wingate's office, closing the door gently behind him. The old man greeted him with a smile.

'My son, we thought we had lost you.' He slid the book in his hand back on to its shelf. 'Have you encountered our visitors?'

'I've been avoiding them.' Magnus kept his voice low. 'You said you'd give me time to prove Jeb innocent.'

'Events have moved on.'

Father Wingate eased himself into the same high-backed chair he had insisted on, on the afternoon when Jacob had persuaded Magnus to stay and help with the harvest. He nodded towards an armchair.

Magnus ignored him and leaned against the desk where he

could see the door. Father Wingate's boyish smile was wide, but there was an excited edge to the priest that Magnus did not like. He said, 'Why are you so keen to execute Jeb?'

'I hope I'm not giving the impression of being over-eager.' The priest was unfazed by the question. 'Jacob acknowledged that the sweats were a sign that we should return to Old Testament times. He would approve of what we are doing.'

Jacob had used the phrase 'Old Testament times' in the cornfield when he had confided his doubts about Melody's death, but he had been uneasy; weighed down by sorrow and responsibility. Magnus said, 'Jacob might have feared a need for harsh punishment, but he would never have considered using it as entertainment. These men are building a stage on the lawn and you're planning on serving refreshments.'

Father Wingate let out a scandalised laugh. 'It does sound bad when you put it that way. But what you fail to recognise is that death can also be a joyous occasion.'

'Joyous?'

'We can incarcerate your friend indefinitely or we can grant him the opportunity to cleanse his sins and offer up his life as a sacrifice to God. Until recent times such occasions were always a public spectacle.' Father Wingate's voice turned grave. 'It is a serious thing to take a life. The whole community must be involved. We are all guilty of survival.'

Magnus faltered, grasping for words the priest would understand.

'Jeb maintains his innocence. He's not Jesus Christ, he isn't going to offer up his life to God. He's more likely to go raving blasphemies.'

Father Wingate leaned forward. His face was sympathetic,

as if Jeb were already dead and Magnus a bereaved relative. 'Do not worry about your friend's dignity. There are ways to ensure a solemn end.'

It was like talking to a madman. Magnus said, 'What are you going to do? Hypnotise him? It's possible that the person who really killed Jacob murdered other people too. Doesn't that worry you?'

The old man clasped his hands together and rested them on his lap. 'Death is not as important as what comes afterwards. We had lost sight of that before God, in His mercy, chose to visit the sweats on us. I am eighty-two years old, but I remember my youth, my childhood, as if it were yesterday.' The priest paused, as if he could see the house in full splendour. 'Life is a blink of the eye, eternity is everlasting. Will you pray with me?'

Magnus pushed himself off the desk and stood up straight. 'I'd rather get up on that platform with Jeb than go down on my knees with you. I didn't agree with everything Jacob did, but he was a good man who was trying to build a community. If there's an afterlife then he deserves to rest easy, but what you're doing is enough to call him back from the dead.'

Father Wingate crossed his legs. 'Jacob was a good man and he will have his resurrection, but he was only human. He believed that if we built a community people would come and join us. Malachy has taken a more dynamic approach. He has gone to the people.'

'What people?' Magnus had started to pace the floor, moving like he did on stage. It was a waste of energy, but anger had blasted him with adrenalin and it was impossible to sit still.

'Malachy and his group have been touring the district looking for somewhere to settle. There are pockets of survivors all around the parish.'

'And you think they'll come to Jeb's execution? The idea's sick.'

'When I was a boy, harvest was the most joyous festival in the countryside. It was more popular than Christmas. In those days there were fewer crops and so farms reaped them at the same time. When it was done, communities came together to worship and celebrate.'

It was like one of his father's reminiscences. Magnus perched on the edge of the easy chair, trying to make up his mind about what to do next. The old man's words rolled on.

'Some corn would be taken from the final sheaf shorn and made into a corn dolly to be presented to the prettiest girl who had taken part in the harvest.' The old man looked up, suddenly anxious. 'Do you know what a corn dolly is?' Magnus nodded and Father Wingate continued, satisfied that his story was making sense. 'You can imagine the feuds that were caused by that.' His laugh was gleeful. 'They all wanted to be queen of the harvest.' The priest looked at Magnus, suddenly serious. 'You're a country boy. You must surely understand the natural cycle of things.'

Magnus recited one of his mother's favourite verses: 'There is a time for everything, and a season for every activity under the heavens: a time to be born and a time to die, a time to plant and a time to uproot, a time to kill and a time to heal, a time to weep and a time to laugh, a time to mourn and a time to dance.'

Father Wingate beamed and nodded his head. 'I knew you

were a good Christian, but you forgot, "a time to tear down and a time to build".'

Magnus said, 'I lost my faith a long time ago, but my mother is a good Christian and she would be appalled by you.'

Father Wingate closed his eyes for a moment, as if drawing on his stock of patience. He spoke slowly. 'If your island was subjected to the full force of the sweats, your mother might be inclined to agree with me. God has had His own harvest. It is coming to an end and we must mark it.'

Mention of his mother threw Magnus off track. He struggled to make sense of the priest's argument. 'You were never interested in whether Jeb was guilty or not.'

The old man nodded. His voice was soft and reasonable, as if he recognised that Magnus was a bomb that might suddenly explode. 'You are the kind of man who needs journeys and quests. But your search for so-called justice was always a distraction doomed to failure. There is only one judge and He will weigh each of our sins in due course.'

The realisation was horrible. Magnus whispered, 'You want to sacrifice him.'

'That's exactly what I said.' Father Wingate's smile held a boyish lack of guile. 'We will offer up his life as a sacrifice to God.'

Thirty-Nine

Magnus was done with skulking in cupboards and passageways. He walked boldly across the lawn. One of the puppies rushed to greet him, but he ignored it and it gambolled away. The noise of banging and sawing drew to a staccato pause. Viewed from the house the four men had seemed out of kilter, but as they turned to face him Magnus wondered if they might be more united than he had thought.

He muttered, 'Midwich Cuckoos,' under his breath and raised a hand in greeting. A couple of the men nodded warily in response. Magnus drew close and asked, 'Anyone in charge?'

The platform was coming along, but perhaps the men had forgotten a spirit level, because the supports were uneven and the dais listed to one side. Close to, the group had a hungry, hollow-eyed look. If Magnus had met them before the sweats he might have assumed that they were drug addicts and he wondered if that might still be the case.

One of the men said, 'No one's in charge,' at the same time as another said, 'Malachy's not here.'

Magnus nodded, as if it were possible for both answers to be correct and asked, 'What are you doing?'

Something caught the light in one of the high windows of the house. Tanqueray held enough deserted rooms and sly passages for generations of ghosts. He thought of Belle saying, *I'm always frightened*, and hoped that she was all right.

'We're restoring law and order.' The tallest of the men spoke. The sun had darkened his already dark skin, but it had a dusty sheen that made it look gun-metal grey. 'You Scottish?'

Magnus nodded. 'From Orkney.'

'Were you up there when the sweats hit?'

'I was in London. Did you hear anything about how things are in the north?'

There were murmurs of 'no' and a few shaken heads. The man said, 'The same as down here, I reckon.'

'I'm heading in that direction, so I guess I'll find out for myself soon enough.' Magnus included the group in his smile. 'Is this stage for a trial?'

'Trial's over.' The tall man was unabashed. 'The scumbag's a child-killer who broke out of jail when the sweats started.'

A pale, thin man with the dogged look of a tax inspector said, 'He murdered a priest.' He pointed towards the back of the house. 'Shot him against a wall over there.'

Magnus said, 'Sounds like a maniac. Were there witnesses?'

'Who are you?' another of the men asked. He was bald and bespectacled and was holding a hammer loosely by his side.

All the men still had tools in their hands, Magnus realised, an arsenal of hammers, screwdrivers and mallets. He held his hands out palm up and said, 'A survivor, like you.' A door slammed. Magnus looked towards the sound and saw Malachy walking across the lawn towards them. He had the busy air of a man scoring things off his to-do list; a venue manager or a wedding planner. Magnus said, 'So what's the squinty stage for, if the trial's over?'

The bald man shifted the hammer to his other hand. 'We're going to make an example of him.' He was around sixty years old, dressed neatly in beige slacks and a pink, short-sleeved shirt. 'Things need to get back to normal.' He raised the hammer in the air, marking the beat of his words with it. 'Thugs like him have to be shown that decent people are willing to take a stand. I had three daughters . . .' His voice broke and he let the hammer fall to his side. 'Three daughters,' he repeated and the fat-thin man Magnus had noticed from the window put a hand on his shoulder and whispered in his ear. The bald man nodded. He walked a short distance from the group, took something from the pocket of his slacks and put it in his mouth.

'Poor guy.' Magnus had feared that the hammer was meant for him and his voice wavered with unspent adrenalin. 'I guess you must be certain this bloke's guilty if you're making an example of him. No one wants a wrongful execution on their conscience.' He looked back towards the house. Malachy was almost upon them. 'Is this the boss?'

The man who had told him there was no one in charge said, 'There is no boss,' and the tall man said, 'Malachy's what you might call a natural leader.'

'You're making a good job of that.' Malachy seemed not to notice the platform's lopsided legs. 'It'll do the job nicely.' He held out a hand. 'I'm guessing you're Magnus.'

'You guess right.' Magnus ignored the hand and Malachy dropped his to his side without any obvious embarrassment.

Magnus said, 'I was just saying to the boys here, you must have pretty concrete evidence if you're confident enough to hang a man.'

Malachy's hair curled over his collar but his beard was neatly trimmed and there was a pen clipped to the top pocket of his shirt. 'What made you think we were going to hang him?' For a dazed moment Magnus thought that he had got the whole thing wrong. Then Malachy said, 'There's more than one way to skin a cat, if you'll excuse the expression. Have you got time for a quick chat?'

'I'm not sure. When's the big event?'

'Tomorrow at noon.' Malachy handed the bundle of paper he was carrying over to the tall man. 'Paul, do you think you could see your way to distributing a few more of these? Junctions are probably best. Stick them on trees and lamp-posts, wherever you think people might see them.'

Magnus held out a hand. 'Do you mind if I have a look?'

'I thought you were a new recruit.' Paul passed Magnus one of the pages. 'Who are you?'

'Someone who would like to be sure the cat was guilty before they saw it skinned.'

Paul said, 'We're not fucking vigilantes.'

'Really? I thought maybe you were Fathers for Justice.'

Paul's fist knocked Magnus to the ground. He lay there, watching the tall man's boots walking away, his head ringing.

Malachy said, 'You deserved that. All these men are bereaved fathers and all of them are passionate about justice.' He held out a hand.

Magnus shoved it away and struggled to his feet. He shouted after Paul, 'Killing Jeb won't bring anyone back. You

317

can mount all the fucking crusades you want and all you'll have to show for it is more dead bodies.'

The man gave no sign of having heard him. He kept on walking, his back straight, shoulders square.

Magnus's nose had started to bleed, but he could already tell that it was not broken. He searched his pockets vainly for something to mop up the blood. Malachy handed him a cotton handkerchief. Magnus held it to his face and tried to slow his breathing.

'Killing an innocent man won't avenge the sweats.' His words were thick and nasal.

Malachy said, 'Jeb's guilty, don't worry about that.'

Magnus had dropped the poster when Paul hit him. He bent over, spotting it with blood, and picked it up. It was neatly printed in black marker pen.

TOMORROW
12.00 Noon

EXECUTION!

---

at TANQUERAY HOUSE

of MURDERER, CHILD-KILLER & ESCAPED CONVICT

JEB SOAMES

SUPPORT A RETURN TO LAW AND ORDER

A simple map and list of directions followed below.

Magnus spat a gob of blood and snot on to the grass. 'You forgot to mention the refreshments.'

'Father Wingate said you were a bit of a joker.' Malachy patted Magnus on the back and steered him towards the house, keeping an arm around his shoulder as if they were old friends, enjoying a walk home at the end of a long, boozy lunch at which Magnus had been the booziest. 'You used to be a comedian, didn't you? I think I saw you once at the Hackney Empire. You were good.'

Magnus pulled free of Malachy's grasp, resisting the urge to elbow him in the ribs. 'I never played the Empire.'

'Are you sure?' Malachy's face wrinkled. 'I was certain it was there.'

Magnus tipped his head back, trying to staunch the blood. 'Maybe you meant the Comedy Store. People often get them mixed up.' The venues had been different in size, style and clientele and had been located in different districts of London.

'That sounds right, the Comedy Store.' The Irishman grinned. 'You did a routine about not fitting in.'

All of Magnus's routines had, in one way or another, been about his inability to fit in. But most comedy routines were. The trick was to make the audience believe you were both ordinary and extraordinary; a misfit-dynamo who held the stage feeding the absurdities of their lives back to them.

Magnus said, 'On second thoughts it couldn't have been the Comedy Store.'

'No?'

'No.' Magnus gave him a fuck-you stare, still holding the

319

blood-soaked hanky to his nose. 'I never performed there either.'

Malachy was unfazed. 'Ah well, I'm sure I saw you somewhere.'

The bleeding had almost stopped. Magnus spat on a corner of the hanky and attempted to clean the blood from his face. His nose and eyes were throbbing and he knew from experience that they would bruise. 'What did you do before the sweats? No, don't tell me.' He held a hand to his forehead, as if he were receiving a telepathic message from another realm. 'You were a double-glazing salesman.'

'I was a lawyer.'

'I'm guessing you worked for the prosecution.'

'You're wrong about that too. I always stood for the defence. I spent decades keeping villains like your friend Jeb out of jail. I guess they took their toll.'

'So now you've decided to become judge, jury and executioner.'

'We'll draw lots to decide who carries the burden of the actual act.' Malachy turned to face Magnus. They were almost at the house but the steady sound of hammering followed them, like nails going into a coffin. 'I know you think I'm a manipulating bastard who sees this crisis as an opportunity to grab some power—'

Magnus interrupted him. 'I couldn't have put it better, except I wouldn't have used the word crisis. Cataclysm is closer to the mark.'

Malachy put his hands in his pockets and walked across the gravel where the line of motorbikes was parked. 'You're right, cataclysm is a better word. The sweats were a cataclysm which has imposed a level of equality on everyone. We're all bereaved and we're all frightened. Everyone has lost their sense of purpose. Those of us who were in the cities have all experienced lawlessness and most, with the exception of those hoping to profit from it, recognise the danger of anarchy.'

Magnus said, 'Killing Jeb will be murder. An illegal act can't signal a return to law.'

They had reached the house. One of the pups was lounging in the shade, its tongue hanging out. Its tail gave a couple of weary beats and it shut its eyes. Malachy sat on the stone steps that led up to the front door.

'I disagree. Whatever that man told you, he is guilty of killing the woman and her child and probably of killing the priest. Okay, there are hundreds – thousands more people who have committed equally horrible crimes during the sweats. We can't punish them all, but we can punish Jeb Soames. Public execution is an extreme measure, but it will serve as a warning to others and a rallying call to the districts around here to unite. Ultimately it will save lives.'

Magnus sat on the step beside Malachy. It was the kind of day his mother described as heaven-sent. The sky was hung with cottony clouds that put Magnus in mind of white sails against a calm sea. Swifts reeled and swooped, performing Spitfire antics above the lawn, and promiscuous bees hummed as they pressed themselves into flower after flower. He touched his nose gently with his fingertips. It was tender and his nostrils felt crusted with blood, but the bleeding had stopped. 'You're forgetting that capital punishment isn't legal in this country.'

'Not under normal circumstances, but these are not normal circumstances. Execution also has the virtue of being popular. It may not have been legal before the sweats, but people wanted it.'

'You're as mad as the old priest. He believes sacrificing Jeb will appease God.'

Malachy leaned forward and rested his elbows on his knees. 'I'm not a spiritual person, but Father Wingate is expressing through religion exactly the same argument I've just put to you.'

Magnus stared towards the drive. The avenue of trees was still and bound in shadows. Rooks cawed in their upper branches, black-coated and out of sorts, like puritans distressed by the festive weather.

'You spent years defending people, now you're about to kill a man who maintains his innocence. Don't you have any doubts at all?'

Malachy looked off into the middle distance. 'The time for doubts is past.' He got to his feet, scuffing the palms of his hands together, as if they were dusty. 'Father Wingate said you and Jeb met in jail. What were you in for?'

Magnus had half expected the question. He said, 'I tried to save a woman from being attacked. It got messy and the police picked me up. It was just after the sweats took hold. Special measures were in place and I got thrown in Pentonville without a trial.'

'Quite a string of bad luck. Some might say an unbelievable string of bad luck.' Malachy tossed Magnus a set of keys. 'I heard you were headed north.' He nodded to the row of motorbikes standing outside the house. 'These are for the

322

Honda on the left. I imagine you want to hit the road as soon as possible.'

'Are you telling me to leave?'

'I'm telling you to be careful. You don't want to end up in the same situation as your friend.'

Magnus said, 'He's not my friend.'

'So why are you defending him?'

'I don't know.' Magnus watched the swifts' quick climbs, their sharp turns and swoops. No matter how many there were, cutting through the air, they never collided. 'A friend of mine once wrote me a letter. It said, *Life isn't worth living once you realise the world is hollow*. Maybe I'm scared of finding out what he meant.'

Forty

The Honda took the country roads' winds and bends with ease. Magnus had left Tanqueray House with just the clothes he was wearing and the rush of air felt cool and reckless against his bare arms and head. He remembered what Raisha had told Belle about homes with children being easy to spot and tried to imagine the kind of house that would contain what he was in search of. It would be an old countryman's cottage, he decided, somewhere neatly painted with a kitchen garden out back and a variety of prize roses out front. He had noticed a likely house, not far from the cemetery, on the way back from burying Jacob. An elaborate model of a sailing ship in full rig sat in its front window. It was the kind of object Magnus had coveted as a boy and he had been tempted to break in and steal it for auld lang syne. The ship had suggested more than his island childhood: it spoke of masculinity, order and patience.

He smashed the kitchen window with a washing pole. A smell of rot and decay reached down into Magnus's throat before he was fully inside and he crouched on the draining board gagging. He was tempted to retreat, but time was against him. Magnus grabbed a dishtowel decorated with a map of the Norfolk Broads and tied it around his face.

The householder sat slumped in the sitting room, his head an explosion. He had used a rifle to do the job and the recoil of the blast had sent the gun to the ground. Magnus kept his eyes from the corpse and tried to shut out the buzz of flies. He reached for the rifle, lips clamped tight, skin crawling in response to the thought that the man might stretch out and touch him, though the man had been dead for weeks. Magnus lifted the gun gingerly, checked the chamber and put on the safety catch. It was fine for killing vermin, frightening bank tellers or shooting your brains out, but it was nothing special.

The gun cabinet was in a room the man had probably called his study. He had been a law-abiding sportsman to the end and had locked the cabinet before he shot himself. Magnus guessed the keys were still in the man's pocket, but there was no way he could bring himself to touch the corpse and so he forced the doors open with the aid of the sitting-room poker. The contents were disappointing, a pair of rifles as unremarkable and short range as the first. Magnus zipped both of them into their cases and scooped up a box of bullets. He left the model sailboat in its place on the windowsill. It was spattered with blood, like a vessel that had sailed into gory waters.

The village felt strange. There were no abandoned cars skewed across the roads or smashed shop windows as there had been in London. The streets were litter-free, the cottage doors neatly closed. It was as if the residents had all gone off on an annual spree and might return at any time. Magnus wished he had never seen a zombie movie. It was too easy to imagine half-decayed villagers stumbling towards him. He muttered, 'Get a bloody grip,' and pushed the Honda down to the green. It was deserted, except for a pair of horses who lifted their heads and looked at him. One of the beasts lowered its head and resumed grazing but the other, a handsome chestnut with a white star on its forehead, walked slowly over to Magnus and nuzzled him. He knew the horse was in search of a treat, an apple or perhaps a Polo mint, but the clean animal scent of it came from his childhood and tears sprang to Magnus's eyes. He stroked the horse's long nose and pressed his brow against its neck.

'I've got nothing for you, boy,' he whispered into its mane. 'Nothing for you.'

The horse gave him a last friendly nudge and walked back to join its companion, as if it had understood Magnus's words.

Paul had reached the green before him and some of Malachy's posters were taped to lampposts. Magnus ripped them down and tore them into confetti. The sun was high in the sky, the execution less than twenty-four hours away. He scanned the houses that edged the green. There was something about them that added to his usual stock of unease. He stared closer, noticing their gardens' trimmed hedges, clipped lawns and tidy beds. Horses did not leave neat edges, nor were they known for discriminating between weeds and flowers.

'Are you one of the judges?'

The voice gave him a jolt. It was high and bad-tempered and belonged to a tall woman in a straw hat and gardening smock. The smock was printed with improbable flowers: blue orchids, neon ferns and purple daisies. Magnus wondered that he had not spotted her before.

'I might be. What would I be judging?'

'England in Bloom.' The woman was standing behind a hedge. She had a pair of secateurs in her hand and looked as if she were tempted to use them on him. 'I'm the only one of the committee available, but I'm happy to show you round, though I must say you're rather late. I'm afraid some of the gardens are past their best.'

Magnus said, 'It's been a difficult year.'

There was a flicker of something behind the woman's eyes, but she tucked the secateurs into the front pocket of her smock and pushed open the gate. 'Perhaps we should start with Mrs Norris's garden.'

He needed to get away from the woman and her madness, but Magnus could still feel the kind touch of the horse's face against his. He said, 'I've already done my inspection and I am delighted to announce that Tanqueray Village has won England in Bloom.'

The woman kept her hand on the gate and gave him a suspicious look. 'When did you do your inspection? I'm always here. I would have seen you.'

'A few days ago.' Magnus took a step backward. He had propped the motorbike opposite her cottage, on the edge of the green. 'Tanqueray won hands down. We'll be sending a photographer to record it for the local paper.'

'Now I know you're lying.' The woman's voice was more menacing for being soft. 'Everyone at the *Gazette* is dead. Jeremy who always takes the photographs is dead. They are all dead. Robin my husband is dead, our son, our daughter-in-law and our little grandson are dead. Mrs Norris is dead and so is everyone else who lived on the green. You have the damn cheek to make excuses about a difficult year. I have had a bloody dreadful one, but I have continued to work my fingers to the bone keeping these gardens in bloom. I demand that you do your job and inspect them properly.'

If it were not for Jeb he would have walked the boundary of the green with the woman, exclaiming at the gardens, but time was running out.

'I'm sorry. I can't.' Magnus's hand was on the saddle of his bike.

The woman said, 'I'll report you to the committee,' though in her heart she must have known that the committee were also dead.

'I'm sorry to dash.' Magnus swung a leg over the saddle of the Honda. 'You really have made an amazing job in what has been a tremendously challenging year.'

He must have hit the right note of pomposity and apology because the woman's mood shifted and she smiled. 'Do you really think so?'

'No doubt about it.'

Her smile widened. 'Please come back. We can have tea outside if the weather holds up.'

Her change of temper was too swift to last, but Magnus risked a question. 'Was your husband a hunter?'

The woman looked confused. 'Robin was a member of the RSPB.'

Magnus said, 'The what?'

'The Royal Society for the Protection of Birds. My husband

328

was a bird-watcher. He opposed hunting in all its forms. He and Mr Perry had a falling-out about it one night at the White Hart. Mr Perry's a firebrand, but Robin stood up to him. I was worried they were going to come to blows.'

'Where does Mr Perry live?'

'Sycamore Cottage, opposite the school, but I'm afraid he's dead too. I took a clematis from his garden. It's thriving.'

Magnus dislodged the Honda's kick-rest. 'Congratulations on your win.'

'Thank you.' The woman's mood was shifting again. She sounded bemused. 'I'm not sure what I'll do now that the competition is over. It's given me something to focus on.'

'You need to start preparing for next year.'

She treated Magnus to a smile that said she knew he was patronising her and bore him no ill will. 'I don't think there's much point in that, do you, dear?'

Forty-One

The primary school was a low, flat-roofed building with abandoned cars jammed across its playground and a makeshift sign marked *Quarantine Centre* hanging from its railings. Magnus remembered the cattle barn he and Jacob had stumbled into, the decaying, swollen-bellied cows, and felt an urge to set fire to the school.

He wheeled the Honda across an empty zebra crossing to Sycamore Cottage. The garden was treeless, but the name was etched in gold in the fanlight above the door and there was a large tree stump in the centre of the lawn that had been sawn into a seat. Magnus guessed the tree had been felled for fear its roots might creep into the foundations. But the cottage had been well named. New sycamore shoots were sprouting, floppy-leaved and resilient, among the weeds in the neglected flower beds and it would not be long before one of them took hold.

Something about the dead-eyed windows of the school unnerved Magnus. He rang the doorbell of the cottage and waited a moment before wheeling the Honda into the back garden and breaking in. There was no sign of Mr Perry, but he had set his burglar alarm before he left and it rang, ear-splitting and urgent, as Magnus made his way through the house.

The interior looked like it might have been inspired by a magazine feature on country living, or maybe a fox-hunting-themed pub. Prints of beagles lined the hallway and a brass hunting horn hung at a jaunty angle over the fireplace. Magnus's low spirits sank another notch. He had been hoping for someone who stalked deer, a lone predator in need of stamina and keen sites, but Mr Perry had been a fox-hunter, the kind of man who needed back-up from a pack of hounds and a mob of toffs. Magnus knocked a picture of red-coated huntsmen on horses from the wall and ground his heel into the glass. The burglar alarm was pulling his already raw nerves to the surface and stretching them to snapping point. He clamped his hands over his ears and went in search of a gun cabinet.

He found it in the sitting room and smashed its lock with a bronze model of a vixen tending her cubs. The quartet of rifles inside was better quality than the ones he had already collected, but their range was still less than he had hoped for. Magnus sat back on his haunches. The sound of the alarm was enough to make a man shoot himself. The thought bothered him and he strode through to the hallway, broke open the alarm's junction box and prised out the battery pack powering it. The silence made his ears ring.

Magnus whispered, 'Mr Perry, I'm going to leave the doors to your house open for foxes to move in.'

He propped the guns in a corner of the hallway and jogged upstairs, his boots clumping. Two bedrooms and a bathroom led off a square landing. The smallest of the pair had been

331

shelved and turned into a library. Magnus lifted a set of binoculars from the windowsill and then went into Mr Perry's bedroom and investigated his wardrobes. The man had been a few inches larger than Magnus around the waist and a couple of inches longer in the inside leg, but it was nothing that a belt and folded trouser cuffs would not fix. He had dressed as Magnus hoped he would, in country colours, muted browns, greens and greys that blended with the landscape. Magnus ditched his jeans and T-shirt and pulled on a pair of khaki walking trousers with zip pockets, a lightweight shirt and a waistcoat equipped with bullet pouches. A black hooded tracksuit was folded neatly on a shelf. Magnus shoved it in a bag along with a navy ski cap and a couple of changes of socks.

He poked around looking for anything else that might be useful. A cardboard carton was pressed in at the back of the wardrobe, behind a rack of shoes. Magnus slid it out, surprised at the weight of it, and undid the flaps. The box was full of magazines: *Muscle Power*, *Physique*, *Adonis*. Judging by the hairstyles and skinny briefs sported by the pumped-up men on their covers they dated from the seventies and eighties. Magnus closed the box and slid it back where he had found it, feeling shabby.

He was pulling on his boots when he heard a door slam. *Fuck*. Mr Perry's rifles were propped downstairs in the hallway. Magnus scanned the bedroom for a hiding place. The wardrobes and double bed took up most of the space. The wardrobes were freestanding and Magnus feared that if he hid inside one, it might topple forward, trapping him for ever like a bride in some gothic tale. The footsteps were on the stairs now. 'Hello?' It was a man's voice. 'Is somebody there?'

Magnus took two paces, swift and silent, to the window, but it was a long drop with no convenient outhouse or clinging ivy to aid his descent. Across the landing, the door to Mr Perry's small library opened and closed. A floorboard creaked. Magnus slid beneath the bed an instant before the bedroom door opened.

'Hello?' The voice was male and hesitant. Magnus lay on his front in the cool dust-bound shadows. Mr Perry had stored things under the bed, and there was barely space for him. The stranger opened and closed each of the wardrobes. He said, 'I think someone may have been here.' His voice sounded less cautious.

Magnus felt the mattress dip as the man sat on the bed. His shoes were brown moccasins, mid-price and unremarkable, the kind of shoe a middle-aged man who did not notice fashion might wear. The stock of a rifle rested next to them, set upright like a walking stick. Magnus held his breath, steeling himself to get to his feet.

'I know you're there,' the voice said and there was something in its tone that made Magnus stay where he was. This was how prisoners felt in the face of death, desperate for one more gasp of air.

'Are you under the bed?' A tease had entered the voice. 'Shall I look?'

A motorcycle engine sounded throatily outside in the street. The man swore and started to his feet. He ran out of the room and down the stairs, slamming the front door behind him.

333

Magnus let out a groan. He stretched out a trembling hand, feeling for whatever it was Mr Perry had hidden beneath the bed, and touched what might have been a musical instrument case. He crawled out, dragging it with him. The lid was grimed with dust. He undid its clips and flipped it open. The rifle inside was a sniper's dream. Relief combined with the weight of having to carry his plan through was too much for Magnus and he let out a sob. 'Mr Perry, I take back everything.' He rubbed his eyes against the bedspread and tried to make himself laugh. 'Never judge a book by its cover.' Magnus reached beneath the bed and pulled out a box of illegally stored bullets. 'Unless the book in question is by Tom of Finland.'

Forty-Two

Magnus pitched a small tent in the woods at the back of Tanqueray House. The tent was olive-coloured, perfect for blending into the foliage he draped over it for camouflage. He lay there, wrapped in a sleeping bag, conserving his energy, the high-performance rifle by his side. The tent and sleeping bag had been stashed in a cupboard beneath Mr Perry's stairs, along with a supply of freeze-dried food. Magnus wondered about the fox-hunter. Had he been ex-military; a spy hiding incognito from enemies he feared would track him down? Or was he a gun freak who, if the sweats had not intervened, would one day have stationed himself in an upper room of his cottage and picked off children, one by one, as they played in the schoolyard opposite?

Jeb had been right, Magnus thought. He should have found a gun sooner, put it to Will's head and forced him to open the dungeon. Now things had escalated. He thought about running away and stayed where he was.

Magnus had mistrusted trees, but now they were his allies. He listened to the wind shivering the branches, the rustle of birds tossing through fallen leaves in search of grubs, the occasional scurry of mice and voles. He let himself be absorbed by the noises of the wood so that he would hear an intruder if they approached.

Magnus tried to picture where Raisha might be and hoped she was safe. He thought about Belle too and wondered if she had ventured out of hiding to meet Malachy. If Raisha was right about the girl's father complex, the lawyer with his certainties might appeal to her. He remembered his last conversation with Father Wingate and the priest's conviction that Jeb's death would nourish renewal. The old man was mad beyond the usual insanity of religion.

After a while Magnus dropped into a half-doze and lay in dreamless dread until the screech of an owl woke him. It was cold and damp in the dark wood. Magnus dragged Mr Perry's black tracksuit on top of his clothes. He shoved the ski hat on his head, pulling it low over his brow and wishing that he had thought to steal some boot polish to blacken his face. He spat on his hands, rubbed earth on them and daubed it on his exposed skin.

The wood was as alive as it had been when he had followed Raisha, but it bothered Magnus less now. He muttered the Bible verse he had quoted to Father Wingate: 'There is a time for everything, and a season for every activity under the heavens.' Harvest was a killing time; the priest was right about that.

When he reached the edge of the wood Magnus realised that the night was not as dark as he had thought. The moon was only a slim crescent, but the air was clear and stars glimmered across a black velvet sky. He looked up and saw Orion's Belt, the Plough and higher still a shimmer that might have been the Milky Way. His father and Hugh felt very close, though they had not been close to each other in life. His father had never warmed to Hugh, although he was his sister's child. 'Sib to the de'il' he had called him half in jest and 'a bad influence' fully in earnest.

He walked down the path to Tanqueray House, hoping Malachy had not posted a lookout. The building was cast in turreted darkness except for the kitchen windows, which glowed with light. At first Magnus thought it was merely Jacob's paraffin lamps, shining in an empty room, but as he grew closer he saw Father Wingate standing over a pair of jam pans that were steaming on the wood-fired Aga. Magnus guessed the priest was making refreshments for the crowd he hoped would come to the execution. He drew closer and saw that the old man's lips were moving as he worked, as if he were muttering a prayer or an incantation.

The side door was unlatched. The hallway smelled sourly of Father Wingate's brew, but it was deserted. Magnus walked quickly to the servants' staircase, his senses so alert he could almost hear his blood pumping through his heart. It was pitch-black inside the passage, but Magnus did not bother with a torch. He imagined the building as a dolls' house, its front walls pulled back to show the rooms within: Jeb lying in the foundations, contemplating his execution; Father Wingate standing hunched over his punch in the kitchen; Malachy and his followers alone in their beds on the upper floors, hearts heavy for the loss of their wives and children. He imagined Belle working on her collage in the attic studio, extending the Dance of Death into a worldwide ceilidh. Then he saw himself, a thin man dressed in black, creeping between the walls.

It was cold on the roof. Magnus hunkered down behind one of the decorative urns that punctuated the balustrade. From this height the moon looked like a slash in the fabric of the sky, behind which everything was silver. He heard a pattering noise and started, but it was only a bat. His eyes adjusted to the night and he saw that there were legions of them, flapping blackly against the darkness. The chill penetrated through his double layer of clothing. Magnus remembered the warm liquid bubbling on top of the Aga with longing, though he knew that anything the priest had made would taste foul.

Forty-Three

Magnus woke to a pink and blue dawn that gave way to a seamless sky. Pigeons had colonised the roof and daylight revealed their guano, white and foul, plastering the tiles and stonework. The house cast a dark shadow across the lawn that receded as the sun moved higher. Magnus lay on his front, among the bird shit and feathers, watching for the moment the shade pulled free of the execution platform, unveiling it like a prize object in a magic trick.

There was a hum of motorbikes coming and going along the drive. Magnus guessed that Malachy's men were trying to spread the word, visiting outlying districts, like busy party activists before a by-election.

The sun caught him in its rays about mid-morning. Flies and insects buzzed around his head, making a feast of him. Magnus wriggled free of the black tracksuit and fashioned a turban from the jacket. He had an uninterrupted view of the platform, but worried that by noon the sun would begin to blind him. His childhood had had its seasons and all of them had included a portion of rain. He wondered if this part of England had always been subjected to such relentless summers. He had shoved a bottle of water in his rucksack, along with the binoculars and a few of the packets of dried food from Mr Perry's house. Magnus felt too sick to eat, but took sips of the water, rationing it to last. He rationed his use of the binoculars too, afraid that the sun would glint against their lenses and give away his hiding place.

Some of the men had started to move trestle tables on to the lawn. Father Wingate fussed among them, dressed in a black cassock. Viewed from above, he reminded Magnus of the bats he had fallen asleep watching. The creatures had appeared fluttery and ill-directioned, but their natural sonar meant that every blind move was sure. The men placed the tables on one side of the lawn and then the other, until the priest was satisfied. Next they brought out tea urns and trays laden with cups and glasses. Magnus was dismayed to see that Malachy's group had grown larger. He counted five new recruits, all of them men. There were not enough urns to hold Father Wingate's refreshment and the men set out a variety of jugs and bowls full of brownish liquid which they covered with cotton cloths against bugs.

Malachy trotted across the lawn followed by one of the puppies. The Irishman was dressed all in black and Magnus wondered if he had raided some dead priest's wardrobe. Someone had fixed Union Jack flags around the platform like a skirt. Malachy stopped to admire the effect before leaping up on to the stage, as jaunty as a new manager about to reassure the workforce that redundancies spelled fresh opportunities. The dog sniffed at the flags and then lifted his leg against them and ambled away. Magnus was unsure what Malachy was carrying until he raised an old-fashioned megaphone to his lips. He had only ever seen one in comedy sketches and doubted it would work, but then he heard Malachy's voice, *Testing, one, two, three, testing,* loud and clear across the lawn.

Magnus whispered, 'I'd like to ram that up your arse, wide side first.'

The drumming started soon after: two slow beats, followed by three swift ones.

BANG–BANG–bangbangbang–BANG–BANG–bang-bangbang–BANG–BANG–bangbangbang . . .

Tanqueray House had proved a treasure trove. There were three drummers. One of them had a massive bass drum, the kind used to mark time in military parades, slung across his body. He hit the heavy beats. The other two were equipped with snare drums and rapped out swift *ratatats.* The rhythm was simple, but it took the men a while to master it and even once they were under way one or other of them would occasionally trip, throwing the rest out of sync and creating a racket of bangs; the sound of a body tumbling downstairs.

Magnus recalled Jacob saying that Father Wingate remembered the way things used to be done, before technology took over.

He muttered, 'You got that right, Captain, trouble is, the old days were fucking brutal.'

People began to arrive. They came singly, in pairs and small groups. Many wore the stunned expression of drivers involved in a motorway pile-up. Most were dressed soberly, though there were a few dishevelled souls who looked as if they had not changed their clothes since the sweats began. There were more men than women and none of the women was alone. Magnus recalled Belle's story about the gang she

341

had seen during her escape from London and was not surprised that solitary females had kept away.

Magnus had rehearsed assembling the gun in his tent in the woods, but his fingers were clumsy and it took longer than it should have. The sun seemed to signal midday, but he had no way of knowing the exact time, or whether Malachy intended to start on schedule. He cursed himself for not thinking to get a watch.

There were about thirty people on the lawn, including Malachy's crew. Judging by the number of cups set out on the trestle tables it was fewer than Father Wingate had hoped for, but it was more people than Magnus had seen since the sweats. He mopped his forehead, trained the gun sight on the platform and then leaned back and observed the crowd. People were beginning to mix and he felt a desperate urge to go down and join them. He watched the way clusters drifted cautiously together, the need for human contact overcoming fear of contamination, and wondered if they had really come to see a man die.

No one was visiting the refreshments tables yet, but Paul and a few more of Malachy's men stood awkwardly on hand, ready to serve. One of them poured himself a generous cupful and took a sip. His face buckled with disgust. Magnus guessed that the brew was alcoholic, because the man raised the cup to his lips and knocked the contents back. He shuddered and offered some to Paul who shook his head. The man forced down a second glass. He grimaced and wiped his mouth with the back of his hand.

The drummers stuttered to an exhausted halt and the small crowd looked towards the stage. Magnus scanned

342

the gathering for Father Wingate and Malachy, but they were gone; in the dungeon, he guessed, preparing Jeb for his ordeal. He scanned the crowd again, looking for Will and spotted instead a familiar slim figure crossing the lawn, hand in hand with a boy of around six years old.

Magnus grabbed the binoculars and focused the lens. Raisha turned her head as if she were searching the crowd for someone and he wondered if she was looking for him.

'Fuck.' He rocked back on his heels. 'Fuck, fuck, fuck, fuck, fuck.'

Raisha crossed the lawn and fell into conversation with a short, slim youth in a cloth cap and tweed jacket. The youth crouched down to welcome the little boy. He tipped his cap back and Magnus saw his – her face. Belle was grinning as if the presence of the child had put the reason for the gathering from her mind.

'Hello . . .' Malachy had mounted the platform without Magnus noticing. Father Wingate stood thin and dignified by his side. Magnus had expected the priest to dress up in embroidered finery, but he had donned a simple white robe and black surplice. The effect was theatrically austere.

Malachy raised the megaphone to his mouth. 'Hello, fellow survivors.' There was a mumble of hellos from the crowd and Malachy nodded in acknowledgement. He looked sure and solid. 'My name is Malachy Lynch. I'm not here to make a long speech. We have all suffered. We have lost the people most dear to us and our hopes and dreams have gone with them.'

Some heads were nodding. Malachy had a strong voice and Magnus wondered why he continued to use the loudhailer for such a small crowd, but then he saw him glance towards the perimeter and knew that he hoped there were other survivors lurking beyond the lawn, listening.

'Our task is to honour those we have lost by building a new England, one they could be proud of.' Malachy left a pause for people to contemplate the dead and the kind of world they might have wanted. 'Law and order are at the heart of a civilised society. Without the rule of law all we have is chaos.' More heads were nodding. 'We are here today to take a step towards re-establishing justice. A few days ago Father Jacob Powe, a man who gave his life to peace and who, despite his own hard losses, was determined to build a community here, in the English countryside, was brutally shot in the back.'

Jacob had been shot in the head, his fine brain full of hopes, plans, pain and memories, blasted across the lawn.

Malachy paused again, leaving space for the crowd to react, but they had experienced too many outrages of their own to be easily shocked and stood in silence, waiting for him to continue.

'The murderer is a man called Jeb Soames. Jeb Soames was a new member of Father Powe's small community, a man who Father Powe had rescued from certain death, a man who he had sheltered and was nursing back to health.'

Raisha was standing with her back to the house, her hands resting lightly on the boy's shoulders. She lifted a hand and stroked his hair. Magnus wanted to tell her to take the child away, before they brought Jeb to the stage.

Malachy's voice was rising. 'What Father Powe did not know was that Jeb Soames was a convicted killer, a man who had brutally murdered his wife and daughter and was serving life for the crime when the sweats gave him the chance to escape prison.'

Father Wingate was smiling beatifically. Magnus followed his gaze towards the refreshments tables and saw that more of Malachy's men were helping themselves to the brew. A few of the crowd had joined them. The drinkers grimaced as the liquid passed their lips. On some other occasion their contortions might have been comic, but now they underlined how desperate people were to escape reality.

Malachy's voice dropped. 'Sometimes fate gives us a second chance. It took the deaths of millions, but Jeb Soames was given just such an opportunity. He used it to kill a good man in cold blood.' Malachy raised his voice again. It reached across the lawn and out into the woods beyond. 'I say that a man like Jeb Soames, a child-killer, a murderer, has no place here. Why should he live, when so many good people have died?'

Malachy's men clapped loudly and one of them shouted, *Hear, hear.* A few heads in the crowd nodded and some people joined in the applause, but there were others who stood with their hands at their sides, or looked silently at their feet.

'Our country has a long and proud history of democracy. This small community has decided to send out the message that murder will not be tolerated.' Malachy's men were clapping again. 'If you agree that Jeb Soames should be executed for the murder of Father Jacob Powe, say Aye.'

AYE!

The shout was loud and masculine, but Magnus had the impression that not everyone had joined in.

Malachy said, 'The ayes have it. In a moment we will bring Jeb Soames to the platform, but before we do I would like to ask Father James Wingate to lead us in a prayer.'

The priest stepped forward and Magnus caught him in his gun sight. Father Wingate had been awake, concocting his refreshment until the small hours of the morning, but his skin had a pink glow and Magnus would have sworn that he looked younger than when they had first met. He whispered, 'Fucking vampire.'

Father Wingate did not bother with the megaphone. He raised his head and his voice carried, thin and high-pitched, across the crowd.

'Our Father, which art in heaven, hallowed be thy name . . .'

Some of the crowd joined in – *Our Father, which art in heaven* . . . – but others were drifting away. Raisha took the boy's hand and walked in the direction of the drive. Belle followed her.

Father Wingate's hands were clasped together. 'Thy Kingdom come. Thy will be done in earth, as it is in heaven . . .'

Thy Kingdom come. Thy will be done . . .

'Give us this day our daily bread. And forgive us our trespasses, as we forgive them that trespass against us. . . .'

. . . them that trespass against us.

A movement caught Magnus's eye. Jeb was being led across the lawn towards the platform. His back was to the house and so Magnus could not see the expression on Jeb's face, but his leg was still in plaster. His steps were limping and awkward and he was supported on either side by Malachy's men. Will walked behind them, slow and sombre in a black suit. Jeb's head flopped forward, as if he were drunk or drugged.

'And lead us not into temptation, but deliver us from evil.'

. . . lead us not into temptation, but deliver us from evil . . .

The crowd was smaller, but the responses of those who remained seemed louder.

'For thine is the kingdom, the power, and the glory . . .'

. . . the kingdom, the power, and the glory . . .

The small execution parade had walked the length of the lawn and was level with the platform. They turned right, but the escort blocked Magnus's view of Jeb.

Magnus muttered, 'C'mon, c'mon, c'mon.'

'For ever and ever, Amen.'

. . . Amen.

The execution party turned and faced the depleted audience. Magnus could see them clearly through the sight of the gun. Will's face was parchment white. He had what looked like a samurai sword in his hand.

'Jesus Christ,' Magnus whispered. It was real. There was to be no reprieve, no backing down, no shout of *Fooled you.* They intended to go through with the execution. He focused the gun sight on Jeb. His chin was resting on his chest, as if his head were too heavy for his neck. 'C'mon, Jeb, chin up, help me out,' Magnus whispered. His vision was blurred. He had shot almost as many barn-rats as Hugh, but it was a different thing to shoot a man, even when you had promised to save him. 'Lift your head, boy. Don't let them have the satisfaction.'

It was as if Jeb heard him. He raised his chin slowly and turned it sideways to look at the platform. Magnus's finger was on the trigger, Jeb's head caught in the crosshairs. The prayer was in his head, *Our Father, which art in heaven . . .*

There was a shout from the other side of the lawn, a thrashing noise and smash of breaking glass.

Father Wingate snatched up Malachy's megaphone and announced, 'Refreshments are being served. Please help yourself to alcoholic refreshments.'

One of the men was lying on the grass by the trestle tables, his body caught in the grips of a fit. The people around him were frozen, but all of a sudden Raisha was there, turning him on his side, making sure that he did not bite his tongue, issuing instructions. Magnus looked for the child and saw him on the edge of the lawn, his legs wrapped around Belle's waist, his face pressed into her shoulder.

There was another shout, the crash of an overturning table. Raisha went to a second man, who was writhing on the ground, his mouth frothing.

Father Wingate said again, 'Everyone, please help yourselves to refreshments.'

Malachy had his hands in the air and was saying something that was lost in the hubbub. Raisha was shouting too, but there was too much noise for her to be heard. She shouted again and then ran across the lawn and on to the stage. She was yelling something at Father Wingate who merely smiled and raised the loudhailer to his lips. 'While these poor gentlemen are being helped I suggest that everyone avail themselves of —'

Raisha wrested the megaphone from him. 'Nobody touch that drink, it's poi—'

Father Wingate took a gun from beneath his cassock and shot her in the chest. And then all hell broke loose.

Forty-Four

Magnus strained his ears as he hurtled down the succession of servants' stairs that led to the ground floor. All he could hear was the rasp of his breath and the frantic echo of his footsteps.

Raisha.

Suddenly he was at the tradesmen's entrance. He plunged into the open; out into an assault of screams and shouts, the gun still in his hand. Sunlight seared his eyes. Magnus ran into the blindness. His vision adjusted and he saw that more people had fallen to the ground. Others were trying to make themselves sick or were tending to the dying. He ignored them and raced across the lawn. He had never seen such green grass; greener than any football pitch, any cricket ground or pampered bowling green. He had thought people's clothes muted, but now he saw that even shades of black were bright and glowing. A woman he did not know grabbed him by the arm. Magnus shoved her away, barely registering the rake of her nails against his bare skin, and sprinted towards the platform.

Father Wingate was still standing over Raisha's body, his white robe streaked with red. The men who had been

349

guarding Jeb had wrested the gun from the priest. They stood stunned and awkward either side of the old man, holding him by the arms, though he offered no resistance. Jeb was nowhere to be seen. Malachy was blood-spattered and shouting at Father Wingate, 'Why? Why did you shoot her?' as if there might yet be a good reason.

Magnus reached the platform and heard one of the guards say, 'Was it her who put the poison in the drink, Father?'

His companion muttered, 'I looked to see who was shooting and when I turned back the murdering cunt was gone. How did he get away so fast, the state he was in?'

Belle stood by the platform, cradling the boy as if he were a much younger child. She put out an arm to stop Magnus, but he ignored her and charged up the steps. Will was crouched by Raisha's body. Magnus pulled him away. Will said, 'She's gone,' and Magnus punched him.

A woman stood below the platform shouting about poison. Most people were too caught up in the confusion of dead and dying to focus on the cause of the tragedy, but she was beginning to attract a few dazed looks. One of the men holding the priest said, 'We need to get indoors.'

Malachy took Father Wingate by the shoulders and shook him. 'Why did you shoot her?' He pointed towards the people lying on the lawn. 'Did she have something to do with this?'

Magnus was kneeling beside Raisha's body. He touched her face and his hand came away red. He said, 'Don't try and pin it on Raisha. This is all him.'

'I am a servant of God.' Malachy's shake seemed to have roused Father Wingate. 'The end of all flesh is come before me.'

350

Will was crying. He whispered, 'I would have done it. I would have brought the sword down. I was ready to. I would have brought it down on his neck.'

Magnus smoothed Raisha's hair away from her face. She was still warm, but her features had slackened and whatever had made her a person was gone.

Paul was suddenly crouched beside him. 'They're going to lynch us.' He caught Magnus by the elbow and hauled him to his feet. Magnus made a half-hearted effort to bat the tall man away, but the fight had gone out of him. 'I've got a bad feeling you might need this.' Paul shoved Mr Perry's rifle back into Magnus's hand.

Malachy's men were jostling Father Wingate down the platform steps. The old man recited, 'The Lord said, I will destroy man whom I have created from the face of the earth; both man, and beast, and the creeping thing, and the fowls of the air . . .'

Belle was running on ahead with the child. Magnus wanted to catch her, but he heard a shout behind him and turned to see a man armed with Will's sword tearing towards the priest. Magnus stood in his path and aimed Mr Perry's rifle at him. 'There'll be no more killing today.'

The stranger faltered to a halt. His eyes were wild. 'I wouldn't be so sure about that.'

'You volunteering to be next?' Paul stepped to Magnus's side and pointed a revolver at the man.

The stranger said, 'You murdering fuckers are outnumbered,' but he fell back.

'Come on.' Paul pushed Magnus's shoulder, urging him on.

They jogged towards Tanqueray House, their weapons

351

in their hands. Magnus scanned the lawn for Jeb, but it was as the guard had said, the condemned man had vanished. It hurt Magnus to leave Raisha alone on the stage. Wherever her soul had gone, he had held her body and it strained his heart to abandon it. He looked back at the platform where she lay and wondered again where Jeb had vanished to.

Malachy locked the kitchen door after them and collapsed on to a chair. He tossed the keys at one of the guards. 'Make sure the other doors are locked.'

The man lobbed the keys back at him. 'Do it yourself.' He left the room, slamming the door behind him, and a moment later they heard the sound of a motorbike disappearing up the drive.

Paul said, 'I'm gone too.' He looked at Magnus. 'You should get out of here.'

Magnus ignored him. Father Wingate was hunched on a chair by the door to the hallway. Magnus put a hand on each of the chair's arms and leaned into the priest, so close he could see the pores of his skin, the three white hairs sprouting on the bulb of his nose. He was not sure why he had saved him from the stranger with the sword. It was an effort not to put his hands around the old man's neck and squeeze. Magnus whispered, 'Did you kill the others too?'

It seemed impossible. The priest was too frail to force a young woman's head into a noose or make a grown man slash his wrists.

The flight across the lawn had tired Father Wingate. His skin was grey, but he raised his face to Magnus's and looked him in the eye. 'Melody recognised that the good Lord

352

wanted to bring an end to the corruption in the world and so she offered her life up to Him.'

'Melody wasn't corrupt.' Belle was perched on the kitchen table, cradling the boy on her lap. 'You brainwashed her.' Her voice was loud and the child whimpered. 'Shhhh.' She rocked backward and forward, stroking his forehead, and said more softly, 'Melody spent hours with that bastard. We thought he was trying to help her, but all the time he was convincing her to kill herself.' She pulled the boy closer.

A stone smashed through the kitchen window. The child cried out and somewhere in the floors above the dogs set to barking. Paul said again, 'I'm gone.' He went into the hall-way, leaving the door open behind him.

Malachy looked bewildered. He made an effort to reassert himself. 'We should all go and leave him to his fate.'

Will was leaning against the kitchen cabinets. He muttered, 'I was going to do it. I would have killed him.'

Belle shushed the child and gave a crazy little laugh. 'I don't know why I ran. This has nothing to do with me.'

Magnus grabbed Father Wingate by the scruff of his bloodied cassock. The old man's bones were sharp beneath their thin covering of flesh. 'I've not finished with you yet.' He shoved the priest into the hall. They followed Paul through the house to the front door where the dogs were whining to be let out. Magnus peered through the hall window. Around a dozen men and a couple of women were standing on the drive. They reminded Magnus of groups he had seen on television, silently waiting outside law courts for the arrival of a child-murderer. They had been robbed of Jeb's death, more than robbed, had innocent deaths forced on them in its stead. They would start shouting soon, working themselves up to do what needed to be done.

Magnus said, 'We're too late.'

The priest whispered, 'It is the end of days.'

Malachy's voice wavered. 'Do you think they'll let us go if we give him to them?'

Paul said, 'I wouldn't like to bet on it.'

Malachy said, 'Why don't they storm the building?'

'They're just ordinary people like us.' Paul ruffled the dogs' heads, trying to quiet them. 'Maybe they don't know what to do.'

Magnus said, 'They know what to do. They just don't have the courage to do it yet.' He pressed the priest into a chair and squatted on the ground, so that he could see his expression. 'What happened to Henry?'

Father Wingate said, 'We have been a terrible disappointment to God—'

Magnus slapped him hard across the face.

Father Wingate touched his reddening cheek with his hand. 'I am a man of God.'

Magnus whispered, 'Do not doubt that I will slice you to pieces slowly and make a fucking martyr of you, if you don't tell me what happened.'

Paul said, 'We should go upstairs and barricade ourselves in one of the rooms.'

Malachy shook his head. 'It's the priest they want. Let's give him to them.'

Magnus snapped, 'What I just told him goes double for you. He's going nowhere until I say so.'

Father Wingate touched his cheek with his fingertips

354

again, as if he had never been slapped before and was amazed at the sensation. Tears had sprung to his eyes, but his voice was resolute. 'Henry was a worldly man. I knew there was no point in trying to make him see what our Lord God intended for him . . . what He intends for us all. But the Lord came to my aid. He gave Henry toothache. Raisha would have been able to prescribe something, but she was absent and Henry was nervous of taking anything stronger than an aspirin without her advice. I told him I had a natural remedy that would help. It was the first time I had tried to make the infusion. I must have got the quantities wrong, or perhaps he didn't drink as much of it as I'd intended.' The priest's smile was wistful. 'I believe it does taste rather foul.'

Magnus said, 'Why did you take his body to the barn? How did you get it there?'

'The body walked there all by itself.' Wingate smiled as if he had said something clever. 'We were looking for harvesting equipment, just as you were on the day you and Jacob found him. I gave Henry the medicine and he drank it as we drove to the farm. He was overcome in the barn, but I could tell that he was still breathing. I was afraid he had merely sunk into a deep sleep and would wake, so I secured his wrists with some packing ties I found in the barn. I went back to the house, took a knife from the kitchen, and then I sent him to paradise.'

'Jesus.' It was as if Malachy had just taken in what the priest was saying. 'You were going to let us execute Jeb Soames for murder.'

'Every life is a sacrifice to the Lord. Jeb Soames too was worthy, as are we and all of those people out there.'

355

Malachy said, 'We brought them here to re-establish law and order, but you planned to poison them. No wonder they're baying for our blood.'

It had been quiet outside, except for the occasional shout, but now banging came from the back of the house. Paul hesitated and then hurried in its direction.

Magnus sensed time running out. He said, 'Why did you shoot Jacob?'

Father Wingate intoned, 'The path that the Lord asks us to follow is often hard and stony. I have cried bitter tears . . .'

Paul strode into the hall. 'They're breaking up the platform.'

Malachy sounded hopeful. 'Maybe they're taking their anger out on it?'

Paul shook his head. He touched Belle's shoulder. 'If I were you I'd take a chance and leave now, make sure they can see that you're carrying the boy. He'll be your protection.'

Belle whispered, 'I don't trust them.'

The priest was still reciting scripture. Magnus slapped him again. The old man started to cry. Magnus said, 'I told you, if you don't answer me I will take the sword Will was going to use on Jeb and shred you to pieces.'

Father Wingate's voice was thick with tears. 'Jacob and I were each other's spiritual advisers. After Henry's death I sensed a change in him. He talked of survival but I knew that, deep down, he too wanted to give himself over completely and utterly to God.' His eyes met Magnus's, and it was not only tears that made them shine. 'It was a joyous moment when I was able to tell him how I had helped two souls on their way. You remember the night.' Father Wingate

356

nodded to Will who was standing by the stairs. 'There had been an altercation, Jacob was tired and I could tell that he was desperate for peace.'

Will said, 'And so you told him what you'd done.'

Tears were caught in the wrinkles in the old man's face, but his smile was saintly. 'He didn't take it in at first, but when he did he put his gun on the table and said that I should be the next one to go.' Father Wingate lowered his voice conspiratorially. 'I knew what he really wanted. I watched him cross the garden. It was almost dawn and he made the perfect target, standing opposite my window, all dressed in black against the white wall.'

Will said, 'You shot him?'

'The Lord guided my hand and steered the bullet towards his blessed release.'

The dogs' whining became more frantic. They started to scrabble at the door. Paul had been sitting on the stairs, watching the crowd congregating outside. He got to his feet. 'Can you smell something?' Smoke was beginning to drift through from the back of the house. 'They want to flush us out.'

Will said, 'This place is built of stone, it won't burn easily.'

Paul said, 'Smells like it's fucking burning to me.'

Malachy muttered, 'I still say we should give them the priest.'

Magnus was leaning against the staircase, trying to absorb what Father Wingate had told them. He looked at Malachy. 'You're the face of law and order. It's you they'll want.'

Paul ran through to the kitchen and came back, his face flushed. 'They must have used some kind of accelerant. It's taken hold. They got two Calor gas canisters from somewhere . . .'

357

Will said, 'Jacob was saving them for the winter.'

'Good for Jacob.' Paul's grin was desperate. 'They've rolled them into the centre of the flames. We don't have any choice. We have to go out through the front.'

Magnus said, 'There's a door at the side.'

Father Wingate chirped, 'The tradesmen's entrance.'

Paul nodded. 'I think they used some of the planks from the stage to nail it shut. These canisters explode at high temperature. We don't have much time.'

Magnus put his rifle on the floor. 'I'll go first.'

Belle said, 'Tell them there's a child in here.'

Malachy said, 'Pick up your gun.'

'He's right.' Paul gave Magnus a tight smile. 'The only way to get through this is *Butch Cassidy and the Sundance Kid* style. All guns blazing.'

Magnus said, 'You've forgotten how that movie ended.' He left Mr Perry's rifle propped in the hallway, opened the front door and stepped towards the waiting crowd.

Forty-Five

Magnus walked out into the afternoon sunlight, his hands in the air. The dogs dashed onto the lawn and made for the back of the house. He guessed they were heading for the woods beyond and wished that he could go with them. He remembered the drugged girl in the alleyway, the night of Johnny Dongo's O2 gig. Trying to save her had set him on the road to here. He could not regret it, even though she was probably dead by now anyway. So many people were dead. Perhaps his part of the story had always been meant to end here.

Magnus braced himself for the sudden impact of a bullet and it occurred to him that it was a shame to die on such a beautiful day. He thought, I would have liked to know how it all turned out. Now that he was closer to the small crowd he recognised a couple of the men from Malachy's crew. He saw their guns and raised his hands higher. 'Nobody knew about the poison except for the priest.'

A woman with an open face and braided hair said, 'Someone should pay.' Her voice was low, but it carried as clear as ice water.

Magnus ignored her. 'There's a young girl called Belle with

359

a small boy in the house. Will you promise not to harm them?' A couple of people nodded. It was not enough for his liking. He tried to summon his stagecraft. 'I didn't hear you. They're innocent. None of this was their fault. Do you *promise* not to hurt them?'

More voices answered this time and he called to Belle. She came out slowly, her face tight, holding the child in front of her, too much like a shield for Magnus's liking. She reached his side just as someone asked, 'Who's this guy anyway?'

One of Malachy's men said, 'He's a buddy of the child-killer they were going to execute. I heard they met in prison.'

The atmosphere changed. Belle took Magnus's hand. He pulled it free. 'Keep on walking.'

Belle whispered, 'I'm scared they're going to kill you.'

He felt bad for thinking she might use the child as a human shield.

Someone shouted 'Murderer!' Belle caught hold of his sleeve. Then everything happened at once. The small crowd surged towards the house. Paul ran through the front door, shouldering the rifle Magnus had left lying in the hallway. There was a pop and a series of explosions from the rear of the building as one gas canister, and then the other, exploded. The crowd scattered and a Transit van spun from the side of Tanqueray House and skidded to a halt at the front door. The van's side panel was open. Magnus grabbed the child from Belle and threw him inside. He pushed her in next and jumped on board. Paul followed close behind. Magnus shouted, 'Drive, drive, drive!' and Jeb pressed the pedal to the metal.

Epilogue

Magnus was not sure that the distant sliver of dark edged between the sea and sky was land. The wind grabbed at the chart he had found stowed in the boat's cabin. He smoothed it against the wheel and checked the route against the compass embedded in the centre of the helm. He thought he was on course, but vision grew tricky confronted with a view of air and water. The eye saw land where there was none, boats where there were only black waves and breaking foam. Magnus focused on the dark edge of shade that hinged the sea to the sky and drew his cap low over his forehead. It was a long time since he had sailed and he had never, not even when he and Hugh had been in their fishing phase, sailed such a distance.

Magnus could imagine Hugh making fun of the orange life jackets he had strapped himself and the boy into. They had never bothered with such precautions when they were lads, but it seemed important now, even though the chances of anyone fishing them from the waters were slim.

The boy was tucked in the bunk below. Magnus did not need to see him to know that he was either sleeping, or staring into space. He had coaxed him to eat almost half a bar of chocolate that morning before they had set out, but neither of them had eaten since. He wondered if he should go below and check on him, but stayed where he was, feet anchored to the rolling deck, hands grasping the wheel. There were moments when he felt awkward around the boy; a representative of an adult world that had screwed everything up.

Jeb had given his guard the slip in the confusion of Raisha's shooting and hidden beneath the execution platform, concealed from view by the Union Jack skirt draped around its edge. 'I thought I was seeing things when I spied you running across the grass with that rifle in your hand and then I realised you'd been there all along, ready to take out those nutters for me. That was a bit of a fucking suicide mission, wasn't it?'

Magnus had not disabused him, but he caught Jeb watching him once or twice during the drive and wondered if he suspected the truth.

The horizon was coming into focus. It was definitely land. Magnus tried to suppress an electric leap of excitement. He had come too far to get shipwrecked on treacherous rocks. He traced a finger along the route to South Ronaldsay marked on the chart.

Belle had persuaded them to take a detour somewhere near York, following a series of colourful banners that led to what looked to Magnus like a folk festival. The boy had already elected to sit squashed next to him in the front seat. He had edged closer to Magnus at the sight of the small cluster of tents and camper vans, worried by the prospect of strangers. 'It's all right, Shug.' Magnus was driving but he had given the boy's small hand a quick squeeze. 'They're hippies. They smoke the pipe of peace.'

Paul said, 'I bet that's not all they smoke.'

Jeb was sitting on the other side of the boy. Magnus glanced at him, wondering if he was remembering his time among the environmental activists whom he had betrayed, but the big man kept his eyes on the road.

Belle said, 'Why did you call him Shug?'

'It's short for Shuggie.'

'Ah, that makes perfect sense – not.'

Belle took a comb from her bag and started to pull it through her hair. She had been subdued since their escape from Tanqueray House, but now Magnus sensed nervous excitement crackling from her, like electricity before a thunderstorm.

'It's another name for Hugh.' He ruffled the boy's hair. 'I had a best friend called Hugh. This wee lad reminds me of him and as we've got to call him something, I thought Shug might do the trick.' He looked at the boy. 'What do you think?'

The child's face remained impassive, but he leaned his head against Magnus.

Magnus smiled. 'Aye, I think he likes it.'

Belle had found a mirror and lipstick in her bag. She looked at her face and dabbed her lips red. 'You're becoming more Scottish.'

'Am I?'

'Yes, the further north we go, the stronger your accent gets. You'll be speaking Gaelic soon.'

Magnus said, 'The only Gaelic I know is *uisge beatha*.' He

guided the van to a halt. People from the camp were walking over to greet them. Belle opened the door and leapt to the ground, not bothering to ask for an English translation, her face split by a smile.

Magnus whispered, 'It means water of life.'

The five of them camped there overnight. Jeb had insisted that now was the time for his cast to come off and, after scouring the small site, Magnus had managed to borrow a craft saw from a man who had been a carpenter before the sweats. Jeb's leg was pale and had lost muscle. It seemed at first that they had removed the plaster too soon, but then the carpenter turned up with a makeshift crutch he had fashioned and Jeb hobbled a circuit of the camp.

Magnus was packing their gear back into the van the next morning when Belle announced that she had decided to stay. He had not spotted any other children at the camp and some of its inhabitants had a hungry look that made him uneasy. 'I can see why you want to be with folk your own age,' he said, making an effort to keep his voice reasonable. 'But I'm not sure this is the best place for the wee lad.'

Belle laughed when she realised his assumption. 'I can't look after a child.' She was smiling, but there was an edge of panic in her voice. 'You know me, Magnus, I'm far too selfish. Anyway, it's you that he's fallen in love with.' It was a typical hyperbole, designed to get her what she wanted, but Magnus felt a leap of gratitude. Belle said, 'Raisha would want you to look after him.' Magnus hoped that she was right.

Belle was a grown woman, in charge of her own life, but Magnus was relieved when Paul said he was staying too, though the campers were mostly younger than him and he and Belle not an item.

'He'd like to though, wouldn't he?' Jeb had said, with a grin. He smiled more now, Magnus noticed.

It was cold on deck. Magnus rubbed his hands together and blew on them, wondering if there was a pair of gloves tucked somewhere in the cabin below. Something broke the water on his leeward side, huge and black. Magnus swore. He killed the engines, his heart beating a tattoo. 'Shug!'

The boy must have heard the urgency in his voice because he came up on deck straight away, rubbing his eyes. Magnus was relieved to see that he had kept his life jacket on as he had told him to.

'Look.' He pointed at the shining mound of black as it broke the water again. There was another beyond it and another beyond that. Magnus laughed, though there was danger in the sight. 'Minke whales.' The boy stood by his side and leaned his body against Magnus. His head rested against Magnus's ribs. 'Do you know what they are?' The boy stared out into the sea. Magnus started to explain, but how did you explain a whale? 'They're big sea-beasts. Gentle creatures, harmless.' Unless they tip the boat, he thought but did not say. 'We'll find you a book on them when we get there. I'm betting you're a good reader.'

He looked at the boy, but Shuggie kept his eyes trained on the school of whales, swimming towards their mating grounds in the North Atlantic, and gave Magnus no clue. The boy had not spoken in the time they had been together, though once or twice Magnus thought he had seen his lips moving when he was playing alone.

'You speak when you're ready, son.' He ruffled the boy's hair and then, thinking he might be cold, took off his cap and put it on the boy's head. 'Most folks talk too much anyway.'

The van had felt quiet without Belle's chatter and Paul's attempts to impress her. The roads were quieter too. He and Jeb had stopped three times, lowered the van's windows and exchanged news that was no news with other survivors.

Most of the world was dead.

There were fires in the cities.

Tribes were beginning to form in the countryside.

Women, guns and food were currency.

It was best to be careful.

Magnus suspected that children might be currency too and so each time they had encountered someone, he had told the boy to hide in the back of the van beneath a blanket. He and Jeb kept their guns loaded and near to hand.

Magnus let out a cheer when they passed the Old Man of Hoy, the skinny finger of rock, narrowed by aeons of wind and rain, pointing tall and steadfast at the sky. The boy caught some of his excitement and jumped up and down on deck, one hand clamped to the too-big hat on his head.

Magnus saluted him. 'Not far to go now, Cap'n.' Fear of what he might find when they got there knotted his stomach.

Newcastle had lit up the night sky, a blazing orange glow. Magnus and Jeb had been forced to take a detour and found themselves on a hill above the town. They got out and looked down on the furnace. They were miles away, but the

366

throat-scraping stench of blazing chemicals and charred flesh reached them.

Magnus said, 'What do you think causes the fires?'

'Who knows?' Jeb's voice was soft. 'Electrical faults, arson, a power surge. Maybe they're a good thing. They'll dispose of a lot of bodies and help clear the place of infection.' He nodded at the van where the boy lay sleeping. 'You should wake him up. This is the kind of sight he'll remember for the rest of his life.'

Magnus shook his head. 'I think his memory bank is probably full enough for now.'

Jeb said, 'You could be right. Do you remember the Angel of the North?' He did not wait for Magnus to reply. 'I wish we'd been in time to watch it burn. I hated that smug bastard.'

It amazed Magnus that he could still laugh. But they laughed a lot on the journey, even though he felt the loss of Raisha, the loss of the world, heavy and cold, like a stone in his belly.

It was deep in the night when Jeb told Magnus about Cherry. The boy was curled beneath his blanket, asleep in the back of the van and they were driving through the dark, along a narrow country road bordered either side by dry-stane dykes.

Jeb said, 'Raisha died a good death.'

Magnus kept his voice steady and his hands on the wheel. He stared into the blackness; on the alert for the shining eyes of a rabbit, deer or pack of roaming dogs. 'I can't think of it like that.'

'You should try. She died trying to warn people what Wingate was doing. It was fast too, she didn't suffer, not like the poor sods he poisoned or people who caught the sweats.'

Magnus was driving without headlamps, for fear of attracting unwanted attention. It was tricky anticipating the road's turns in the dark. He pressed the brake pedal gently.

'Do you still miss Cherry?'

Jeb was silent. Magnus wondered if he had overstepped the mark, but then the other man said, 'Part of me is glad that Cherry and Happy escaped all this, but a bigger part wishes they were here.' He paused. 'What happened was my fault. I was sick and tired of the deceit. That's the real reason I told Cherry I was with the police. I should have known she wouldn't be able to handle it, but I told her because I thought it would make me feel better.' He drifted into silence again. Magnus thought the subject was closed, but then Jeb said, 'It was like she was possessed. She screamed at me to go. I tried to calm her down, but everything I said made things worse. Eventually I went into the bedroom and packed a bag. When I came out, Cherry was sitting on a chair on the balcony with Happy in her arms. I don't remember what I said, but she turned and looked at me. Her hair was wild. I thought of it today, when we watched the city burning. She looked beautiful, but I was sick to death of everything.

'Cherry stood up and pushed the chair against the balcony railings. I knew that she wanted me to tell her to stop, but I just stood there, even when she climbed on to the seat, still holding Happy in her arms.'

Magnus kept his eyes on the road. The moon was hidden behind clouds and the night was pitch-black, but he could see the woman in his mind's eye, her untamed hair catching the breeze as she mounted the chair.

Jeb's voice thickened. 'She told me that she was going to

jump and I said, 'Fucking do it then. Let's see if you can fly.'
Jeb sniffed and Magnus realised that the other man was
crying. 'I turned to go. I honestly didn't think for a minute
that she would do it. She loved that child.' Jeb took a deep
shuddering breath. 'I was at the sitting-room door when
Cherry let out a shout and I heard the chair falling over.
When I looked back, she was gone. I told her to jump and
she did.'

They drove on in silence. After a while Magnus said, 'You
couldn't know—'

Jeb interrupted him. 'I bloody know now though, don't I?'

They had gone their separate ways the next day. Magnus
had wondered if Jeb had waited until he had decided to go,
before telling the rest of his story. Or if it had been the other
way around and once the tale had been told, Jeb had no
choice but to move on.

They had dropped him where he had told them to, on
a deserted roadside. Magnus had offered to help him find a
vehicle of his own, but Jeb had been determined to walk.
'I'm not in a rush.'

'You know where we'll be, if you need us.'

'Sure.' Jeb had shaken Magnus's hand and then the boy's.
'Maybe I'll see you there some time.'

There was a stile by the road. Jeb climbed it awkwardly
with the help of his crutch and crossed into a field where
some scraggy-looking sheep were grazing. The sheep raised
their heads, but Jeb kept a city boy's distance from them and
they turned their attention back to the grass.

Magnus sat Shuggie on the bonnet of the van and they
watched Jeb limp away. His jacket and gun were twenty-first

369

century, but his receding figure might have come from an earlier age. They waited until he passed over the brow of a hill and then Magnus helped the boy down and they continued their journey.

Magnus steered the boat for one of the natural coves where he and Hugh had often landed. The sands were holiday-brochure white. He sank anchor, helped the boy into the dinghy and rowed them towards shore, jumping out when they reached the shallows and pulling the rubber craft with the boy in it up on to the beach. He reached for Shuggie, but he was standing up in the dinghy, pointing at the sands beyond.

Magnus turned and saw a tall, slim woman with *café au lait* skin and cropped hair, standing on the dunes. She had a rifle in one hand and was holding the collar of a large dog with the other. Magnus held up his hands to show that he was unarmed and then turned and lifted Shug from the boat. They walked hand in hand across the sands to where she stood. Magnus said, 'I'm Magnus McFall and this is Shuggie.'

The woman had a London accent. 'I'm Stevie Flint.' She nodded at the dog. 'And this is Pistol.' Her expression gave no hint of how she felt about the arrival of new survivors.

Magnus said, 'I'm looking for Peggy and Rhona McFall. Do you know if they're on the islands?'

Stevie's eyes met his. 'I'm sorry, they're not here.'

Magnus looked at the ground. The boy's hand tightened in his and Magnus smiled at him, to show things were okay, although they were not. 'Are there any McFalls that you know of?'

She held his gaze. 'I know everyone on the island, there's

370

no one of that name.' They stood there for a moment, the tall sea grasses on the dunes bending to the wind. Stevie said, 'I've got a van. If you come with me we can find you a change of clothing and something warm to eat.'

Magnus would have liked to have filled his pockets with stones and walked back into the water, but he had the boy to think of and so he followed her, over the dunes, towards the road.

Acknowledgements

The Black Death may have been named for the way its symptoms affected its victims' bodies, or it may have been so called because of its scope and dreadfulness. It is impossible to know true figures for how many people died, but it is generally agreed that the first wave of the pandemic (1340–1400) killed at least a third of the population of Europe. The Black Death was a democratic killer. The young, the old, the poor and the rich, the educated and uneducated, religious and irreligious were all at risk. Everyone who survived had lost someone they were close to and had lived with the imminent prospect of their own death.

The first wave of the plague pandemic left the world altered. There were more jobs, higher wages and increased social mobility. Some people with no expectations of ever inheriting anything became wealthy as a result of the deaths of successive relatives. A lack of manpower meant that women were able to access economic and social freedoms previously denied to them. The arts were also changed; inspired by the knowledge that death is everywhere. I am fascinated by the survivors of the Black Death. How must it have felt to still be alive in such a changed world?

The Bubonic Plague still exists in parts of China and America. Its final outbreak in Glasgow, the city where I live, was in 1907 and was quickly dealt with. We need not fear another mass outbreak of the disease. But scientists are agreed that there will be another pandemic at some point in the near future. What it will be, when it will hit, and how many will die is uncertain. All we can be sure of is that it will come.

Thanks are due to several people who helped me during the writing of this book. Roland Philipps and Eleanor Birne of John Murray have both been enthusiastic supporters of the *Plague Times* trilogy. They have given me invaluable care and editorial advice.

My agent, David Miller of Rogers, Coleridge and White, cast his beady eye over the manuscript several times and discussed it with insight and good sense. He has saved me from devastating geographical mistakes and much more.

As usual I have neglected my friends and family in favour of books and the blank page. Thanks once again to them for sticking with me.

Special thanks are due to my partner, the writer Zoë Strachan who has been living surrounded by plagues and pandemics for a few years now. She read this book at the early and later stages and it is much improved for her rigour and expertise.

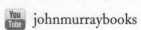
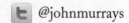
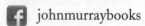